Hurricane of the Heart

Hilton Head Island

Farley Dunn

THREE SKILLET

HILTON HEAD ISLAND, Dunn, Farley L

First Edition

Hurricane of the Heart, Book 1

 THREE SKILLET

www.ThreeSkilletPublishing.com

Cover design by Farley L Dunn

ISBN: 978-1-943189-17-5

Hilton Head Island

Prologue

"HEY, SIS!"

Sand flung itself over Carolina DeAngeles as a handsome young man clad only in board shorts crashed into the beach just in front of her, his momentum gouging a trench in the sunbaked sand.

"Edward!" Carolina brushed the sand from her arms and reached a hand to work her fingers into the roots of her hair. Drawing out the tangled strands, she shook her head to get it to fall cleanly at her shoulders. It wasn't as if she cared if Edward liked the way it looked. He had seen her much worse. Little brothers were just that. They were simply there, fixtures in one's life.

She let her eyes rest on his face for a moment, then she looked off down the beach as if searching for someone.

"Well, aren't you the sour thing!" In a scramble of flying sand, his golden body flung itself from the trench and stood just for a moment, the foam football in his hand raised over his shoulder, and his muscles bunched. Then, like an over-tensioned steel spring, all the young man's energy was released in one smooth snap that sent the ball flying into the midst of a group of similar golden boys just down the beach. With a quickness that only extreme youth can offer, he flung himself to the sand to sit at her side.

"A penny for your thoughts." He cupped a handful of warm sand in his palm and let it dribble across her knee.

She reached to brush it off, and when he laughed and continued, she sighed and gave up. "A dollar, shouldn't it be?" She pursed her mouth and chewed the corner of her lip.

Edward laughed, punching her playfully on the shoulder. "At first I thought it was my wonderful older sister dragged down by the thought of summer school." Picking up and dumping a second handful of sand on her leg, he finished and wrapped his arms around his own legs, resting his chin on his knees. He watched the people on the beach, smiling as several girls, probably still in junior high, were chased by the incoming surf, squealing when it caught them off-guard. "Now I see the truth of the matter."

"What truth does my Antarctica-bound brother see here on this warm, Carolina beach?" Carolina cut her eyes to him as she reached once more to work her fingers into the roots of her hair. She wasn't exactly tugging at it, revealing her internal feelings, as her mother would say, but she pulled her hand away when she realized the action was telling her brother more than she intended.

He laughed soundly. "That's just a dream, sis. Mum and Dad won't turn loose of me just yet." He looked at Carolina, chuckling. "If I could, however, I'd be there now. Enough of me, though. Where's that boy you've been looking for?"

Carolina snorted her laughter at him. "Edward! You can't tease me as if I'm fourteen all over again." She reached for a handful of sand of her own, and she dumped it across his back, watching as it skittered across his bronzed skin, the grains chasing themselves back toward the beach.

He just grinned. "I deserved that. Most of it went inside my shorts, though. Thank you, Carolina."

"You're very welcome, little brother." She wasn't ready to let go of his earlier remark, though. "What truth?"

Edward reached a finger to his side to trace out geometric shapes in the sand. "I can see cause and effect, you know. Sis, you love this beach. You come home, and you light up with anticipation until you get on the sand. Then, I see you here today with that hangdog expression on your face, and your eyes keep roving up and down as far as you can see. Look at you, even now!" He reached and slapped her on the leg.

"What!" Carolina glared at him for a moment, then turned her eyes back to the shore in front of her.

He laughed. "See? You can't look at me for even two seconds. You've met a boy, haven't you? A man, I should say, right, sis?" He flipped sand on her. "Do I know his name?"

Carolina sighed. Edward always could see through her. She reached both hands up, worked her fingers back into her hair, and looked at the sand between her feet. She laughed, but it carried a sound of disappointment.

"I don't even know his name, Edward. Rather, he doesn't know mine."

Edward brushed his hand off on his shorts and placed it on his sister's shoulder. He squeezed it in a brotherly fashion and spoke quietly, "A man of mystery."

Carolina pulled her hands from her head and shook her hair back. She took a deep breath and laughed at her brother's words. "A man in an airplane cowling was more like it. He said he lives here. I'd just hoped . . ." Her voice caught.

9

"So, he's not come to find you, yet." His hand dropped, and in one quick motion, he was standing. He reached to grab his sister's hand. "The beach is huge, sis, and you're one tiny girl. He'll never find you if you sit here and mope. There's a Frisbee on the sand. It's waiting on us."

Carolina worked her hand free, and she dropped it to the sand at her side. "I don't think I want to play, not today." She motioned with her head to where the football game was still going on. "Your friends. They're still playing."

"Better not let Mum and Dad see you like this. Margarete, either. They'll grill you like toast on a Sunday morning, even if Mass has to wait. See you, sis!"

In a flurry of sand, he was gone, his skin glistening in the brilliance of the coastal sun. Carolina's eyes followed him for a moment, his slender body belying the strength and quickness she knew he had. Then she let her eyes flick to others who were out on the beach, looking for a golden head of hair streaked with the summer sun, and a face with dimples a mile deep in each cheek. She looked, because she remembered his words to her. She'd seen his name on his shirt, and in the few moments they had stood in each other's presence, she had felt an attraction that had taken her by storm.

Now, in a blur of longing and emotion, two words were sharply in focus in her mind, and they were all she could think of.

"Alaska? Cool."

Tears blurred the beach around her. He'd also told her something else. "Hilton Head? I'm from there." With those words, she'd known hope, and today she was learning disappointment.

She stood and laughed sourly. Her father would tell her to quit moping, to pull from the strength of the Southern iron in her blood. Her mother would say to use her good, Southern breeding, and not feel sorry for herself. Carolina would say she had a lack of choices. She couldn't make Alaska come to find her, could she? She'd have to buck up and go on without him.

However, as she brushed the sand from her legs, readying herself to go to the house, she did leave herself one small remnant of hope. She was only home for this one weekend. When she flew back to Atlanta for the upcoming summer school session, she'd look for him again. Perhaps he'd be on the tarmac, and he'd be searching for her.

She knew it was silly, but she could hope, couldn't she? After all, she was only nineteen, and she could still dream.

As she walked toward the house, she heard her name called from down the beach, and a sudden, bright hope grabbed at her. Then she remembered she hadn't told him her name. She turned to see Edward waving. As she waved back, he smiled at her and turned back to his game just in time to catch an incoming football and fall laughing into the sand.

Carolina remained standing, watching her brother, and tears filled her eyes. Her Alaska boy wouldn't come find her, and although she knew it was silly, it left her feeling empty inside.

She reached her hands to her face and brushed the moisture away. She sniffed and laughed at herself. Narrowing her eyes at her brother, she muttered, looking at him as he scrambled to his feet to throw the ball back to his friends, "Edward, you'd better keep this to yourself, if you know what's good for you. Mum doesn't need to know, or Dad, and especially not Margarete."

That made her feel a little better, and she turned and marched toward the house.

Chapter 1

"I WANT to be the one to buy the flowers."

Carolina whispered her words as she stood and looked through the window. An executive assistant at one of the top electronics companies in California, she was adept at dealing with stressful situations where other people were concerned. However, this time the events that pressed in on her were more personal. She searched but couldn't find the Southern iron her father had always said ran in her blood. Instead, grittiness rubbed her eyes raw, and she felt as if her soul was torn in two. How she needed the God she had been taught about so many years before in her parents' church in Hilton Head!

She didn't feel Him with her today, though.

For some strangely cruel reason, it was another void that ached inside, a loss from a decade earlier that unaccountably gripped her soul. She liked to pretend she'd long ago excised that day from her life. Her lie hovered in the glass before her, the image of a man she'd run into on the Savannah airport tarmac. His face was as clear as the time she'd spoken with him, and he'd promised to come find her. Filled with an ill-defined longing, she reached her hand to the shimmering surface and placed it there, the heat of the afternoon just on the other side of the glass wrapping around her fingers as if to draw the sorrow of the day's news from her skin.

Guilt at thoughts of this boy rather than her parents' deaths churned her thoughts. She'd finally come to realize she'd run to California. She'd deny that to anyone who asked, but it was true. After he didn't come to find her on her beach, she'd continued to look for him. Unable to bear the memories of her foolish searching, she'd fled, leaving her home and parents far behind. She hadn't escaped, though, as evidenced by his smiling face in the window at her fingertips.

Feeling the warmth of tears start down her cheeks, the image of her parents took his place, and she felt the first vestiges of real grief begin to take hold. The unexpected accident in far-away Hilton Head! How could something so horrendous have happened? Carolina repeated her words to the image of herself she could see reflected in her office window.

"I want to be the one to buy the flowers."

THE SUN filtered through the polished glass windows, and the sea glittered across the sand. Carolina was home for a short visit, and her mother's news was a surprise to her.

"Your cruise! Oh, Mummy, I'm so jealous." Carolina laughed, placing her hand on her mother's arm. The paperwork strewn across the dining room table was filled with glossy photos showing a glamorous ship filled with exciting venues. One pamphlet centered on an elegant couple dining in a star-studded restaurant, the gleaming brass rail at their side opening to a vast cathedral of shipboard banqueting experiences. Another was filled with sun-drenched activities centered on

14

poolside locations, with a glittering sea in the distance. All the participants were young, toned, and laughing. "That'll be me." Carolina's mother pointed to the glossy image of one young couple. She cocked her head to the side. "I'll be thirty again. The travel agent has assured me so." "Daddy, too? Thirty?" Carolina stifled a smirk, her pleasure in her mother's teasing making her glad she'd traveled all the way from California to her family home on Hilton Head Island.

Her mother leaned in, her voice husky with mock conspiracy. "Your father only thinks he's thirty. He forgets he's been married now for that many years." She chuckled, her eyes twinkling.

"Your anniversary." Carolina turned and looked out the window. Her mother's words were a wake-up call. She was nearly thirty herself, her younger brother Edward was in Antarctica doing research—on a perpetual basis it seemed—and she'd been in California as Mr. Warner's executive assistant for years now. "Thirty years of marriage, Mum." She turned back and smiled, forcing her pensive thoughts out of her mind. This was a vacation, not a time to feel sorry for herself.

"And they've been wonderful." Her mother's laughter tinkled. "I've finally got your father to let the reins of the business go. Charlie is very capable, I told him. That's why you hired him as manager. Let him manage, and let's take that cruise you've always promised. Now, we're off. First Class, too. A suite with all the amenities." Sweeping the cruise information from the table and standing to put it into a drawer, she turned to her daughter. "How is that puppy we gave you? Is he keeping you from being lonely?"

"Getting bigger every day." Carolina pursed her lips, stepping to the window. Ricotta. The puppy had carried its unusual name to California, and Carolina hadn't had a choice in the cumbersome moniker. Rotten Ricotta Cheese should be more like it.

"Puppies do that, my dear." Her mother stepped to her and gave her a kiss on the cheek.

"Daddy's at the dealership today?" Carolina truly loved Ricotta, in spite of her complaint, but the dog wasn't what she wanted to talk about right then. Her mother's reference to the airport reminded her of that boy she'd seen so many years ago, and the memory surprised her. She'd thought him long forgotten.

"Do you wish to call him, Carolina? I left my cell phone in the next room, but Margarete can bring the house phone for you. I'll be glad to ring for it." She reached her hand to let it hover over a small device on the table at her side, the red light on its top just beneath her finger.

Carolina turned and gave her mother a hug. "Leave poor Margarete in peace. I think I'll go walk the beach for a bit, Mum. I always forget how beautiful the island is, and you get to see it every day. I want to take some of it home with me, even if I really can't."

Her mother gave her a second kiss as she shooed her out the door.

On the beach, Carolina walked along the surf, the pale sand underneath her feet warm in the afternoon sun. The wind swept her hair across her face, and she reached a hand to pull it back, tucking it behind one ear. When a seagull barked at her, she laughed, knowing it had claimed the beach as its home, and Carolina wasn't welcome to intrude. However, it was her beach, too, and the seagull could certainly share for the few hours until she returned to her California life.

Tears crept unbidden into her eyes. She claimed California as her residence, for she worked there, and her good friend Sha'Cretia Washington waited on her return. Even so, each time she left her Carolina beaches, she left a little bit of her heart here, and when she was in California, this was always where she wanted to be.

There was one other thing. Each time she stepped onto the tarmac at the Savannah airport, her eyes invariably searched for that boy from so many years ago. If only he'd come to find her as he'd promised a decade before, she'd never have run away. With a laugh, the heat of the sun-drenched sand bringing out the Southern fortitude flowing through Carolina's veins, she brushed that boy away. It was summer, she was on her beloved beach, and her mother waited on her to return from her walk. What better life could she ask for?

As Carolina once again pushed her hair from her face, her palm brushed against windblown sand caught in the dampness on her cheek. She would have denied it if asked, but it didn't seem that boy from the Savannah tarmac had been banished so very far from her thoughts after all, even if her bright expression claimed he had.

THE WIND whistled through the Alaska hills, and as it slipped through the trees, it calmed, reaching slender fingers to caress an unnamed stream. With a soft touch, it lifted Kodiak Leberge's fly-fishing line in a dance of sparkling beauty. Scattering the surface of the water into a million wavelets, it sang its melodies to the lone fish shimmering just under the surface of the stream.

"Beautiful girl," Kodiak whispered, winking at the scaled creature. "If I ever met you on an airport runway, I'd not let you get away again."

The young man, sandy blond and not yet thirty, let his eyes jump for a moment to the brilliance of the blue sky visible between the mountain peaks in front of him. His hair was a thick mass atop his head, unruly and filled with the sun and the wind. He smiled at the feeling of the day against his back. It wasn't winter today. The cold had been brutal this year, for the last two, actually. Today, though, he could endure all the brutal winters in Alaska, if only for a handful of days like this one.

17

His line tightened, and his reel sang. His offering to this beauty before him had been accepted.

"Today, you will be mine!"

His vibrant words broke the crystalline air as he began to work his line, and pulling his rod high, then letting it fall, teasing the fish, tiring it as they played, he began to step forward, planning his final gambit. At last he released his line, and it stilled its dance to float on the surface of the stream. His opponent had tired, relinquishing its freedom, giving it up to the master of the catch.

"Gotcha!" Kodiak called, unable to contain his enthusiasm. "Wahoo! I am the best!" He leaped over the stones in the riverbed, scrambling to get his net under his fish. This would be a day of feasting, that was for sure, and he would eat well.

He reached into the net and pulled out his prize, shaking the hook from its mouth. He held it up in the sun, and as its rays flashed along the moistened scales running down the finned creature's side, he was taken back to a time years earlier. His wife. His ex-wife, now. When he'd felt his childhood faith pulling him back to the Church, she hadn't joined him. He'd felt trapped with her, just like this fish he held in his hand.

In that moment of reflection, before he could stop himself, his fingers opened. As if in a slow motion sequence, each second stretching to fill minutes, the scales of the creature shimmered in the sun, and with a splash, it was gone, free to live another day.

Kodiak looked around at the beauty of the Alaska wilderness. He grinned. Reaching into his bag, he pulled out a new fly and attached it to his line. He would eat tonight, even if his hand had turned his dinner free. He knew everyone needed a second chance now and then, but he wanted a meal. That fish had better watch out. There'd be no third chances. He had a frying pan waiting, and it wouldn't be patient forever.

"YES, MR. WARNER?"

The day was early, yet, and the news of her parents hadn't yet assaulted Carolina's morning. Her voice was bright with enthusiasm. Even so, it was her formal business face she wore. It had been weeks since she'd been home, and she missed her parents unmercifully.

"Carolina, please come in." Her boss stood, stepping around his desk. "Please, have a seat."

She moved into his office, letting the door gently swing closed behind her. Mr. Warner took her elbow, guiding her to a pair of chrome and leather chairs that sat next to each other. As Carolina lowered herself into one, he dropped heavily into the other. Just behind, banks of curtained windows wrapped two walls of his corner office. His voice had been warm and gentle, but there was something else, and it caught her attention.

"There's a problem, Mr. Warner?" Carolina pushed her hair back from her face, tucking it behind her ear. She thought of her parents, even though there was no reason to do so. Still, an image of them at home in Hilton Head flashed through her thoughts, their house on the beach, her mother driving one of her father's Cadillacs along the tree-lined streets searching for the shops she wanted, barely able to see the signs that were no higher than the hood of her massive luxury car. Pushing the familiar memories aside, she smiled, crossing one leg over the other.

"Your parents, Carolina." Mr. Warner paused, taking a deep breath. "There's been an accident." He stood, and he grasped the front of his slacks along the creases, shaking them out. Then he quickly sat again, licking his lips.

She laughed, relieved it was something so simple. She imagined her mother forgetting her glasses and sideswiping another car as she looked for a new store she had heard about. Carolina had complained for years about her hometown's refusal to allow signs any taller than the hood of her mother's big car. She was forever turning in at the last minute because the sign she searched for was hidden behind a low shrub.

When her boss didn't elaborate, Carolina reached a hand to rest it on his suited arm. "I'm sure everything's all right, Mr. Warner. What did they say happened?"

"Carolina, neither of your parents survived." The words were choked out. He reached to her, taking her hand in his.

Carolina felt the sudden and gray world of disbelief wash over her. She woodenly stood and walked to the window. Pushing the drapes aside, she rested her forehead against the glass and watched the city around her, one hand unconsciously tugging her hair. The sun glittered in the summer sky. Each building stood in the same location it had occupied on the way to work that morning. Cars filled the streets below, and people scurried along the sidewalks, going about their busy lives.

Carolina loved this city, or at least she did when her memories of Hilton Head weren't pulling her home. She loved the sounds of the traffic, the people carrying on their public conversations without regards to who might overhear, and even the smells of the traffic that filled the streets.

However, as she looked out over the great metropolis that made up the sprawling city of Los Angeles, it was all a world of gray fog to her.

How could this vast and cold place ever be home again?

KODIAK was just out of high school, and he wrestled with the engine of the prop-driven passenger plane. It was a warm day, even beautiful, and he felt lucky to have gotten this job at the Savannah airport. Mechanical work had always been easy for him, the skills learned as a teen working on his father's old airplane. The pilot of this small commercial craft had radioed in an unusual noise, unwilling to risk taking it aloft again without it being checked out. Kodiak could find nothing but a loose cable that might have been bumping the engine housing. He used an industrial zip tie to snug the cable to a bracket and backed out to close the cowling. He turned to see a stunning girl watching him, and he grinned. Her eyes glanced at his shirt and back to his face. A sparkle was in her eyes, and she was beautiful.

"Alaska!" She called the word to him with a laugh and a wave. It was just a word, but to Kodiak, it was so much more. When she spoke, her voice was the ripple of a summer stream across glistening smooth stones. The wind caught her hair, and she reached a slender hand to tuck it behind one ear.

"Alaska?" For a moment he was caught off guard, but that didn't stop him from noticing the girl's shining hair, the cast of her eyes, or the cut of her lips as she smiled in return.

"Your name. I love it!" She pointed to his shirt.

His name! He laughed. "You'll be on Hilton Head all weekend?" It was where all the small planes were headed.

"I live there."

"I'll come find you. Look for me on the sand." He turned, startled as the pilot sounded the airplane's horn at him. He didn't remember airplanes having horns.

The scene began to shift, and Kodiak opened his eyes to the underside of his old truck. A vehicle's horn blared again in the silence of the cool Alaska morning as someone called to him.

"Kodiak! Is there a Kodiak in here? If so, where are you?" The loud honking reverberated a third time.

Kodiak rolled out from under his old truck, shaking his head to bring himself back to reality. Here under his truck, attempting to tackle his ancient rust bucket, Old Red, he'd dozed only for a moment, and that girl from all those years ago had been back with him. He thought he'd forgotten all about her. He had no idea what brought her to mind now. At this exact moment in his life, he had other fish to fry. His transmission had been giving him fits, and he'd wondered whether he should pull the entire thing, or if he could drive it a while longer. It was only func-

21

tional now because most of the rugged Alaska roads he drove rarely required him to shift any higher than second. Forcing it into third had become a workout, and he'd already decided that if he was going to sit in the shop with no work to do, then perhaps it was time to tackle this.

Wiping a hand across his face, he grabbed the truck's step rail and pulled himself to his feet. He noticed the grease smeared across his palm, and he knew it was now all over the side of his face. There was nothing to be done about it now, though. There sitting outside his single garage door was the longest white limousine to be found anywhere on the Alaska Coast. He had work to do. Old Red would have to wait yet again.

He smiled at that.

He stepped outside the door, glancing back at the sign he'd just installed the week before. Kodiak Leberge, it read. Master Mechanic. In smaller letters he'd added, Aircraft, Cars, Small Machines. If It Runs, I Can Repair It.

"You're Kodiak, right?" The man next to the white car narrowed his eyes, only relaxing when Kodiak nodded.

This man might not know Kodiak, other than his name from the sign overhead, but Kodiak had dodged this vehicle a few times. This man was a reckless driver, taking corners at fantastic speeds.

"I need my brakes checked on this limo. I have it rented at three for a cruise tour, and it's squealing like a woman with her credit card cut off." The pristinely dressed man looked down at his watch and then up to the sky, pursing his lips as if expecting the unlittered expanse of blue to cloud up and rain just to make his day more difficult.

Kodiak moved his truck and pulled the limo onto the rack. From watching this car as the driver hauled his tourists around, he wasn't surprised to hear the brakes were gone. Not only was the limo huge, and Kodiak understood that meant heavy, but he knew what to expect any time he saw it coming down the road.

Move out of the way. Everyone moved out of the way of this limo owner. He was fast, and he was dangerous.

When he pulled the first wheel off, it wasn't a revelation to find that in addition to the pads, the rotors also needed to be replaced. Getting new rotors in this remote location was going to slow this car down for a while. He had none in stock and would need to fly to the next town to get them.

Kodiak whistled as he walked back into his small office. He placed a worn brake pad on the counter. "Gone," he said, looking up to the man's face. He tried to stifle a grin as he continued. "The rotors, too." He glanced down and rubbed a fingernail across the edge of the worn pad to draw the man's attention to just how bad they were.

"Rotors? Are those important?" Panic invaded the limo owner's face.

"Well," Kodiak drawled in his best Low Country voice, "Only if you want to stop to avoid hitting any errant caribou that might be wandering across the road. If you're out with a group of hunters, maybe not so much." Kodiak glanced up at a clock on the wall. "Might be tight on time, but if I took my plane, I think I could fly to Koko's Auto Supplies to get your new rotors, as long as I leave now. It'll be extra, though." There would be plenty of time, but this was an opportunity to get up in his airplane, and he suddenly wanted to be there.

"Koko's? That's up in the next town, isn't it? How much extra?" The man had pulled his wallet out, and he made as if to drop it back into his pocket. "It'll be a lot, won't it?"

"Gas for the Cessna sure hasn't gone down the last few months." Kodiak nodded across the road where his small plane could be seen tied up to a dock. He opened a drawer underneath the counter and flipped through his latest surfing magazine. Pursing his lips, pretending he was evaluating the cost, he shook his head as if the total was surely too much. He continued, playing up the expense angle. "Two-fifty would just about do it,

I think. Is it worth it to you? If not, I could get the rotors delivered tomorrow, if you can do without the car that long." Gently, he closed the drawer.

"Two-fifty? You can guarantee it by three? I lose nine hundred if I have to cancel." The limo owner nervously glanced at the airplane and back to his car. The beading sweat on his brow told Kodiak just how much he wanted this.

"Guaranteed? No, I can't promise that. Too many variables when I'm flying. Try. That's all I can do. Is it a go?" Kodiak looked back at the clock. "Gotta go now if I'm going to have any chance to do this."

"Do it. You have a phone around here, a land line? My cell's dead. Never gets reception off the main street, anyway." He grinned with relief when Kodiak pulled an old, black rotary phone from under the counter. "I need to call my partner to let him know I need to be picked up."

Kodiak watched his visitor dial in the number, then he rapped the counter with his knuckles to let the man know he was on his way, heading out the door. He'd call in the order on the shortwave radio as soon as he got in his plane. Koko's would have it ready for him when he arrived. The man nodded to Kodiak as he began his conversation into the old, outdated phone.

With his checkbook and wallet in hand, Kodiak stepped briskly to the dock and his airplane. He was unworried about the shop. Bears were more of a concern than any thieves in this part of the world.

He breathed in deeply. Alaska. He'd hated the past two winters, but this was a day he didn't regret being here at all, even if it wasn't the Low Country he'd been born to. The weather today was faultless, and the sun glistened on anything that had been sprinkled with the morning's moisture. The crispness in the air would make for a perfect trip. It wasn't often he got paid two bills plus some just to take his airplane up.

In addition to having plenty of time to cruise by his cabin and see how things were going, with the cruise ship coming in, he'd get a really good view of the tourists' activities, too. More importantly, he'd get to watch it from high in the air, and that was just where he wanted to be, away from the commotion that would overwhelm his small town while the cruise ship was docked. He'd have the freedom of the skies, even if only for a couple of hours, unlike the life he'd lived in that hated condo on his ex-wife's beloved East Coast beach.

He brushed that reminder from his mind, letting his enjoyment at prepping his craft for the flight occupy all of his attention.

Soon aloft, he glanced around, lowering the visor against the brightness of the morning. The clarity and warmth of the weather during this time of year was uncommon but very welcome. Laughing at a series of breaking waves in an otherwise calm sea, he recognized them for what they were, a pod of whales. His father should be here now. If not for him, there'd be no plane and no Alaska.

Touching down in the protected cove near Koko's, Kodiak idled up to the dock and was soon off for the limo's needed rotors. He'd gotten through on the shortwave while en route, and he fully expected the goods to be packaged and waiting when he stepped through the door.

As he climbed the dock's ladder to reach the level of the street, he looked back at the float to admire his Cessna floating in the water. His heart swelled. The winters could certainly be brutal in this wild land, but seeing his love there, his airplane floating in the gentle swell of the cove, made it all worth it.

A motion caught his eye, and Kodiak laughed. It was Old Man Tuck from down by Kodiak's place, and he was pulling up to the waterfront in his old Cherokee. He had a reputation as having the ugliest four-wheel drive in the state, and Kodiak had to agree. Not only was it four different colors—unintentionally, from several body parts that were mismatched—but rust had painted it a tie-dye red. The old man had probably spent the better part of three hours navigating the back roads to get here, and it'd take him just as long to get back home.

"Hey, Tuck!" Kodiak raised his hand to greet the old man. "God certainly gave us a beautiful day today." He laughed when all he got was a snort and a mumbled reply.

"New-fangled planes. Give me a good old Jeep any day." Tuck glowered as he walked by. He ignored the comment about God. He always did.

Poor old Tuck, the younger man laughed silently to himself. He was stuck on the back roads, and he didn't even know what he was missing.

Kodiak loped up the final few steps to the parts store to find they had indeed followed through. His packages were wrapped and ready for him as promised. With a flourish of his name on a check and a humorous joke to the cashier, he was back out the door into the sunshine. He closed his eyes in the brightness of the glare, letting the warmth wash across his face.

The girl's remark that day. Alaska. He supposed it had stuck with him because of his mother telling him of how he was as close to her dream of Alaska as she'd ever get. When Julianna had demanded his plane be sold in the divorce, he'd taken off for the one place in the world that he considered his.

You were my worst nightmare, Julianna, he muttered. However, he wouldn't be in Alaska if it weren't for her wanton lifestyle and outrageous demands. After all, he was flying the skies of the most wonderful state in the Union, and today, there was no better place to be.

Chapter 2

"OH, SWEET baby!"

Sha'Cretia Washington barreled through the door, dropping the files she carried into a convenient chair. Her coal-black hair was piled high on her head, and she wore a perfect coat of polish on each hand. Her white blouse boasted ruffled sleeves over a tight burgundy skirt. Dark skin set off her equally red pumps. She was perfectly refined, with every outrageous element neatly matched.

Today even her eyes were red, although it was unintentional. She held her arms out, ready to offer consolation.

Taking a deep breath, Carolina laid down the report she'd been reading. Since leaving Mr. Warner's office an hour before, she'd tried to focus on her work. She really had. Reports were piled on her desk, ones she felt responsibility for. Disbursements were waiting to be sent, and overtime pay needed to be credited. People had to be taken care of, even if a disaster had taken her personal world and shredded it to clippings.

On the other hand, she couldn't deal with someone else's issues through her fog of disbelief. She knew she needed to buy a ticket to return to the East Coast as soon as she could arrange it, but it was as if it were someone else's ticket, not hers.

She took a deep breath, pushing away the throbbing in her temples. Grief would hit her hard. It just wasn't here yet. She must be in shock. She must.

"Yes, Sha?" Carolina ran her slender finger along the edge of the thin folder in the middle of her desk, the report captured inside. Someone's life was in that folder, someone who hadn't had the best part of everything they knew ripped from them. She felt her eyes burn, and she couldn't even greet her best friend properly. Numbness kept her from running to those welcoming arms just across her desk.

"Honey bunch, I'm so sorry." Her friend moved around the desk, with each step a graceful waltz across the floor, and put a carefully manicured hand on her friend's shoulder. "I was just at the manicurist getting a polish, and when I walked in, I heard the news. You know you've been my best girlfriend here." She reached to flatten a crease in her skirt, and she looked up with tears trailing mascara down her face. She laughed, whispering, "I can't even see myself, and I already know I should have splurged on the waterproof stuff. If my daddy hadn't been black, then I'd really look a mess."

Carolina drew in a deep breath, and in that moment she felt something ease inside. Just seeing Sha'Cretia's brightly made-up features was the rainbow of life through Carolina's gray gloom of acid-washed sorrow. She reached out her arms and gave her friend a big hug, certain her presence would keep the tears at bay for a little while, anyway.

"Sha, you know you always brighten my days, no matter how bad they are. How can I endure the East Coast this time without you?" She gave her a kiss on the cheek, reaching her thumb to wipe some of her running mascara away. "Let me get you a tissue."

"Girl, you are a winner." Sha'Cretia's brushed her long, polished fingers across one side of her face, and she stroked her cheek softly to make sure the moisture was gone. "You go give those people in the East a piece of your mind. Make them do your parents proud." With those words, her eyes welled up again. "Oh, Carolina," Sha'Cretia wailed. "I wish I could go with you. Just thinking of you going alone is breaking my heart."

Carolina smiled, truly warmed by her friend's giving nature. She turned to the sound of a voice at the door.

"Ms. DeAngeles, the driver is on his way."

"Driver?" She turned to Sha'Cretia.

Sha'Cretia stepped to Carolina and cupped her elbow in her hand, moving her toward the door. "You were kinda out of it, sweetie. Mr. Warner called his car for you. Go. I've got this handled. I'd be there with you, but then this place would fall apart." She smiled and patted Carolina's shoulder. "Go. Stay until you feel better. I've got your house and that big lug of a dog under control." Then she grabbed Carolina and gave her another firm hug. "I only met your parents once, and I loved them like my own."

"Oh, Sha," Carolina whispered, her face going numb.

Sha'Cretia smiled and looked directly into her friend's eyes. "Sweetie, I loved your parents even more than my own, actually. Mine showed me the front door and took my key the night I put my first designer dress on, and it was a classic Dior A-line. However, even I can see that you'll never cope with just my silly stories. What can I do for you, baby?"

Carolina's voice was ragged as she turned to the window. "Sha, I want to be the one to buy the flowers."

Sha'Cretia wrapped her arms around her and hugged her for a minute. Then she called another assistant to help her out. With her most cheerful face, Sha'Cretia moved to shoo Carolina out the door. The driver arrived to meet them at the office and assisted Carolina toward the company car waiting just outside.

Out of the presence of her friend, Carolina felt her energy drain from her like melting butter in the heat of a California summer. Exiting the building, Carolina's feet dragged along the sidewalk, lifeless, and she tugged at her hair, barely able to cope. At the car, she placed one hand on the door, soaking up the heat in the metal. What did it mean, her parents on one side of the continent, and her on the other? Now, they were gone, and she wasn't there.

Before climbing inside the long, black company car, she put on her best office smile and teased with the driver. "Just be glad you have me and not Sha'Cretia to drive around today."

"Sha'Cretia is a handful, I'll give you that. My condolences on your sad news today, Ms. DeAngeles." The driver tipped his hat.

That reminder was a blow to Carolina's false front. Dropping into the luxurious automobile, she felt her momentary bravado collapse inside of her. She desperately wanted to say a prayer, but that never seemed to work for her. Even the sumptuous smells of leather and exotic woods that usually triggered her love of fine things had no effect on her. Her life had begun unraveling around her, and all the extravagances in the world could not repair the damage that had been done.

KODIAK was able to pick up the parts and get back to the shop to get the new rotors on the limo with plenty of time to spare. Of course, he would've had even more time if he hadn't stopped by his favorite backwoods stream on the return for a quick bit of fly-fishing.

Looking out from his airplane, the sparkle of the sun on the stream had called to him, a beautiful siren with a voice of beauty beyond compare. It would only be a quick hike from the small lake he could land his airplane on. The scramble through the wooded hillside would use up precious fishing time, but driving there would take even more. He hadn't been able to resist. If he didn't get the brakes fixed because he was out on his stream, he hadn't exactly promised, had he? And anyway, his airplane was gone from the dock. Who would be there to tattle on him?

The tradeoff was worth it.

It wasn't until he caught his third fish that he remembered Old Man Tuck. "Drive a Jeep!" He'd been seen at Koko's, and there was no doubt Tuck would vent to everyone he met about that darn airplane that had invaded his precious Alaska coastline.

Kodiak pulled his line in and gathered his fish. He now regretted they'd seen each other. All because Tuck preferred Jeeps. Why, when an airplane was much better?

Flaming bear turds!

The tension was broken, and Kodiak laughed aloud as he scrambled through the brush back to his airplane. He'd lost his garbage to marauding bears three weeks in a row. One morning, he decided no bears were going to get his trash again. He'd burn it from then on. He'd followed through just that once. He hadn't known several cubs had been sleeping in his metal drums and leaving him gifts afterwards. He'd dumped his trash in, doused it with a good jug of gasoline, and thrown in a match. Talk about brutal! Those bear droppings had wafted their awful odor for two weeks, and the wind had been kind enough to blow it directly towards his cabin the entire time.

Once back at his shop, and after gladly accepting a well-padded envelope of money for what amounted to a simple brake job, Kodiak pulled down an old box from on top of a storage cabinet, putting a portion of the money inside. After the divorce he'd had trouble making his alimony payments as well as paying rent to his friend for the shared room he called home. Now he wondered if he'd ever save enough money to buy his freedom back. He'd run to the only place no one knew about except him and his father, their old fishing shack in Alaska. Weeks passed as he'd continued flying west, working his way farther and farther toward the Pacific. He'd worked temporary jobs at the airports he stopped at along the way, from repairing engines to washing the aircraft, anything to make money.

His own airplane had finally given up on him, and he'd left it behind in Edmonton until he could earn the money for repairs. Eventually he'd stepped off a bus, and he'd been in Alaska. It was only Tok, but still, Alaska!

Anchorage had come later, and there'd been a job at a mechanic's shop to earn money to repair his airplane. At first it had been everything he'd hoped. Then, he'd barely survived his first winter in the old fishing shack he and his dad had once cobbled together. After that, he'd found the motivation to put together his own much-better-built cabin. It was small, but it was warmer than stuffing wads of cloth in knotholes to keep out the winter wind. He'd even managed to salvage much of the old shack in the new cabin's construction.

Now, here he was in Alaska with the things he treasured most. He had his father's old fishing cabin, completely rebuilt; a mechanic's shop of his own; and his father's airplane, now his, of course. However, on quite a few cold nights, he'd trade it all for one pretty girl to smile at him as he drew his head out of an airplane cowling, only this time he'd insist on her name. He might have to give up living in Alaska to hold her in his arms, but it'd be worth the cost.

He was certain of that.

"MS. DeANGELES? We're here."

Carolina looked out the window to see her house coming up. "Pull beside the house, if you don't mind."

"Yes, ma'am." The driver turned into the drive, the front wheels dipping into the depression along the curb, and the rest of the massive machine sliding after it into the driveway. No more did Carolina have her car door open, than Ricotta barked twice, bounded over the fence, and leaped through, his enormous body filling much of the back seat of her boss's massive limousine. Carolina laughed through her tears, grabbing his furry head.

"Ricotta, you rotten thing! How I've needed you!" She wrapped her arms around the animal's neck, pressing her face against his fur. "I have to get my things, and no, you can't go with me. Sorry, you rotten cheese."

She laughed again when he began to lick her face.

She stepped into her house and packed a light bag, letting the driver load her single case into the limousine's trunk. After she entered the car, the driver stood, holding her door, and asked about her dog.

"Ms. DeAngeles, I believe I've been told your pet is welcome to accompany you."

"To the airport?" Carolina wadded her tissue in her hand and looked up at the man holding the door. She'd been fighting her tears, and she didn't wish him to see.

"Certainly. Mr. Warner has approved the animal's transport. I can return him here afterwards."

Now, Ricotta was with her, and she could cry into his fur, and no one need know.

The window separating the passenger compartment from the driver slipped down. "He missed you, I see."

Carolina glanced up to see a smiling face watching her in the rearview mirror. "I've missed him more. Thank you for all your help." The black window rose smoothly into its track, sealing her into the back of the long car. With barely a sound, she felt it begin to move down the street, taking her toward Hilton Head.

She jumped at a piercing beeping from just to her side. Her attention was quickly riveted to the blackened glass separating her from the driver's compartment. It slipped down, and the driver held up a corded phone. "Ms. DeAngeles, the call is for you. If you'll look in the armrest, you'll see a phone like this one." He caught her eye in the mirror, and he waited until she looked down and saw the blinking light on the armrest. She opened the compartment to see the phone. "Just pick it up and you may begin speaking. Hang up when you're finished." He glanced away and the window was closed, even before Carolina could reach beside her.

Next to the phone was a small container of tissues. Pulling a fresh one out, Carolina dabbed her eyes and then her nose. Lifting the receiver, she tried to be bright and brave as she spoke to the unknown caller.

"Carolina speaking. How may I direct your call?" Immediately she felt silly. She wasn't at work, and besides, who even knew she was here?

The voice was Mr. Warner's.

"Oh, Carolina!" She heard him laugh out loud. "You may not direct my call anywhere. You're not at work, and I expect you to focus on yourself. When my wife died, I was inconsolable. Then, after Gabriella was killed in that horrible carjacking, no one could make me see farther than the end of my nose. You'll be the same. I've arranged for you to take the company airplane. Your pet can ride anywhere with you, even in the next seat."

"Ricotta's going to the East Coast with me?" Her eyes welled with tears of gratitude. "Mr. Warner, you're too good to me." She pressed the tissue to her eyes. It was as if the flow would never cease.

"My driver tells me you just left your house. When you reach the airport, he'll help you carry your things. Please have a pleasant trip, if that's possible. This will be a time of extreme sorrow for you, and I hope my arrangements will make it as easy as possible. Take your time and come back when your affairs are in order."

Carolina could barely whisper her gratitude before hanging up the phone. If Ricotta hadn't been at her side, she didn't think she could have stood it at all.

KODIAK climbed up and leaned onto the wing of his airplane. He glanced up at the sky and could tell that the weather was due for a change. He looked around and grinned. He knew he'd had a treat with the clear flying conditions he'd lucked into the past few days. It had been great to be able to get up in his airplane, and at someone else's expense, too. Sometimes he cursed the way the cost of fuel had put a crimp in his flight time, but when someone else paid, then, well, it just didn't matter.

As much as he hated winters here, he accepted the tradeoff. Being up north was a major factor in being able to fly regularly. It was the distance between towns, and the inaccessibility created by poor roads and severe terrain. Flight was often the only way to get from place to place.

He reached to make sure the fuel filler cap was tightly secured. On one occasion—and one only—he'd flown with water in his fuel lines. He'd had his ex-wife with him, and she hadn't really wanted to be there that trip.

She had been the reason for the water.

He'd worked extra-long hours that summer to make some needed repairs on his airplane just so he could get it up in the air. When his ex had wanted to spend a week in Naples, he'd offered to fly them down. She'd fought him, preferring to travel First Class in the style of her preference, having filet of some-thing and a saucer, er, glass of bubbly. That was her idea of a fine trip, not riding the winds of a hurricane in a tin can for two. Her words, not his, he told people when he shared the story of his life.

On that trip, he'd filled the wings with fuel, and when he'd stepped down to put the filler hose away, she'd done something very unusual. When he moved to secure the cap, she smiled, very pleased with herself, telling him she'd already replaced it, so please get his tin can in the air in order for them to get there.

"Wine, well-seasoned fillet, and a nicely salted bath. Just get me to the hotel." Her smile had quickly turned into an irritating whine.

Kodiak hadn't felt right about it. He always made a practice of checking the airplane himself, never trusting anyone else. However, it had been the first time she'd done anything to help prepare for a flight, and he'd wanted to show her he trusted her and appreciated what she'd done.

Then came the rains. All the way down into Florida. After that came the spitting and the coughing of the engines. Every highway had started looking good to him about that time. It had cost him a bundle to have the tanks and fuel lines flushed, too. That's why he twisted the fuel cap just to be sure.

Nearly biting the dirt just because of a loose fuel cap was not his dream way to land a plane.

Chapter 3

CAROLINA stepped from the company jet. Savannah! She closed her eyes and drew in a deep breath. The salt in the air, and the smell of the greenery. The greenery! The brilliance of the light! Oh, how she forgot each time she was away! The air was so moist, and the smell brought back such memories. She could, she *would* put her grief away just for this moment. Her parents would want that from her. They would expect her to grieve, but they would expect her to continue to live and love life, also.

She smiled, soaking up the intensity of the experience, her eyes kept tightly closed. In her mind, she saw something no one else could: a golden-headed boy; his sun-kissed skin. It'd been nearly ten years, but he could have stayed on, even still be single, possibly still looking for her. It was conceivable in her dreams that the pilot had radioed in an imperceptible problem with the airplane, demanding a mechanic be on the tarmac to check it out, and her boy would come running. He'd see her and wave. She'd find his face breaking into a smile, and the dimples she'd dreamed of so many times would split his cheeks in two. He'd ask if she was going to the beach, Hilton Head, of course, and she'd take him home with her.

"Ms. DeAngeles?"

Carolina jerked, catching herself, opening her eyes, the late afternoon sun suddenly harsh on her face. Her boy faded away, and she caught the attendant looking at her. She smiled as if caught exposed, her embarrassment written in the warmth crawling up her neck. She put her hand to her collar, pulling it close as if cold, although the air was quite warm.

"Missed it, huh? I understand you've been away quite some time." The flight attendant smiled at her. "I feel this way every time. Stop and smell the sea air. It never gets old. You'll be on the island soon enough." He patted his pocket. "I've been given a list of your local contacts, and I'll be on the phone immediately to take care of your needs." His face sobered, and he took a moment to reassure her. "I'll be available your entire visit if you need me. I've been asked to reassure you of the love of all your coworkers."

"My dog, Ricotta. I mustn't forget him." Carolina turned to the airplane, her grief building inside, as the memory of why she was here flooded through her. How could she have forgotten Ricotta? He was the one love left in her life.

The attendant reached at his side to pick up Carolina's case. "The pilot will be bringing him. Don't you worry." He paused, and seeing a long black automobile drive up, he nodded. "Your car. You'll be staying on Hilton Head. However, I also understand there are some stops for you to make here in Savannah. Now, your Ricotta." He nodded his head towards the airplane.

Hearing a familiar whine, Carolina turned to see the pilot being tugged along by her dog.

"Our pilot was a woman? She flew so well, too. She's very

pretty." Carolina covered her mouth and laughed, her thoughts of her parents set aside for a moment. She glanced at the attendant. "I wish I'd known. I might have asked to go forward to say hello."

The pilot, a petite woman in a dark suit, wrestled the large dog up beside Carolina. She was laughing. "He certainly knows his master. He couldn't wait to get over here to you." She handed Carolina the leash. "He's a cutie. I noticed his name on the kennel's tag. Isn't that a type of cheese?" She stepped up to the attendant and slipped her arm around his waist.

"Only in the world of fine cuisine. In this case, Ricotta means rotten dog. He's pedigreed, though, no matter how wicked he is."

"Seriously?" The pilot laughed. "Pedigreed, with a name like that?"

"His name's really Rotten Ricotta Cheese Soufflé Flambé. It's those crazy AKC names. I couldn't imagine calling him Rotten except in teasing. Cheese? Even worse." Carolina rubbed the animal's ears as he leaned hard against her legs. "I never even considered Soufflé or Flambé."

"I understand why." It was the attendant responding this time, and he leaned down and kissed the pilot on the forehead.

Carolina knelt, rubbing both sides of Ricotta's head, looking directly in his eyes as he opened his mouth and let his tongue hang out in excitement at all the special attention. He gave three sharp barks. "Actually, now that I've had him a while, I've figured out that he really is rotten, but I'm used to Ricotta. So, Ricotta it is." She continued to peer into the animal's eyes a moment before she stood. "You two are a couple?"

The pilot smiled. "Married. We pilot together. This gig with the company's been a dream come true. I fly and Marcus stewards. Then we switch. I steward and Marcus pilots. On the way back, you'll have me in the cabin with you."

Carolina paused, hesitant to suggest their apparent mistake. "I haven't made any return plans, yet. What if I don't fly with you when I return?" She reached to Ricotta, rubbing his ears pensively. The thought of breaking even the tenuous connection with the airplane's crew was suddenly very distressing to her, as if she were suddenly being forced to face the details of her parents' impending affairs all alone. She couldn't share her grief, not really, but this was just one more layer of isolation added to all the rest. She felt her eyes begin to burn, and she looked away to keep her composure.

A hand reached to Carolina's arm, and a voice soothed her fears. "We have no return plans, either. Mr. Warner has requested we stay here at your convenience. I thought you'd been informed. We'll bring the airplane onto the island for the return leg of your trip."

Carolina knew she might have been. However, with the fast-moving events of the day, not everything had stuck with her.

The pilot continued, "When you've completed all you need to take care of, just give us a call." She looked at Marcus. "Have you given her the phone, yet?"

"Oh," and he smiled, reaching a hand to his jacket pocket. "Your satellite phone. Our numbers are preprogrammed in. Press two and it calls me. Number three calls Melissa. That's my wife. Number four is your driver. He's yours for the trip. Mr. Warner really must think a lot of you. This is first class all the way."

He nodded at the car, reaching to tap on the glass. An older, suited driver wearing a military-style cap emerged. With a smile, he stepped up to Carolina.

"Such a pretty miss you are, my bonnie lass. Carolina DeAngeles, I hear. My name is Bill White, and I'm yours for your time here in Savannah and on the island." He stepped forward and reached to take the bag from Marcus. "I'll put this in the trunk, and we can be on our way." He nodded with a continued smile, running his free hand over Ricotta's snout, getting a lick in the process. "Plenty of room for a good dog like this. Looks to be a good breed, too."

Carolina just laughed. A good breed? She didn't know about that. However, Ricotta was good for lifting her spirits. "Rotten Ricotta Cheese, that's what he is. Thank you, though. He's my emotional bastion on this trip. Good old Ricotta will get me through. Won't you, boy?" She rubbed the side of his face and down his neck as he looked up at her.

Turning to her transporters, she took one of each of their hands in hers. "The both of you have made this leg of my journey so much easier. I'll eagerly anticipate joining you for our return flight. I suppose the kennel can remain on the plane? It's rented, you know." At Melissa's nod, she smiled at them, wrapping her grief into a small place in her thoughts as she let Bill help her seat herself in the limousine's rear accommodations. She held up the satellite phone. "I'll keep you abreast." She smiled again and waved as the door enclosed her into the buttery leather of the machine's luxury.

Just then the opposite door opened, and in bounded Ricotta with a yelp of excitement, putting his paw on her lap and nuzzling her around the face.

"You thought I'd forgotten you again, you rotten dog. Too bad. Just like rotten cheese, I'm stuck with you forever." She patted the floor, and he obediently lay down for the ride. She snorted. If he'd just behave that well outside of a car, she'd find him much more agreeable, but then that wouldn't be Ricotta, would it?

As the car pulled away, Carolina's eyes unconsciously looked to the front of the airplane in which she'd flown across the country. Just for a moment, her breath drew in a fraction more quickly, and she blinked her eyes a little faster. There was no boy walking around from the other side, though.

She settled back and reached one hand to Ricotta's head,

41

letting him lay it in her lap as she idly scratched the base of his ears. She whispered to him, "Ah, well. He's probably married with three kids, has a potbelly, and is half bald by now. I wouldn't know him if I saw him." Then she closed her eyes, and within moments he was there with her, running in from the surf, the water glistening on his skin, and a surfboard under his arm. He laughed with the joy of being on the water and with the pleasure of returning to his found-again love. He leaned down to Carolina as she sat on her chaise, and he kissed her wetly on the cheek. Carolina's breath came faster as she reached her hand to laughingly brush him away. Her hand met with a bearded face, and she opened her eyes.

She sat up laughing, and then she sighed, her eyes burning. "Ricotta, get down. Can't a girl even have a good fantasy without you putting your muzzle in where it doesn't belong? Now my parents' deaths are on my mind again."

She pushed him back into the floor just as she noticed a light blinking on her armrest. Remembering the limo in California, she reached to open the compartment she knew must be there and wasn't surprised to see a similar phone nestled inside. She picked it up. "Yes?"

"Ms. DeAngeles, this is Bill. Marcus just called, and the funeral home would like to know if you feel up to stopping by on your way to the hotel. What should I tell them?"

Carolina paused for a moment, soaking in the information, her chest suddenly tight. It had been such a relief to be on the airplane with others responsible for the moment. Then, in the limo, she'd felt the same relief. Now, her parents' death was once again real, an intrinsic part of her day, and even the fantasy world of luxury jets and dream cars couldn't intrude for long.

Taking a deep breath, barely able to push aside the rising grief, she replied, "Of course, Bill. We can stop by."

"Thank you, Ms. DeAngeles. I'll let them know."

"Bill?"

"Yes, Ms. DeAngeles?"

"I didn't know Mr. Warner had a hotel for me. I'd thought to stay at my parents' house. Do you think that will be all right?" Her tears were threatening again. She needed the comfort of her parents' beachfront home, and as she rubbed her dog's forehead, poor Ricotta looked up at her with his great, sad eyes, his tongue hanging from his mouth in a slow pant.

"I'm sure that can be done, Ms. DeAngeles. May I make a phone call for you to see that the house is ready?"

By this time, Carolina could no longer contain her tears. Barely able to speak, she whispered into the phone, no longer wishing to push Ricotta away as he sensed her distress and began to edge into her lap, his front paws and head threatening to overwhelm all the space poor Carolina had available.

"They have a housekeeper. Full time. She'll be there. Do you need the address?"

"It's already on my GPS screen, Ms. DeAngeles. Would you like to bypass the funeral home at this time?"

"No, no, Bill. I'll be fine. This is hard, that's all." She sniffled, reaching inside the armrest for the tissues she knew would be there. "I'm already better. Carry on, James." She said the words with bright enthusiasm, mimicking an old movie she'd once seen.

Bill chuckled over the phone. "Bill, Ms. DeAngeles, but you may call me by any name you wish."

Carolina exhaled soundly, and she smiled, glad for the feelings of distress to be momentarily broken. "Bill, thank you. I'd like for you to call me Carolina. Will that be okay with you?" She could hear the pleased expression in his voice as he assured her it would be more than acceptable.

Carolina hung up the phone gently, grateful that Mr. Warner had so thoughtfully gone out of his way once again to care for her. Now if only that boy would make himself known. Then her life would be just what the doctor ordered.

She took advantage of the quiet of the limousine to lean her head back and close her eyes, letting her hand gently run over Ricotta's furry head. In several minutes, they would make a quick stop by the funeral home to tidy up matters, and then to her parents' home on the island. However, in the soft hum of the tires on the pavement, she was finding her boy from so long ago to be an escape from this hard time, and she was discovering a certain amount of pleasure in her memories of him.

This time, though, she tried to imagine him not as an overweight father of three, but as the older, more mature single man he would surely be. Perhaps married, but now divorced, he'd never been happy, because he'd been constantly looking for a girl he'd once seen as he'd completed a final checkup on a small airplane as it had headed out from Savannah for the island of Hilton Head. He still liked to ride the surf, keeping his full head of hair bleached to a golden blond.

She dreamed, warmed as she remembered those long-ago words.

Alaska? Cool.

CAROLINA was finally at home, her real home. The funeral arrangements had been depressing, but that was quickly concluded. Bill had watched Ricotta in the car, and the staff had made her visit as painless as humanly possible.

She stood in front of the open window, letting the ocean breeze brush past her into the interior of the house. Her mother would have a fit, she knew. "Carolina! The moisture will warp all the inlays on the furniture." Then her father would laugh. All the times he had opened the windows in the house only to have her mother follow after him, shutting them all. Today, Carolina's grief kept her from doing anything other than what felt good to her.

The window was open.

She glanced to see Margarete walking down the hallway,

44

her white apron neatly tied behind her into what Carolina knew would be a deftly snug bow. Carolina sighed, well aware what was coming. Her mother and Margarete had been so well suited for each other.

"Oh, my sweet girl. You must miss your mother so." The mature, lined woman reached up and patted Carolina's face. "But she would tell you to close her windows. The salt air will ruin all her fine furniture. Would you make your mother turn over in her coffin?" Margarete paused, looking up at the ceiling, crossing herself. "God rest her poor soul." She tugged the great window closed. Reaching to the console table sitting in front of the window she'd just sealed, she ran her finger along a section of inlaid ivory and exotic woods. "Good. Nothing is pulled loose, yet. Your mother can sleep soundly." She looked at Carolina. "Your father, he would not care so much. Get new furniture, he would say. So wasteful!"

Carolina reached and gave the housekeeper a hug. "You make me feel at home, Margarete. I just needed to feel the air. At times, my grief overwhelms me. If you didn't chide me, I wouldn't know you. Thank you for being the strength that will help me to get through."

Margarete reached in her pocket and peeled off a tissue from an ever-present package. "Here, dear. Use this. Do not stain your mother's furniture. Your family will be here soon." Then she smiled. "Do not ask me to tell, but one surprise is waiting on you. My favorite, too." When Carolina gave her a bemused look, the old woman began to smirk. "No, Carolina. You will not get the admission from me, but the surprise will cheer you up. You go to your room and get yourself ready. Shoo, now. Your parents would want you to be at your best."

Up in her old room, and without Margarete to close her windows, Carolina sat in the window seat, her finest black A-line lying on the bed across the room. She glanced at it for a moment, thinking it was no Dior, but still she wouldn't cut a

Vera Wang up, as Sha'Cretia had done with her Dior, no matter how good her legs looked.

She turned to the window, her humor buoyed by her memory of Sha'Cretia's rendition of the night she'd been thrown out by her parents. If only her friend had been able to fly out with her, then Carolina would be able to bear all that this week would surely entail. Her spirits began dropping as fast as they had soared a moment earlier, and she leaned her arms on the windowsill and rested her chin on them. Her eyes caught a father and daughter throwing a Frisbee across the sand. On Little Estero in Ft. Myers Beach, the water was far across the sand. Here, it was just outside the window. The sound of the surf washed over her, and she could see the laughter on the little girl's face as she grabbed for the flying disk. The sand flew, and she scrambled to retrieve it as it darted just out of her grasp.

Carolina felt the muscles behind her eyes tighten and her vision blur. She and her father had played those very same games in that exact spot. Now they never would again. Carolina rolled over, resting her head on a pillow, letting the sounds of the little girl and her father flood over her, bringing to mind memories of times that could never be lived again except in her thoughts. At least she still had the memories, and lying here would not get that A-line over her busty chest, as Sha'Cretia would say. Tonight when she was alone would provide plenty of time to cry into her pillow. Now, she must present her best face.

Standing, she reached into her closet for a black slip, the very one she'd worn to her parents' thirtieth anniversary celebration just last year. She knew it would still be hanging where she'd left it. Dropping her lightweight shorts and blouse, she dusted her face lightly to remove the shine, gave herself a dose of Chanel, and slipped the black lace over her head, watching in the mirror as it settled into place over her ample chest and somewhat less ample hips with nary an extra ripple in

46

place.

Smiling, she reached for the Vera Wang, and with the same motion, she slithered it over her head, knowing it would fit just as well as its undergarment. Glancing at her dressing table, she saw where Margarete had laid out her graduation clip-ons. Oh, these would hurt, she knew, but her father had loved their old-fashioned glamour. The gold was like filigree. The diamonds were what added the weight.

She clipped them to her earlobes and glanced at herself. She smiled, and running a comb through her hair, she returned it to the table just as the doorbell chimed its first warning of the events to come. Her guests were here to offer her their condolences. She wondered how many of them she'd have to console, instead. Her strength would be taxed today.

Then she remembered Margarete's surprise.

A surprise for me? Come on, Margarete. Do your best. Surprise me, then, old girl. I might even surprise you by not acting surprised at all. Ha!

It was a childhood game, and she and the housekeeper had played it many times. Sha'Cretia was the one time Carolina had truly seemed to catch the old woman off guard, and then Margarete had fallen in love with her just as everyone else seemed to do. Carolina blinked, grabbing a tissue to dab the moisture pooling in her eyes at the thought of her old friend. She needed Sha'Cretia here with her.

Steeling herself with a bright smile on her face, she pretended she was in her office, and she had a business meeting to attend. Yes, she could do this. It was just another gathering of the office personnel. She stepped to the door and grabbed the knob. She whispered with barely a quaver in her voice, "So, who wants to be voted out of the office today? Beware!"

Her face was tough, and her smile was bright, but behind it was hiding a tender woman who was feeling very crushed, indeed.

THE STORM beat at the windows. Kodiak took another log and slipped it into the wood stove, jumping back as the sparks flared. One landed on his hand, burning his finger, and he dropped the log inside.

"Flaming turds, that was close!" He used the poker to latch the glass door shut, then he sat, sucking on the burned place on his finger. He couldn't even see his airplane out the window through the heavy weather, and it was cold!

He ran his free hand through his thick hair and fingered the wetsuit draped across the stool at his side. He glanced up at his surfboard hanging on the wall above the stove. The heat wasn't good for the wood, but he didn't know if he would ever ride it again, anyway.

Alaska! He couldn't imagine what he'd been thinking. That first winter, the surf had been huge, and all he'd been able to think about was getting out there. All he'd needed was a wetsuit and his surfboard.

He could have bought a new board for what it'd cost his friend to ship this one to him. He never imagined courier costs would be so high. His board, however, was custom built of light-weight and exotic woods in a small shop near his home on Hilton Head, a very particular style special to that shop. To most people, a surfboard was a surfboard. Longboard. Shortboard. Surfboard. Not to Kodiak. He wanted his, and his good friend obliged, as long as Kodiak was paying.

The wetsuit hadn't been much cheaper.

Then, he'd gone out onto the ocean, and he thought he'd be dead before he got back to shore, a human Popsicle. How the townspeople had laughed at him, but then that spring was when he'd started to get a little business at his shop. The people would stop in just to talk to him about his crazy antics.

"Hey, how are the waves, today?"

"Great," Kodiak would reply, and their lawn equipment

48

would be back to them in a day or two. Soon, a truck would drive up, or sometimes be towed in.

"Hear the surfing's good out past the breakwater."

"Yep," he would reply, and the truck would soon be running again.

He'd gotten his first airplane repair that way. That man had wanted to know if he'd ever windsurfed the Alaska coastline, and Kodiak had invited him up to check out his board. Now, he had his sign up. But he'd never surfed again.

Now he wished he never had to face another Alaska winter again. Fly-fishing on a warm day? He'd take that. This storm? Gads! And it was still summer! He closed his eyes and laid his head back.

"Give me a Southern beach and a girl with a soft, Southern drawl. If one should walk up to me, I'd snatch her away, and Alaska would be history."

As much as he might dream, he knew that would never happen. Good Southern girls never made it to Alaska, and besides, there was always Julianna, with her hands out and her lawyers on call should he ever set foot on his Low Country shores ever again. Kodiak guessed he would be stuck in this freezer forever.

He opened one eye and was glad to see the log had kicked the fire up. It was burning brightly. Warmly? It was working on it. For now, he guessed brightly would have to do.

THE SKY glowed outside the windows.

Carolina was slightly tipsy, but she poured herself another shot. Then she passed the bottle to Margarete. She leaned in to whisper conspiratorially, "I'm not a decorator, but that sunset is beautiful, Margie. If I were a decorator, and we all know I'm not, I'd name that particular hue Sunset Salmon, and they'd put it in a can. I'd have so much money, I could pay God to give me that view every day."

49

Margarete hiccupped. "Easy, my girl. I have another way to get that sunset every day." She reached behind her and opened a cabinet door. Putting her hand inside, she pulled out a small video camera. "Set this in the window. Then put a really big TV in the place of that window. When you want a sunset, just turn it on." She beamed with her suggestion. "I like that idea. Is it as good as my surprise?" She reached out and patted the hands on either side of her.

Carolina laughed. "You turned my tables, you old woman. Last time I sprang Sha on you, and this time you surprised me with her. How did you get her out here?" She looked over to see her friend blinking her eyes, not entirely focused on the two women's discussion. Sha'Cretia had imbibed far more than either Carolina or Margarete. Carolina leaned in to whisper in an obvious stage voice, "And I think that's her Dior from her sixteenth coming out party."

Margarete's eyes were wide with humor. She nodded her head in the affirmative as she poured herself another nip, the liquid not quite all making it into the glass. "I stitched the top. She was not careful with her scissors at all, but it now makes a nice Dior skirt." She giggled.

Finally, Sha'Cretia gathered herself enough to speak. "Girls, I think I've had enough. I'm sleepy." Then, her head crashed to the table.

It was later that night that Carolina lay in her room just down the hall from the woman who was her very best friend, listening to her light snore through the wall, and thinking of what she would choose, if she could pick the man of her dreams. He'd be a manly type of man, outdoorsy and with a touch of southern charm, Carolina Low Country style.

She watched the ceiling in the dark, lonely. If she ever got a man, she guessed God would have to dump her on the side of the road and let him almost run over her. Otherwise she'd never see him coming. The only man she could claim was a boy working on the engine of an airplane, and she'd only seen him once. She realized what she'd done. She'd built up an ideal that no man could ever match, and so no man ever would.

She sighed and laughed to herself. At least she had Sha'Cretia and Margarete. And Ricotta. She reached out a hand to find him sprawled on the bed at her side. Only then did she realize it wasn't Sha'Cretia she'd heard snoring. It was the dog.

She rolled over and snuggled up next to him. He was warm, and the breeze through the open window was cool.

In the darkness, the alcohol from the evening's merry-making made Carolina's head buzz, and she knew it also helped her to push the emptiness of her parents' deaths aside. The crushing burden of what had happened to them would return in the morning, but she could be at peace for this one night.

As she snuggled, she heard her pet making the small sleeping sounds that animals make, and it was comforting. She felt herself slipping into a dream, one that was full of warmth and companionship, but it was not of the people under her roof. Her dreams were of a surfboard, golden hair, and an airplane, one that was just the right size to carry two people far away to a land where love could be found. For some reason, as she dreamed, she shivered with the cold, and only her companion next to her was able to warm her skin.

Her heart, however, was another matter. It would take a different kind of companion to warm her there.

SHA'CRETIA moaned. She'd joined Carolina in the early hours of the morning, claiming it was too cold to sleep alone. "Sunlight in the heavens, girl, turn off that sun!" She rolled over and covered her face with a pillow.

Carolina laughed loudly at the complaints of the woman in her bed. "No one told you to drink two full bottles last night." She reached and yanked the covers off her friend, leaving her lying in a set of bright pink undergarments.

Sha'Cretia turned and threw her pillow at Carolina, missing by half a room.

Carolina laughed again. "Open your eyes and you might actually be able to aim next time. I saved your Dior, by the way."

Sha'Cretia's eyes popped open. She sat up in a befuddled panic, looking around. "My Dior? I still had it on at the drink fest last night? I didn't spill anything on it, did I?" She looked down at what she was wearing. "Oh, you haven't seen my new things, have you? I have on the matching thong underneath. What do you think? You can order them through Neiman's."

"I don't think so, Sha." Carolina reached to a hook and took down a robe. She tossed it onto the bed. "Put that on. Sorry it's not pink." She smiled. "Your Dior is in the closet."

"Thank my lucky daddy." Sha'Cretia sat up on her elbows, the robe just covering her feet, and she wiggled it around. "My daddy was really lucky, you know. First, he married my momma, and then he won the lottery." She glanced up, smiling when Carolina gave her a disbelieving look. "It wasn't a big lottery. We held it each year at the church, you see, and it paid out in good deeds. House cleaning, frozen turkeys, and the like. Then the big payoff happened, and he was really lucky that time." Sha'Cretia dropped her head back to the bed, luxuriating in the finery of comfortable linens, the sun across her bare limbs, and the sounds of the sea just outside.

"And, Sha?" Carolina walked over and sat on the end of the bed, shaking Sha'Cretia's foot under the robe. "What was the big payoff?"

She sat up and grabbed Carolina's hand, kissing it before releasing it. "Me!" She jumped up and walked in her slinkiest shimmer toward the bath. "He'd have to be lucky to get me, sweetie! See ya' in a bit. I need some shower time, and I need it alone." She began to close the door, and then she peeked back around one last time. "You're good for me, sweetie. I love ya',

Carolina. I love ya' a lot." She blew her a kiss and gently shut the door.

Carolina sat on the edge of the bed as the sounds of water started up a symphony in the shower. She smiled as she heard Sha'Cretia add her own vocal accompaniment. She looked out the window at the clear, blue sky, and she ran her hand over the bed where her friend's warmth still lingered.

"No, Sha," she said, knowing her friend couldn't hear her words. "You've got it all wrong. You're the one who's good for me, and for that, I love you more than anyone I know. Even more than Edward. At least you came when I needed you most, and for that, I love you most of all."

She stood and walked to the door, stepping out onto the beachfront deck. Leaning against the railing, she looked up and down the beach, knowing she still had a funeral and a meeting with the lawyer today. Her parents were gone, and somewhere inside, she knew she must be numb. She felt like she was being strong, or she at least hoped so. After all, she had no choice. Her brother couldn't be with her, and this was a day she'd have to be outside of herself. She didn't know if even Sha'Cretia would be enough to buoy her once her day came crashing down around her.

She did know of one person she could love even more than Sha'Cretia, someone who could console her in her grief, but he was there for her only in her imagination, and besides, he had three kids already. He was also fat and bald. If he still had a head full of hair and rode that surfboard, he'd have come for her already. Surely he'd have come for her already.

A level of frustration crept over her. She really did want a man in her life. That hadn't been her luck, though, and her loneliness was intense sometimes. Now, with her parents gone, it was overwhelming. She'd gone to the beach and waited all weekend. Every airport, and she still looked for him. He was never there. Had he only teased with her? Alaska! May Alaska freeze until it was frostbitten! She'd take her warm, Carolina beach any day.

She felt a hand at her shoulder. "Those are tears, baby girl. Oh, you let Sha'Cretia wrap her arms around you. You've got no parents anymore, no brother here for you, and no man to warm your heart. Only little Sha'Cretia is here for you in your time of need. Oh, my poor baby. You've got nothing except me, and I ain't much, I know that. But I'll give you all the hugging you can take."

As Sha'Cretia wrapped her arms around her, Carolina hugged her back. "Sha, right now, you're all the friend I need. Thank you for being here. My parents are gone, and I have no one. I love you, you know." Sobs began to rack her body.

"Yes, girl, I do. I love you, too. I also know I'm not all the friend you need, but that you'll have to fix on your own." She laughed. "A girl as pretty as you will get someone going, though. Trust me, you pretty thing. Just relax. You never know. Someday you may be walking along a road, and your knight in shining armor might just come up and run right over you."

"Sha, what did you say?" Carolina sniffled and froze, her tears momentarily put aside.

"What, honey? I said a lot of things. What part?"

"The last part, the one about a knight in shining armor."

Sha'Cretia paused, putting her hand to her chin, her brow furrowed in thought. Then she brightened. "Oh, that part. I said a man might just run right over you, and you'd never see him coming."

Carolina kissed her friend on the cheek, feeling better already, wiping her damp eyes and clearing the last of her tears. "I'll be looking for him, Sha. He'd better watch out, too, because then I'd never let him go."

Sha'Cretia brushed her girlfriend's hair away from her face, smiling when she saw her tears were gone. "That's the spirit, girl. You give him what all it's worth. He'll love you the more for it."

"He'd better." Carolina laughed. "Come on inside, Sha. We've got a funeral to attend."

"MARGARETE, honey, you *are* family. Where else would you sit if not with me?" Carolina looked out the car window at the passing greenery, the occasional glimpse of a business or resort entrance visible past the living wall that her beloved island provided as a screen against all that humanity had slashed across this beautiful Low Country land. She turned back to Margarete, and seeing the redness in her eyes, reached to place her smooth, pale hand over the old woman's dark, worn one. "It'll be okay. Mummy and Daddy would have been so happy at this beautiful weather for their final service. Going out in the best of style, Mummy would have said."

Carolina laughed at her jest, and the sudden sound finally got a rise from the mound of brown fur lying in the floor at their feet. She reached and rubbed a hand around Ricotta's inquisitive ears. "You know something's wrong, just not what, huh, boy? You just be good today, and it'll soon be over." Carolina looked up to see Margarete smiling at her.

"He cannot understand you, you know. He is a dog."

"He knows my tone, and it soothes him. At least I think it does." Carolina closed her eyes and smiled at the chiding. She knew that in her grief, she needed someone to reassure her, and Ricotta had become her outlet.

"Yes, you are probably right. I hope so on this sad day." Margarete's pursed lips showed she understood the younger woman's motivation and was willing to admit it.

The muted sun flickered through the tinted windows of the long car heading toward Holy Family Catholic Church. Carolina opened her eyes and watched outside the car, oddly disoriented in her jumble of thoughts. She lifted the armrest at her side, reaching to pick up the phone inside. She waited with it at her ear for a moment, trusting Bill to answer. He'd told her this was their method of communication when the window was up.

"Yes, Ms. Carolina? How may I help you?" The unseen voice was helpful and reassuring, and she could picture Bill's kind face as he voiced his question, his eyes crinkling with pleasantness.

"Bill, Holy Family. You know it's on Pope, right? At Woodhaven? Don't go to 24." She could feel her palms growing moist with the uncertainty in her question. "I'm sorry, Bill. I'm just at loose ends today. I've lost my concentration, and I haven't been home in a while. What street are we on?"

"Cordillo Parkway. We'll be turning on Pope in about two blocks. I have it right here on my GPS. Trust me, Ms. Carolina. You're in good hands. The services start in about twenty minutes, and I'll have you there in ten. By the way, Ms. Carolina, you're doing just fine."

Carolina looked up to see the glass divider sliding down into its recess. She smiled when she saw a suited arm show itself in the opening with a thumbs up hand signal flashing at her. As the glass closed, she spoke softly into the phone, "Thank you, Bill."

"You're very welcome, Ms. Carolina. One more thing. Will Ricotta be attending the services with you?"

She looked up at Margarete, covering the phone receiver with her hand. "The dog. Inside the church or outside?" Seeing the woman's perplexed look, she clarified her question, "During the services."

Margarete looked aghast. "The dog! Inside? What would your mother say? Your father, him we will not ask." She dabbed her tissue at her eyes and pursed her lips in disdain for the very concept of having a dog, no matter how treasured, attend memorial services inside the church building.

Carolina smiled, finding Margarete's refusal humorous in its intensity. Still, Carolina knew that with Ricotta in her thoughts, she'd be able to hold herself together.

56

She spoke into the phone, "Bill, may he stay with you in the car?" After a moment, she replaced the phone into its recess and turned to Margarete. "He'll remain outside, Margarete. The church will remain sacred."

At the woman's satisfied expression, Carolina closed her eyes and sat quietly for the remainder of the trip, her thoughts on seeing her best friend once again. Sha'Cretia would also be a reservoir of strength for her. She had gone on ahead, and then Bill had returned for the two remaining women.

In her reverie, Carolina smiled. Those society matrons who didn't know Sha'Cretia wouldn't recognize her for a lowly office worker today. She was in one of her mother's finest outfits. Sha'Cretia had been pleased to find the two wore exactly the same size, and Carolina had been glad to let her look through her mother's closet, even offering to let her take home anything she thought she might wear. She'd chosen a beautiful sequined Gucci for the day, one of her mother's favorites. Carolina hadn't the heart to tell her it wasn't really appropriate for the events they'd be attending. She'd seemed so pleased as she'd run her hand down the glittering fabric, and it did look very flattering on her.

Carolina laughed, and she opened her eyes to see Margarete looking at her with a mystified expression on her face. She just waved her attention away, letting her know the unexpected laugh was nothing to pay a mind to, and she reached to rub Ricotta's ears. What would she do if one of her mother's friends tried to match a bachelor son with the beautiful, exotic friend of the deceased's daughter? Even bowed under the grief this day had already begun to slash her way, Carolina had no trouble imagining the absurdity of the situation. No doubt Sha'Cretia would jump at the opportunity.

However, Carolina knew she'd have to keep her friend reined in. Sha'Cretia was no debutant, and she had a job waiting on her on the West Coast. Three people depended on her friend to be here for one reason only, to support Carolina in her time of need. Well, four if she counted Bill. Five if Ricotta were included. She reached to rub her friend's ears one more time.

"You count, my friend, as rotten as you are. You can be in on the joke, too."

Margarete smiled. The car slowed to pull into the Holy Family Catholic Church lot, and the parking was packed. That was very satisfying. Everyone should be here.

Carolina's parents deserved that.

"SWEETIE, I'm so sorry to attend your services and run. I could only take these two days, and I have to be back to rescue Mr. Warner from the workaday wolves." Sha'Cretia wrapped her arms around Carolina and reached to wipe the remains of tears from her friend's watery eyes. She stepped back and brushed Carolina's nose with a manicured fingertip. "I only spent time with them that once, but I loved your mother and father so much. You take your time, you hear me? I've got you covered back in L.A. No worries for you, and I hope you don't mind that I'm still wearing the Gucci." She ran a hand down the front of the skirt. "I never wore a complete designer outfit before."

Carolina laughed, turning to glance around the church lot, folding the tissue she held in her hand. She touched it to one eye. "Sha, I'm glad you want to wear the dress home. Mumsy would be so pleased. Everyone seems to be waiting on me, though. I'll be watching you, you know. You leave all those college boys here." Her eyes crinkled in mirth, the burning around her eyes at odds with her forced humor. "Even if they do seem attracted to you like flies to candy. You're so sweet to have come all this way for me." She reached her hand to press it to Sha'Cretia's face as her eyes misted once again. "Thank you, Sha. I wish you could be with me when the will is read this afternoon, but I do understand."

Sha'Cretia grabbed her hand and kissed it as a taxi pulled

up beside them. "Be a beast, my beautiful Carolina. When those lawyer sharks show their teeth, growl back and make them do it your way. Ship your momma's wardrobe to me, girl. I want every outfit." She laughed and dropped into the taxi, waving as the door closed behind her.

Reaching the lawyer's office and stepping out of the limo, Carolina moved aside as Ricotta unfolded from the car, his leash attached to her hand. At Bill's raised eyebrows, she smiled, her voice unnaturally bright. "Bear with me, Bill. With Sha gone, I cannot do this without my second-best friend. The lawyers can tolerate him being at my side just this once. Margarete would like to be taken home. She'll need to finish preparing for the events this evening. I have my phone if you're not back when I'm finished." She patted the handbag she had draped over her shoulder.

Stepping toward the building, she heard the limo as it pulled away. Pausing, she gathered her strength, then she took a deep breath and let it out. She patted Ricotta's head. "Let's go, you rotten dog. You must help me be strong. I just wish I had Edward for support. A handsome airplane mechanic would be even better, but the one I found ran away from me before I could tell him my name." She knelt and let Ricotta lick her face, laughing as he did so. He was certainly proving himself to be the bastion of strength she had hoped she would find in him.

"You're all I've got, my friend. You must be strong for me. This will be the hardest part of my day, even worse than the services. At least Sha was there to entertain me. Can you do any tricks? No?" She stood and sighed. "I thought not. On to the wolves! Forward, Ricotta! Rotten cheese and all!"

CAROLINA leaned toward the desk, Ricotta raising his head as she did so. "But this is a great deal of money. You mean it's all to be wasted?"

"Ms. DeAngeles, your parents were in excellent health. The

trip had already fully funded before their deaths, and they felt they had no reason to purchase trip cancellation insurance. My office has gone over the details of the contract, and there are no applicable conditions under which the cruise line will accommodate our requests for a refund of any already paid monies. I'm so sorry." He shrugged. "If the dates for the trip were further out, then perhaps, but not within the current timeframe."

"Transfer? Can I at least give the trip to a friend of the family?" She thought of Sha'Cretia and how she would love to take a cruise to Alaska. She was out there covering for her at her job, and this would be an excellent way to repay her for coming to support her in her time of need. "I could do that, couldn't I?"

The lawyer pressed his lips together and shuffled the papers on his desk as if hoping to find the answer his client so wanted to hear. Then he looked up at her.

"Only an immediate family member can substitute for the original purchasers of the tickets. You and your brother," and he looked at his forms to find the name, pointed with a finger, and continued, "Edward, I believe, are the only two people who fulfill the requirements. If the two of you, or just you alone, Ms. DeAngeles, cannot go, the tickets will be forfeit, and the cruise line will be legally free to resell the accommodations. I understand your brother is in Antarctica for the summer?"

Carolina nodded. "Researching. I've been in contact, but it has to be by email. He's there until October or November. I forget the exact time the ice opens back up. He goes every year, you understand. It's just that I needed him this time." She looked around, blinking the moisture from her eyes, finally settling on Ricotta. She reached to rub one furry ear between her fingers. "Good boy, you rotten soufflé, you. Even old cheese is better than no cheese at all." She looked up to see the lawyer smiling at her. "Can I get the mail and the phone services forwarded for a time to my address in Los Angeles? There are bound to be items I can't plan for, and I must return to the West

Coast within the week."

That was something he could do. He reached for a pad and started to make some notes. "Phone and mail services. What about email? If you'll provide me with your address and home phone, I'll get these requests taken care of. In addition, my firm will be at your disposal for any additional questions or services you might require. You've not asked about your father's business. However, not to worry. Your father was very forward-thinking in this. A trustee will be appointed to run the business, with your approval, of course. Your brother's, too, if he can be contacted. The house should transfer into your name within six weeks or so. I'm afraid it will be in yours and your brother's names jointly. If you decide to sell eventually, it must be a joint decision." He looked up, catching her eye before going on. "You've requested your housekeeper to remain in residence. We'll be paying her from your parents' accounts, yours and your brother's, now, of course. I do hope a quarterly statement will be satisfactory. If you'd like us to provide a monthly accounting, just let us know. Is there anything I haven't covered?"

He paused, watching Carolina for a moment, before sliding a slim checkbook across his desk toward her.

"You can access the funds in your accounts after twenty-four hours. Just give my office a call when you need to replenish your supply of checks. I can set up a debit card on this account if you wish."

Carolina reached to take the leather book from the desk. "No, this will be fine." She stood, holding the checkbook up as if to hand it back to the lawyer. "Nearly thirty years, and this is all I have left of my parents. It doesn't seem fair, does it?"

He stood and pursed his lips before speaking. "No, it doesn't. It doesn't seem fair at all."

Carolina turned, dropping the checkbook into her purse. She felt it bump the satellite phone, and she reached to adjust it so they fit side by side. At least she had that. She could call and fly home anytime she wished. She could just leave all this behind. She felt pressure against her leg and looked to see that Ricotta had stood and was leaning against her, providing the support that somehow he sensed she needed.

"Do you think I'd forget you, you rotten thing, you? No. Today, I'm lost without you." She turned to the lawyer. "I can see myself out. You've been very helpful. Please continue to work with the cruise line. My parents will be losing a great deal of money . . . I'll be losing a great deal of money. I'm sorry. This is just hard."

She turned, her eyes burning, and let Rotten Ricotta Cheese escort her from the room.

Chapter 4

CAROLINA dropped her things into a chair. It had been a long trip back from the East Coast, and she was exhausted.

In spite of that, Melissa had charmed her, and Carolina had enjoyed getting to visit in the cockpit. Sitting in the copilot's seat had seemed almost as if she were flying the airplane herself. She hadn't been, of course, but it had been fun to pretend for a short time.

Margarete had offered to keep poor Ricotta. Carolina had been glad for that. He was too much for her right now. The next time she flew out, she'd bring him home, or she just might put her feelers out for a business position and possibly move back to the family home. Of course, she would have to find the job there first.

She reached into her purse for a tissue. She'd taken to carrying a small package there. She smiled at her memory of why.

"Child," Margarete had chided her. "Take these. Then you never have to ask to borrow. Here, take them."

Carolina would continue to carry them for a time longer. The drizzly eyes weren't always under her control yet.

As she fished for the tissues, Carolina's hand bumped the checkbook she'd been given. She pulled it out and looked inside. She snorted. Have to find a job? Her parents had been very good to her, indeed. She could just quit. However, she knew that was a way to lose herself. Her identity was here in Los Angeles with Mr. Warner's company, and she could no more leave the company behind than she could leave herself behind.

Her extra week after the services at Holy Family had left her detached and drained, with even her beautiful beaches unable to ground her to anything solid. Her loneliness at the loss of her parents had torn at her inside, and she'd been miserable without Sha'Cretia. She'd found herself watching all the boys on the beach, just hoping one would walk by and turn to her, those dimples splitting his face in two.

Then, one afternoon, she'd been at her bedroom window, her legs curled on the window seat. She'd seen a glistening in the surf, and when it had drawn close enough, she'd been able to tell it was a surfer, a golden-haired man riding the waves in.

Her heart had taken her by storm, and she'd grabbed her beach sandals. Her pulse had pounded as if it were that day all those years ago. She'd been blind with need for him. Running downstairs, she'd waved at Margarete and called for Ricotta. Fumbling her sunglasses onto her face, she'd wrestled the leash onto Ricotta's collar and rushed from the house.

She was just in time to see him carry his surfboard from the water. He'd flexed his sun-kissed, bronzed arms. The muscles in his back had rippled as he lifted the board to his side, and the reflection of summer on his wet shoulders was bright. She'd seen the back of his sun-bleached head of hair, and her heart had sung. When she'd stepped to speak to him, to make sure she told him her name this time, he'd turned to her. He'd greeted her dog, even knelt to roughly rub Ricotta's neck. Then he'd wished her a good day and run off to meet his friends.

He'd been no older than seventeen. Carolina had stood in the sand and watched the surf without any hope at all. She'd still be standing there, she knew, if Ricotta hadn't finally tugged at the leash, a group of birds pulling his attention away from his duty. Carolina had released him and let him run, but she hadn't returned to the beach again. Instead, she'd taken her satellite phone and called Marcus and Melissa. She'd wanted to go home.

Dropping the checkbook on a side table, she looked at the pile of mail that had built up from her stay in Hilton Head. Moaning at the prospect of sorting through it all, she idly reached for the basket and began to flip through the items. Her heart pounding, she pulled one item from all the rest. Altessa Cruise Lines. She turned the thick packet over to see who it was addressed to. Mr. and Mrs. Delcroy DeAngeles. It boasted a yellow forwarding tag to her Los Angeles address.

She set the basket down. Her folks. Mummy and Daddy. This was from their planned cruise, the one that would be wasted. She remembered her mother telling her she was expecting tickets and an itinerary. This must be it. However, she couldn't deal with this now.

She stepped to the window and pushed the curtain aside. The brilliance of a Southern California summer made her blink and squint. She could not stay trapped inside with this grief. She glanced at the clock. Four. Too late to go to the office this afternoon. Then, the plant she kept by the window caught her eye, and for the briefest moment, it shifted her attention from her own problems.

"Oh, you poor thing. I've almost let you die."

The thought of the plant's wilted leaves brought back the

moment Mr. Warner had first told her of her parents' accident, and Carolina sank to the floor in tears. With her repressed grief suddenly flooding from her in gasps of tearing pain, her wails reverberated throughout the house. However, there was no one there to hear, and the lonely, grief-stricken woman bled her sorrow alone, finally curling into a ball underneath the window with only the puddling of the drapes to cover herself. Exhausted, she lay on the hardwood floor and slept the entire night through.

KODIAK stepped through the grass as he walked down the slope to the water. There was a tree down over the walkway he'd built to the dock, and clearing it away would take more time than he had today.

He needed to check on his airplane.

He paused, the freshly bright sunlight flickering through the rain-moistened trees. His little Cessna bobbed next to the float as if it hadn't stormed a single day. Three days Kodiak had been trapped inside. Three days of cold and torture, memories of this past winter when snow was all he could see for weeks at a time.

Jumping over a limb he thought was small enough that he could get past it without stumbling, he hopped and slid the last few yards to the dock. Walking out, he stepped onto the float and began to inspect any possible damage to the airplane. He knew storms often caused small issues that had to be looked after. If he were lazy, those same small things could easily grow into larger problems that could ground his craft. Up here in Alaska, that wouldn't do at all.

His first concern was the fuel cap. Was it still tight? His hand twisting it, he was soon comfortable with its seal, and he climbed inside to make sure no water had created any problems that needed his attention. That was when he noticed something that made him smile. It was a tiny bird, a Kinglet, and it'd become trapped in the cockpit of his craft. He recognized it from the few red feathers in the crown of its head. Apparently, it had been blown in by the storm.

He reached for it, only to have it hop away. Kodiak's eyes crinkled in mirth. It was afraid of him, not realizing he'd never hurt the poor creature. As he cupped it in his hands, he felt it struggle against his skin, and he knew its bid for freedom. He'd felt that himself, and he'd run far across the country to the only place he'd known to run. Oh, at first, he hadn't even considered where he was going, just from airport to airport, looking for whatever work would keep him afloat. Then one day he'd realized who had sent him to Alaska. It hadn't been his mother. It had been a girl on a Savannah runway. She'd looked at him, and she'd seen his name, and she'd told him to go to Alaska.

Deep inside, he also knew she hadn't really told him to go to Alaska. What she'd done was made him start thinking of his name differently. He was no longer a Kodiak bear, his high school mascot taking his mother's name from him. He had become an island in Alaska.

Kodiak stepped from the airplane, and holding his hands high in the air, he opened them. Just for a minute the small Kinglet stood, and then it hopped. Kodiak watched as it turned its head to look directly into his eyes as if to say thank you, and then in a blur, it took to wing and was gone.

Kodiak stood, his temples suddenly tight, and he felt his eyes tear up. He wanted what he'd just given that bird. He wanted for his life to release him from its clutches, and he wanted to be able to hop once, look around, and be able to look his rescuing angel in the eye to say thanks. Then he, too, would fly free, his life finally his own, not some sticky-fingered woman's who wanted him to sell his airplane to pay her alimony, all so she could party with her society friends.

He stood and looked around. The world was beautiful on this special day. The storm had left everything bejeweled, and he was glad he was here. If Alaska was to be his home, he'd take it, and he'd breathe a daily prayer of thanks to the pretty girl on the tarmac who had started him on his way here.

Now he needed to check on his shop back in town. Hopefully his tools had survived three days of stormy weather, too. He couldn't afford to replace them any more than he could come up with the money to buy a new airplane.

He drew in a deep breath. The air even smelled good today. He was glad to be alive, and he was thankful Alaska was his home.

SHA'CRETIA put her creamy brown hand on Carolina's white one. Carolina had only been back at work for three days, and already Sha'Cretia could tell her best friend was still stressed by all that sadness from back East.

"Just do what I do, sweetie." She wiggled her fingers and smiled. "Go get a new manicure. Do you like this new cinnamon color?" She walked to the window to let her latest polish sparkle in the sun. Turning to Carolina, she quipped, "Notice how they don't call them womanicures? Makes you wonder, doesn't it?"

Stepping back to Carolina, she handed her the printout from a recent sales conference. "If you don't feel like looking at this, Mr. Warner has said I could pass it on to someone else." Sha'Cretia winked at Carolina. "I'd pass it on, if I were you. It's not very interesting."

"Let me think about it." Carolina smiled at her friend and waved her towards the door. She had other things to think about at the present. She'd just gone online and checked her email from home, and she'd been most distressed to find one in particular. It had been forwarded from Altessa Cruise Lines. She'd even printed a copy. It lay on her desk, and she set Sha's report aside to look at it.

The cruise was boarding in three days, and her parents' cabin was waiting on her confirmation. If she didn't call in today, the cruise line would release it for resale. She hadn't even been able to think about work for remembering how this had been her father's dream, her mumsy's, too, and now it was being wasted.

"Honey, are you all right?" Sha'Cretia was back at the door, a new stack of folders in her hands. She walked over and placed them on the corner of Carolina's desk, and she stepped around to put her arm around her shoulders. "Girl, you haven't moved since I was here last."

Then she pulled the email from under the report it was partially hiding under.

"Sweetie, what's this?" Sha'Cretia stood and carried the paper to the window, flicking it in the light, and reading it to herself. She glanced at Carolina. "I get it now. I remember you talking about this weeks ago. Now the cruise is here, and your parents aren't. Honeybunch, this must be tearing you up. You know you have to go."

Tears flooded Carolina's eyes. "Sha, how can I? I just got back to work."

Sha'Cretia fell onto Carolina's desk, resting her chin on her elbows, and she stared into a startled set of eyes. "Honey, how can you not go? This is your parents' dream. How far did this place go while you were gone? It'll be right here when you return, too. Go on this cruise, sweetie. Go and make me proud of you." She stood, a mischievous grin growing on her face. "In fact, I intend to call and confirm this trip for you right now." She reached for the phone, only to have Carolina snatch the email printout away.

"I can do it, thank you very much." She released a long-held breath and laughed. "You know, I've doubted whether I should let this trip go back to the cruise lines. My parents, my father, really, wanted to go on this trip more than anything. If I don't use it, the money'll all be lost. I think I will go. Where is that phone?"

Sha'Cretia laughed as she stepped out the door. As she closed it, Carolina's words drifted through after her.

"Altessa Cruise Lines? I'd like to confirm a reservation. However, I need to invoke special condition number four. Yes, I'm the daughter of the ticket holders . . ."

"THIS." The word was a sentence in its own right. Sha'Cretia pulled a heavy sweater from Carolina's closet. "You'll certainly need this, and the cabling will show off your bust line to a most scrumptious effect." She stepped to the bed where she began to fold it for placement in one of the opened cases spread around the room.

Carolina's voice called from the living room, "A coat, Sha? Do you think I'll need a coat?"

"Only for the spring cruises, sweetie. Let's stick with your thickest sweaters."

"I only have the one. This is Los Angeles, remember. My other home is South Carolina. I have no thick sweaters."

"Sweetie, you have thin ones. You can wear two at a time. We'll just pack them all." Sha'Cretia began picking up stacks of lightweight sweaters, placing them in various suitcases. "Now for all the other things you need." She looked at the cases she'd nearly filled and pondered aloud. "Too many sweaters." She reached in and grabbed a stack. "These can stay here. Now we have room for underwear." She called to the other room, "You do wear underwear, Carolina?"

Carolina laughed. "Of course I do. You'd better leave me room for some." She stepped into the room and opened a drawer. "They're right here. Put in enough for two weeks." She laughed again, her pleasure in the packing easing the reason for going on the trip at all. "I'd never get this done without you. Hurry, though!" She turned to look at her watch. "The time! The taxi will be here any moment."

She started grabbing items, and she flung them inside the empty places in the cases. Eventually finding them full, she grabbed Sha'Cretia's arm. "Just two more things. I have a checkbook I was given. I put it on a table in the other room. I also need my cruise packet. It has my ticket and itinerary. My purse, Sha'Cretia. Grab my purse."

"That's three, but that's okay, girl. I've got it all." The beep of a horn sounded outside. "It's here. Girl, you are going to have such a good time. Love it for your momma and your poppa. Give me a hug before he gets inside." Sha'Cretia grabbed her friend, and pressing her cheek to Carolina's face, she whispered, "I can't fly up with you this time. Find you a good man and bring him home. Love ya', baby." Then they were broken apart by the repeated ringing of the doorbell. In a flurry of answered doors and moving cases, Carolina's things were transferred into the waiting vehicle, and the taxi was gone.

Sha'Cretia was left all alone in the middle of Carolina's living room with not even a rotten piece of cheese for company. She walked into the kitchen preparing to lock up the house when she saw a slice of cheesecake sitting on the kitchen table.

"Hmm, girl. I said I love you, but right now, I think I love this piece of cheesecake even more." She glanced around, knowing no one was inside the house, but checking just in case. She didn't want to be seen stealing Carolina's food. However, she knew the dessert wouldn't last until Carolina returned.

Sha'Cretia called out to the house, "Sweetie, I can't let this ruin. I'll lock up in a minute, after I sample this little snack." She did sample it, too.

As she lay in the spa tub later that evening, she decided Carolina wouldn't mind if she stayed the night, so she turned the jets on and stretched out. If Carolina were only a man, she'd marry her, and as soon as Carolina got back from her cruise to Alaska, she'd tell her that, and in those very words.

However, before long, she'd fallen asleep. Sometime later, the jets automatically turned themselves off, and Sha'Cretia bobbed in the water for the rest of the night. The next morning, she found himself to be very pruned, indeed, and it was some

71

time before she plumped back out.

She took it on the chin, however. Carolina was her friend, and she was worth all the inconveniences she had to put up with for her, even being turned into a prune.

Chapter 5

CAROLINA smiled at the young couple sitting across the cabin from her, and she turned her head to look out the window. She scanned the airport and used the back of her hand to wipe her tears from her eyes. If her parents had been going on this flight, they would have been taking those two seats. Instead, she'd chosen to sit off to herself, letting the young couple have the opportunity to be together in the more private seats that were hers originally.

She reached and rubbed the richness of the leather seat. This jet seemed to be nearly new, and the interior was quite pristine. In spite of changing seats, she longingly hoped for a companion. It was only a couple of hours to Seattle, but it would be a long few hours if she had no one to visit with. A distraction would help her keep from bleeding these tears the entire trip. She leaned her head back and snorted a rueful laugh. She was a crying fool, and no one would understand what it was all about.

She'd watched the other passengers board the aircraft, and she'd been amazed at the variety of individuals. Some she could see were obviously dressed for business, perhaps to spend the day in a northern city with plans to return before nightfall. Others were clearly returning from vacations, their sunburns telling of time in the California sun. However, it was the ones holding hands, the man carrying two items, and the woman selecting their assigned seats, that told Carolina of love. That would have been her parents, she knew. Her father would have struggled with too-heavy carry-ons, and her mother would have prattled on about her anticipated vacation plans. The flight hadn't even left the airport, and Carolina was already feeling lonely, wondering if she shouldn't have stayed home.

Then, just as the attendants were closing the door, a voice could be heard calling for them to hold on, and in popped a pretty young thing about Carolina's own age. She smiled as she stepped inside, and she stopped to catch her breath as she showed the flight attendant her ticket. With a pensive look, the attendant glanced up and down the airplane, then paused to question another of the attendants. Together they pointed at the empty seat next to Carolina.

"Do you mind? We seem to be completely full this flight."

This girl wasn't what Carolina had expected, but she was company. Carolina smiled and picked up her purse. She hadn't bothered with a carry-on. It had all gone in the hold, extra charges and all. It was all included in the itinerary. Her parents had paid for the top of the line, and that included all the luggage she wanted to carry.

"Hi! I almost didn't make it." The girl sat next to her, her excitement bubbling over. When she saw Carolina paying attention, she smiled and continued, "I had a screen test, you see. Out at the studios." She took a deep breath as if her day had gone very well indeed.

Carolina smiled. She wanted to hear more. She adjusted her

seating position and propped her chin in her hand, watching the expressions flash across the girl's attractive face.

"Did it turn out well?" Carolina smiled to see the girl's eyes crinkle in pleasure as she prepared to answer the question.

Turning in her seat to find a more comfortable position, a mischievous glint seemed to dance in the girl's eyes. "Very well. You know, my great-grandmother was an actress." She looked at her hands, and she smiled as if they were extra special. "No, no one's ever heard of her, but she did act once. With John Barrymore. You know, the old man who played Scrooge in *It's a Wonderful Life* John Barrymore."

In watching the girl, Carolina guessed she was younger than she first thought. Her makeup and clothing, and the bright flush on her face from running to board before the door was closed had added maturity to her appearance. As Carolina watched, she could see the years melting away. Now she guessed maybe nineteen or twenty. At the most. She was very pretty, too, and fresh. Carolina's eyes were glued to her as she watched her features flicker with the emotions of her story.

The girl's impromptu audience impelled the tale along.

"Was your great-grandmother in that movie?"

"*It's a Wonderful Life*? You've seen it? It's ancient, you know." The girl seemed incredulous that someone almost as young as she was might have actually watched the old production.

"Dozens of times. It's one of my favorites." Carolina smiled at the girl's youthful presumptions. "So, what part did she play?"

"Oh, she wasn't in that one. John Barrymore, you know, the old man?" The girl twisted in her seat to face her companion as she warmed to her story. "He was young once. That surprised me when I found out. I thought he was always old. He was tall and quite the charmer, my grandmother used to say."

"So, was it your grandmother or your great-grandmother

75

who used to act?" Carolina smiled at the girl's fractured story. "Or both?"

"Oh, it was my great-grandmother, for sure. She was dead before I was born, though. My grandmother used to tell me the stories. She remembered Mr. Barrymore, as she used to call him. He used to pick her up and carry her around. She was just a baby, though, so I don't really see how she could remember that. I think she remembered her mother's stories."

"So, what parts did your great-grandmother used to play?"

The girl giggled. "I always thought this was funny. She played a black slave girl. She used to tell my grandmother how they wiped black polish all over her face, and she had a terrible time getting it off at night."

"Blackface," Carolina offered.

"What?" The girl looked puzzled.

"Blackface. That's what they called it when a white actor played a black role. He or she was acting in blackface."

The girl looked thoughtful for a moment as if unsure whether this was a joke or not. Then she smiled. "Blackface. I never knew that." Her expression shifted, and she laughed, her hands moving as she continued her story, her motions telling part of the actions her words were describing. "Anyway, I always wanted to do that. Not the blackface part, you see, but the other part, the acting. I had an audition in Hollywood." She rolled her eyes. "At least it was close to Hollywood, but I always say Hollywood. For a face cleaner." She brightened in her best commercial persona. "Do you know there are one hundred forty-two germs that live on the human face alone?" She paused and frowned. "Or is it one thousand forty-two? I forget, but certain antibacterial soaps can kill all but two percent of them. I'm not allowed to say which one, though." She looked conspiratorially at Carolina. "That's in my contract. They can fire me if I tell before I get the job." She leaned over and almost whispered her best news. "I think I got it, though. When I left, they smiled really big at me and said they'd be calling me. I feel really good about this one."

Carolina smiled and patted her arm. "Good for you, dear."

The girl looked appreciatively at Carolina and smiled. "You have a pretty voice. Sort of soft and Southern. I like it. If you don't mind, I might close my eyes for a moment. I've been up a long time."

Before a response could even be offered, the girl's eyes were closed, and a soft snore could be heard. The sound was pleasant and comforting, and Carolina smiled, looking back toward the window. It's so simple when you're young. People can smile, and the young can sleep with the assurance of a contract earned.

Carolina thought about her own job. Her parents had wanted her to stay on the East Coast, but she'd needed her independence, chasing it all the way to the far side of the continent. She'd made the most of it, too, and she lived well. There was no car, but she hadn't needed one. Taxis were available, and occasionally Mr. Warner would send the company car for her.

Then there was this trip. In spite of Sha'Cretia's assurances, she was already having misgivings. She'd been in Hilton Head for over a week, and now she was taking two more. She had the sales figures to go over and the upcoming yearly retreat. Who could do that as well as she could? Sha'Cretia would certainly give it her best, but Carolina knew it inside and out.

She leaned her head back and closed her eyes. She also had her parents on this trip with her, for their memories were bound to crop up at every turn. That would be very hard. Would that she could sleep like the young lady next to her! Then the trip would melt away. Even so, sleep was not likely, that was for sure. If her parents were here, what would they think of her melancholy attitude? In fact, the last time she'd seen them, her father had quipped about how distressed she seemed when he picked her up from the airport, almost as if she'd been expecting someone else as she got off the airplane.

"Sweet girl of mine, who were you looking for?" He'd reached and hugged her as he took her bag.

"No one, Daddy. Why do you ask?" She'd searched, though. She remembered, and she always looked.

"Well, pumpkin, you glanced at me and smiled, and then you turned to look around the front of the airplane. I know that expression, young lady. You can't fool me with that wide-eyed innocence." He'd laughed to let her know he wasn't bothered by her answers.

Her mother had kissed her when she got to the house. "Carolina, come home. We love you. All the good boys live here, you know. You'll never find one in California. Also, your father and I love that Sha'Cretia. You know she charmed us, and we want you to bring her back again. Still, a friend can't love you like a man."

"Man?" Carolina had laughed. "Mummy, you act like I want to marry Sha'Cretia. She's my best friend, not my fiancée."

"That's what I mean, Carolina. A woman should be a best friend. A man is what you need for a companion."

Carolina had truly laughed then. "Mummy, that's what Sha is for."

Her mother had given her one of those looks, but Carolina had just hugged her and forgotten it. Later that weekend she'd hugged her parents farewell, not imagining she would never see them again.

Carolina pulled herself awake, looking to see the young woman beside her still sleeping quietly. Suddenly her parents and what they must have gone through in the moments before the accident made Carolina's heart ache. Putting a hand to her face, she leaned her head back to look out the window. She knew she needed to let this go, or she wouldn't survive this trip.

After a short time, she felt herself relaxing into a settled rhythm as the airplane droned on, enjoying the feeling of warmth the leather seating provided. Her eyes grew heavy in the solitude of the flight, and she let them close. A small sound caught her attention, and her eyes popped opened as suddenly as they'd slipped shut. She was surprised to see she was on a small airplane flying across a forested wilderness. She held her breath, knowing this surely couldn't be real. On either side of her were the canopy windows of a tandem cockpit, her view impeded only by the cinnamon-gold hair of the pilot sitting directly in front of her. She studied him for a moment, feeling he should be very familiar to her. She knew no pilots, though, and she'd certainly never flown in an airplane this small. There were only seats for two. Around the pilot's head of thick hair, she could see the blur of a propeller as it thrummed its steady rhythm pulling them through the skies.

She reached to touch the pilot's shoulder, wanting to ask where they were. She was surprised to feel his muscular frame clearly evident through the thick fabric of his shirt. Her pulse quickened. She had to know this man. He seemed so familiar. As he moved his head to see what she wanted, his shoulder flexed under her hand, the muscle rippling with the movement. Carolina's heart caught in her throat. She could almost place him. If she could just see his face. Then his profile turned to her. Frustration began to mount as Carolina's anticipation was dashed. His heavy headphones and aviator glasses shadowed much of his face.

"Where are we?" Carolina yelled over the beat of the propellers. That was when she saw something she'd know anywhere, something that told her she did know this pilot. He opened his mouth to speak, and his face broke in two as a huge dimple split his cheek in half.

"Alaska, ma'am. Cool, huh?"

Carolina awakened and sat up in her seat. There next to her was the young actress with the assurances of a new job selling antibacterial face chemicals. Just across the aisle were the young couple she had given her seats to, and she could see the attendants moving silently, pausing occasionally to see if a passenger could be helped, perhaps with a warming blanket or a cushioning pillow.

Carolina's heart raced and her skin burned with the flush she knew must be visible to anyone watching. He'd been here. He'd spoken to her, and she'd actually reached out and touched him. She didn't want a blanket or a pillow. She wanted that boy from ten years ago. He'd become a man now, and he wasn't bald or fat. He was youthful and muscular, and his face had broken into those dimples she had learned so well in all her dreams, and he'd spoken to her in a Southern drawl she recognized from her own Carolina coast.

Tears burned in her eyes, and she turned to see the waters of the Pacific coastline shimmering under the midday sun. She'd left her boy back in Savannah, and she'd stayed as far away as possible. He hadn't come to her on her beach that weekend, and she'd run to the most distant coast of the continent that she could reach.

Admit it, Carolina. You were afraid he'd never come for you, and you didn't want to face that. Now you're imagining him in the farthest location you can possibly go, and he won't be in Alaska to rescue you when your world breaks down around you. Don't expect any knight in shining armor. An old pickup truck will be more like it. Any knight that rescues you will bounce up covered with rust, and he'll ask if you need a ride. He probably won't even tell you his real name, and you'll never know who he really is. Ha! He'll certainly be old and fat, and his three kids will all be bouncing around in the back of the truck.

Won't that be some rescuing angel!

Her mood somehow buoyed by the image of a gaggle of kids in the back of a rusty truck come to rescue her, she smiled and wiped the tears from her face. She turned to see her companion stirring in her seat. This was real life. Living was more than some dream-world Lancelot who'd never come to rescue her. She'd become fixated on a figment of her imagination, one that she'd bumped into for five minutes ten years ago. Her parents had died, she'd attended their funeral, and now she was going on their cruise. How much more real could life get than that?

Reaching a thumb to catch a final tear, she spoke to the waking face next to her. "Did you have a nice nap, dear?" Carolina smiled at her pretty seatmate.

Brightly, the girl answered. "I did, thank you. I dreamed I was in a big movie, and everybody loved me. I even had to sign autographs for everyone." The girl stretched and smiled. "There was this boy, and he invited me to the beach to go surfing. We had the best time ever. I wish you could have been there."

Carolina turned to look out the window at Seattle in the distance. "Thank you, dear. That's sweet of you to offer." Inside, though, her thoughts ran a different direction. She imagined a small aircraft, two seats preferably, with a golden-haired pilot and muscular shoulders. A Southern voice would split his dimples across his cheeks when he spoke. Then there were those words: *Alaska? Cool.* He was all she had right now to push her grief away.

Carolina took a deep breath. She was strong. All her life she'd proven that. She could do this, and she would show her Southern iron. Good breeding would win out. She turned to the girl at her side, putting her best office face on.

"So, my dear. What are your plans now that you're arriving back in Seattle?"

Chapter 6

CAROLINA stood looking around her at all the bags assembled along the drop-off curb, the results of Sha'Cretia's packing. There was so much, and most of those at the landing had only a bag or two. She was appalled to know this entire lot was all hers. Now she felt lost and alone, stranded with more luggage than anyone could possibly need.

A massive ship was just off the dock, and she wondered if that's where she needed to go, or if she was meant to head inside to a check-in counter of sorts. She watched people swirl around her, and for a time, she felt the heat of embarrassment tingeing her face brilliant red. However, what could she do? She couldn't move all her luggage on her own. She had no car, and her taxi had gone. She was stuck with all of it.

She sat on her biggest and sturdiest. Checking her watch, she knew she was very early, but then she hadn't wanted to miss her boarding call and had allowed plenty of transfer time from the airport. After a time, she closed her eyes, the waiting becoming a welcomed interlude in the passing of her day. She was startled as a hand touched her arm. In that moment of surprise, she opened her eyes to find her makeshift seat an unsteady one. With an unexpected snap of stressed plastic, one wheel went flying, and the whole affair flew out from underneath her. Her arms swinging, and her legs flying, Carolina's traveling cases were soon scattered into a dizzying disarray, and she found herself planted on her backside right in the middle.

An elderly voice tried to soothe the damage.

"Oh, my. I did not mean to do that. Not at all. My dear, let me help you up."

Carolina looked to see a hand wearing a white glove reach to her. The two of them were the only ones around.

The elderly voice continued, "And then we shall call you a porter."

"A porter?" Why hadn't she thought of that?

As Carolina stood, the person attached to the arm peered around, her broad-brimmed hat shading her face from Carolina's view. "I see you have only a few things. Perhaps my porter can tote them with mine. That would be so much simpler."

"A few things? I have so much. I feel so embarrassed." Carolina reached to brush her clothing off, and then she turned to get a good look at her new companion. She was wearing a classically tailored suit of heavy fabric, even though the Seattle afternoon was quite warm. Under the enormous hat was a very round, carefully made up face, one that must have been quite pert and attractive when younger.

"Now dear, if you don't mind waiting just a moment, my porter's around here somewhere." The old woman patted her on the arm.

"I'm so sorry. It was silly of me to be sitting on my case like that."

"Oh, no, dear." The manicured face smiled. "You mustn't apologize about your things, and I cannot let you take the blame for what happened. I startled you. You looked so peaceful there that I just hoped you were going my way." The old woman glanced around at the port, and she got a wistful look on her face. "So many people these days aren't."

"Where are you headed?" Carolina inquired politely as she pushed her hair from her face. The few people she'd seen earlier had disappeared, and she hoped she hadn't missed her boarding call.

The older woman put her hand to her mouth as if in deep thought. "Let me see. Umm. How shall I put it?" As if deciding Carolina was a kindred spirit worth trusting, she smiled. "My grandson, you know. He's my favorite. He's A.W.O.L, you know, and I miss him. I'm off looking for him." She chuckled.

Carolina watched as the old woman's eyes misted. "I can see you really wish to find him. He must be very special to you." Carolina felt herself drawn to this finely dressed old woman. With a smile, she bent to begin straightening her luggage, and the old woman grabbed her arm.

"No, my dear. My porter will get those. See? He's just over there. I'm traveling light this trip. He can add your things to mine. That will be fine with you, won't it?" She was already waving one gloved hand at the porter, pointing with the other at Carolina's things scattered across the ground.

Carolina started to refuse. She didn't want her things to get mixed in with the woman's items, especially as she wasn't sure they were embarking on the same vessel. When the porter arrived, his cart was piled high with matching cases, and Carolina reached her hand to cover her involuntary reaction of amazement.

"Are all those yours?" Carolina tried to count them, but there were too many. The woman's reply made Carolina smile.

"Of course, my dear. One must dress for dinner, you know." She reached to speak to her porter, directing him to put certain items in very specific places. Then she turned back to Carolina, waving her hand to dismiss the man she'd been directing.

"My dear, I'm amiss. I've not introduced myself. I'm Mamie. My grandson calls me that, and I'd like for you to do the same. You're about the same age as my grandson, you know." She laughed. "I'm told I'm not supposed to have favorites, but forget that. This one is special. I'd still have him too, if it weren't for that money-grubbing woman he married. He's on the run from her, you see. She wanted him to sell his little toy, the one he got from my son, and my grandson put his foot down and just ran away. I'd have helped him, you know, but he never even asked. Very independent. I like that in a man."

Carolina was charmed by the story, and the more Mamie talked, the more Carolina could hear hints of a Southern drawl in her voice. It might be hidden by Harvard, or perhaps Yale, but it was definitely there. However, Carolina had something more important on her mind. Her baggage. It couldn't be allowed to wind up on the wrong ship.

"Mamie, I also haven't shared my name. Carolina, and I'm pleased to meet you. I'm intrigued by your story, but I don't know where you're going, and my luggage is mixed in with yours."

"Why, dear, if you're here to board a ship today, I don't have to tell you where I'm going. We're going together."

"Together?" This had been her parents' cruise, not hers. She had no idea how Mamie could know they would be together.

"Dear," Mamie prattled on, "Only one ship leaves today, and it goes to find my grandson." The old woman reached to adjust her hat, and she moved forward. "Come, dear."

Carolina hurried to keep up, still not satisfied. "If your grandson's missing, what makes you think you'll find him on a cruise ship?"

"His favorite phrase, my dear." She waved Carolina on, not slowing a step. "I thought he was telling me how cold it was for a long time, but you're about the same age, so you'd understand, I think. My neighbor, that's Susan Cotton, of the Atlanta Cottons, explained it to me, and even then it didn't make sense. Now I understand. It wasn't intended to make sense. It was no more than an expression."

They approached a big warehouse-type building, and as they entered, Mamie began to articulate her story with her hands, throwing them up in the air as she spoke, something Carolina recognized from her own Southern grandparents. "It was the excitement. Young people are like that, you know, all wanting excitement in everything they do. When he was young, he said it to me over and over for the longest time. That was some special grandson. You should meet him sometime. You'd like him."

Carolina laughed. "His phrase, Mamie?"

"Oh, dear! I didn't tell you?" Mamie glanced her way, and her pert red lips smiled. Then she turned once again and marched ahead, calling the phrase back as she waved her white-gloved hand in the air. "Alaska? Cool. That's what he said to me, and that's where I'm going. To Alaska!"

Carolina stopped, frozen. Then she laughed to herself. It was ten years and a continent away that she'd heard those words. She chided herself. Her boy from Savannah couldn't be Mamie's grandson. He was fat with three children. Real life fantasies didn't come true just because you wanted them to, especially in the middle of Alaska. She was running as far from that boy as she could get, and he wouldn't be anywhere near her cruise ship.

She could take that to the bank.

Yet, before resuming her walk, she did glance around, perhaps to see if there were any golden-headed men around, ones about her age, even though if someone called her on it, she'd have said she was simply taking the opportunity to look around the facilities one final time.

She was startled when Mamie called her name. "Carolina! Come on, dear. You can't just stand and obstruct traffic all day."

Carolina laughed, striding forward, determined to leave all her silly dreams in Los Angeles, or at least here in Seattle, and as Sha'Cretia had suggested, she planned to find her a man in Alaska to bring home with her. She was pretty sure it wouldn't be Mamie's grandson, either. He was running from his own wicked witch, and Carolina didn't need any of that.

She pressed along with a smile, pleased to have found a new companion, and she was certain she would get her allotment of exercise just keeping up with this engaging woman, much less chasing after a man her own age.

CAROLINA opened the velvet box Sha'Cretia had thrown into one of her many cases. She'd been so amused to see the volume of luggage Mamie had jostled, wheedled, and tweaked into her suite of rooms. Afterward, although Carolina had expected to spend the cruise in a much smaller room, however luxurious, she discovered her own cabin was right next door to Mamie's. Her parents had indeed opted for first class. No wonder the monies she would have forfeited on this trip were so much! She didn't have a room; she had a suite to equal Mamie's.

Carolina's cabin swallowed her own cases that had looked so numerous out by the curb, and now she was glad her friend had insisted on packing so many items. She wouldn't have to do without anything at all over the next two weeks, and she could indeed double up on her sweaters if it got cold.

Tonight, though, she had signed up with Mamie for the formal dinner with the captain. She needed to look her best. She opened the box, and there they were, her graduation earrings from her parents. Somehow, Sha'Cretia had managed to get these all the way from her parents' home in Hilton Head, and

Carolina wasn't upset at all. These earrings for the evening were certainly a nicely chosen accent.

Slipping her freshly laundered Vera Wang over her head, Carolina tugged it down, thinking she wouldn't be able to indulge herself too freely on this cruise. She didn't imagine the cleaners would have taken in the dress, and it had fit perfectly in Hilton Head. She looked at herself critically in the full-length mirrors filling one end of her bathroom, one of the perks of a top-of-the-line cabin. She turned to get her profile, raising her arms to shift the dress on her body. Yes, she had to admit, it was snug, but it still moved beautifully, just as Vera Wang had designed it. It would dazzle Mamie tonight. Carolina's newly found friend was obviously a very well dressed personage, but Carolina could make that leap when she wished.

Picking up one of the earrings, she held it against the fabric of the dress. If only her skin were Sha'Cretia's creamy cocoa, then these diamonds would flash with the fire of the brightest stars on a velvety summer night. No, her own skin wouldn't set them off like Sha'Cretia's, but then Sha'Cretia wouldn't be wearing them. She would, and she smiled. They'd set off her skin's Southern peaches-and-cream in a different way, but it would still be beautiful. Subtle was the effect she would present, a bold black Vera Wang, and a subtle cascade of diamonds.

Not even Sha'Cretia could top that.

Slipping her feet into her shoes, feeling the extra height in her calves, Carolina reached to work one strap over her hose, rubbing the silky threads to press them flat. She loved the feel of good nylons, and she especially loved the ones that shimmered. Shifting her feet to settle them into her shoes, she adjusted her dress and stepped to the door.

Catching sight of herself in a small bureau mirror just inside the door, she paused. "Oh," she murmured to no one in particular. "My hair is a wreck." Shrugging in resignation, knowing it was too late to give it any real attention, she reached a hand

and worked her fingers in at the roots. Shaking her hand to jostle the strands of hair into some sort of order, she pushed her fingers through her hair and shook her head to get it to fall gracefully.

Noticing that the satellite phone the cruise line had given her for the trip was attached to its charging cord on the bureau, she unplugged it and dropped it into the too-large purse she was leaving behind in the cabin.

"Don't want to misplace that," and she laughed.

Looking back into the mirror, she smiled. She blew herself a kiss and stepped into the corridor, calling out to her new friend who was already outside her door waiting to head to dinner.

"DEAR, A BEAUTIFUL girl like you cannot survive on a salad and water. It doesn't matter if you have chicken shredded all over that lettuce." Mamie pressed her lips together and bobbed her head smartly. She turned to the waiter. "My dear friend here will also have the lobster bisque and a vegetable platter. Please bring your freshest. Nothing frozen, please. White wine." She turned to Carolina and confided, "Only white with fish. Never red. Too overpowering." She pulled Carolina's salad from her charger plate, handing it to the waiter. "Take this back. Real food will keep up our energies tonight."

Carolina let her eyes peruse the room to see the massive plates of food being served to the other diners. "Mamie, I cannot eat all you're ordering. And the cost? Lobster?"

Mamie patted her hand. "Cost? On board this ship, your ticket covers everything. You have your pass? Remember? The one with your name on it. I keep mine here." Mamie reached to her chest and pulled a cord from inside her lace collar. Out popped a white card with Altessa in bold colors across the top, and her name plastered across the bottom. The card flew through the air, restrained only by the cord around the old woman's neck, and it bounced back and hit her in the face. Twisted around it was a gold cross on a chain of its own.

89

"Oh, my!" Mamie grabbed at it, rescuing both just before they dropped into her tea. She slipped the cross back inside, holding the white ID tag out to the woman at her side. "This, dear. See this black strip on the back? They scan it through one of those machines of theirs, and you don't pay a thing. Cool, huh?" She leaned in close to Carolina. "That's the word I got from my grandson. What do you think? Did I use it correctly?"

"Yes, you did." Carolina watched Mamie drop the card back inside the collar of her dinner attire, and she smiled. "I'm afraid I left my card in my room. I'd forgotten we were told to keep it with us."

Mamie assured her the ship wouldn't charge her for her meal, even without the card. The card was mostly to ensure the identity of the passengers and to pay for items that weren't part of the standard meal ticket. She nodded, telling Carolina that with their staterooms, everything was covered.

"You buy the best and the rest is free. Unless you want to get plastered, of course. Then they expect you to pay."

Mamie let out a laugh at that, and she fanned herself with her hand. She asserted that no one got plastered on white wine, and she reached for her glass to take a sip.

CAROLINA didn't intend to become "plastered," and she also didn't want her dress to become any tighter. She was determined to leave most of what was soon to be placed in front of her, no matter how ardently Mamie pressed her to imbibe.

Later that evening, Mamie praising Carolina's looks and claiming an old woman's exhaustion on the cruise's first full day, she sent the younger woman off to "make merry with the boys," and Carolina was alone. Walking the corridors of the ship, perusing the shops that were available, she was amazed at the variety of things to do. She smiled, remembering Mamie's remark that with her card, everything on the ship was free. Not exactly. Carolina could easily see that there were opportunities to spend money that could total far more than the original tickets must have cost.

Tickets. Not singular, but plural. Just that one word stopped the beautiful young woman in her tracks, and the lifeblood of the ship, the people who drove the cruise, the passengers who were her peers, flowed around her, deftly avoiding the beautiful statue that was on display in the middle of the concourse. For a time Carolina was just that, frozen, with only her eyes watching, seeing but not really seeing, and it was the lovers who caught her attention. Her thoughts followed those walking hand in hand, his arm wrapped around her waist, the occasional kiss of sensuous lips against a freshly shaved cheek.

It was her tears that signaled this was no statue, no mannequin strategically stationed to model the latest in evening wear available in the shop just across the way, the jewelry on display from the merchant watching from next door. No, she was real, and the heartbreak was genuine. The events of her life had continually contrived to keep Carolina busy with the activities they required, allowing her to hide the pain deep inside, but when they let her alone, the heartbreak once again bubbled to the surface.

It was heartbreak, too, the pain of a lost love she'd never really known, and one that she'd never admitted even to herself. Her family had been a bastion of support for her, and her work had consumed her identity. Now her parents had been cruelly taken from her, and she needed comfort that her job couldn't provide. She was a drowning woman grabbing at whatever emotional handholds were out there, and the one that kept reaching back was one that had never truly been hers. He'd floated into her world that one day she'd stepped off that tram. Then he'd flexed his arms from behind that engine cowling, and she'd become infatuated.

It hadn't been love. Even she knew that. It had been the idea of love, a perfection that had leaped out at her and grown in her mind from a chance meeting to something much more. From that moment she had searched for him, and now she knew he'd never be found. Not by Carolina. Not in Alaska. Not in her lifetime.

Then her world snapped back into motion, and Carolina began to move through the ship crowded with chattering people. She passed through the maelstrom of their voices, those sounds that formed the background of life for all aboard. The reverberations of that life flowed around her, unable to touch her thoughts as her feet carried her body along. Eventually she made it back to her cabin, and her filigreed diamonds were nestled back into their velvet box. Her Vera Wang was shaken out and hung gently in the closet. Carolina slid between sheets that were silky to her skin, but she drifted off with a new thought skittering through her mind.

Three kids might be all right, if only he still has muscular shoulders. I'd make that trade.

As she turned in her bed, her hand reached beside her for an arm that wasn't there, and with that realization, her tears began to flow.

"CAROLINA, dear? We're stopping today. Will you join us?" Mamie stood outside the younger woman's door, her white-gloved knuckles gently resting against the wood.

Inside, Carolina sat on her balcony, the day finally warm, the sun streaming across her pajama-wrapped legs, the chaise lounge for her alone. The sliders to her room were open behind her; she hadn't had the energy to close them when stepping outside. This particular day had been hard for her. Over the course of the cruise, except for those rare occasions when Mamie had pulled her from her increasingly pensive moods, she'd been overwhelmingly aware of what her parents would have been doing each day aboard the ship. Each activity available had thrown itself at Carolina to haunt her moments, and more days than not, a good deal of time had been spent wrapped in a blanket staring out to sea, her trusty box of tissues at hand to stem the flow of distressing tears.

She heard her friend's voice through the door, and she called back, "I'm sorry, Mamie. You have a good time, you hear? I can't bring myself to dress today." Carolina looked out at the water, the edge of the harbor just within her view, as a new eruption of tears chased itself down her face.

Mamie's voice called to her once more, chiding her about her reclusive behavior. "Get it all out today, dear. Tomorrow you must go with me. I cannot find that grandson without you, you know. You're a magnet for handsome men. If I have you, that grandson will come find me. Toot, toot, my dear. You're missing Alaska!"

Footsteps in the corridor faded as Carolina watched the water. The cool sea breeze brushed against her face as she smiled. She reached up and pulled her hair back from her cheek and rested her chin in her hands. Mamie was certainly the dear. If Carolina didn't know better, she'd swear the old woman was from her own Carolina coast. However, she never talked of the Low Country, and Carolina had never pressed the old woman for her history. There were too many other things on Carolina's mind at this point.

She was startled as the ship's intercom announced the final tender to shore in ten minutes. Suddenly, she couldn't bear the thought of remaining alone on the ship all day. In an impulsive rush, she leaped from her chaise and grabbed her outdoor things. The steward had laid them out the previous evening, but Carolina had simply stacked them in a chair. Now, they were in her hand, and she threw her pajamas to the side.

Stuffing her laces into her walking shoes, knowing she could tie them on the smaller boat as she was ferried to shore, she grabbed the small wallet that held her shipboard tag. She remembered Mamie telling her to keep it with her at all times, although Carolina hadn't gone so far as to tie it on a cord around her neck. Opening the door, she remembered how bright it had been on the deck. As the announcement rang throughout the ship that the last tender was leaving in two minutes, Carolina hesitated, then stepped back inside to grab her larger purse. She had a secondary pair of sunglasses there, and she simply couldn't take time to look for her regular ones.

Her feet carrying her as fast as she could run, she was out of breath by the time she reached the ramp to the tender. "Hold!" she cried. "Don't leave."

"Ho, miss. You nearly got a day aboard ship. Come this way. The boat is waiting for you." There was no one else in the corridor except Carolina and the very helpful man.

At his smile, Carolina slowed to a walk. "Oh, thank you for waiting. I decided at the very last minute, and I do need to see something besides the interior of my cabin. It's my first time ashore. The walls were starting to grow on me."

An announcement echoed throughout the corridor, "Final boarding now for the mainland."

The man at the ramp frowned, telling her, "Miss, if you only just decided, then it's probable you've not been logged out. That presents a difficulty, as the boat is leaving now."

"Surely you can log me out." Dismay washed across Carolina. Now that she'd decided to go see this wild country her cruise had brought her to, it seemed too much to be dashed by the simple matter of logging out. She tried to smile, only to feel her eyes burn with an upcoming eruption.

The threat of sudden tears in her eyes must have tugged at the man's heart. He whispered, "I can let you on, but I'll have to log you off the ship manually. I must see your ID card to do so."

"My ID card?" She had grabbed her purse for her sunglasses, but what else was inside, she couldn't remember in such a rush.

"The small card we ask you to carry. You know, with your name?"

"Oh!" Carolina laughed. "I do have that." She reached into her small wallet. "Mamie, that's my friend, wears hers around her neck. This is my first time off the ship."

"Don't like the small boats, miss? We'll come to a real dock later on. You won't mind so much, then." The man looked at her card and asked her to say her name aloud. He smiled. "Thank you, miss. I'll enter you after you're gone." He nodded at her conspiratorially. "They don't really like us to do this. However, as it is your first time ashore, how can I not? Don't forget to be on time to catch the tender back. I like my neck." He handed her card back to her.

Carolina laughed as she walked onto the boat for her ride to the shore. Her run had energized her. She could feel it in the heat on her face and in her racing pulse.

Once on shore, she glanced about for Mamie, and not seeing her, wandered through a couple of nearby shops alone, hoping for some time to think. She looked around at the town and the wilderness she could see in the distance. It wasn't cold at all. The sky was blue, and the sun was bright. She knew she must find a way to wrestle with her issues, with her parents' deaths; and if there was a God-given day to do so, this seemed to be it. If she couldn't, she was lost. She was too strong to let that happen.

It didn't take Carolina long to understand she'd have no time to think as long as she stayed in this very touristy location. Several hundred of her shipboard peers were gathered right here by her side, and their magpie conversations weren't allowing her any quiet at all.

Strolling down the road, she was surprised to see a lone man standing beside a trail-worn Jeep. He was holding a sign up, and when she read it, she laughed. He was offering to rent his off-road ride for the day, and apparently there had been no takers.

Carolina knew off-road rentals were an option in the cruise line's literature, but she would have certainly expected more than one Jeep.

"Miss? Do you wish to rent my Jeep? You can drive it anywhere you wish for the day. The tank's already full of gas. One price covers all." The man looked at her hopefully, and Carolina turned to watch the crowds she'd just left. She'd driven a Jeep before, or a sort of Jeep, anyway. An ancient Samurai, her brother's, before he'd let it get caught in the ocean surf one day. After that, no one had driven it ever again. The thought intrigued her. With a Jeep, she could get far from the crowds, and she could think as much as she liked.

"One price? How much?" She had money, but she could see it was a very old Jeep.

"One hundred?" At Carolina's sudden look of dismay, the man quickly stumbled to a new price. "Seventy-five for you, though. Just seventy-five. It's for the entire day."

Carolina took a deep breath, thinking of the cruise ship and all its people. She couldn't go back, not just yet, and the idea of enduring the town for hours and hours was claustrophobic. She smiled and reached to her purse, glad she'd grabbed her larger one. That was where most of her ready cash was. She reached inside and counted out three twenties, a ten, and a five. When she held it out, the man took it with a bobbing bow and backed up, patting the hood.

"The keys are inside. Just leave it here when you get back, keys in the ignition. No one'll bother it. Thanks, miss." Then he was gone, and Carolina was alone with the freedom she so craved. She walked up to the well-worn machine and suddenly hoped she'd not just thrown away her seventy-five dollars. Surely this machine would start.

She looked, and sure enough, the keys were there, teasing her with the prospect that the old machine would at least try to lumber to life. Stay running? Carolina smiled. At least she didn't plan to take it far, and if she needed, she could always walk back. She reached in and brushed dirt from the seat. She sighed. The ship had laundry facilities. She could do this. After all, this was Alaska, and if they were here, her parents would be out on the hills whooping it up.

Carolina threw her purse to the passenger's seat and reached to the bar running where the top of the door would be. If it had a door, she thought. She stepped up and used her arms to hoist her body into the seat. Settling back, she reached for the gearshift to make sure it was in park, only to realize she'd rented a standard.

"Oops!" she said out loud, cringing at the thought of using a clutch. Then she reached a foot down, pressed the pedal partially to the floor, and turned the key. She groaned when nothing happened. Looking around for the man she'd rented from, she wasn't surprised to see him nowhere around.

Reaching for her purse, her hand bumped the gearshift, and she was surprised to feel it wobble at her touch. She laughed. It had to be in gear to start. She pressed the clutch back in and forced the shifter into what she thought was first. Turning the key, all she got was silence.

"Oh!" she cried, her frustration at the day finally breaking through her calm exterior. "No!" She would not give up so easily.

This time, she moved the seat forward for a better grip, and wrapping one arm around the steering wheel, she pushed the clutch in as firmly as she could and turned the key one more time. This time it responded. The old machine's starter ground for a moment, and the engine growled to life with the snarl of a sturdy machine designed for off-road service.

"That's more like it," Carolina muttered. "Now let's get out of town." She revved the engine and let the clutch out, only to have the vehicle jump backward and die.

"No wonder that man ran away as soon as he took my

money. He didn't want to watch me tear his transmission to pieces." She laughed and tried again, the process finally making sense to her. She had to push the clutch all the way in and then make sure it was really in first gear. At last she was on the road, headed out of town, and the glorious solitude of a perfect Alaska day was hers for the taking.

CAROLINA had spent the day exploring in the Jeep, but clearly, no more. It was dead in the water. Rather, dead on the side of the road, but dead was dead, nonetheless. The day had been beautifully distracting, but she should have saved her seventy-five dollars and found something to do in town. She should have faced her boredom head on and made the best of it.

She climbed out and stood next to the broken vehicle, holding her purse under her arm and looking around her. She glanced up and down the road. No one. The air had grown chilly, too. She let out a frustrated breath and turned to face the Jeep. Then, with all her strength, she pulled her foot back and kicked the tire on the stubborn vehicle that refused to run. She knew where her cell phone was, too. It was in her cabin on board the ship. She'd been charging it overnight to keep access to her email account. A lot of good it was doing her there, although she did distinctly remember being told that personal cell phones probably wouldn't work reliably for phone service away from the immediate coastline. Whether that referred to onshore or offshore, she wasn't sure. But it seemed to be a point not worth worrying about in her case. She had no cell phone at all.

Carolina sat on the running board below the Jeep's missing door, only to slip and fall, hitting the road hard. Standing, she almost cried. The road wasn't even a road. It was dirt, with mud scattered throughout the shaded areas. And she'd just found the wettest place of all. It was all over the backside of her clothes. She felt ready to just lie down in the road and let a truck run her right over, and she would, too, except there was no one around to do the odious deed for as far as her eyes could see.

98

Chapter 7

THE BLEATING of a faraway horn brought tears to Carolina's eyes. That was a sound she was very familiar with. She'd heard it at every stop they'd made. It was the horn that signaled the ship was nearing its final departure time. She guessed she could try to run back to the boat, but she knew it'd be useless. She'd not intended to get so far from town, but one interesting sight had led to another, and she'd soon found herself on a remote road.

She certainly wasn't lost, but she was much farther than she could run.

She looked up at the sky. At least she didn't have to worry about it getting dark soon. It seemed to remain light forever up here. The first few mornings of the cruise, she'd awakened with the rising of the sun only to be distressed by how tired she was. It wasn't until Mamie had told her about being so close to the top of the world that Carolina realized what was happening.

She'd learned to go to bed when the sun was still up, and remember to always, always close the light-darkening drapes in her cabin.

When the ship's horn blared the second time, the sound overwhelmed her. With a wail of frustration, she pulled herself up into the Jeep to try one more time. She didn't know why it had died on her. Just like that, and then it had refused to start. Throwing her purse into the seat next to her, she wrapped her arm once again around the wheel and pushed the clutch to the floor. Turning the key, she heard the engine grinding as it turned over and over. However, no matter how long she held it, it wouldn't catch. She pumped the accelerator with her foot to no avail.

"Oh!" She reached to slap the steering wheel. "I cannot start this machine. I might as well walk." Crawling down, she considered taking the keys, and then she decided it might be best to hide them in the vehicle just in case she could somehow get back in time to catch the boat. Finally she laughed. No one could start it anyway. How would they steal it?

Her deal-with-it nature beginning to win out over her problems, Carolina reached in and grabbed her purse. She'd dealt with similar situations before, and she knew what to do. She could hear her father's words from when she'd been eighteen. *Think it through, Carolina.*

One time had been the day an old boyfriend had taken her to a party on the beach. It'd been some distance from home, and there'd been a large crowd there. During the evening was when Carolina had learned that the boyfriend had quite a taste for the wilder side of partying.

Many of his friends had been there, and they'd started a slugfest. Slugfest. That was a definitive term. They'd taken slug after slug of whiskey, just to see who would pass out first. Well, Carolina had picked the loser, and she'd been stuck without a ride home. Her boyfriend's buddies had packed him up, leaving his car behind. She'd somehow expected them to come back for her, but when the last person was gone, and she was the only one left, she'd followed her father's advice. She had no ride. She had no key. *Think it through, Carolina.* So, she'd struck out on the road. It had been late when she'd gotten home, but she'd gotten there. That boyfriend had been history, too.

Here she was again, and she knew which direction she needed to head. Toward the coast. Standing, shading her eyes against the afternoon sun, her sunglasses some help, Carolina looked back at her old Jeep. "Go, friend. For a moment you gave me freedom. Then you abandoned me, just like all the other men in my life. Sha'Cretia, I could sure use your company now."

Then she started on the long walk back to town.

KODIAK checked his burn barrel, flipping on his flashlight just to be sure. He wanted to make sure there were no bear deposits inside the heavy-duty drum, and then he began to drop his branch clippings in a handful at a time.

He'd been at this for days. At least he'd had only one small repair at the shop to pull him away. The big jobs would come at the end of the season when people were getting ready to pack away tools and summer toys. Of course, they'd also be pulling out winter toys then, and those that hadn't been stored properly would need his attention. Until then, he'd get only the occasional emergency.

Shaking his gasoline can, he realized most of it had gone into an earlier burn barrel, and he still hadn't cut the largest sections of the tree from his walkway. In addition, especially down closer to the water, there were plenty more piles of trimmings already cut and waiting. With the downed tree in his way, he was still having to slip and slide down the grassy slope to get to his dock.

He glanced up at the sky. It would be light half the night, but that didn't mean the station would be open for him to get fuel. He gauged he still had plenty of time to make it in and back before it started getting too cold. The weather had been exceptionally cooperative the past few days, and he didn't want to waste any of it.

He dumped the last of one pile of cuttings in the barrel and shook his gasoline can, hesitating before tossing in the rest of his fuel. He felt one pocket for his matches, considering whether he should light the fuel now or wait until he returned. He had only so many barrels, and it usually took several hours for each one to burn down. That decided him, to get this started so he could reload it when he returned. He dumped the rest of the liquid in the barrel and reached in his pocket for a match. With a whoosh, it was soon blazing hot enough to make him stand back and give the flames space.

"There. That'll burn down a bit while I'm getting ready to head to town. Good going, Kody, my friend."

He laughed at his self-imposed nickname. It was like having a friend at his side, even if it was just the man he saw in the mirror each day. He turned and set the empty can by a tree, and he loped to his cabin. Bounding up the steps, he burst through the door, bypassed the living room, and vaulted directly into the adjoining bedroom. Pulling open the door to the bath, he flipped the water in the sink on. When it'd warmed, he lathered up his arms and rinsed them, splashing the soapy rinse water over his face, and shaking his arms to dry them without a towel.

Looking in the mirror, he realized how stained his shirt looked, and he reached over his head with both hands to pull it off. Tossing it to the side, the dirt residue at his collar line was apparent. Sighing, he glanced at the shower. He'd just cleaned it last week, and he hated to get it dirty so soon. Still, he'd have to rewash any fresh clothing he put on after just this one wearing. No way was he going to do that.

He rubbed his hand along one arm and looked in the mirror at his stomach. Clearing the trees the storm had taken down had given him his old high school six-pack again. He sighed and grabbed a bar of soap, then he stepped back into the bedroom to grab a clean set of clothes. He looked at his stack of clean towels and decided he could do without one of those. It would just be something else to wash.

Walking back outside, he stood on the front porch for a moment, admiring the view out over the water. His Cessna bobbed dutifully in the water. It wouldn't be going into town with him tonight, though. He'd be driving Old Red.

The truck had originally been blue, but there wasn't much of that anymore. It could truly vie with Old Man Tuck's, except that Kodiak kept a can of rust-colored spray paint in the back. Rust preventative, it said on the can. He didn't know about that. From the rust the truck had grown over the past two winters, it seemed the spray paint could easily be causing much of the problem.

The flames were blazing in his burn barrel. Good. He placed his clothes and soap on the porch railing and hopped over the side to where the ground was almost level with the cabin's floor. Reaching and pulling his clothes and soap after him, he leaped around back. He set the things in his hand on the shelf he'd installed just for that purpose, and sitting on a large stone, he untied his shoes and tugged them off, balancing them behind him.

He stood and stepped to the shower deck. It was still in full sun, the better to shower in, because it was warmer. He flipped the water on to let it heat, jumping back to keep from getting wet before deciding that his clothes were so filthy, it surely didn't matter. He stripped them off, kicking them to the side of the deck. Stepping to the shelf, he shivered as he moved out of the sun. It looked to get cold overnight. Even now the air had grown quite cool in the shade. Grasping the soap firmly, he stepped under the spray, glad to have the sun wash across his shoulders.

He was glad the water was warm, also.

He lathered up, pleased to feel fit again. It was almost as good as being eighteen, he thought, and all it had taken was a few days with a chain saw. Working outside had also given him some color. He felt energized, too. As he worked soap into his hair, he closed his eyes and let the sun warm his face. Then, his hair rinsed, he flipped the water off and shook himself, drying off as best he could without a towel.

Grabbing his fresh clothes, he slipped them on, sitting on the stone to put on his shoes. The clothes he'd kicked aside? They'd keep. Now he needed to check on his fire, and he sprinted back to the far side of the house.

Seeing the flames burning merrily away, Kodiak headed to his truck. He'd put it inside during the storm, and now he wrestled with the barn doors, forcing them open. It was an old building, here long before his dad had bought the property. He'd have to put on new hinges someday, but that time hadn't arrived just yet, not as long as he could still wrangle the doors aside.

Once inside, he dropped the gas can in back. Then he yanked open the truck's door, catching it, careful to not let it swing back all the way. The hinges were rusted, too, and he'd had it fall off in his hands more than once. He climbed in, only to find the ignition empty. Then he remembered. His keys were in his other pants.

Heading back up the slope, he tucked into the back of the house and grabbed the wet clothes, picking them up and digging through the pockets. There, sure enough, were the two keys on their old, wire ring. He hung the pants and undershorts on the towel hooks beside the shower, even though he doubted they'd dry overnight. With the cool evening already in the making, they'd still be dripping when the sun came up. He picked up the soap and took a deep breath. Inside or outside? He took the cabin steps two at a time and slipped the bar into the bathroom where it belonged.

Then he noticed the aftershave he rarely used. He was clean and headed into town. He might as well smell good, too. Maybe he'd meet a pretty woman, and it'd be like those commercials he remembered from TV. She'd just smell him, and she wouldn't be able to keep her hands off. He dumped some in one hand, and lifting up his shirt with the other, liberally splashed the lotion over his torso. He finished up by rubbing his damp hand over his face, slapping his cheek with a laugh, just for good measure.

At the truck a second time, making sure he had his wallet, he climbed inside. Throwing the key in the ignition, he pumped the gas vigorously, aware of the old truck's lack of fuel injection. He'd never had to pump a vehicle to get it started until he'd moved to Alaska.

As he backed out, he began to whistle a tune. The old truck had no radio. Rather, it had one. It just didn't have an antenna. Or a power cable. Or a speaker.

Shifting into first and dropping the truck into four-wheel drive low, Kodiak began to crawl up the slope behind his cabin. Yeah, he knew what Old Man Tuck was all about. Kodiak was able to walk the walk, or at least drive the back roads, but he still felt getting around in an airplane was better.

It was also much more fun.

CAROLINA brushed the seat of her pants again. Several more chunks of mud fell to the ground behind her, and she sighed. Alaska wasn't turning into all that the brochures had built it up to be. It wasn't the state's fault. It was her fault. She hadn't thought out this trip, and it had been overshadowed with all the issues she needed to work through.

She knew the real problem. She suspected the cruise ship was long gone, and no one was missing her. Perhaps not even Mamie. Oh, eventually, but with all the hiding Carolina had been doing, probably not until tomorrow, and they'd be heaven knows how far up the coast by then. She didn't know the next stop. Good heavens, she didn't even know this one. She hadn't paid any attention at all when she'd exited the ship, and the signs in town? If they'd been there, she hadn't noticed.

Carolina looked ahead of her. There were trees ahead. That wasn't what she wanted to see. Trees meant shade, and her sunglasses were all the shade she wanted. The air was definitely getting cooler. No, she amended, it was more that the sun was not as warm. The air had been cool all along. What would she do when the sun went down? This walk to town was taking longer than she thought.

Hearing a noise, she turned to glance behind her. She didn't see anything the way she'd come, but just the same. There were bears in Alaska. Black bears? Kodiak bears? She just knew they were big and would eat people if they got too hungry. Her pulse quickened. She tried to imagine what she'd seen on how to deal with rogue bears. Climb a tree, she thought. However, she was getting tired and hungry. She wasn't sure she could make it up a tree. Play dead? If she did that, she was sure she'd be dead.

She turned to look behind her again. She saw a bit of dust in the air, and soon the rattle of metal banging against metal accompanied it. Finally, a truck that didn't quite look safe to ride in climbed over the top of the hill. She laughed, relieved actually, and she turned and continued walking ahead.

"He'll be old and fat, too. If I see three kids in the back, I'll never believe in God again." She laughed again, her voice higher in pitch, just on the edge of hysteria. "Or maybe I will."

When the truck squealed its brakes, coming to a stop beside her, she froze. Not knowing what to expect, she crossed her arms, resting her hands on the purse she'd pulled to her stomach, and she looked at the ground. She knew she shouldn't be afraid of who was in the truck. She should be very grateful. It was the person she'd imagined seeing inside, fat and bald. If she looked, it might be true.

Finally, a deep, resonant voice called out to her, "Ma'am, can I offer you a ride?"

With those melodious Southern words, Carolina's breath was nearly stolen from her. It was the wash of a Southern summer breeze over her bad day, and she was home once again. She felt safe. She raised her head and smiled, her eyes closed.

"Ma'am?" The voice caressed her once again. "Do you just enjoy walking, or is this too fine a day to miss out on? I saw your Jeep back there. Rather, I saw Tad Simmons' Jeep back there. It has a broken gas gauge. I bet you rented it for the day, huh? And he told you it had a full tank." When she nodded, he laughed the golden chuckle of the summer surf on a Carolina beach. "He always thinks it's full. He doesn't even know the gauge is broken. He told me one time he just keeps it topped off, that it never falls below full. Come on. I'll give you a ride into town."

Carolina stood, her muscles unable to respond. She still hadn't looked in the truck. Unable to think of anything to say, she turned her head and glanced inside. She laughed, and her words surprised even her.

"You've got hair!"

KODIAK closed his eyes and laughed. "Yes, ma'am, I do. Too much of it, in fact. It's kind of rough with me cutting it myself, but hair I think you can say I've got."

He watched her, warmed by her response. She didn't feel like Alaska, that was certain. Low Country, maybe. East Coast, for sure. He was unaware of the passage of the minutes. Instead, he soaked up the moment.

"I'm sorry." Carolina flushed, the silence broken. "You say that I can ride with you?"

He grinned at this woman who had yet refused to look at him for more than a quick glance. He hoped his addition of aftershave wasn't having the opposite effect he'd intended.

"If you're going my way, and it sure seems you are. The air's getting colder, too. You know, that sweater looks good on you, but once the temperature drops, beware. You'll want more." He leaned over and tripped the handle, encouraging her. "Come on. I don't bite. Besides, ever been to Alaska? Cool at night, even in the summer. You don't want to be out much longer. Come on. Don't open it too far. Hinges are rusted out. The door might fall off. Just slam it to close it, if you don't mind."

Climbing in the truck and slamming the door behind her, Carolina set her purse beside her. As the truck pulled away, she leaned forward to rub her calves through her pants.

"Sore legs?" Kodiak grinned. She didn't look like much of a walker, and she'd managed to travel quite a ways by foot.

"A BIT. YOU live here?" For the first time Carolina really looked at her rescuer. His voice was warm and familiar, but that was probably the melodic lilt she seemed to hear in his words.

"I have a place behind us. Just a cabin. I stay there and run a small shop in town when people need me. It's a good life." He looked at her. "Cold in the winter, though."

She couldn't keep her eyes off him. He grinned.

Carolina's heart jumped as she watched the man. If only he wasn't from Alaska, she'd be certain she knew this man. She'd placed his voice now, one that she'd heard only once, and that had been on a long-ago airport runway. She could hardly expect this man to be the same, though. How could he?

Her voice shook as she broached her next question. "Do you have a name?"

"What sort of question is that?" He laughed. "I guess if a man lives in Alaska, he's just a wild, unnamed beast, one that roams the wilderness freely with no need for any kind of identifying moniker." He looked at her sideways, his attention glancing to the road in front of them only enough to keep them from going off into the trees. With one eye, he winked, although it was too quickly done and over to be sure it was real.

"No, that wasn't what I meant. I'm just out of sorts. I was on this cruise, see, and I think I missed my boat." Carolina cut her eyes to her hands in her lap, once again aware of her stupidity. What an idiotic question! And she was a fool to chase an old dream, seeing that boy from so long ago in yet another stranger. Truly, she was a fool, and she felt her face warm with humiliation.

"No *think* about it."

She looked at him. "What does that mean?" She recalled the repeated blasts of the ship's horn, and she was pretty sure she knew.

He propped one arm in the window as he pushed the clutch in and wrestled the old transmission into a new gear. He didn't answer her question, asking a different one, instead.

"Where are you from? You seem East to me." He cocked an eyebrow as he waited for her response.

"Los Angeles. I work there. Have I missed my boat, the ship, I mean?"

Turning his head to look out his window, he made a tsk sound with his mouth and then replied, "About two hours ago."

"What can I do? I have no one I know here. All my things are on board." Carolina was overwhelmed. She shouldn't be surprised, because she'd heard the horns, and she'd known. It hadn't been a fact for her, however, until his words made it real.

"All my good friends call me Kody." He reached a hand to her. "Now you know someone, so you're not alone."

"You know what I mean." Carolina reached to wipe threatening tears from her eyes. She had also caught his name, Kody, not Kodiak. Of course this wasn't the same man. How stupid of her!

Kodiak kept his hand out. "Before long, I'm gonna have to shift, and it might be rough if you don't shake and tell me your name."

Carolina drew in a ragged breath and reached her hand out. "Carolina, like the Southern states."

"Carolina from California. That's good. You've got both coasts in you."

Carolina laughed, the tension finally broken. "You don't know the half, Kody from Alaska. You don't know the half."

"Miss or Missus?"

Carolina turned to him with a grin. "Miss. You?"

It was Kodiak's turn to grin. "One ex on the other side of the continent. We don't speak. I like it that way." He released Carolina's hand. "Our gas is coming up. Can I give you a ride back? Or is this as far as we go?"

Carolina looked out the window. This station was not anywhere near the town. In fact, she couldn't see the town at all.

"Who else would I get a ride with?"

Kodiak's smile grew wider, and that was when Carolina noticed for the first time how his dimples seemed to split his face in two. Her heart lurched as she waited on his answer.

"Well, there's the other cars here at the station, or you could hitch with that semi coming down the road just now."

Carolina glanced outside the truck. "I don't see anyone."

Kodiak looked away, obviously trying to force his grin from his face. Then he looked back at Carolina, working his jaw, his amusement clearly evident.

"Well, ma'am, you just made my point for me."

"Oh." Carolina's face dropped. "I'd appreciate riding back with you."

As he clambered from the old truck and walked away, she turned and watched her knight in shining armor, the man who'd been her rescuing angel. He was certainly friendly. She'd give him that. He'd also given her a comforting, unidentified warmth, although in her current distress, she wasn't certain just what it was about him that made her feel that way.

Well, he's not a pilot, and he's not from Savannah, but he's not fat, either, and it's certain, he's got all his hair. Then she chided herself for what she was thinking. She didn't even know him. He was a wild man from Alaska, and he had an ex-wife. That alone should tell her he had problems under all that Alaska charm, no matter how appealing he seemed.

There was something he had said, though, something that was stuck in her thoughts. She didn't know just why she remembered it more strongly than all the other things he'd said, but she couldn't let go of it. *Ever been to Alaska? Cool at night.* Now why should those words stand out to her?

Finally she gave up and let it go. She was tired, her ship was gone, and this man she'd never met before was walking back to the truck.

This had become a very long day.

Chapter 8

"HERE! CATCH!"

Carolina jumped and turned just in time to intercept a can of soda flying through the cab of the truck at her.

"Thought you might be thirsty." Kodiak stood outside the window and leaned to rest both arms on the sill. "You'd be surprised how much liquid you sweat out in this warm weather. You don't even know it, either. Back home, we used to sweat buckets. Here, we sweat, but we just don't know it, and a body is dehydrated before it's even thirsty."

He stood and turned, leaning against the truck, and Carolina heard the snap of his own soda opening. She watched his back as he lifted his arm to put the can to his mouth, and her heart raced at the flexing of his muscles as they rippled under his shirt. If she didn't know better, she'd recognize that arm, only the arm she knew was back in Savannah, and this man had never been in Savannah. He was Alaskan, a wild, Alaska man with an ex-wife who had run all the way across the continent just to get away from him.

Even as that thought crossed her mind, Carolina understood she was creating her own version of this man's life, but why else would his ex-wife be on the East Coast when he was up here? He also had a home and a business of some sort. He wasn't new to this lifestyle. Then, this truck. It was twenty years old if a day, and probably twice that.

He'd been here a while.

After a long moment he shifted his position, dropping his arm, and holding the emptied can in his hand as he rested it on the windowsill. Then he turned and looked in the truck.

"Not thirsty, huh?"

Carolina jumped at his words, realizing she was still watching him, her attraction to him far more than she should feel for a man she had known perhaps twenty minutes. She dropped her eyes to the can in her hand. She smiled, holding it up.

"It's not diet. I always drink diet. I . . . um . . ."

She looked around, flustered at her inability to handle this very minor gaffe. His thoughtfulness had charmed her, and now she was treating his graciousness as if she were insulted. She felt herself growing red. He just laughed, causing her to look up to find what had caused such an unexpected response.

"Trust me, Carolina from California. You don't want diet up here. The caffeine will cause your core body temperature to drop, and the lack of sugar won't ramp it back up again. The sugar is the benefit up here." He looked at her and chuckled. "Just because I look like an unnamed wild Alaskan doesn't mean I haven't had some schooling. All us Alaskans have to go at least one day a year." He grinned and dropped his head. "I'm sorry. That was uncalled for. You've had a hard day, and you don't know me." He reached his hand through the window, stretching his frame toward her. "Shake again? When you shake, you know, all is forgiven." He closed his mouth, pressing his lips together as if trying not very successfully to restrain his mirth.

Carolina looked at him with a bemused expression. Nothing seemed to faze this man. Now he was standing outside his old, rusted truck, he had his body twisted through the open window, and his arm was stretched out toward her. In addition, he was trying not to laugh at her.

Finally, she smiled and reached to her can, popping the lid. She kept her eyes glued on his as she raised it to her lips to take a sip. Blinking, she realized she really was very thirsty.

Lowering the can, she reached her free hand out and took his, and an electricity she hadn't felt the first time they'd shaken sent its tendrils through her body, lighting up every nerve in her being. She couldn't take her eyes from his face. That hair, roughly hewn and thick, his cheeks cut in two by those enormous dimples, and those eyes. She'd not noticed his eyes before. They were that crystal blue that seemed to draw her right in. Slowly, she noticed her hands were cold, and his were very warm. With a ragged breath, she felt herself sink into the touch of his skin as his warmth melted her inside.

"Carolina? My hand? It's attached to my body, and this door isn't very forgiving." Kodiak chuckled. "I've paid for the gas, but I still need to pump it. My can's large enough for both my chainsaw and Tad's Jeep."

"Money. I didn't even think of that." She released his hand and grabbed for her purse.

"Tad Simmons will pay me back. Don't you worry about the cost."

"Thank you. I'm stuck here since I missed my ship, and I don't have much more than pocket change until I can get back aboard." The thought suddenly occurred to her, "I can get back aboard, can't I?"

Kodiak stepped to pull the can from the bed of the truck. He leaned over to speak through the window. "I don't know about that. I do know that Jeep back there isn't moving without fuel. One step at a time. Can we do that?"

When Carolina smiled, he slapped the edge of the door, startling her, and he turned to fill the can.

CAROLINA stood by the Jeep watching Kodiak pour gasoline from his can into the empty fuel tank. As he lowered the can and tapped the spout against the tank's filler nozzle, he turned to her. "Keys?"

She cleared her throat, feeling guilty about that. "Um, Kody, the keys are inside. I left them there. You see, I wasn't sure if I'd be back."

He smiled. "And you didn't want to steal them. I appreciate that. You want to try it, or would you rather I take the honor? You start it, you can drive it." He grinned, setting the half-full gas can in his truck. "I start it, I drive it." He leaned back against his truck. "Mine's harder."

She laughed. "I got pretty good at starting this Jeep. I'll give it a try. I'm not sure I could drive your truck in any case."

"Probably right, there." He motioned toward the Jeep. "At least you got Tad's Jeep this far."

Tossing her purse in the passenger's seat, she turned her eyes to him, and she reached her hand to the grab bar above the door. "After I jumped it out of gear a few times."

Kodiak laughed as he moved forward to offer her a hand into the Jeep. "What do you drive at home? A little sporty coupe?"

"Nothing."

"You drive nothing?" Kodiak raised his eyebrows. "How can you drive nothing?"

Carolina settled herself in the seat and put her hand on the key. She looked to make sure her feet were on the proper pedals before she replied. "Taxis. Also, there's a company car I use sometimes. It comes with a driver." She reached her arm around

115

the steering wheel. "You sure this will work?"

"Pump the gas a few times. When it runs dry, you've got to get some gas up to the carburetor."

Carolina laughed at what sounded like a misused word. "Carburetor? I've got a brother. Cars don't have carburetors."

"These old Jeeps do. Just pump it. I know this engine. Pump."

Carolina gave him a hard look and stomped the accelerator several times. Then she turned the key. She looked at Kodiak in appreciation when she heard it roar into life.

"Follow me," Kodiak yelled, and he ran to climb into his truck. When he took off, he spun his tires on the dirt surface, and the detritus showered Carolina's Jeep.

With a disgusted grunt, she brushed her arms off. "Well, at least now I know why he has an ex-wife. I guess this comes from growing up in the Alaska wild. Men!" Then she shifted the Jeep into gear, and she made a shower of her own, the dirt and rocks flying as she took off after the man who had rescued her.

CAROLINA pulled the Jeep up behind the old rusty truck she'd been following into town. The drive had surprised her. When she'd been touring that morning, it seemed she hadn't gone very far. An unexpected waterfall she'd seen coming out of a rock wall by a stunningly beautiful gorge had been exquisite. She'd found a trail and driven closer to get a better look. One trail had led to another, and she'd forgotten the time. The weather was so beautiful, with not a rain cloud in sight, and she'd felt refreshed.

Then the real hills had started, the grass and dirt trails twisting through ravines she thought were hopeless to navigate. She'd driven her brother's four-wheel drive years before, and she recognized the levers in the Jeep. She'd reached and pulled the low lever, and grinding the gears, the vehicle had leaped forward. It had lurched, one tire had grabbed, and it had twisted through the ravine in a perfect imitation of a dying crab.

She'd only brushed one small tree, and she hadn't looked, but she didn't think it'd done any damage. That had taken her to another dirt road, more of a track, really. She'd followed it, and it had topped rises where she'd seen magnificent vistas of the cruise ship in the distance, and at other times, of stunning mountain valleys.

She'd actually felt better. Wrestling with the rough-driving vehicle, the gears grinding under her tutelage, and the wind in her face, had seemed to breathe life into her day. Then, she'd found the road that had the same numbers as the one she'd originally been on, and she'd started toward town.

She would have never made it walking. She realized the little station Kody had stopped at wasn't really in town. It was miles away. She must have been able to hear the ship's horn because of the mountains. They trapped the sound like an amphitheater and threw it back at her.

Then had come the surprise of her life. Kody from Alaska. A rust-red truck. What was left of a rust-red truck, anyway. What the rust hadn't eaten away. Now, this place. She didn't recognize it in any shape, form, or fashion. It was nothing like the town she remembered from that morning. She killed the engine, not sure if she'd need to drive the Jeep again to get someplace else, and she dropped the keys in the floorboard, uncomfortable leaving them in the ignition.

"Kody," she called out, waving her hand to get his attention. "I've got a question." She fought to stand, but the seatbelt didn't want to release.

He opened the door of his truck, lunging to grab at it as it swung out of his hand. He grinned, calling to her, "This one is rusted through, too." He slammed it and walked back to her, undoing the belt and helping her from the Jeep. "What else can I do for you?"

Carolina looked around. "I don't recognize this place. Are you sure this is the right town?"

He peered one way up the street, and then he turned his head the other way down the street. "Hmm, Carolina from California. I don't see any other towns."

"Stop that," she cried, her eyes beginning to burn. "I can't take much more of today. This morning there were crowds and shops open, and I wanted to be alone. Well, you're telling me I'm back, and I'm still alone. Where are all the people?"

Kodiak rubbed the back of his neck, looking at the ground for a moment before answering. "Carolina, when the cruise ship leaves, it takes all the people with it. Only a few hundred people live in this whole area. The town shuts down except when the ship's in."

She turned, her hand to her mouth. Leaning back against the Jeep, she sat, aiming for the running board, missing, and thudding to the ground. At that, she wrapped her hands around her knees, put her face down, and began to sob.

It was too much to be expected that she should deal with this, too. She simply couldn't take any more.

"COME ON, girl." Kodiak reached and pulled on one of her elbows. "It'll be light for hours, and I bet you haven't eaten since breakfast. The town's shut down, and I don't see a ship in the bay, but I bet Marv's is open. It's mostly for the local crowd, but they do have some choice burgers. Come on." He pulled her until she began to move. "Leave the Jeep. It'll be my treat. I'll drive."

He put his arm around her shoulders. He knew this wasn't his girl, but he also knew she fit very well against him. There was that Southern lilt, too. Kodiak didn't know how a California girl got that, but he'd take it any way he could get it. Somehow, he felt like she belonged right where she was.

With him.

He swung the door to the rustic establishment open, leading Carolina into a small foyer. Another set of glass doors separated

118

them from the chaotic scene inside.

Catching a glimpse of her reflection in the glass, Carolina wailed, "Kody, I appreciate you trying to help, but I can't go in there. I'm a wreck. I've sat in the mud, and my hair's a mess." She reached her hand to work her fingers into the roots, attempting to pull through the windblown tangles.

Kodiak leaned in, pointing her the direction of the people sitting inside. "See them? See anyone who looks any better than you? This is Alaska, and these are not tourists. They are loggers, fishermen, and dock workers. They're lucky to have clean underwear on." He straightened back up before going on. "Besides, I think you're very pretty, and tonight, it's my opinion that counts." He smiled. "Ready?"

CAROLINA took a deep breath, intensely aware of how good Kody smelled, and she looked at him critically, unsure whether she was still being charmed, or if he actually meant all those words he'd said. That Southern smoothness in an Alaska man was throwing her off. Then she relaxed, admitting to herself that she was very hungry, and that as much as anything was probably skewing her judgment. She'd determine this man's guilt or innocence after she had finished off a dinner. Or two.

As she stepped through the door, Kody spoke one more thing, something Carolina suspected wasn't intended for her ears, and he was lucky not to be able to see her face. He mumbled, "I'm lucky *I* have clean underwear on tonight." It made her smile, and her mood was truly buoyed by his little slip of the tongue.

Perhaps it was what he'd said, and perhaps it was that hint of a Southern drawl, but as she stepped inside that Alaska diner, although she was far away from California and had no idea how she would manage to get back, she felt like she was right where she was supposed to be. With this man at her side, she felt right at home.

"YOU DIDN'T eat your sausage." Kodiak picked up a slice, popping it whole into his mouth. "At least the cigarette smoke's cleared. Not a vice I care for. Makes my clothes smell. Have to wash them, then."

"You have to wash your clothes, do you?" Carolina smiled, picking up her platter and setting it directly in front of her companion. "Kody, this is more food than I normally eat in a week. Help yourself."

"Tonight, don't complain when you get really cold. All these calories go onto your plate for a purpose. There's a very real danger in freezing to death up here. Eat up while I'm paying." He picked up another sausage and leaned back. The place was almost emptied, and it seemed the sun might actually go down sometime soon. He glanced outside to see the exterior lights flicker on.

Carolina tapped the table. "Besides, I thought you said this place had great hamburgers. Those scrambled things were funny-looking burgers, unless you want to try calling those little sausages burgers. They sure are small to be Alaska burgers, though. I'd expect something a bit larger." She smiled. "So, what happened to the burgers you promised?"

He licked one finger and peered at her. "I'm saving the burgers for your next visit." Then he leaned in and pointed to the back. "Julie's not in tonight. She's the burger queen. Everybody knows to order the eggs when Mabelle cooks."

Carolina looked down and toyed with her napkin, and she glanced up as she asked, "What if I'm gone when Julie comes on duty?"

"Don't see how. Town's closed. You're not going any place." He shook out a toothpick and put it in his mouth to chew. "Julie comes on at four on the days she works. That's A.M. She'll be here the next time this town opens for business. You leaving before then?"

Carolina looked around the empty room. Only two people were left, and they were talking to each other at her table. "I see what you mean. I might need a place to stay tonight."

Just then, the waitress came up, pulling her glasses from her nose and dropping them to a chain around her neck. She slipped the check on the table. "Closing in ten."

Carolina interrupted her, asking, "Ladies'?"

"Through those doors, honey. You're a cutie. Hope you're here to stay. This boy here needs a better half to keep him in line."

"I've got you to keep me in line, Claudine." Kodiak took her hand and kissed it before she could pull it away. Carolina laughed as she stood and walked toward the back of the establishment.

The waitress gave the man a hard look. "She's pretty. Hope you can hold her." Then she tapped the check. "It's late, Kodiak. You want to pay tonight, or can I just put it on your tab?"

"You're wonderful, Claudine. I love you." He stood and gave her a peck on the cheek. "If she won't stay, I'm moving you in with me."

Claudine frowned, putting the check in her pocket. "Not in that cabin you've got up there. I'm not slipping and sliding out of there all winter. You move into town, and I might think about it."

"Claudine, you're impossible." He gave her another peck as he saw Carolina coming back inside the room.

As they walked outside, Carolina pulled Kodiak's sleeve. She had a smile on her face. "You should see the toilets they have in there. They have chains you pull from the ceiling."

"It's Alaska, Carolina from California. We can't all be modern."

She stopped at the truck and turned as the diner's neon sign flickered out, quickly followed by the exterior lighting. She laughed. "The lights just came on while we were inside. Now they're out." She shook her head. "There's not much nighttime here in Alaska. Well, I need to see about a room."

Kodiak looked at her. He hadn't really thought this far. Oh, he admitted to himself, he'd thought this far, but they were thoughts he couldn't share. Now he had to break the news to her.

"Carolina, I might not have good news for you."

She looked at him sharply. "What does that mean?"

He didn't want to say there was nowhere for her to stay, not unless it was in a private home. And there weren't all that many of those around.

"Just say it. Spit it out. Now that I've eaten, I think I can take whatever you have to tell me." She had a look of determination on her face.

"Look around you. You can see that the town is shut down. All the way. You need a place to sleep. I can ask Claudine if you can use her sofa. She's a good soul. I'm pretty sure she'll say yes."

He watched Carolina's face, not sure just how she'd react. She'd had a hard day, that was very clear to him, and he suspected it wouldn't take much to push her over the edge. He didn't want this to be it.

Carolina was quiet for a minute, then her words were so low Kodiak had to strain to hear. "My ship is gone. I have dirty clothes on. This town is asleep, and my only option for a bed is a sofa from a waitress I don't even know."

"She's a good woman. She wouldn't . . ."

Carolina's next words lashed out, low and firm, her tone reminding Kodiak of his ex when she'd really had all she could take. For his ex, that had been all the time at the end.

"I'm tired, Kody. You have no idea. This hasn't been a good month. I cannot sleep on a stranger's sofa. I just cannot. There have to be other options."

He took a deep breath. "I have a sofa," he started.

Carolina's response slashed his sentence from him. "No! I thought I just said that. I cannot sleep on a stranger's sofa."

"Carolina," he whispered. He cringed when she whipped her head to turn to him. "Carolina, am I a stranger?"

It was an eternity before she answered. Then she seemed to change, gaining control of her emotions.

"No, Kody. You're not a stranger, not anymore. You've been incredibly helpful in every possible way. I'm sorry I snapped. I'm very tired, and I'm feeling very lost right now. You've made yourself into my friend, and I didn't respond in kind." She raised her hand to her mouth, looking away, her eyes shimmering in the dark. "I'm so sorry." A catch in her voice exposed the depths of her distress.

Kodiak reached and took her hand, and with that touch, Carolina leaned into him, and her tears began to flow.

He whispered, "Just cry it out. That always helps. I only meant that I'm willing to share my cabin. I could sleep on my sofa, and you could have my bed. It would all be very proper." When she raised her head and looked at him with a smile, he continued, "The bedroom has a door and everything. I'm pretty sure there's a lock on it. You can just lock me out, and you'll be safe from any big bad wolves that might be sleeping on the sofa. Perfectly safe."

Carolina stepped back and patted his chest with her hand. "How could I have been so lucky to be picked up by an angel like you? I rail at you, and you offer me your bed." She laughed. "A lock, too, just to make me feel better. Thank you. I'll take you up on your offer." She stepped around him to open the door of the truck, turning to face her benefactor. "Let's go. It's a long drive, I bet, and it's already dark. I've learned this much about being in Alaska. If it's summer and the sun goes down, that means it's really, really late."

Kodiak grinned, running around the back of the truck, slapping the tailgate as he did so. As he opened the door, he replied, "You have no idea!"

Chapter 9

KODIAK yanked the lever to throw the truck into four-wheel low. Carolina held on as they slipped and pitched down a slope past barely-glimpsed and quite-frightening obstacles. He did live a long way from town, although she'd had no idea it would be this far. In the depths of the forest they'd come through, it seemed they'd slid over most of the interior of the state.

He'd carried on a running and somewhat one-sided conversation with her about how much he enjoyed living in Alaska; that it was predicted to cloud and rain tonight; but, he'd brightly encouraged, the weather should clear by morning. Then she'd see how beautiful his place was. It would also make it cold, but then it was already cold, so she understood that.

It wasn't much better inside the truck. The heater didn't work when the headlights were on. Even then, the headlights barely illuminated the road, and the dash lights didn't work. The only glow was from the old radio that Kody said also didn't work. No power cable, he'd explained. When she'd asked about the glow, he said that was from the dash light cable he'd mistakenly wired incorrectly.

She gasped as he slid the old truck down a mysterious slope through the trees, missing every one. Then the rusty old machine was still.

Kodiak reached to the dash and flicked the lights off. In the darkness he asked, "Ready?"

Carolina could hear her breathing in the stillness. "Ready for what?" She didn't know if she was expected to hike a mountain or canoe a lake. Just the ride alone had shaken the sense out of her.

"The house. My cabin."

"Where? I can't see a thing." Carolina had fallen for this idea back in town. She was now wondering just how far away Claudine lived.

"Sit tight, and I'll come around and help you. I'm used to navigating all this in the dark." He paused for a moment, and then he laughed. "There are some steps to walk up. A lot."

Carolina put her hand out to stop him before he could get out. She fumbled and grabbed his wrist. "Steps?"

"I live on the side of a mountain. It's the reason I have a four-wheel-drive."

Well, she got that. She'd been jarred to pieces every mile of the way.

KODIAK popped the door, and noise flooded inside. "Insects," he yelled. "I've got those, too."

He clambered out, slammed his door, and ran to Carolina's side of the truck. He stood a moment before opening her door, willing his heart to slow down. "Father above," he whispered, "give me strength." He wouldn't allow anything out of line to happen while Carolina was here, or at least he wouldn't intend it, but he might need the help of a higher power for

125

reinforcements. He took a deep breath, and he reached and tugged the door free.

"I thought you'd forgotten me. I'm ready," she yelled into the thrum of the insects' song.

Kodiak took her hand, enjoying the touch of her skin. At the same time he reminded himself that he'd only known this woman for a few hours. Tomorrow she'd be gone, and he wouldn't see her again. Navigating the steps brought a few chuckles, as he talked her up one at a time. She almost tripped once, and he pulled her tight, apologizing that he hadn't left a light on. Once at the cabin, and reaching inside the door, he flipped on the light switch. Several lamps flickered on, and he heard his cabin's generator gently start up, the hum a sound that was comfortable and soothing. Carolina glanced around the room as Kodiak hurriedly closed the door behind them. She turned as the door banged shut.

"The insects," he said. "The light draws them. The door can't be left open at night."

Carolina laughed. "At home, too." She glanced around to see a wood-burning stove. It was dark, explaining why it was as cold in the room as it was outside. Above it was something that caught her eye. She turned to her rescuer. "A surfboard?"

He laughed. "I have a wetsuit, too. Never again! The Alaska surf is phenomenal, but the water's freezing. The one time I went out, I didn't know if I'd survive. But it brought me enough fame to jumpstart my business."

Carolina paused, smiling. "So, I've been rescued by some-one famous. Amazing. I can take the sofa, you know. I was just tired back in town." She snorted, shaking her head. "I was being a baby, and I feel embarrassed."

Kodiak opened the bedroom door. "No, you were worn down. You still need sleep, though. Let's get you in bed." He quickly moved into the room, opening several drawers, search-ing. "I've got clean sheets here somewhere. At least, I think I do."

Eventually he stopped and took a deep breath, unsure of where else to look. At his sheepish appearance, Carolina stepped to him and placed a hand on his arm. Energy surged through him, and finding fresh sheets no longer mattered as long as her hand was on his arm.

"I'll be fine. If you can sleep on those sheets, then so can I. Do you have a bathroom? Sorry, Kody. Let me rephrase that. Where is your bathroom?"

He smiled. "I deserved that. In here." As he stepped inside, he broke the contact with her hand, and he felt embarrassment rush over him once again. He grabbed his dirty shirt from earlier and tossed it into the bedroom where he could later kick it under the bed. He glanced at his towels, glad he hadn't used them earlier.

"May I shower?" Carolina pushed her hair back from her face. "Also, I have no clean clothes. Where's your washer?"

Kodiak hung his head sheepishly. He glanced up, even as he felt his face reddening. "Now you can ask if, because shower, yes, but as for your clothes, the answer is no. I take my laundry into town. That or wash it by hand."

"I can't wear these tomorrow, or to sleep in tonight, either." She sighed heavily. "Please help me. I can't think past all these things. My brain's gone numb." She sat on the edge of the bed, then jumped up, wiping crumbled dirt from her pants onto the floor.

"Wash them." He paused, thinking. "I can do that for you while you shower." He looked around, remembering she would need something to wear. "Here." He reached into a drawer and pulled out a shirt and striped boxers. "You can wear these." Then he grabbed the boxers and stuffed them back into the drawer. "Sorry."

Carolina took a breath and smiled. She reached, accepted the shirt, and felt in the drawer for the boxers. "These are greatly appreciated. I'll wear them proudly. And warmly, I hope. It's chilly in here."

Kodiak was apologetic. "I'm very sorry. When I invited you here, I didn't think about clothes or washing machines. Claudine has a washing machine at her place. I borrow it sometimes." His eyes had grown scratchy, and he didn't want her to see his frustration. He'd felt a connection with her, a connection with his childhood home, and that had been comforting to him. Then he'd felt more, a connection to his heart, and to the man he was. Now, he felt the fool. "I'll leave you alone. The bath is yours. I'm sorry for bringing you out here. Your clothes. I'll take them in the morning and wash them for you. Will that do?"

Seeing the distress on his face, Carolina reached for his arm. "I can wash out my own clothes. They'll dry overnight. I'll snuggle under more blankets than I've ever used in my California home, and I'll be fine. Thank you, Kody. This is a castle to me."

His eyes burning but his tears contained, he sniffled. He could barely think past her hand on his arm. Anything, he thought. Anything you say, Carolina. Aloud he mumbled, "Really? Do you mean it?" At her nod of assurance, he clicked back into gear, the bumbling boy inside the man assuaged by Carolina's reassurances. He also patted her hand, pressing it against his arm, just to feel it against his skin. "Let me grab a few things. Then you can lock me out." He reached behind him to the doorknob, clicking and unclicking the locking mechanism. "See?"

Carolina smiled. "Your things, Kody? I can figure out the lock." She pulled her hand free and turned away.

Newly energized, he grabbed a set of clean clothes, an item from each of several drawers, and backed toward the door. Just before he closed it, Carolina reached to him and put her hand on his chest. "Good night, Kody." Then she gently pushed him into the other room.

With that touch, all Kodiak's misgivings and apologies were forgotten. He only knew that there was a woman in his cabin and on the other side of that door, and she'd touched him. Well, not really, not in a suggestive way, but he was energized, just the same.

He also knew he'd never get to sleep unless he took a cold shower. Oh, if only he'd never met his ex-wife. This should have been the woman he'd married. He took a deep breath, dropping to sit on the sofa, with his eyes glued to the bedroom door. His heart pounded in his chest, and all he could think about was that door, and the woman just on the other side.

"God," he muttered. "I don't deserve this."

It was going to be a long night, but it was his own fault. He'd invited her out. He moved outside to the porch and jumped over the rail. Carolina might want all the hot water, but at least there'd be plenty of cold. Stepping to the shower deck, he pulled off his shoes and tossed them at the rock. Flipping the cold water on, he stripped his clothing, kicking the bundle to the back edge of the deck. When he jumped underneath the spray, it took his breath away. For a moment, he couldn't say a word, but his curses flowed anyway.

When shivering drove Kodiak to flip the water off, he stood in the darkness, rubbing his arms. Blackness blanketed the sky. The only light came from a sliver of a window just above his head, the one that opened to the warm bathroom on the other side of the wall. Then, hearing the sound of running water from inside the cabin, he was jolted into action.

Stepping to the shelf for his fresh clothes, he felt in the dark, and was momentarily surprised to feel bare board. The sofa. He remembered putting his stack of clothes on the sofa, and he'd brought nothing outside. Not even a towel.

He did have the clothes he'd worn to town. The pants would at least get him inside. As soon as he touched the fabric, he knew he couldn't put them on. He lifted them, and water dripped to the deck. He reached for his clothes from earlier that day. Squeezing them, they hadn't even begun to dry.

The running water inside gave him an idea. With Carolina in the shower, he was perfectly safe retrieving his clothes. He grinned, and he flung the wet pants back to the deck. He moved to the porch, and grabbing the railing, he vaulted over, grabbed the doorknob, and twisted, pushing the door open. He called out softly, "Carolina," aware of the risk he was taking. When there was no answer, he swung the door wide and stepped inside, reaching for the clothes on the sofa. He heard the bedroom door latch click, and he froze. The front door slowly swung to and snapped shut.

"Kody, are you in there?" The bedroom door began to open.

He grabbed at his clothes, and he looked desperately for a place to hide. Before he could come up with a plan, Carolina began talking again.

"I heard water in the pipes before I started the shower, and I decided I'm very thirsty. Do you mind bringing me a glass of water?"

Kodiak cleared his throat, his blood throbbing in his temples. "Um, Carolina. Can you hold on just a moment?"

She let out a short laugh. "That's okay. I'm still dressed. The water's warming in the shower, and I don't want to waste it by letting it run too long. I can get it myself."

Kodiak was horrified to see the door swing wide, and through it stepped the beautiful Carolina from California. He had his clothes to his chest by then, and he did his best to cover himself in one swift motion. However, he fumbled his pants and shirt, sending them flying across the room, only hanging onto his boxers. Horrified at the impending debacle, he bunched them between his legs. His eyes locked with Carolina's, and the moment was frozen for them both.

Carolina whipped to face the wall. "I'm so sorry, Kody. I should've known you had a second bathroom. That was the water I heard. Since I've taken your bed, this is your bedroom for the night. I've been most inconsiderate. I'll return to my room and let you dress. Knock when I can come out again." She stepped through the door, vainly trying to hide the laughter on her face, and latched the door after her.

Kodiak let his arm drop, his shorts falling to his side. Boy, had he royally fouled things up. He really liked Carolina, and he'd wanted her to be impressed with him.

He took a deep breath. At least he couldn't do much more to look like a fool in her eyes. If she didn't write him off now, she never would. As he began to dress, his mood slowly improved. It could only be uphill from here, he decided. Also, she hadn't seemed all that upset.

He delivered Carolina's requested water. It did occur to him that her thank you had more of a laugh to it than serious appreciation, but that was fine with him. He could only hope she found him as attractive as he found her. The morning would tell.

As he lay on the sofa, pulling the throw from across the back to cover himself, he stretched out. The room had grown cold, but he couldn't tell. Just the thought of Carolina in the next room was enough to keep him warm. He listened to the sounds of her showering and then washing out her clothes, and he breathed in deeply. It was worth it all to have her here tonight. It didn't matter that she would be gone tomorrow, or that she was on the other side of the door.

Besides, he'd heard her lock the door when she'd taken the glass of water from him. What choice did he have?

Kodiak flipped onto his stomach, wrapping his arms underneath the sofa cushion, bunching it up for a pillow. He turned his face sideways, staring out into the dark room. As he finally saw the light under the door flick off, he heard the gentle hum of the generator fade to silence. Soon his eyes closed, and the warmth of his body seeped into the sofa's softness. He smiled, and he curled up with his arms wrapped around the cushion. To the sleeping man, it felt very much like he was holding the woman in the other room, even if it was just an old sofa cushion. It was what was in his dreams that counted, and at that moment they felt very real.

Chapter 10

CAROLINA stood in the darkness with her hand pressed against the light switch. She released it and pulled her collar tight against the unknown, pausing before stepping to the bed, taking a deep breath in the blackness as her skin betrayed her.

She was very aware of the feel of Kody's clothes against her skin. There was a roughness to the boxers, a manliness she couldn't deny. Earlier she'd held them upon getting out of the shower, running her fingers around the waistband, and it'd made her breath shorten to think the man in the other room had worn them. However, it was when she'd slipped on the shirt that she'd closed her eyes, absorbed in the moment. The fabric, well worn, had brushed against her unprotected skin, and she'd wanted him. She'd stood there, wanting this man she didn't know. He'd teased her, and she'd agreed with him, telling him he wasn't a stranger. However, no matter how much she felt at ease with him, no matter how closely she felt her Low Country roots every time he spoke, he was indeed a stranger to her.

Still, she had wanted him. Desperately.

After showering, she'd walked back into the bedroom, and seeing the dirty shirt he'd tossed out of the bathroom, she'd laughed. It was still lying in the middle of the bedroom floor. He'd been embarrassed by it, and then he'd forgotten all about it. What did that say about him? A lot, she was certain. It was proof she knew nothing, really and truly nothing about him. His ex-wife? Who knew but what she'd left him for a very valid reason. His surfboard hanging on his wall? Only a fool would bring one of those to Alaska.

Yet, to Carolina, it only made him more and more fascinating, a man of mystery, a man she wanted to know more than she wanted anything else in her life.

As she stood in the darkness letting her memories and regrets carry her back, tears crept to her eyes. Why hadn't she met this man ten years ago, instead of that boy who'd never come to find her? He could have been the one who'd backed out of that airplane cowling, couldn't he? If she'd flown to Alaska that summer instead of to her childhood home, he could have been at the Anchorage airport.

He could have been working on her airplane.

They would have made a connection, and he'd be hers in a way he could never be now. He had a life in Alaska. She had one in California. That alone made them incompatible on so many very different levels.

She smiled through her tears. She could make the what-ifs grander than that. It wasn't too much to imagine. Why couldn't this man have been the one at that airport in Savannah, working on an airplane she was getting ready to board? It was only a continent away from where he'd built his life. Then she'd have never felt the desire to run to California, and she'd have been there for her parents when they needed her. They might even still be alive. Then they'd be the ones here in Alaska, not her, and she wouldn't be stranded because of a broken-down Jeep, and sleeping in the house of a man she barely knew.

She drew in a ragged breath, and she admitted she'd not trade the truth for her imaginings. If her life had turned out that way, then she wouldn't be here in this man's cabin in the Alaska wilderness, and she wouldn't be sleeping in his bed tonight.

She remembered the gentle humming that had suddenly ceased as she'd turned the light switch off, although she hadn't really been aware of it before. Then the insects from outdoors had seeped their gentle drone through the cabin's walls. Carolina smiled. The background of nature instead of her pounding city felt nice.

She sat on the bed, reaching to where the sheets were pushed aside, showing the shape of where Kody had lain only that morning. She traced where his face had pressed against the pillow, and she gently straightened the creases his body had made the last time he'd slept. With great care she gently and carefully lay just where she'd smoothed the wrinkled sheets, and she laid her head right where his had been. Then she carefully covered herself with the blankets he'd carelessly thrown aside only that morn-ing.

Finally, warm in the embrace of her rescuer's bed, cocooned in his world, she breathed deeply of the musky aroma that spoke of the man in the other room. She felt a tingling in places she knew she had no right to be feeling anything at all, and just before she fell asleep, she whispered to herself, "I should really unlock the door."

But before she could move to throw the covers back, she'd already fallen asleep.

CAROLINA turned, and the sun sparkled through the trees. Everything glistened in the morning light, although she didn't remember getting out of bed. Still, she was up, and that was what mattered.

She looked at the magic prisms of light as they flashed at her, realizing they were drops of water. Obviously this man who'd brought her home with him had known what he was talking about. It had rained, although she must have slept through it. The showers were very recent. The flashing droplets of water everywhere spoke to that.

She gazed across the grass to see the ocean off against the horizon. She knew it was the ocean, although she didn't know how. It just was. Perhaps it was the whitecaps, or the person she could see surfing the swells in the distance. That didn't seem unusual to her, although she recalled she'd recently been on a vacation to Alaska. She didn't think she could have gotten home to her Carolina coast so quickly, though.

She heard a noise from the trees, and she turned. It was Mamie. She was dressed in her white gloves and her warmest suit. Carolina spoke first, laughing. "Why, Mamie! Did you miss the ship, too? You must hear all about my adventures." Carolina ran to her and gave her a hug.

"No, Carolina." Mamie smiled at her. "I must tell you my news first." She reached and pulled the younger woman down to her, leaning her head in and whispering directly into her ear. "I have found my grandson."

Carolina stepped back and looked at the old woman. Then she hugged her, remembering the grandmother's assurances she would find her grandson if only Carolina were with her. Carolina spoke very gently to her. "I see no one, Mamie. Where is he?"

Mamie pointed a white-gloved finger. Carolina followed it with her eyes to the surfer far out at sea. Then the old woman looked at Carolina with tear-rimmed eyes.

"I told you he would find me. With you by my side, he wouldn't be able to resist. I knew he would come find you no matter where you were, and then I'd have him back again. He's my favorite, you know."

136

Immediately, Mamie put her white-gloved hands to her mouth as if in dread, and she spoke again. A note of desperation was in her words. "Hold him tight, or he'll fly away, Carolina. Hold him tight." Then the old woman reached and patted Carolina's arm. With a smile, she stepped away and returned to the trees.

Carolina thought nothing of Mamie walking away again, and she looked back to the water. The surfer was riding the wave as if it were the easiest thing in the world, and he was coming straight at her. Carolina's eyes narrowed, and even though she knew he was still far away, his face was as clear to her as if he were right at her side, and it was the face of Kody from Alaska.

Carolina jerked, and she stared into the darkness. The insects were still singing their melodies, and her bed was truly warm. It was the middle of the night, and she must have been having a very strange dream.

Slowly, the musky Kody smell that was part of the bedding permeated her thoughts, and she drifted off to sleep once again.

KODIAK ran his fingers through Carolina's hair.

He kissed her forehead as the silken strands of her glossy tresses melted away under his touch. The stars above told him where they were. He'd grown up with these patterns of light, and they only happened on his warm Carolina beaches. He reached to run his fingers along her neck, and she turned her head to him.

"Kodiak," she whispered.

He thought nothing of her using his real name. She must know it, even though he'd never told it to her.

"I've always wanted you, Kodiak."

His breathing deepened. He wanted her, also, and he nuzzled her ear with his lips. Her skin was both salty and sweet to him. He knew she was his if only he asked her.

"The sand's warm, Carolina. The beach is ours alone. Will

you lie here with me until the sun rises?"

She reached to him, brushing the day's unseen sand from his chest. She ran her other hand over his back, removing still more sand, her body brushing up against his, sending pinpricks of fire straight to his core.

"I barely know you, Kodiak."

He breathed his truest wishes and dreams. "I've known you all my life, and I can no longer live without you. This is my home, Carolina. Not Alaska. I know it must be yours. It will be yours. Just give me a chance."

She smiled in the darkness. Kodiak was not surprised to be able to see her face, even though it was enveloped in the shadows of the night.

She stroked his cheek. "In California, we'd make a movie of this, and then the whole world would know the beat of our hearts. Do you wish the world to know how much you love me? Smile." Then, Carolina reached her arms around him and kissed him firmly on the lips.

As she did so, he looked up, and they were surrounded by banks of floodlights. A camera was pointed directly at them.

A man's voice yelled, "Cut!" Kodiak's heart pounded in terror. Then he jerked erect, reaching to rub his eyes. There was Carolina standing with her hand on the wall switch, and the light overhead was blinding. He squinted and shaded his eyes with his hands, struggling to drag himself awake.

He managed to squeeze out, "Carolina?" He swung his feet to the floor, realizing the room was really cold.

"Oh, Kody! I'm so sorry. I was hot, and I wanted another drink. I must have become more dehydrated than I thought yesterday." She reached and turned the light back off. Through the quiet of the darkness, she whispered, "I've become good at intruding on you. I won't bother you again."

Before she could get away, he called out, "Wait." The thoughts of his hometown beach were still fresh in his mind, and his body still felt her remembered warmth. She couldn't disappear so quickly. He jumped to where he knew she must be. Taking her arm, he whispered, "Come talk with me for a few minutes. I dreamed of you."

She laughed quietly. "So did I, of you."

When he tugged her arm, she relented, moving through the liquid darkness to nestle at his side. "Carolina," he murmured as he put his arms around her. He could still feel his dream, and he reached up to touch her hair. He put his lips to her forehead, and everything was just like he remembered.

Carolina reached a hand and rested it on his chest, brushing it across his skin. She held her hand still, pressing it against him. He was certain she could feel his heartbeat if she wished, and then she'd know how much he was attracted to her.

She placed the side of her face against his shoulder and whispered, "Can it truly be we met only half a day ago? I feel as if I've always been looking for you."

Kodiak knew he couldn't sit with her next to him this way without taking her in his arms. He struggled with his promises of propriety. His senses screamed for her touch. If she'd give him just one sign she wanted more, he'd be hers for all time. She'd taken him back to his Carolina beach with her melodious, Southern voice, and he couldn't return to this life he'd built here in the Alaska wilds without her at his side. He let his lips find her face and tasted the saltiness of her skin.

"Carolina," he croaked, his breathing barely calm enough to be called breathing anymore. He wanted to hold her the night through, everything he'd felt in his dream.

Then, he'd get it all, wouldn't he, including the bright lights and the camera recording his actions. That had felt very real, too. Anything they did tonight would be exposed in the upcoming light of morning. With a cry of frustration, he pulled himself away and threw himself onto the far end of the sofa, releasing Carolina to sit untouched.

"Kody! What's wrong?" She reached a hand to him, touching him on the arm, and then holding it. He jerked his arm away. "What is it, Kody? What did I do?"

Kodiak wailed, "It's what I want to do." His voice ripped from him with the intensity of his desire. "I want to betray my promises to you, and that would make a fool of you for trusting me. I don't want to stop what we've already started, and if you touch me again, I won't be able to." He rolled over and curled into a ball, his internal torment bleeding from him in his words. "I hate this. I hate myself for what I want to do."

Carolina sat for a few moments, and then Kodiak could feel her rise from the sofa. She spoke slowly. "I'm a woman, Kody, and I'm an adult. You wouldn't have taken anything I wouldn't have given willingly. But, thank you. I know what you just did was very hard. However, all you've done is show me I can trust you without reservation."

He heard her step toward the bedroom door, and just before the door clicked shut, he heard her say very softly, and, he was certain, with a small laugh, "Perhaps it's best. What I'm wearing is yours. You wouldn't want to remove your clothes twice." Then the door clicked shut.

Kodiak did notice as he wrapped his arms around his cushion once again that the lock didn't make a noise, and that meant she hadn't engaged it. However, he wouldn't go to her, even if he had to fight it all night. He also noticed that his cushion didn't feel so very much like Carolina any longer.

She had felt much, much better.

Chapter 11

CAROLINA'S eyes opened. The first thing she noticed was the brittleness in the air. Shifting her position slightly, drawing in a deep breath, she coughed as the cold air scoured her lungs.

She would not be able to get up, not and survive.

She hadn't felt this intensity of cold the entire time she'd lived in Los Angeles. She moved her arm to change her position again and jerked it back. Not all was warm underneath the blankets, just where she was presently positioned.

Her eyes moved to the uncovered window. The sun was shining outside. That brought back memories of her dream, and she chuckled. Had it actually rained, and would Mamie really wander out of the woods? The thought made her smile, and it also made her wonder how she was going to get out of this prickly situation. She had to be on her ship, and she had no idea where it had been headed, except farther into the deepest heart of Alaska!

She glanced around the room. The steep, vaulted ceiling was of wood, and an old, wooden airplane propeller hung at the opposite end of the room. There was a rough, wooden shelf lined with outdoor footwear, much of it well worn. She smiled at the opened drawers in the dresser. As tired as she'd been, she remembered the man in the other room digging frantically through them last night. She stretched her body at the memory, drawing in at the cold, and then deciding she could stretch and return her limbs to their warm nesting places immediately afterwards.

Then, with a catch in her chest, she also remembered sitting with him on the sofa. She'd wanted what he'd seemed to offer. She'd wanted the press of his lips to hers, and the feel of his hands on her arms. She'd wanted more, but that was put aside in the light of the morning, and she was glad for Kody's surprising self-control. She might have enjoyed it last night, but this morning would have been a different matter altogether.

What made her eyes tight with regret was the knowledge that she'd gone into the next room with some degree of intent. Hope was all she'd felt as she stood at that door. The sight of him so clumsily bumbling with his clothes when she caught him off guard had created a longing she hadn't found easy to put aside.

She thought of that airport from so many years ago, and the boy she'd seen. She'd dreamed of him for years. At times she'd felt a sense of betrayal when she spent time with other men, as if he were still out there, waiting on her, searching for her. She hadn't felt that sense of betrayal with Kody. He'd seemed a completion of that boy from so long ago.

How could that be? Did she want him to be the same person so much that she'd convinced herself of something that wasn't true?

She squeezed her eyes shut, her efforts to keep the tears from flowing only making them come more quickly. She knew she was letting herself be too strongly attracted to a man who would never be part of her life. No, she admitted, she wasn't letting herself. She was being swept along in a river of attraction, of completion in her soul, one that she couldn't battle against. He was something she needed, and she didn't know how she could deal with that. She'd walked into that room last night with hope, and when he'd pulled her to the sofa, she'd allowed him. He'd assured her of his good intentions, and she'd gone to him wanting, no, needing him to throw those good intentions to the wind.

Carolina opened her eyes and turned her head to look back out the window, biting at her lip as she did so. She had to be honest with herself. She hadn't wanted him to throw his good intentions to the wind. She had intended to shred them with claws of passion, rending his good intentions until he wanted her, too. When he'd pulled back from her, her emotions had been devastated.

She'd seen his pain, though, and she'd seen the gentleman in him. For a wild, Alaska man to show himself to be the gentleman she thought could only be found in her Carolina Low Country had endeared him to her more than ever. She'd taken her rampaging emotions, and she'd left him in his torment. She hadn't locked the door, though, and if he'd come to her, she would have welcomed him. Now she knew he must feel ashamed. She'd seen him at his most vulnerable, and she'd been the one to force him to his knees.

Carolina knew herself for the wicked woman she was, and she could not face him this morning. Yet, her hated honesty threw reality back at her. She was in his home. His most private items of clothing were on her body. She was nestled in his bed. Even though she'd shamed him, she must depend on him for transportation back to town.

She jumped at a knock on the door.

"Yes?" Her heart seemed to stop. He'd rail at her, sending

her packing. He'd call her names she'd never forget. And they'd be true, every one. She'd wanted to be those names last night, and he would know her for what she had never before wanted to be, yet what she had desired to become while nestled with him on that sofa.

She was overcome with mortification, and the shame made her face burn.

"It's very cold outside, Carolina."

She was surprised to hear that his words weren't harsh at all.

"The rain's also gone. I have a fire on this side of the wall, but your room must be freezing. May I open the door to share?"

She heard the door creak in its frame as if he were leaning against it, his weight shifting as he waited for her answer. He didn't sound upset, easing her dread, and she couldn't very well avoid him all day. She tested her voice.

"Please, Kody, the door's unlocked." She paused, listening for the sound of the latch, then she called louder, "You're right. It's freezing in here. I'm covered up. You can open the door, if you want."

When he swung the door wide, it was much more than heat that assaulted her. The sudden crash of odors that poured through the door were of the things she truly needed this morning. Coffee and eggs and frying bacon. Just the smells were enough to wash aside her earlier trepidations, and it was only moments before the air began to grow warmer.

Sunlight flooded through the doorway and filled the room with the promise of a beautiful day.

Against the dazzling sunlight, she noticed the shape of a man cutting through the brilliance. He was deeply shadowed, and she traced his outline with her eyes. In that moment, seeing his profile, she knew without a doubt that Kody was her boy from long ago, and it made her smile. His hair was that same golden halo, and his skin seemed kissed by the morning light.

He raised one bare arm to rest it against the doorframe, and she could see the muscles move under his skin. It was the same as she remembered from all those years ago. Then he dipped his head and smiled, the small movement cutting through the brightness, leaving him glowing in the light.

Carolina nearly called to him, *Alaska! Remember Savannah? It was me.* Still, it couldn't be true, and she caught the words as they formed in her throat. He couldn't have stepped so easily back into her life after all these years.

Then the apparition in front of her moved forward, and the boy from her dreams became Kody once again. He reached to her, and in his hand was a steaming cup of coffee. As he navigated around the bed, he told her it was black, and he apologized he had no milk or cream. Shrugging, he set it by the bed, and with his golden hands, gently tucked the covers around her face. It would soon warm in the room, he assured her. Finally, he stepped away, telling her he must attend to breakfast.

She watched him as he moved around the room. Kody's hair was that same golden brown she remembered so well, but the streaks of summer sun weren't there. This man's face did dimple when he smiled, but then so did many others. His arms, she told herself. They definitely weren't the same. These were a man's arms, not those of a college boy.

She smiled at having seen what she wanted to see in her rescuing angel. She'd dreamed of her imaginary boy ever since seeing him just that once for that very brief moment so very long ago. Could she even say her memory was true any longer? Perhaps her mental image of that long-ago boy was changing into the man Kody was, even as she pictured him speaking to her from an airplane engine.

She laughed, and Kody reappeared in the door. She reached a hand to wave him away. She would get up, and she'd eat this man's cooking. This was Alaska, and how many of those people on that cruise ship could ever say they'd truly seen this wild land? She had, and she'd spent the night with a wild Alaska man. She'd almost enjoyed his bed. She threw the covers aside, and she thought back on the night. She had indeed enjoyed his bed, but she'd almost enjoyed even more. Now her chances were lost, and she'd find her way back to California as chaste as ever. That was as it should be, she knew, but today!

Today was her one and only chance to live her wild Alaska adventure.

CAROLINA pulled her chair closer to the stove. She held her plate in her hand as she warmed herself. She hadn't known she could be so hungry.

"Kody, this is very good." She reached to take another bite.

He smiled. "I told you. The calories aren't something to avoid. Here, they're survival. Your body craves them, and then it burns through them to maintain warmth. You'll feel better with a full stomach."

"Also with the bacon grease and the butter in the eggs," Carolina smirked.

Kodiak laughed. "Calories, Carolina. This is Alaska, remember."

She reached to dab a bit of egg from the side of her mouth as she smiled. "How could I forget?" She glanced to the display on the wall above the wood-burning stove. "Tell me about the surfboard. I remember ones very similar to it on the beach where I grew up."

Kodiak raised his eyebrows, and then his smile broke his cheeks in two. "I surfed forever. Not any longer, of course. I can't take the cold of the Alaska surf. Now I surf in a different way." He nodded his head toward the window. "Look to the water."

"The water?" Carolina had ridden in with Kodiak in the dark, assuming his was some backwoods cabin landlocked in the Alaska interior. The window in the bedroom opened to a forested slope. The sun had been too bright to even try to see out front.

Water?

She stepped to the window, rubbing her arms at the chill near the glass. She shivered as she slipped a slice of bacon into her mouth.

"There." A voice whispered in her ear. It was Kody at her side, and his arm pointed over her shoulder through the trees. As she moved her head to let a shadow from a tree block the sun from her eyes, the scene before her jumped into her heart.

"Kody, this is beautiful."

There were trees taller than anything she'd ever seen before, some kind of pine or spruce. The ground sloped away, and far down the hill were a dock and a small airplane tied to a float. She could see the ramp shifting as the float bobbed in the gentle surf. The sun sparkled on the wings of the craft as they caught the light filtering through the trees. Just on the other side was a small spit of protecting rock with the ocean beyond.

She turned to her breakfast chef. She'd seen his ragged truck. She hadn't expected this scene outside his window. "You own this?"

He laughed, and his eyes twinkled at her amazement. "Well, ma'am," he started in a fair imitation of a Texas drawl. "When they run us plowboys out of the Texas Piney Woods, they just send us on up here, telling us the land is free. Just go! It's yourn." He smoothed his face, but his mouth revealed his fight to keep from laughing. "I'm sorry. It's the tourists, you see. They bring it out in me."

He pointed to several other things, the garage, his old truck, even his burn barrels that they could barely see down the steep slope. "My mother always wanted to live in Alaska, and she died before my family could get here. My father brought her here in his heart." He turned and looked around the cabin. "After he died, I built this using much of the wood from his old hunting shack, although," and he laughed, "I had to buy other materials, too. I did winter over once in that shack. It didn't even have insulation. This is much better."

Carolina smiled at him, enjoying the animation of his face as he told his story. When he slowed, she prompted, "The airplane. Surely you didn't build that?"

Kodiak turned back to the window. He stood pensively for a moment, and he whispered almost inaudibly, "I nearly lost that airplane. Once when she tried to take it, and then when it quit in Edmonton." He turned to Carolina, his face visibly brightening. "It was my father's. We'd travel together in it, and when he was gone, I began my own adventures, flying the skies in my wonderful machine." He chuckled at that.

"May I see it later? I've always had a love of small planes. When I fly, I request prop driven ones if they're available."

Kodiak reached a hand and tapped the glass with a fingernail. "I honed my skills on that little jewel. It was old when Dad bought it, and we had to work to keep it running. I've torn that engine apart and put it back together more times than I can count." Carolina could hear the pride in his voice. "It's dependable, though. Necessary up here, too." He turned, sitting on the windowsill. "You're going to fly in it today. That is if you want to . . . if you can spend one day before you run off back to California." He grinned, and there was a sparkle in his eyes.

Carolina turned and walked back to her warm spot by the stove. She sat and stared through the glass doors to the flame inside, glad for the heat. She glanced at Kodiak. "I'm supposed to be on my cruise ship for another week. I don't see how I can get back to California just yet, not unless your airplane can fly me there."

"Not likely," he remarked. "I fly by sight only, without using instrumentation. Well, I have to have some, but none that would help me get to California. I don't even have a radio

148

inside, not the type used for navigation."

Carolina knew enough to understand control towers and running into things in the dark. "How do you fly without a radio? Isn't that dangerous?"

Perhaps she didn't want to fly with him. She glanced out the window to see if she could find the red truck, to make sure it was still available, but the ground sloped too sharply, and from where she sat, the trees and sky were all that were visible.

"Just you wait and see. I fly during daylight hours, and we have a lot of that here in the summer. It's only seven, you know, and the sun's already been up for hours. Notice my plane doesn't have wheels. For dry touchdowns, I have to trade my pontoons for wheels. That limits where I go."

"You don't fly to airports?" Talking about airplanes was making Carolina think, and she knew this Alaska adventure would have to end sometime. Perhaps it was already reaching that point.

"Only on my journey to get here. Small hops from airport to airport. You'd be surprised to know how many there are. I can update the landing gear to do both at the same time, but that takes money, of which I have very little."

"Hence the red truck." She smiled.

"Hence the red truck." He laughed then turned to the bedroom, shifting the conversation. "Your clothes? Did they get dry?"

"I found some hangers, so I suppose. I didn't check." She sighed. Glancing at the fire, she wondered about his airplane, whether he might use it to get her to her ship. She drew her feet up under her, her legs still chilled. "So, you don't fly to airports, huh?"

"Not unless they have water runways." He stepped to check on her clothes. "Carolina?" He reappeared, holding her pants attached to its hanger. "I don't think you'll be wearing these this morning."

She looked up. They were dark with moisture, and it was obvious they were still very wet. Her eyes went from the pants to Kodiak's face.

"Kody, I can't wear what I have on all day. It's freezing anywhere away from the fire. I won't be able to go outside at all. What about my sweater?"

"Sorry. No luck there, either." He shrugged as he stepped to the stove and hung her things on a hook just above. "I should have done this early this morning when I built the fire. After last night, however, I didn't want to intrude."

"Last night. I'm so embarrassed." Carolina slipped her fingers into her hair, her palm resting on her forehead. She kept her eyes on the floor.

"I have a belt, Carolina. You can use it."

She looked at him, puzzled by his remark. It made her laugh. "A belt? What would I need with a belt?"

"To keep my pants up." He looked at her seriously.

"Why would I need to keep your pants up?" She laughed again at the thought of her putting his belt around his waist to keep his pants up.

"You're going to have to wear something. You can't wear these." He reached and thumped the pants hanging above the stove, the sound very wet. "Mine will have to do." He stepped to the bedroom to retrieve a pair.

"Kody," Carolina called, "I cannot wear yours. That would mean I'd have to bring them back later to get my own. I need to get home."

He leaned out the door, flashing that grin Carolina found so impossible to resist as it spilled across his face. "Thank you. You've made my point exactly." As he stepped to her, he handed her the dry pants. "The part about bringing them back, I mean. The home part? That I can't bear to think about." He pulled a chair up, sitting in it backwards, resting his arms on the back, and watching her. "You may get dressed, now."

150

She reached and put her hand over his eyes. "Not with you looking."

Kodiak pushed her hand away. "You're wearing my underwear. Keep them on. I won't see anything inappropriate. The rules say that when someone wears my underwear, I get to watch them dress."

"Kody!" Carolina laughed at his convoluted logic. He was charming her, and she couldn't resist. However, she also couldn't imagine getting dressed in front of this man.

Kodiak grinned. "Go on. After all, how many chances am I likely to get to watch you putting my clothes on?"

"Okay, Kody. I'll wear your pants and your underwear. However, you must turn your head." She reached and handed him her plate, long since empty, and pushed his face sideways. She stood, and as she pulled his pants on, she knew he was looking out of the corner of his eye, but she couldn't do anything about that, could she?

"KODY, THIS is amazingly beautiful."

Carolina was on the front porch, and she rubbed her arms in the warming sunshine as she admired the view. Who'd have thought anyplace could be as stunning as this? It wasn't something the cruise line showcased in their brochures.

She was surprisingly comfortable wearing this man's clothes. His pants were baggy on her, bunched at the waist and rolled at the hem. His shirt was almost as amusing. She'd rolled the sleeves, and it was tucked in, but it was very loose.

She moved to the steps and wrapped her hand around a rustic pole holding the roof up.

"Watch your step!" Kodiak was ahead of her, and he took the steps two at a time. He turned to see Carolina standing at the top, looking around and admiring the view. He smiled at her appearance and encouraged her to join him. "Come on! Be careful here, but get ready to slide down the hill."

Carolina started down, taking the steps one at a time. "Slide? There aren't steps?"

He ran back to her to take her hand, and he laughed. "That's why I was headed into town yesterday." He pointed. "There. That's what's left of a tree that last week's storm blew down. I ran out of fuel for the saw. I have more now, but you're here, and I no longer care about the tree. When you're gone?" He shrugged. "If I judge by that, I hope I never have to worry about the tree again." Laughing, he pulled her down the slope, the patches of sun flashing in a dappled strobe effect on his skin.

Once at the shore, Kodiak led Carolina along the wooden dock where it hugged the shoreline. Coming to the ramp, he motioned to the airplane at the bottom. "My pride and joy. Come on down. I'll show you." He reached for her hand, and he warned her about not having a rail on the ramp, and to be careful on the float. It was generally stable to anyone with sea legs, he told her. She laughed, telling him she had her sea legs from the cruise ship. He rocked his weight from side to side, causing the float to shift in an ever-increasing arc. When she grabbed for him, he grinned.

"Not quite the same thing," he said.

Carolina hung onto Kodiak a bit longer than necessary, laughing. Then she looked in his eyes and agreed that it wasn't. Turning to gaze back at the cabin, she sighed.

"What, Carolina?"

"I just realized something." She twisted back to him. "We're miles from nowhere. I've heard no cars, seen no ships, and don't remember there being a phone in your house." She took a breath and smiled. "Your cabin. Yet, you must have a phone somewhere, even though I didn't see it. No one could survive without one."

He pointed to one of his burn barrels, the drums he'd been using to dispose of the tree refuse. There were tendrils of smoke rising from one of them, the one he'd lit the evening before.

Carolina looked up at him, mystified. He worked his mouth to keep his smile under control, but he spoke very seriously and with emphasis. "Burn large tree for smoke signal. White man come running."

Carolina slapped his chest, snorting in laughter. "Very funny. You do know I could call someone if I had a phone."

Kodiak looked offended. "You wish to run away so soon? I haven't even shown you my airplane. It's my pride and joy. Taking a tour would be a small price for you to pay considering how much of my food you so readily gobbled up this morning."

"I'll look at your airplane, mostly because it interests me." She teased him, but the phone was a real issue. "You have electricity. You were running lights last night. If you have electricity, you must have a phone."

"And propane. I'm not totally cut off from the world." He paused as if considering, then he backtracked. "Well, actually, I am. No one can reach me up here, save smoke signals." He grinned. "Some of us like it that way."

"But why? Oh, never mind. That's a stupid question and none of my business. The electricity, though. I don't see any wires, and to run it underground all the way here would be prohibitive. How do you get that?"

"Solar panels up on the hill. They heat my water, too, just in case you feel the need to ask. See?" He pulled her to the side to where she could just see a small tank up on the hill. "A low pressure pump keeps it full. It runs off the solar when there's enough. When the weather's bad, or at night, I have a generator. You would have heard it turn on and off last night if you knew what to listen for."

"Oh, I do remember that. It seems you truly are cut off." She smiled, but she felt the promise of a phone fading. "I do have a phone of my own, you know. However, I left it in my cabin on the ship."

"It's useless to have one if you don't carry it." Kodiak

smiled.

"A hard lesson to learn, but you're absolutely correct." Carolina took a deep breath and pushed her hair back, moving on. Or trying to, at least.

"Even if you had it, it'd do you no good up here. You can't get a signal, sometimes not even in town."

"So, it's impossible for me to just call for help." That pulled Carolina two ways. She was getting to see the real Alaska today, and via aircraft, to boot, with a very handsome man for her guide. Yet, all this was sudden, and she hadn't shifted gears yet. She was driven to get back in touch with her world.

"Carolina," Kodiak prodded. "Are you with me?"

She glanced at him, and she reached to run her hand through her hair. "I'm sorry. It's just the stress of not knowing what's going to happen."

"About your call, around here, your best bet is a land line."

"A land line. A hard line, you mean. Dedicated, with wires. Sure. You don't happen to know where one is, do you?"

He reached to open the door to the airplane. "Claudine has one. I think there are one or two others in town. She's the only one willing to share, without paying, that is."

"Oh!" Carolina smiled, teasing. "In that case, I should have stayed with her. I should have taken you up on that offer and just slept on her sofa."

Kodiak's face dimpled, and grinning, he reached to her and wrapped his arms around her, fighting her for her face. Then, he kissed her on the cheek. She pulled away, her eyes burning.

"Please don't, Kody. Not yet."

He drew his hands up, tucking them under his armpits. "Sorry. My apologies. Are you all right?"

She looked at him and smiled, her thumbs wiping impending tears from the corners of her eyes. "I'm sorry. This is all so beautiful, and you're a charming gentleman. I'm afraid I could want this too much, and this is your life. It's not mine."

He looked at her, his dimples stilled, and he whispered in a voice almost too low for her to hear, "It could be."

Carolina wrapped both hands around one of his arms, pulling him to the airplane door. "Could it, Kody? Really? For a Los Angeles office worker?" She forced a bright laugh. "Come, show me your airplane. That I would enjoy."

"You would?" His eyes were red, but he flashed a quick grin.

She reached one hand to touch the gently bobbing craft, and she kept the other through his arm. "Don't mind me. I'm here, and I'm enjoying this immensely. I've also missed my cruise ship and am stranded at a remote Alaska cabin, and I don't know how I'll get home. You know this place, and its every nuance is in your blood. I know Los Angeles. Please be patient with me. Show me, Kody. Teach me. I can perhaps learn to love a part of your world today. Not all, but a part."

She peered encouragingly into his eyes until she saw his lips begin to soften into a smile. Then she turned to the airplane, putting her head inside.

Kodiak leaned inside beside her. "It's very small."

"I expected the seats to be front and back, not beside each other."

He turned his head to look at her, and in the closeness of the space, he inhaled a deep breath. "Umm, you smell good, do you know that?"

"Kody! The airplane." However, his remark pleased her. "Please focus. Do all planes this size have seats like this?"

"No," he replied. "Cessna aircraft do, though."

"This is a Cessna, then." She moved to sit in the seat.

"Cessna 152. You're describing a Piper Cub. I think they have the tandem seats."

"Tandem? One in front of the other, you mean." She ran her hands over the dash and the different controls.

"Have you flown in a private plane before? To know how

they're laid out, I mean."

"Yes, but never in one this small." She laughed as she remembered her dream during the flight to Seattle. "Except in my dreams, of course. When can we take it out?"

"Now, if you want. I have to do a preflight first, though." He grinned. "Do you really want to go?" At her nod, he patted her shoulder. "You climb in and watch. Town's just a few minutes in this. This is what I usually take, not Old Red."

Humming and whistling, he was soon checking fuel levels, flaps, and a number of other things that Carolina couldn't see. He leaned down and smiled at Carolina as he moved around the airplane, stepping on the pontoon struts, and causing the airplane to bob in the water. Her stomach fluttered with butterflies as she watched him scramble over the aircraft.

What Carolina wouldn't admit to herself was the real reason she had butterflies in her stomach. As Kodiak raised his arms to check something on the top of the airplane's wing, his torso stretched, and from time to time, his shirt pulled up over the waist of his pants, showing just a glimpse of skin. The ribbing of his underwear pressing against his flesh had her thoughts embroiled. When his shirt stretched across his back, she felt a chilling tingle run down her arms and legs. As he bent to untie the airplane from the cleats on the float, her body melted in the seat. She was glad she was already inside the airplane and not standing outside. She thought of how silly she would look if she were just now trying to climb inside the cabin of his airplane with her legs filled with jelly.

Kodiak walked up to Carolina's door, and he opened it. She looked straight ahead, unsure of whether she trusted herself to respond to him. However, his musky aroma swelled into the cabin along with the fresh sea air. She had only thought she was filled with jelly before. This time her stomach turned a somersault in her lap. Out of the corner of her eye, she saw Kodiak's face break into a wide smile, his dimples deep and shadowed.

"Okay, now. I'm coming in." He stood for a moment, waiting on her response. "My seat's on the other side." He chuckled and made as if to enter the cockpit.

"Kody, go around. There's no room for you to climb over." Carolina's voice cracked from her throat.

She glanced at him to see if he'd moved, and seeing he hadn't, she looked away again. She knew she wouldn't be able to stand it if he came any closer. She could already feel warmth emanating across her body, and she wasn't sure she appreciated where it was centered.

"Carolina," he prodded. "The water's on that side. I can't swim to my seat."

She drew in a deep breath. She wasn't sure she could stand if she attempted to climb out, but she couldn't let this man, this very masculine bundle of pheromones, scramble over her. Her body wouldn't tolerate it. She'd have to climb out. Then he could make his way to his seat.

She pushed him away. "Let me get out. Then you won't have to crawl over."

He laughed. "I want to crawl over. That's my point."

With those words, he pushed his head into the plane, and he began to work his way past her. She reached with her hands to help him along, and she was dismayed to see that she was only successful in riding his shirt up over his torso. He looked at her and laughed, quipping, "This is much better than last night."

Irritation overriding her earlier giddiness, she slapped his bare skin briskly. When he balled up in laughter, she attempted to shove him away.

"This almost did happen last night. I thought we were going for a ride, not playing hanky panky in the smallest airplane in the world."

Kodiak reached to a handhold on the far side of the airplane and pulled himself into his seat. "Trust me, Carolina." He turned to face her. "They come much smaller. I don't want one any larger, though. Then you'd be too far away from me." He smiled and turned back to his preparations. With quick fingers, he began checking his instrumentation inside the airplane, and then he looked up at the propeller. He groaned. "Would you look at that?"

Carolina glanced up at the cabin high up on the slope, the trees dappling the sun, and the grass as it seemed to sparkle in the morning light. She didn't know what he was talking about, but she knew his world seemed a slice of perfection to her. She turned to look at the man next to her, suddenly aware of his closeness. She whispered, "What, Kody?"

He pointed out the windshield. "I've got a branch there in the cowling. I don't know how I missed it. I'll be just a moment."

With that statement, he released his door and climbed out onto the pontoon, holding the struts and grab handles to climb to the front of the airplane. He grabbed the branch and wrestled with it. Unable to get it loose, he looked back at Carolina and grinned. He unclipped the cowling. Reaching inside, he began to work with the errant limb.

In that moment, as Kodiak leaned into the airplane cowling, Carolina envisioned ten years earlier on the Savannah tarmac, and she was waiting to board a plane for Hilton Head. The engine cowling had been open then, and the muscular back of a young man was there with his head and hands lodged inside. He'd stepped away, and his face had turned to her, splitting into a grin.

Carolina blinked her eyes, and the Alaska shoreline snapped back into sharp clarity. Her eyes began to flood, and she looked away, squeezing them tightly to keep the tears from falling. The memory had felt so real. This man seemed so much like that boy from long ago.

A splash caught her attention, and she looked up to see the branch floating in the water, ripples forming around it.

She watched him bound back along the aircraft, his footing clearly practiced and sure, and his movements nimble. When he got in, she frowned at him, now thoroughly irritated that he'd crawled over her earlier. She looked away, wanting to speak her mind and yet knowing that surge of Low Country pride that would not let her do so.

The man entering the cabin had no such reservations. "A branch in the cowling. Wow!"

She could see his reflection in the glass at her side, and he was smiling in total enjoyment. That did tug her heartstrings, but her irritation refused to leave her alone. As she turned to speak, preparing to lash out at him with Southern iciness, Kodiak beat her to it, and her chance to speak was stolen from her.

"But then, this is the best place in the world. Alaska! It's so cool, don't you think?"

As he reached to pat her leg, Carolina's barbed words melted from her mouth, and her heart pounded wildly in her chest. She must get out of this airplane. She was drawn to this man, and yet, she mustn't be drawn to him. Her home was in California. She'd return there, today if she could, tomorrow if she must. Her cruise ship had gone on without her, and this man was delving into her soul with his charm and graciousness.

She felt torn apart.

Yet, she had no other place to go. Kody was her lifeline, the angel who had rescued her when her errant Jeep had so blatantly floundered, leaving her literally on the side of the road.

She looked into her lap, speaking softly, barely able to force her words from her throat. "You could have walked around, couldn't you?"

"Walked around, Carolina?"

She reached her hand and wiped her eyes. "The airplane." She looked up, suddenly laughing in a desperate sort of way, the tension too much for her to bear. "You could have walked around the airplane instead of climbing over me."

Kodiak grinned again. "What would have been the fun in that?" He looked at her and continued, "Are you ready to fly the skies of Alaska with me?"

Carolina sniffled and smiled. This man had his hooks into her, and she'd be sad when she finally found her passage home. She knew it would hurt, too. However, it was time for her tour, and she could at least have this morning with him. She nodded and turned to the window as the propeller coughed and spat, and then the steady thrumming of the engine kept them from speaking at all.

Chapter 12

KODIAK idled the airplane forward, and once they were past the float, he lined the craft up with the spit of land that protected his small cove. Looking at Carolina, he pressed the throttle in, and with the roar of the engine, the small craft surged forward. She felt the vibration of the pontoons as they rose and began to skim across the water. Holding to her seatbelt, then reaching to grab the handle above the top of the door, she watched the water clip by faster and faster, the trees blurring, and then there was total smoothness.

The roar of the engine also eased, and the trees disappeared from her view.

Kodiak pointed to the ground and moved his hand in a circle. When Carolina gave him a perplexed look, he just grinned. Then the airplane began to bank, and when Carolina looked out her window, there was Kodiak's cabin, the peaked roofline just visible in the green of the trees. She glanced back at him to see his face bright with enthusiasm. He motioned for her to continue to look as he flew down along the shoreline, his dock visible across the spit of protecting land. Then picking up speed, he climbed in altitude, heading along the Alaska coast-line.

"Look for ships," Carolina yelled over the sounds of the climbing engine, her eyes working up and down the coastline.

"Where?" Kodiak yelled back.

"Anywhere. If you see one, it might be mine." She stretched to look all around the airplane, her view of the water not enough for her to see all she wanted.

"Not likely. They go all the way into Anchorage from here. Your ship would have sailed all night. We can fly by the airport and see if anyone has an airplane in. If so, they could perhaps fly you to Juneau. Maybe even Anchorage. You can fly out anywhere from there."

Carolina nodded and sat back in her seat. There was at least hope for her, then, for getting home, at least. Still, she was uncomfortably aware that there was another side to her emotions, and it sitting next to her in the plane.

She glanced over at Kody. He'd certainly charmed her. The thought of boarding an airplane to take her anywhere but back to his cabin was a cold wind driving her hot air balloon of exhilaration to the ground. She wasn't sure what she hoped for with Kody, but she did hope.

She smiled at the unlikely idea of him returning to California with her, and as she did, she saw him glance at her and smile back. In Los Angeles, this wild-woods man would be a fish out of water, and even if he did return with her, he'd suffocate in that urban environment. She knew that, and she wouldn't let that happen to him, not even if it meant she had to bear the pain of separation alone.

Kodiak pointed, and there was the town. "Airport, first," he yelled.

"Thanks," she called back, pointing to her ears. "I can hear you now." The noise level was better since the plane had leveled out.

As they approached the town, Kodiak flew inland some distance, and then he pointed with a shrug. "No planes."

"Where?" Carolina frowned.

"The airport." He pointed again.

"I'm sorry, I don't see it. There's just that field."

Kodiak smiled. "That is the airport. That grassy area is the runway."

"No airplane could land there. It's too small." Carolina looked at him in disbelief.

"Small planes don't take much room. Just no jumbo jets here. They land in Anchorage."

Carolina sat watching the grassy field for a time, and as they reached it and flew on past, she murmured, "So, no Anchorage for me. That other place, either. Juneau. I'm still here in the middle of nowhere."

"Did you ask something?" Kodiak tapped at a dial on the dash before turning to her for a quick look. "The altimeter. It sticks, sometimes."

She glanced at him and shook her head. Then she leaned her temple against the window at her side and looked through the clear surface. Mamie, I did try to find you. No phone, no ship, and no way to get to Anchorage. Are you missing me, Mamie? Am I lost up here forever?

She glanced up as a hand tapped her leg, then pointed to a herd of caribou crowded along a ridge. She looked out and smiled, but it was empty. Carolina felt lost once again, and this time she just couldn't shake the feeling.

CAROLINA was suddenly aware she hadn't seen the coast in some time. She realized she'd been watching with little awareness of what was around her. She glanced around to see a carpet of green, and she realized they must be quite high in the air. She looked at the dials on the dash, but she had no idea how to read them. She turned to the man beside her, and she watched his face for a moment. He was looking intently ahead. She noticed he appeared different, also. It was when he reached overhead to pull down a pair of sunglasses that she realized what it was she hadn't noticed. He was wearing a pair of his own. He turned and gave her a quick smile as he handed her the glasses.

Kodiak pushed his glasses up with one finger, peering out of the aircraft, and letting his eyes focus on the area below. Then Carolina saw his expression shift, and a grin grew on his face. He glanced at her again, and she felt the airplane begin to bank his direction. She looked over to see a fast-flowing stream that fed into a small lake.

"What are we doing?" she called to him, leaning his direction.

"Lunch," he called back.

"You packed something to eat?" Carolina didn't remember him loading anything. She twisted to look behind the seats and didn't see much except some sealed tubes and a couple of small toolboxes. She faced forward, confused. Perhaps this airplane had storage bins that could be accessed from the outside.

"Nah!" Kodiak glanced at her with a smile, his explanation in the word, and he turned back to his descent.

"So what does that mean?"

"We're going to catch our lunch."

"Catch? As in with traps?" Carolina wasn't sure about this. She did have on her walking shoes, but to go trapping wild animals? Then, what about bears? There were black bears in Alaska, and she remembered Kodiak Island. It couldn't be too far away, and wasn't that where Kodiak bears came from? She didn't know if brown bears were found in Alaska, or even if brown and black and Kodiak were all different names for the same animal, but she knew one thing. They were all very dangerous.

Kodiak remained silent for a time, working the controls in the airplane, now on a straight shot for the flat water of the small lake. Then he replied, "Sort of. Nets. Hooks."

Carolina was no longer concerned with lunch, though. Rather, she was distracted with what she could see just ahead of them.

"Kodiak, is there room to land on this lake?"

"Small airplane. Small lake. They go together." Then he looked at her with a grin. "Kodiak?"

Carolina gave him a quizzical look. She wasn't sure what he meant.

"You called me Kodiak."

"I'm sorry, Kody." She felt sheepishly stupid. "I worry about bears, and I know there's a Kodiak Island somewhere up here. Kodiak bears are from there, right? I was thinking that they might be the same as black bears, you know, the same species with a different name." She worried her seat belt, uncomfortably aware of how fast the water was coming up, and she knew she was rambling incessantly. "The water, it's getting really close."

Kodiak laughed. "My high school mascot was a bear, a Kodiak, we claimed. No, there are no Kodiaks on this stream. Other kinds? Well, we'll just keep a close watch. And don't worry about the water. I've got it under control."

It did seem they were slowing, but not enough to actually stop in the small amount of room the lake seemed to provide. Carolina couldn't keep her voice from its incessant fumbling as they approached the water. "Hooks? Nets? What are we trapping, Kody? I've never trapped anything in my life." Then she let out an involuntary gasp. "Kody, don't kill us, please."

She closed her eyes just as the pontoons gently touched the water's surface. Friction grabbed at the small craft, and Carolina felt herself surge forward against her seatbelt. When the airplane stopped, there was just the gentle whup, whup of the prop. She looked over at Kodiak, her face turning red. "Did I really say that?"

He grinned. "About killing us? I never heard a word. Let me taxi up to the dock." He revved the engine, and Carolina felt the airplane slowly move forward as the picturesque view around her shifted.

As the airplane stopped, she realized the dock was built differently. "Kody, you had a floating platform. This is more what I think of as a dock. Why's it different?"

"This is a lake. My float is for the tide so it's always level with the water." He killed the engine. "I've got to tie it up. Give me just a minute." He popped his door open, and he nimbly clambered out. Carolina watched him, this time not quivering with excitement. Something else grabbed her attention; she needed to relieve her pulsing bladder, and she hoped she could exit the airplane soon.

She reached and fiddled with the catch until she managed to get the door opened. Holding it just cracked, she called to him, "Kody?" She'd left her wet clothes back at his cabin. She didn't want to wear wet clothes, anyway.

He looked and waved, then turned back to his cleats. "I'll be right there."

"This might not wait." What had been a pulsing pressure now seemed to be a raging hurricane. It was readying to come out, too. She simply could not sit still. "I'm climbing out, Kody."

Carolina reached to push the door open, gingerly drawing her legs up to step onto the dock. Then she realized the dock was on the other side. "Kody," she wailed. "I have to go pee!"

He rushed to the door, opened the opposite side, and stood shamefaced. "I'm sorry, Carolina. Climb out this way. I should have thought about this." He reached his hand to her.

She was distraught. "I don't know if I can. I really need to go badly." She pulled the door closed on her side and looked across the airplane desperately. "Help me, please."

At her groans of discomfort, he did offer her words of sympathy. Once she had maneuvered out of the airplane, he pointed up the hill just a bit to a small, enclosed space. He told her there was an open-air toilet just there. It had walls of a sort, he assured her, and he'd try to not look through the cracks.

In spite of her urgency, she did find the time to shoot one fiery look his way before she crab-walked up the hill to the small enclosure.

When Carolina emerged from her rendezvous with nature, she saw Kodiak with one of the tubes and the smaller of the two toolboxes. She smiled, calling to him, "Lunch is inside that?"

He waved to her from the dock. "Sure. Let's go see what we've got." He picked up the tube and toolbox, and headed off into the trees. He turned to encourage her with, "Follow me. The stream is this way. We've got lunch to catch."

Not wanting to be left behind, she took off his direction with a speed she'd never have managed just moments before. She didn't know just where he was taking her, but she didn't intend to be left behind, not for the second time in less than a day.

KODIAK fed his line out and flicked his rod. As he did so, he talked quietly to Carolina. "This is a friend's place. His cabin is in the woods up where you can't see it unless you know where to look." He paused, twitching his line. "He only uses it some in summer. No insulation. He lets me land and fish."

She watched him, finding enjoyment in his motions. "That's very kind of him."

Kodiak grinned. "He wants my airplane. Says it's the best-maintained 152 on the West Coast of Canada." He looked at her and laughed. "This isn't Canada. It's Alaska. I won't sell, but he hopes. And lets me use his place."

"Does the lake we landed on have a name? It's very picturesque."

167

Kodiak made a motion to be very quiet. He whispered, "No name. Most lakes up here don't. It's just his. Got me a girl to catch."

"A girl?" Carolina suspected that's what he'd been trying to do with her all morning. However, she didn't think he was talking about her at this point.

Kodiak smiled. "Found her once, and I had her just for a minute. Right in my hands, too. I should have kissed her, then she'd still be mine. Instead, I opened my hands, and she was gone. I've been coming back for a second chance ever since." He froze and twitched a finger for silence. His eyes were glued to his line. Then, he yanked the line hard, and he whooped, "Got you, old girl! We're going to eat tonight!"

"Eat what, Kody?" Carolina laughed at the man's enthusiasm and backed up as Kodiak began to thrash the water, dancing with the fish on his line. "I don't think your fish wants to join us for dinner." She covered her mouth, and her eyes watered with mirth as the lake crawled up his clothes.

When he was finally stilled, his breath coming in gasps, he looked at her and grinned. "Look in the box. There's a collapsible net inside. Hand it to me." He reached for the line, pulling the fish close.

Carolina dug inside, finding something that had netting on it, and she handed it to Kody. He took it and flicked it in his hand, and it blossomed into a mesh net hanging from a metal frame. He stepped forward, the line held next to his pole, and reaching, he swooped the fish inside.

He brought it to Carolina. He held his catch up in the net, letting her admire it, and grinning with his accomplishment. "Trout. I told this one that I'd not give her a second chance. Others have come to me here, but this one's been wily. Now, she's dinner."

Carolina laughed. "Take it out. I want to see it without the net."

Kodiak reached inside and grabbed the fish by the mouth. He raised it out of the net, working the fly from its lip. He held it high, letting the sun flash from its scales.

Carolina's eyes began to water. It was beautiful.

"What is it?" Kodiak smiled. "You don't approve of my fish? I've worked hard to catch her again."

Carolina smiled. "I approve, Kody. I approve heartily. It's beautiful. Let it go."

He looked at her, an appalled expression crossing his face. "Let it go? Carolina, I came all this way just to catch this fish."

"Oh? I thought you came all this way to spend time with me." She did, too, or at least she hoped he had.

"True enough, but just to turn this fish loose?" He pouted, but it was playful, and he had a twinkle in his eye. He still held the fish, though. "I did that once, let this girl get away. Why should I release her again? This is lunch."

Carolina reached to stroke the fish with one finger as it curled for its life in Kodiak's hand. "I want it to have another chance." She looked at the man holding the fish, his knitted brow showing a lack of understanding. She tried to explain something that she'd never told anyone. "I want a second chance, Kody. I never got one. You see, I met a man once. More likely a boy, but he seemed a man to me at the time." She turned from the fish and the man holding it, her voice quiet in the telling. "I never got to know him, and I never learned who he was, not really. I've loved him for years, looking for him wherever I went. Now I know I'll never find him. I still love him, though." She turned to Kodiak. "I know it's a silly girl's story, but for me, Kody. If your fish gets another chance, it'll be like I get one, too. Please."

"But Carolina, I'm very hungry, you know. If I release my catch, I may not have the energy to fly back to the coast." He looked at the fish as if considering whether to even bother cooking his meal. His expression said raw might be a viable option. "We'd have to stay overnight, maybe even forever in my friend's cabin, and he only has one small bed. Not even a sofa. We'd have to sleep very close." He furrowed his brow as if considering that a fair trade, one he might give up his fish for.

His teasing bought him more of a reaction than he bargained for. "Kody! Just turn it loose. It'll die out of the water, and then I'll feel I've lost my second chance forever. Do it now!" Carolina's eyes began to water with frustration. She reached and slapped his arm.

He jumped back. "Okay! I was going to let it go anyway." He knelt and dipped the fish into the stream, holding it a minute to let the water rush over its gills. After a few moments, it flicked its tail, jerked out of Kodiak's imprisoning hand, and with a flash of sunlight through the surface of the water, it was gone. He stood. "For you, Carolina. May you find your love again." He smiled at her, and then he turned to gather his fishing gear, whispering, "Even if it isn't me."

Carolina heard, and she looked at him as he knelt to break his gear apart, storing it in its proper places. He had done that for her, and she'd certainly not expected him to. Her request had been an impulsive response to a very strong memory. Would she have been irritated if he'd kept the fish? Only for a moment, she thought, and then she would have laughed it off.

Watching him, not sure what it was about this man that kept that boy from so long ago in the forefront of her thoughts, she was sure it would fade once she was on her way home. There was a phrase she'd heard, and it seemed to fit these few days in her life. It's just a summer thing. She was sure that Kody would be that for her, just a summer thing. As soon as they went their separate ways, he'd be gone from her thoughts. Surely.

She didn't think she'd be able to bear it otherwise.

"KODY, I THOUGHT we were headed back to your place. I'm getting very hungry."

Instead, they'd returned to the town from the day before. Carolina climbed out of the airplane. She felt much more comfortable this time. She'd remembered to visit the open-air toilet before leaving the Lake of Second Chances. Kody had laughed at her when she'd called it that, telling Carolina he'd have to tell his friend about the lake's new name. Carolina had stopped him. No, she'd said. It was for her, alone. Her and Kody. He'd liked that, he'd said, something private that could be theirs forever. The Lake of Second Chances.

"Food, Carolina. Remember this morning? You devoured my week's supply." He laughed as he secured the airplane. "I must get more in town."

She smiled at that. She had eaten quite a lot. It was all gone, too. "Nothing looks open. How will you find food here? A rod and reel?"

"Perhaps," and he grinned. "If you'll let me keep the fish."

"I'm sorry. I shouldn't have asked you to put it back."

"Oh, no." His dimples still split his face. "It gives me something to look forward to."

"Now, though, a real lunch. I don't see a grocery store." The place looked almost as deserted as it had the previous evening. "Is Claudine's open?"

"Marv's," and he chuckled. "But Claudine will thank you. Just don't let Marv overhear."

"Who is Marv, anyway?" They walked along a rough street that bordered the shore, and Carolina asked her question just to make conversation, at the moment wanting nourishment more than answers.

Kodiak held a finger to his lips and clicked his tongue. "Marv is Claudine's ex. She got the diner. He got the young waitress. Now, Claudine is the waitress. They should name this town Peyton Place." He grinned at Carolina. "I actually suggested that to Claudine once. I didn't get to use her washing machine for a month. I think it was the smell of my socks that caused her to forgive me."

Carolina smiled. She could learn to like this little place on the Alaska coast, or she could if only she didn't already have a life in California. Peyton Place, Claudine, and a wild Alaska man. Who'd have thought she would ever find all this on her last-minute excursion from the cruise ship?

"Kody, why are we still walking along the shore? Is this the way to Marv's?"

"Marv's is closed on Thursdays. See those steps there? Go down them." He reached and put one arm around Carolina's neck, leaning his face to hers, while pointing to a series of flat stones that led downward from the level of the street. "Right there. Go down to that gravel beach you can just see. Dinner is waiting there."

"Kody, is this like the friend's cabin? Just a chance to get me alone?"

Kodiak stopped, and he put his hands on his waist as if very offended. "You malign my honor, good woman. As General Lee would say, 'Do not run from the fray. We might yet save the brocade draperies.'"

She reached for his hand and laughed, wrapping his arm around her neck once again. That had felt nice, and she was enjoying her day with this man. "You know full well that General Lee never said such a thing." She laughed. "He might have more likely said, 'Atlanta's burning! Run for your lives!'"

Kodiak laughed. "A Southern woman after my own heart."

Carolina chided him, "After your Alaskan heart, you mean. I liked your reference, though. General Lee. Who would have thought?"

Kodiak whispered, "I am very well rounded, ma'am. I know the rules of gracious conversation."

She patted his flat stomach. "Not so very well rounded. Still, we'll work to save those brocade draperies you're so fond of. However, speaking of well rounded, when do I get food?"

172

They stepped up to an old wooden wire spool attached to the ground with steel cabling. There were several wooden deck chairs also loosely tied down. Kodiak opened one of the chairs and set it at the spool.

"Your table. Let me just rustle us up some vittles." He grinned. He walked to a ledge that opened to the water, and he turned to Carolina. "The town keeps a little holding pen here. The tide comes up, and the fish swim in. The tide goes down, and we have dinner." He pulled a net off a pole in the ground, and he dipped it into the water. With a swift movement, he lifted it, and inside were two glistening bodies. He turned to Carolina with a wink. "Do these two need a second chance, my lovely Scarlett?"

Carolina laughed. "Frankly, my dear, no one gives a damn." She blushed at the obscenity. She covered her mouth with her hand and tried to explain it away. "From a movie. I've seen it forever, and that phrase is one of my favorites."

"A film buff!" He grinned.

"I'm sorry, Kody. You've probably never watched it. It's not the exact quote. It's from . . ."

"*Gone With the Wind.*" Kodiak laughed, his words cutting her off. "It's also one of my favorites. I haven't seen it in years, but when my mother was alive, we used to say those words together whenever Rhett would stand at the bottom of the stairs and glare." He grinned at her. "We'd say the original, though." He pulled free a knife that was also hanging from the pole. "Since there are no more second chances tonight, it's time to have dinner." He reached into the net and grabbed one of the fish.

Carolina laughed. "That pole is a complete fish cleaning station, I see."

"And a kitchen. Out here, you can't always run to the store or head back for something you forgot. This is handy for emergencies." He carried the fish to a large stone out near the

173

water's edge.

As she watched Kodiak prepare the fish, she remarked quietly to no one at all, or at least to no one who was listening, "Or handy for romantic interludes. I like this better than any emergency I can think of, thank you, Kody from Alaska."

CAROLINA undid the final roll of her sleeves and buttoned the cuffs snugly. "It's cooling off, Kody."

"Come closer to the heat. It's very warm here by the flames. This fish smells good, too." Kodiak looked up at Carolina from his place by the fire. "Shish kabobs. Can't beat this, can you?" He drew in a deep breath. "Mussels, salmon, and wild onions on a stick." He turned back to his meal and reached to shift a stick over the flames, the moisture dripping in a sizzling dance of splatters.

Carolina stepped up beside him. She'd been content to just watch this man, this intriguing person who could bring her to this rocky beach and make this meal from nothing. Even the fire. He'd collected small sticks, and his kitchen, the pole she'd found so amusing, had provided a small waterproof container of matches that was hanging by a wire. The fire had blazed for a moment, then quickly settled into a glowing bed over which this resourceful man had mounted his cleaned fish to sizzle with aroma. The day had been full of activities, and she'd felt her emotions war within her, but now there was no indecision. Her nerve endings were alive with anticipation, both for food and for the time she would spend with this man. She reached her hand to let it rest on his shoulder.

"Kody, what about when we're finished?" Carolina looked up and down the beach.

"What do you mean?" He prodded at the fish with a stick. "After we leave town?"

"No, now. This is beautiful and unspoiled, but I don't see any refuse bins. Where do we dispose of our trash?"

"We won't have any trash left over." He readjusted one of his shish kabob sticks to cook the opposite side of one of the fish.

"We won't eat the bones, at least I won't. We're in town. There must be receptacles for our refuse when we're through eating. However, I don't see them anywhere."

Kodiak stood and turned to her. His face broke into a spontaneous smile, and his arms wrapped around her in an equally unplanned hug. He looked surprised as she relaxed into his embrace. When he released her, she stepped back, her expression a pleased question.

"What was that for? I enjoyed it, but what did I do to deserve that?"

"It's all about being here in the wilderness, you know. Free. Clean. Taking care of nature and things. Tourists don't get it. Sometimes they act as if it's their right to throw trash down and let others clean it up." He turned to look across the gravel beach and out across the water. "The tide will come in and clean this for us. Anything organic we can leave." He faced her and smiled. "The pole and the other items that are attached, we don't want the tide to take them. We keep them above the tide line or fasten them to the ground. That way anyone can come use these things."

"But, there are receptacles for refuse?"

"Farther into town. Not on the beach. Storms carry the containers away." Kodiak bent to adjust a fish on one of his sticks. "From time to time, I've volunteered to clean here after the cruise ship has left." He turned to Carolina and gave her another big hug.

She laughed as she leaned her head back. "You still haven't told me what that's for."

Kodiak pulled her tight, pressing his face into her hair, and then he whispered into her ear, "Respect. You have respect for things other than your own, even if you're trying to run away from them."

"Run away?" Carolina pressed the two of them apart and looked at him in dismay. "What am I trying to run away from?" The very idea horrified her. She'd never considered herself one to shun a problem. She preferred to tackle them head on, or at least she liked to think she did.

"Me. This place. This town. Alaska."

He turned to look to the sea, but before he did, Carolina could see the pain in his expression.

She paused. His words hit home hard, and they twisted as they stabbed her heart. She had thought she was running home to her California responsibilities, but she'd been doing as Kody said. She could see that now. She'd been trying to run, ever since Kody had picked her up on the side of the road. This man reminded her too strongly of a lost chance at love, one she'd never really had, and she'd become afraid—afraid she would grab at the chance for renewed hope, and it would be taken from her as it had been when that boy had walked away from that airplane on that Savannah tarmac so long ago.

She stepped to him, putting her arm around his waist, and looking out to the sea with him. "I'm here now, Kody. I'm not running away from this charmingly touching meal you've taken the time to prepare for me. We'll both feel better when we've eaten." She reached her free hand to take one of his. "Join me? I can't eat all this alone." Smoke from the fire twirled toward them, carrying the delicious aroma of the fish their way, and she smacked her lips suggestively.

He turned his head slightly and peered at her, catching her eye. "You won't run away until tomorrow?"

Carolina was relieved to see a smile playing at the corners of his mouth, and she laughed. "How would I run away? I have nothing, not even my cell phone. All I have to my name is my clothes, and I'm not even wearing them. I have on your clothes, and you've even loaned me your sunglasses. Mine are still in my purse." With those words she froze. Then she turned, her eyes raking what she could see of the town. "My purse. I've not seen it since yesterday. Kody?" She felt panic rising as a tangible entity, and she heard it as it crept into her voice.

Kodiak reached and touched her arm. "Are you sure you brought it off the ship?"

"Of course, I'm sure. I carried it with me. It had my sunglasses inside, not my best ones, of course. I was afraid I'd miss the boat, and I just grabbed it from the bureau."

Kodiak stepped up to her and wrapped his arms around her for a third time. "Food, Carolina. We'll both think more clearly with food, and it'd be a shame for these fish to have given their lives in vain. Can you at least share this meager offering with me?" He reached and put a finger under her chin, lifting her head to look into her face. "Carolina?"

She nodded, reaching to wipe her eyes. "Is it cooked, then? I'm famished." She looked around and laughed. "I really do need to eat. I get like this sometimes when I go too long."

"People get like this when their world is yanked from under their feet. You've had that happen to you." Kodiak paused, and he knelt to pull the sticks from the gravel, carefully holding each fish so it wouldn't fall to the ground. "Look at this. Perfection." He pulled a piece off and put it in his mouth.

Carolina watched the man before her, and she looked across the beach to the water gently lapping the stones, whispering the romance of the soon-returning tide in its gentle sweep. She felt the distant sun as it tried to beat back the encroaching cold of the coming evening, and she shivered, hugging her arms around her. She whispered her thoughts, "This is as perfect as it comes, isn't it?"

Kodiak turned to her, licking one finger, then a second. "It sure is. Do you want a bite, also? I've never tasted better. If any fish have ever cooked up any more perfectly than this, I've never tasted them."

Carolina felt her spirits lift. They were on completely different pages, and she found that supremely endearing. She took the stick he offered her, and she lifted it to her mouth. It was every bit as good as he said, and the fish was perfect in every way: flavor, texture, and nourishment.

True to Kodiak's prediction, she did feel much better once her stomach was filled.

KODIAK and Carolina sat on the beach with the coals from the fire at their backs and the evening sun in their faces. Carolina snuggled next to Kodiak, and he had his arm wrapped around her for warmth. There had been no other people in the town, and the evening had been theirs alone.

Thursdays, Kodiak had told her. No cruise ships. Everyone takes the day off. Carolina was glad. However, the loss of her purse stymied her, and she couldn't let it go.

"Kody, I've wracked my brain. I cannot exist without my purse. It's like a third arm to me. I always have it at my side. I'm lost without it." She ran a hand along his leg, the fabric of his jeans thick to ward off the cold. She could feel the warmth of his body through the material, and it felt good to her exposed skin.

"You haven't been lost without it, Carolina. You've been right with me the entire time." He turned to her and smiled. "In fact, it seems to me, you've finally been found. If losing your purse will keep you found, then I hope you never find it." He looked back to the water, tightening his arm around her shoulder just for a minute.

Carolina sat up. "I remember. I rented the Jeep. I paid the man with money. I counted out three twenties, a ten, and a five. The money was in my purse."

Without turning his head, Kodiak said, "And, Carolina?"

She got up on one knee, and she looked Kodiak intently in the face. "I never took it out of the Jeep. I was so distraught and tired, I simply forgot. Then, you paid at the diner, and we went to your cabin. I had no need of it, and it never crossed my mind. Kody, it will have been stolen."

He sighed. "Stolen? Not here. If you left it, it's still there."

"But, the Jeep. The man will have taken it away by now. It's been a whole day."

"Carolina." He reached to slow her down. "That's a Jeep Tad Simmons saves to rent. He only drives it in the winter when the snow gets bad. Tad hasn't moved it since yesterday. If he has, I know where he lives. He won't bother your purse. He may not be good at filling the tank with gas, but he wouldn't bother anything a tourist left behind."

Stepping up off the beach, he led her to the place where they'd left the Jeep. Sure enough, there it sat, and when Carolina ran up to it, her purse was just where she had left it.

"Kody!" She reached inside the old off-road vehicle and pulled it to her. She opened it and glanced inside. She pulled out her sunglasses and laughed. "See? I have my own." She looked at him with undisguised glee on her face.

Kodiak smiled. "I'm relieved you located what you thought was lost. However, it was like I said. No one's bothered it. If it were left here a week, it'd go untouched. This is my town, and the people here can be trusted." He turned to look at the sun. "It's time to go. I need to get the plane home before dark."

"Kody," Carolina started, and she looked at him and hesitated, grateful to him for all he'd done, and aware of his disappointment. It was written all over him. However, they were in town, and she did have a cruise ship she needed to be on. "You said Claudine has a phone. Do you think she'll mind if I use it?"

He smiled, and it was tight and forced. "It's Thursday. Claudine will be at home. No one comes in on Thursday. However, I cannot get to her house without my truck."

Carolina looked at the Jeep just feet away. "The keys are

still there, Kody. I can leave the man extra money."

She had her purse. Carolina couldn't believe her good fortune. She'd leave the man all the money she had, if he wanted it.

She had her life back now that she'd found her purse!

TAD'S JEEP.

Kodiak struggled against the blackness threatening to consume him. He felt each thread of the past twenty-four hours as they snapped one by one. The purse Carolina was holding too tightly, that was what had done it. They'd been on the beach, and the fish had been cooking, and the day had been perfect. Then she'd remembered where she left that purse.

She'd seen Tad's Jeep as a solution. He saw it as the problem.

Without the Jeep and the purse it had held, she'd been his for one magical day. She'd eaten with his money, ridden in his truck, and slept in his clothing. All day they had done those things that were important to him, and none of her California life had been there to intrude. Now, here was this purse, this thing of leather and brass. It held items that were sure to pull her away from this life that wasn't really hers, and the idea of that unnerved him. He didn't know what else besides those glasses was inside, but he was sure this purse was not something he'd be glad she found.

He smiled through the unwanted tightness at his temples, giving in to the inevitable. It seemed to him the purse being lost was the magic that had kept this woman at his side, and the magic had begun to unravel the moment she'd remembered it was missing.

Now, though, he had to deal with Tad's Jeep.

"Carolina, trust means not taking a person's vehicle unasked. Besides, the sun looks high, but it'll start to drop quickly. We won't be able to make it to Claudine's and return in time to get the airplane back. I will not drive Tad's Jeep all the way to my place. In the morning, Carolina. We'll bring the truck in. Claudine will expect me then, anyway. Friday is when I usually come in to wash."

Then Kodiak remembered something else. He'd let the fish go, and he'd wished for Carolina's second chance. He wasn't a man who believed in luck or magic wishes, but he felt this was a good case for anyone inclined that way. He'd wished for luck for some unknown man, that boy Carolina had loved so long ago, and now she was no longer interested in him.

It was a long ride back to his float, and most of it was used up in pensive silence. Kodiak spent the trip looking out the windows, his sunglasses still on long past when they made it difficult to see. He wouldn't remove them, though. If he had, Carolina might have seen the moisture brimming in the corners of his eyes.

KODIAK tossed on his sofa. He couldn't sleep. He was distraught with the thought that this woman might have access to a phone tomorrow. In desperation, he'd imagined every possible solution he could come up with. Perhaps he could disengage the starter from the truck. She wouldn't know how to fly the airplane. She'd be trapped here. In time, her ship would return home, and she'd give in to her life with him. They could live together here. He'd built a good life in the time he'd been in Alaska, and Julianna didn't know where he was. No one would bother them.

Yet, even as he wrestled with his ideas, he could see the danger in his thinking. Julianna had tried to force him to be something he wasn't, and he'd struggled until he was free. Now he could see that very thing in how he was thinking of Carolina. He couldn't force her, but he didn't see how he could let her go. Together they were better than they were apart. In only one day he'd seen that. Surely she must, too.

He'd planned his hot water better this time. He told Carolina he'd be using the extra bathroom, and he'd shower early so she'd have plenty of water. The fire had burned down, and the house was cold, so she'd smiled and asked if she could sit on the porch and watch the last of the evening light. She'd borrowed a coat of his and wrapped herself into a rocking chair, still wearing his borrowed clothes. Her clothes were dry, but she didn't want to change. She wanted to save hers so they'd be fresh in the morning.

She'd waved away his offers of repellant, saying insects never bothered her. When he stepped out to head to the back of the house, she'd given him a puzzled look.

"My extra bath is out behind the house." Kodiak had grinned. In that moment, he hoped to rekindle the spark that had nearly taken them by storm the night before.

"You can't get to it from inside?" Carolina smiled, but it wasn't a real smile, not like the one from earlier on the beach. "Use the one inside. I won't intrude. I did enough of that last night." She looked down, her purse still at her side. "I feel better with this, although there's nothing inside I really need. A small amount of money, but not much." She looked up at him. "I can get you more to repay you when I get back."

His heart sank. It wasn't money he wanted. He wanted her. He smiled, telling her the inside bath was hers for the evening. Enjoy it, he said.

He'd brought a towel and clothes this time, and he even had his aftershave. After he stripped and stepped under the water, with the heat steaming around him, he leaned his forehead against the wall. He squeezed his eyes shut, pretending the water from his hair was the moisture running down his face, unwilling to admit to his tears. He had hoped for so much in the past twenty-four hours, and now she was pulling back from him. Eventually he turned the water off and looked to the sky, watching the stars overhead. Surely God cared enough to step in and keep Carolina here.

Finally, his skin starting to feel the chill, he laughed with a renewed sense of devil-may-care. He didn't know if it was that purse or that fish, or maybe inspiration from God, but this was not out of his control. Not yet. Purses could be lost again, and fish could be eaten. With renewed determination, he grinned and reached for his towel. He would put up a fight, yet.

Then he'd returned to the porch in the near darkness to find the chair empty, and stepping inside the house, the bedroom door was shut. Kodiak's wind went out of his sails, and now he tossed once again, and he couldn't sleep. His eyes turned to the door where he knew she was, and he knew there was nothing he could do. That purse had won. That, or maybe the fish. He didn't know which, but in that moment, he knew she was already gone.

Carolina would never be his.

CAROLINA watched Kodiak walk around the back of the cabin. She knew there was no bathroom there. She'd watched from the airplane, and she'd seen the outside platform where he showered. That was why he hadn't had his clothes with him the previous night.

She knew why he used that shower even when she'd offered the one inside. He didn't want to be with her. He'd been distant ever since she'd remembered where her purse was, as if she'd done something to offend him. She reached to the purse and pulled it into her lap. It was just a purse, and it held nothing important.

Perhaps he'd hoped she'd have money to pay him. She had a few dollars. She'd told him that, and that she would get him more. Yet, he'd still seemed uninterested.

She'd found her ID tag in her purse. Altessa Cruise Lines. They'd left her, and they hadn't even tried to find her. Shouldn't there have been *Missing Person* signs posted all over town? By the morning, it would be two full days. What did they care about one passenger who couldn't bother to get back aboard on time?

She held the card with her name on it. They hadn't even scanned it into the machine. The man had simply looked at it and sent her onto that small boat, almost as if he was glad for her to be off the ship.

She was drained. The sound of the shower in the night air carried over the cabin, and she couldn't bear to think of him standing on that platform, the steaming water coursing over his bare skin. It was torturing her, and as the evening began to dim, she could take no more.

Struggling to contain her tears, she stood and stepped inside the cabin. In the darkness, she stumbled into the bedroom and closed the door. She angrily dropped the ship's ID card into the trash can beside the bed. It was useless to anyone, and she didn't want to be reminded of the disaster this trip had turned into.

This time, she made sure the lock was securely latched. Then she took off Kodiak's outer clothing. As she stood there in the darkness, she rubbed the lightweight shirt and shorts she'd worn all day under his heavier things, and she knew she couldn't remove these. They were as close as he would ever get to her. With tears streaking her face, she thought of how he had jerked away from her the previous night.

"He probably thinks I'm ugly," she whispered, and with those words, she threw herself into the bed, stretching her limbs to suffer against the cold of the bedding. It was only a few moments before she drew her legs and arms up to curl into a ball. She stifled a sob as she listened to the sound of the shower outside. She waited to hear it turn off, but she was very tired.

She was already asleep by the time it did.

Chapter 13

CAROLINA wrapped Kodiak's thin shirt tightly around herself. The trees outside her window were brilliantly green in the morning light. It was certainly cold in the bedroom, and she really wanted to get dressed. However, she stood and looked at the door in front of her with dread. Her pants were hanging above the stove in the other room. So were her sweater and socks. She shivered, and she realized she couldn't stand on this floor much longer in her bare feet.

She reached and unlocked the doorknob. Carefully and slowly, she turned the handle and pulled the door to her. She blinked as the early morning sun slashed across her face. She was surprised even after yesterday to feel little warmth from it. At this early hour, her California sun would already be cutting into her skin with enthusiasm.

Stepping into the room, remembering the warmth that had flooded through the door the previous morning, she somehow imagined it would be warmer, but the cold was just as severe. She looked at the sofa to see Kodiak's back toward her, his torso uncovered, and the waistband of his shorts showing beneath the throw he'd slept under. She was surprised at the amount of muscle across his shoulders. His waist was very trim, making her breath catch in her throat. Asleep like this, she could almost imagine he cared about her. She knew that was all it would be, though, her imagination.

She stepped to the window to see the sun cutting through the trees. She glanced up, calculating. She knew the cabin sat at an angle to the water, and in the airplane yesterday she'd also been able to tell the shoreline was not aligned north and south. She'd been surprised to find the morning sun could cut into the house, and later, the evening sun could also give her a sunset, all from the same room. This brilliant man had wisely built windows into three sides of the cabin. He'd known to place his cabin to take advantage of the sun and to give him the best view possible. Even his airplane was there for him to see directly from his cabin windows. When she looked out the side windows, she was even able to find the old red truck.

Then she glanced to the tree still lying across his walkway to the dock. He'd been working on that, she remembered, before she'd gotten in the way. He was probably looking forward to her being gone.

When he didn't stir, she tiptoed up to him for no other reason than to look into his face. His eyes were closed, and her heart caught, stripped of last night's anguish. At this angle, with his jaw covered with stubble, and his face unmoving, she'd know these features to be the same as those from ten years ago. How two people could look so much the same, she didn't know. Different they certainly were, though. A continent apart and a lifestyle of difference. "All that you love, Kody, you keep close to you. I wish that could be me." She murmured her words, not wanting to wake him. As she finished speaking, tears leaked down her face. She wiped them, careful not to make noise, as she looked to the stove, realizing it needed a fire to warm the room. She chuckled at something else she just realized. She needed to use the bathroom, but it was too cold for that. It would have to wait.

Looking around, she remembered how he'd built the fire on the beach the previous evening, and she gently opened the stove and began to prepare. When she had the kindling stacked properly, and her igniter fuel in place, she reached to a box of matches. Just as she started to strike one, a voice startled her, causing her to drop them on the floor. She watched them scatter, appalled.

"Close the box," Kodiak said, his final word drawn out in a yawn.

She turned to see him sitting up, his hair askew, and his hands over his shoulders rubbing the upper portion of his back.

"This sofa gets to you after a while. Be glad you had the bed." He stood and let the throw slide off, one end of it landing on the floor. He glanced at her and pursed his lips before speaking again. "It won't start unless you strike the match."

"I'm sorry, Kody," Carolina apologized. "You were asleep, and I was cold."

"Don't apologize. At least I didn't have to build the fire. I think I will use the inside toilet this morning, thank you." He walked groggily into the other room, turning as he came to the bedroom door. "I'll start the truck after while. We'll get breakfast in town. It's Friday, and Marv's will be open." He turned and was gone, the bathroom door clicking shut unseen.

Carolina turned to look at the materials she had so carefully assembled. She'd prepared the fire because she was cold, but she'd expected him to at least show appreciation for her efforts. Thoroughly irritated, she picked up the empty matchbox and ran her hand along the floor, gathering up the scattered slivers of wood in her fist. She dumped them into the opened box, and taking one, she angrily dragged it along the striker panel. She threw it into the stove and watched it quickly catch fire. Closing the stove door, she muttered, this time not quietly at all, "There, and I didn't close the box. I hope your cabin burns down, Kody No-Name from Alaska. It'd serve you right." Then, she reached to grab the throw from the floor, and as she wrapped it around her shoulders, she began to cry.

"WHAT ABOUT the fire, Kody?" Carolina looked straight ahead through the windshield of the truck. It was still very early. Kody had said it was about six, and as tired as she was, she'd believe it.

"The stove is made to let burn, even when no one's here. Thank you for doing that. It gets old when you have to build a fire every morning. I'm glad to let someone else do it once in a while." He pumped the accelerator, and the truck roared into life. He flipped on the heater on high, although it hadn't warmed yet. He shivered. His coat was being worn by the woman sitting next to him.

"You're welcome," Carolina replied dryly. She also wondered how many other women had prepared his morning fires, or lit his nightly ones for that matter. She watched the truck climb up the slope she had ridden down in the dark two nights earlier, and she thought about how she'd never see this place again. She had to admit it was beautiful, a wonderful interlude in her life, but she had a phone on the way. Hopefully, if Claudine was as considerate as this man claimed, she'd also have a place to stay if she couldn't get a ride out today.

Passing the station where they'd stopped to get gas two days ago, she noticed a phone outside in a blue metal and Plexiglas alcove. "There's a phone, Kody. We could stop there."

He put his hand to his forehead and leaned his elbow on the window ledge. Without emotion, he replied, "Doesn't work. A tree took out the line in the last storm. Takes about six weeks to get a repair crew up. Took all summer the year my father died. I had to drive all the way into town just to take my calls." He rubbed his eyes. "We'll stop by Claudine's on the way in. You seem anxious to get to a phone."

Carolina could feel herself twisted up inside. She wasn't anxious at all. Yet, she was. It was her life to be connected, and yet this man had hooked her like a cocklebur on a dog. At this moment she felt like the dog, too. She didn't know how to fix this, either. He was going to take her to a phone and drop her off, and she would never see him again.

"Kody," she ventured.

He glanced at her. "Yes, Carolina?"

She hesitated, and seeing him raise his eyebrows, she tried again. "Could we go to Marv's first?"

"Claudine won't be there, yet. She's a night person. She's fine at home, though. Just ask simple questions, and you'll leave with both arms and both legs intact. Complicated questions? Just warn me so I can step outside first."

Carolina smiled at imagining that. She glanced over in hopes that the ice that had begun to form between them had broken, and was relieved to see his dimple had at least deepened. "Marv's first, please." Maybe they at least wouldn't part as enemies.

"Got it," he said, and they rode in silence the rest of the way.

CAROLINA set the purse on the seat beside her, trying to tuck it out of Kodiak's sight. She'd seen how he looked at it, as if it were something evil, something that was making his life miserable. She wondered if his ex-wife had carried a purse like this. Perhaps it triggered unpleasant memories. She shrugged at that. She couldn't control how he responded to a purse, for heaven's sake. When the waitress came up, Carolina stood to go to the ladies' room while Kodiak ordered.

The food smelled good when it arrived, and she anticipated

the eggs the waitress picked up to set on the table. Then they were placed in front of Kodiak. He looked at her with a hint of a smile, and the waitress placed a massive hamburger in front of Carolina. At her horrified look, Kodiak laughed.

"I promised," he said as he continued to grin. "Julie's in back this morning."

"In back?" Carolina frowned, at first not understanding.

"Cooking. You can't leave without one of her burgers." He reached over and pushed the platter her direction.

"Thank you, Kody." She shook her head at the size of it, but rather than argue, she decided to give it her best. After eating in silence and unable to finish but a portion of it, she was distracted by the sound of an unfamiliar phone. She looked around the room, glancing through the window as an equally unfamiliar Jeep pulled up outside. It was the ugliest vehicle she'd ever seen. She made a face before she caught herself.

Kodiak watched her, and without turning his head to look at what she'd seen, he grinned, leaning back and putting his arm on the back of the seat next to him. "I see Old Man Tuck's here."

Carolina looked at his face, glad to see an expression that wasn't the sour one she'd come to expect this morning. "Old Man Tuck?" She idly rotated the burger platter with her finger as she watched the strangely attractive man across from her.

"In the Jeep. About four colors, right? Mostly rust?" At her nod, he smiled. "Old Man Tuck. Shows up at this time every morning. Everybody makes that face the first time they see that Jeep." When the ringing started up again, Kodiak looked away and mumbled, "Aren't you going to answer that?"

Carolina looked away to see who he was speaking to, and then she realized it was her. She snorted at him, "Answer what?"

"Your purse. It's calling you."

She waved his words away. "Kody, that's a phone, and I have to have one for it to be ringing in my purse. I distinctly remember leaving my phone in the cabin on the ship. It's long

190

gone by now. Besides, you said cell phones don't work here."

"Satellite phones do. You have one? Your purse seems to think it does." He looked at her, the ringing still going on. Several other diners had begun to look their way, one motioning with his hand to his ear, and pointing their direction.

Carolina froze. Her memory crystallized, and she recalled stepping out to dinner with Mamie. The ship's satellite phone was there beside her purse, and she'd picked it up and dropped it inside so it wouldn't get lost. She grabbed her purse and began searching inside. Then, the ringing stopped. She looked up at Kodiak.

"Keep looking," he said. "Just because it quit calling you doesn't mean it's disappeared. It's in there."

Then, inside one side pocket she rarely used, one that was open on the top, she felt an unexpected bulge. With a sheepish expression on her face, she withdrew a small case with the words Altessa Cruise Lines in small letters across the back. It was gently beeping. She laid it on the table between them.

"I had a phone with me all the time." She looked up at Kodiak to see a frown deepen across his forehead.

"Did you know about this, Carolina?"

She'd never heard his voice so gruff, so hurt. She also heard the blame. It irritated her. Whatever was bothering him wasn't her fault, and she was tired of it. She snapped back, "Do you think I would have spent two days here if I'd known this was in my purse? I would have called the minute that old, broken down Jeep left me stranded. I would have been back on my ship where I belong. I'm just a tourist, remember? I'd be having dinner with Mamie, and I'd be adoring her Southern charm, not eating a burger that could swallow me, and doing it in an unfamiliar diner at the crack of dawn."

Kodiak watched her tirade. "Mamie, huh? Southern charm? That sounds like a very familiar person to me."

"How?" Carolina was looking at the phone, wondering if

191

she would have used it if she'd known it was there. Oh, she knew she would when that Jeep broke down. After she'd met this man? She looked at him only to find him staring at her, and she blushed. Would she have called last night while they were in town? At his cabin? When he was showering, and she was crying in his bed? She reached and picked it up. She wasn't sure, and she wasn't jumping to use it now.

"My grandmother."

"Your grandmother?" She looked up from the phone.

"My grandmother's named Mamie. She's the one thing I miss living up here. She told me once, 'You do what you've got to, and that means not giving up what you love. Never, never give up what you love.' So, I brought my airplane here, and that's my life."

Carolina chuckled to think there were two grandmothers out there called Mamie, but she hadn't really expected the one aboard ship was the only one.

"My airplane is funny?"

"No, that's not it. Something else." She smiled and looked to see Kody's Old Man Tuck walking into the restaurant.

"Then what?"

His tone was pleasanter, and she rubbed her hand over the phone, asking, "How many grandmothers out there go by Mamie? Two? A hundred?"

"Thousands, but none like mine." His eyes were red, and he looked out the window.

"Do you ever see her?"

"We all have rough spots in our lives. Let's talk about you."

"Perhaps my Mamie's the same as yours. Don't you want to talk about that?" She started to say that her friend was looking for her grandson, but she didn't get the chance.

Kodiak laughed. "My grandmother's not in Alaska, and no one in my family knows where I am. I'm sorry, Carolina. I'm not what you expected, am I? This is my home, Alaska through

192

and through. Backwoods to the bone, and I couldn't live anywhere else, even if I wanted. I'm off to the men's room. That beeping means you've got a message, you know."

Carolina watched him stand and walk across the room, feeling those familiar butterflies once again in her stomach, and she murmured, "No, Kody from Alaska. You're not what I expected. You've been what I needed, though."

As he walked out of her sight, she opened the phone and put it to her ear, not sure just what message it might have for her.

KODIAK stepped back into the dining room to see his table empty except for a check partially covered with several folded bills. He looked around, and Old Man Tuck motioned to him with a gnarled hand.

"Outside, boy. This one's gone on you, you know." Tuck's eyebrows drew together as his voice grew stern. "Don't let her get away." When Kodiak didn't move quickly enough, he motioned with his hand, "Go! Now! Don't waste your chances like I did, boy. Grab her, and I might even forgive you that danged airplane. Chances're not for wasting. Chances're for taking, that's for sure."

Kodiak waved at the old man, thanking him, but he paused as he stepped into the vestibule, thinking of Tuck's words. Carolina, gone on him? He'd have hoped, yesterday, but after last night, he didn't think so. He pulled his shirt around him and flung the door wide. It was still cold, even in the sun, and he shivered. He caught a glimpse of Carolina, and she was already sitting in his truck. He ran to it and climbed inside. She was holding the phone in her hand looking at it.

"Well?" he said.

She looked up at him, and her eyes were red-rimmed. It looked as if she was about to cry.

CAROLINA'S choices were being taken from her, and in fact

they already had. She'd so wanted this, to call, to be rescued, and now she didn't want it at all. She pressed her lips together without speaking. Reaching to the dash, she laid the phone there where they could both see it.

"Carolina," Kodiak began. "What is it? Is it your parents, or has something happened to your Mamie, perhaps?"

At the mention of her parents, tears began to run down her face. She'd told no one of them, and his casual mention of them caused her emotions to boil over. Kodiak slid next to her, and he wrapped his arm around her shoulders, pulling her close. He reached a hand to brush her hair.

"Was the news bad?" He touched her chin to turn her face to look at him. "Tell me, girl. I'm here to help if you need it."

She sniffed and choked out, "A helicopter, Kody." Then she just closed her eyes.

He pulled her close. "I'm so sorry, Carolina."

She pulled back in confusion, her voice sharper than she intended. "Why should you be sorry? I've been sleeping in your bed, and I've given you a backache on your sofa. I should think you'd be glad to get me out of your cabin."

"Were your parents involved in a crash?"

His question was very surprising, and now it was Carolina's turn to be confused. "Yes. How did you know?"

"You just told me. A helicopter." He made an expression as if that should be obvious.

"Helicopter crash? Kody! I did not say that!" She'd fallen back into her grief, but now she was perturbed, and her grief was pushed aside. "The phone message gave me a number to call. The ship's been trying to reach me for two days. I just didn't have the phone with me, so I didn't know. They didn't call last night because it was after nine. They started calling again this morning at seven. That was the call you heard. My cruise ship wants me back." She laughed when she saw his face drop. "Seriously. They're sending a helicopter to meet me at the

194

waterfront. My ship is scheduled to leave Anchorage this evening, and I can meet it if I go now."

"Carolina." He took a ragged breath before going on. "You'll break my heart and leave me heartbroken. As long as I thought I had a chance, I could hope. Now your cruise ship and your California siren have won out. However, you must know that I'll suffer greatly." He laughed, but his smile faded as quickly as it had come. "When? It'll be very soon, won't it?"

Carolina smiled, once more buoyed by his ever-present charm, and also by the fact that she was now reconnected with a more familiar world, that of her cruise ship and an eventual journey home.

"An hour. It'll ferry me to a high-speed transport ship to take me to Anchorage. The captain insisted they give my phone one last try before they left port." She looked at the morose face next to her and reached her hand to him, touching his cheek. "Kody, you've been the Southern gentleman I didn't know could exist in Alaska. Remember, we'll always have General Lee."

He laughed, turning his head to look away. "And Rhett." He shifted to look at her. "I've always been a gentleman, Carolina. You have an hour, you say? There's more I must show you." He opened the truck door. "Come, my Scarlett. Tara awaits."

Carolina smiled. Once again, this man had found the perfect way to charm her, and she wondered how he did it.

"I don't mind if I do," she quipped as she climbed down, realizing the sun was finally beginning to pull the chill from the morning. She turned and placed Kodiak's coat inside. "Take my hand, Rhett, and let's take the grand tour."

Kodiak smiled, and he did just that.

"WHEN A STORM rolls in, this part of town will actually vibrate," Kodiak intoned. He was being very melodramatic, and Carolina found him exceptionally entertaining. "It's like one of those movies where the old Victorian house is perched at the top of the cliff, and there's a huge squall. Then the camera cuts to a close-up of the house, and with each crash of the sea, the shutters shiver and the windows rattle in their frames. It really is like that here when the storms roll in off the open ocean." He turned to look up the steep incline behind them where a roof could be seen just at the top, and he grinned. "Except our Victorian is really an A-frame the owner refuses to stay in except during the prettiest of weather."

Carolina looked out over the channel where it cut into the cliff face, and she could actually imagine the water from a storm funneling itself into the narrow chute. She pictured it pounding at the apex of the gorge like the hand of a great sea god demanding to be let through.

"Your cabin, Kody. Is that why it's so far up the hill?"

"My father chose that spot. Remember that spit of land? Solid rock. It acts as a breakwater and cuts most of the storm's fury before it hits shore." He nodded to the area in front of them. "Here's where I surfed."

Carolina looked at him in a new appreciation. "You actually did that? Here? Seeing this is impressive. I can also see why your board now hangs above your stove. It feels it can never get warm enough ever again."

He looked at her with mirth in his eyes. "You may be right. I know one thing. I made a fool of myself in front of the whole town." They stood, watching the surging water in this one part of the ocean as it struggled in and out of the slender opening cut in the rock.

"You, a fool? I never heard such a thing." Carolina smiled as she glanced at him.

"I'd do it again, too, if you'd stay to watch. I miss it." Then his uncharacteristic and very brief moment of melancholy broke, and he smiled at Carolina. "Except the cold. Even with my wetsuit, I really thought I'd die out there."

He turned and began to walk with Carolina back toward the town. "California, what do you do there? Something certainly seems to be drawing you back, and when I think of Los Angeles, I only know what I've seen over the years on the news." He looked directly at her for a moment, pausing. "It is Los Angeles, isn't it?" When she nodded her head, he continued, "Riots and carjackings. Lots of concrete, and it's always hot. Am I close?"

Carolina chuckled. "Pretty much, except the heat. Sometimes it cools off. Just sometimes. However, my boss's daughter was killed last year in a carjacking. He thinks of me as a substitute."

"Is that good?"

"Mostly," she whispered, remembering the tense meetings, the anger Mr. Warner had sometimes thrown out at his employees since his daughter's death, with only Carolina understanding the grief behind it. Then there was his understanding generosity when her own parents died. "It has its bad points and its good."

"Like life." Kodiak stopped and looked at Carolina as she turned to him. "May I put my arm around you, sort of as a last time?"

"I'd enjoy that. Tell me something of you."

"My mother. She's the reason I'm here."

She laughed. She was giddy with him this close, and she could feel a silliness stirring inside, the butterflies trying to fly out. "I understand all about that. In California, we call it reproduction. Remember? We were tempted our first night together."

He paused and smiled. "My mother always loved Alaska, even before I was born, and she died before my father could buy a place here. That's why I love this so much. When my father died, he was here. He'd come up for the summer, and we knew it was his last one. He said she was here with him, looking out over the ocean. Then he was gone. I have a part of her as long

197

as I stay."

"And you say your family doesn't know you're here? How could they not know? I'd know."

"You would?" He chuckled, pulling her tighter for a moment. "Only my dad and I knew about this place. It was our secret, for my mother. No one else needed to know."

"That's sweet."

A distant whup, whup caught their attention. Off at sea a speck could be seen in the sky, and they both knew what it was. They pulled each other tighter, knowing this was Carolina's rescue from the accidental stranding that had brought them together. Her ship had deposited her here, and this helicopter would carry her away, tearing them apart with a finality that couldn't be undone.

As they walked, tears came into Carolina's eyes. She knew the upcoming separation would be no simple breaking apart. Even in her moments of frustration, and she would say it, anger, she knew this was the man she should spend her life with. He was the one she could enjoy a lifetime alongside and never regret a moment, and she felt a hollowness inside at the thought of boarding that machine coming in over the waters that bordered this wild land. It was a prison machine, coming to take her back to the jail that was her life in California. She'd never seen it as a penitentiary before, but Kody and his wonderful Alaska had opened her eyes to a reality that had always been invisible to her.

She paused in her steps, and Kodiak paused with her, looking down to see if she needed anything. She just smiled and looked out to sea. She needed him, and she needed him to ask her to stay. Not beg. No, she wouldn't want that from him. Just to ask, to let her know he felt the same as she did. If she could pause here, give him time to ask her, then she could send that infernal machine back to its home somewhere else, and it wouldn't take her away from him.

Then Kodiak smiled at her and whispered, "Your ride, Carolina. You don't want to miss it." He looked down at her empty hands. "And don't forget your purse this time."

After he completed his gentle admonishment, he placed his right foot in front of him, and he pulled her forward. Then there was another foot in front of that, and another, and another, and Carolina could no longer think. He was taking her to give her up. He wasn't asking her to stay. He didn't want her to remain with him, and that was all she wanted. She didn't want her ship or Mamie. She didn't care about her home in California or her job at the company.

Carolina wanted Kody.

She wanted to be at his side, riding in an old, rusty truck. She wanted to look out from her window each morning to see the ocean and an airplane floating on the water, and when the mornings were cold, she would fix the fire in the stove to warm her man before he arose from their bed.

Yet, he was still walking, and he was taking her to send her away, and he didn't care that she was being ripped apart in her heart. She tucked her head even closer to his body so she could hide the tears she couldn't stop, and she walked with him, and she refused to look to the water to see the thing that was coming to take her away.

Chapter 14

KODIAK stopped on the side of the road, pulling his truck into the exact same spot where he first met Carolina two days before, and he leaned to the far window. He spoke the words he'd spoken then.

"Ma'am. Can I offer you a ride?"

He watched a beautiful girl turn to him with frustration written across her features. The afternoon sun caught in her hair, and her skin was fresh with the Alaska summer day. He looked into her eyes, and he could see deep into the depths of the love that had grown in his heart in just two days.

However, he knew there'd be no answer. She wasn't really there. She was in her magic flying carriage that had come to carry her away over his beloved Alaska seas, and he'd never see her again. He closed his eyes as he sat in his truck, and after a moment he took a deep breath.

Perhaps it was the determination of a tough, Alaska life, or perhaps it was a Southern stalwartness that prompted him to open his eyes and drive on. Perhaps it was the rush of pure Alaska air that poured into his lungs.

Kodiak thought it was none of those things. He felt a great emptiness, and he knew he had nowhere to go. He just knew he didn't want to be there.

THE BREEZE flowed over the spit of land protecting Kodiak's airplane from the ocean's upcoming winter fury, that mighty fist of destruction that could come crashing on the shore at a moment's notice. Today it swept gently across the water where his dock hugged that dividing line between land and sea. Finally, it reached tenuous fingers through the trees to wrap a gentle touch around the cabin perched on the side of the rise. On the porch sat a man, and he was wrapped in the coat Carolina had last worn in this very chair, and the breeze wasn't felt at all. If it weren't for the garment being filled with the smell of the woman that consumed his mind, he'd be sitting with no coat at all, and his arms still wouldn't feel the cold. He stared ahead, and he felt nothing but emptiness.

He'd tried to step into the cabin. It was his home, one that he'd built with his own hands. He'd lived within its walls, and he'd loved this place. Yet, every step, every chair, and every surface within the space screamed Carolina to him.

The light grew dim, and the buzzing of the insect population assaulted him. With frustration, he finally drew his legs up and stood. He stepped inside the door and paused in the dark. He smelled the scent of that wonderful, painful woman still embedded in his private world.

He knew he really just smelled his cabin, but she'd been there, and she'd built a fire. It was cold, now, but the ashes were from wood she'd placed inside with her own hands. He drew in the smell of the smoky residue left from the stove, and he knew it was his Carolina. He walked forward, reaching to the matches he could just see, and he smiled to find she hadn't closed them as he'd asked. He reached and placed the box on a shelf, still opened the way she'd left them.

He walked to the bedroom and dropped onto the cold sheets. His eyes traced the shadows of the propeller hanging high on the wall. He reached a hand and ran it over the bedding. She'd lain here, and she'd pressed her body to these sheets. She'd looked up, and her eyes had rested on the propeller. It was one he'd built. It was old, and it was new. The central hub was metal, and it was old. He'd found it, and he'd cut and carved the blades his first year here. It had given him something to do that first cold winter, and he'd liked it when he was finished. Knowing Carolina's eyes had seen it made it new and special to him.

His sense of loss overwhelming him, Kodiak flung himself from the bed. He knew he had to act or die, and many of his choices had been taken from him. He hadn't been able to hold Carolina. Her purse, that hated purse, had rung, gathering her helicopter to her, and she was on her ship in a world he didn't want and couldn't chase. Julianna had him trapped here, and until this moment, it had been a trap of most exquisite beauty. Now, it was a trap keeping him from going after Carolina.

Kodiak reached to his bed, and in one motion, he flung the bedding to the floor. He'd sleep on nothing if he couldn't share it with Carolina. His eyes caught the shape of his sofa through the door, and his quick, sudden anger deflated. He couldn't even sleep there. He'd remember how she held him, and how she told him she respected him.

He could do one thing, though. He could return his life to the way it once was, and he could do his best to try to forget. It would take time, but then what else did he have?

Kodiak kicked the bedding to the side, knowing he would take it to town tomorrow. He grabbed each item she might have touched, and he moved it, set it at a different angle, or dropped those he could do without into the trash can. He worked rapidly and with sure motions in the gathering gloom. Then, he carried those items he'd been able to dispose of to one of his burn barrels and dropped them in. He'd set them alight tomorrow, and his world would be cleansed. Tonight he'd sleep on the floor, and he'd be uncomfortable. He wouldn't notice, though. What was discomfort to his body when his heart had already been ripped out and carried away?

Gathering himself in the cold, his body still clothed in the wrappings he had worn all day, Kodiak curled up beside his bed. As he turned, his back pressed against the bed frame, and it seared him with the flame of heartbreak. It was where she'd slept, and he'd let his love get away. This time, he didn't fight the tears, and he remembered an old, treasured woman from many years before who'd loved him very much. He hadn't followed her advice, and now he was living with the consequences.

I'm sorry, Mamie. I couldn't hold her. I let her get away. I'm so sorry, Mamie. I'm so sorry.

He lay on the floor as the room grew colder, and his sobs gradually muffled into ragged draughts of air taken more and more slowly. Then, his exhaustion complete, Kodiak felt his senses fade until sleep finally overtook him. Even the hardness of the floor couldn't compete with his need for escape from the broken heart that still beat steadily inside his chest.

CAROLINA wrapped her blanket around her and looked at the covered platter at her side. The air on the open deck was cold. The food had also grown cold as she sat there, and she hadn't touched it.

She couldn't bear the thought of eating.

She glanced at the lights of Anchorage twinkling against the hills rising in the background. Another time, she would have seen them as beautiful, the shimmering of fireflies in the dimming mist of evening. Now, it was just another place in a land that could never be hers, and she couldn't care.

She held a new ID pass in her hand, and she thought of the one she'd imagined she'd never need again. It was gone now, thrown away, and it didn't matter. Her life was the same, gone, taken from her with the phone call that had pulled her back to this ship.

She thought of the man she'd held in her arms, and she felt the claws of despair stripping her soul from inside of her. She'd touched his hand, and she'd kissed his face. She'd let him hold her, and she'd let him send her away.

Once inside her cabin, she'd thrown the hated phone across the room. Mamie had seemed so glad to see her, and her steward had apologized profusely. Even the captain had been there to welcome Carolina back aboard, although he had also let her know the responsibility for the cost of the transport back to the ship would be borne by her. She'd nodded, telling him the cost didn't matter. It seemed to Carolina that each handshake had been enacted from the motions of necessity. She'd smiled at gray faces, and she'd walked gray corridors. Then, in one burst of brilliant fury, she had thrown the phone across the room, and it had disappeared somewhere on the far side of the bed.

She couldn't even bear to have her purse in her sight any longer. She'd longed for it when she'd known it was missing, and somehow, when it had returned, Kody had started his long journey away from her. She'd seen his looks and heard his words. The purse had driven them apart, and Carolina didn't know why.

She heard the sliders open, and the warmth of the cabin washed over her. She didn't care, and she kept her eyes on the view that was receding as she watched.

"My dear," a sweet voice spoke, and in her gray world, Carolina knew it was one she could trust. When a gloved hand pressed to her shoulder, she reached and grabbed it, releasing herself to the turmoil roiling inside.

"Mamie," she sobbed. "I couldn't hold him. I wasn't strong enough, and I let him send me away." She pressed the gloved hand to the side of her cheek as her tears soaked its surface.

"Who, dear?" Mamie slowly and gracefully settled herself onto the chair next to Carolina, never releasing the grasping hand. "Who sent you away?"

Carolina could hold it in no longer. "Kody," she wailed, as the old woman reached to wrap her arms around the tearful younger woman.

Mamie patted Carolina's back, and then she reached to push the hair from her tearful face. "Now, tell me, Carolina." She smiled gently. "Who is this Kody?"

Carolina sat up and snuffled, suddenly aware of the intensity of the impending cold. She focused on her confidant, and she felt compelled to tell it all.

"He rescued me, Mamie. I was on the side of the road, and he was there, my knight in shining armor." Carolina laughed at the absurdity of it all, the old red truck not shining at all, and remembering her frustration with the old Jeep. "He was an angel. He bought me dinner and flew me in his airplane, and Mamie, I think I fell in love with him."

Mamie's look turned stern, her brows furrowing to valleys, and she spoke to Carolina very sharply. "Then why are you on this ship? If you love him, you should be back there with him."

Carolina froze, stunned. She wished someone had told her that before she'd boarded that helicopter to return to the ship. Then she sagged with the realization that someone had, and more than once. Sha'Cretia. Precious Sha'Cretia had told her that very thing. Not in those words, of course, but it'd been the same. Mamie, too. She just hadn't listened, and now he was gone.

"Tell me about him, my dear." Mamie looked longingly to the room through the sliding doors. "Would you like to go inside where we can be more comfortable? I do want to hear it all, every word, too. Inside, my dear Carolina?"

Carolina's Southern graciousness jumpstarted her into action, and she moved to assist the old women into the heat. She could hardly wait to start her story.

"Mamie, he was an Alaskan pilot with the charm of a Southern gentleman. We joked of General Lee. I was Scarlett, and he was Rhett." Carolina was filled with a level of vitality that had been absent since returning from her sojourn.

Mamie chuckled. "You must have spent quite some hours with him, dear."

"Oh, there's one thing I must tell you." Carolina gave the old woman's arm a squeeze. "When I told him of you, he said he had a grandmother named Mamie, and you sounded just like her."

Mamie pursed her lips at that. "What did you say his name was again, dear?"

"Kody, Mamie. He has a cabin in the woods and a shop in town." She laughed. "I never got to see his shop. I have no idea what he does there." She laughed. "He surfs, though. Here in Alaska. On a board I've only ever seen in the Low Country."

Mamie's eyes perked up, and she pressed the younger woman. "Low Country, Carolina?"

Carolina laughed. "Carolinas, like my name. Kody called me Carolina from California, and I called him Kody from Alaska. Mamie, he took me fly-fishing in his airplane, and the fish he caught for dinner, I made him turn loose."

That brought a smile to the old woman's face. "He must love you, too, Carolina. He must, indeed."

"Why do you say that, Mamie?"

"My grandson, you know the one I told you about? He loves to fly-fish. His father taught him. He'd have to really love someone to release a fish that was intended for dinner. I tell that grandson of mine, hold on to what you love, because it may never come your way again. My dear, you really should not be here on this boat, you do know that?"

Mamie's eyes turned to the cold dinner plate still outside on the veranda. "Dear, have you eaten anything since coming back aboard?" When Carolina shook her head no, she clicked her tongue and stood. "I'm going to get that steward in now and give him a piece of my mind." She crooked her finger at Carolina. "We might just save those brocade draperies, yet."

KODIAK stumbled into his living room. He reached one hand under his shirt and rubbed the flat of his palm over his ribs where the leg of the bed had pressed against them during the night. He blinked into the glare from outside and ran his hand over his hair. He yawned. Looking outside, he squinted, noting the fog that had moved in, nearly obscuring his dock and airplane.

The cabin did feel better after a night's sleep. He remembered his frenzied reordering from the previous evening, and he found he was able to walk the floor this morning without being hit by the dreams that had attacked him so vividly the night before. His bedding would have to be washed. He wouldn't be able to sleep there without remembering Carolina, not without laundering the linens first.

He realized he was a day late for Claudine's machine, but he didn't think she'd mind too much. Sometimes he worked for her around her house while his clothes washed. It was a good trade, he felt. Claudine's house was kept in good repair, and Kodiak had clean clothes to wear.

He thought of his burn barrel. He knew his sanitizing of this woman from his life would not be complete until those reminders were also gone.

He peered through the wall of windows that opened onto the porch. Glancing down, he cried in frustration, "Flaming bear turds! Not again!" His trash was spread across his property. He threw open the door and ran outside. He slipped down three wet steps in his bare feet before he could catch himself, and he scrambled back inside. He found his shoes where he'd kicked them off in the night, and he slipped them on, hopping toward the door as he did so.

"Bear turds," he cursed again. "For this alone I'd move back to Hilton Head and face Julianna. All bears should be shot when they do this."

In his anger, all Kodiak wanted was to be left alone. He saw himself as maintaining a successful history of obliterating bad experiences from his life—Julianna had been one—and in his sudden frustration at the mess the bears had left in his yard, he was determined that this new woman would be gone from him with her exit. His night had been a bad one, but he was a man of action. If she didn't want to stay with him, he wouldn't let her memory destroy everything else in his life.

However, that didn't mean he didn't care. Expunging this woman meant he would have no patience for anything else. He wouldn't be easy to live with for a time, and people would have to deal with that.

Now, this. Bear turds, and flaming bear turds at that.

He took the steps down to the grass two at a time. Reaching the bottom, he stopped. The debris was everywhere. The marauding animals that did this must have had a heyday for half the night. It would be a good half day just cleaning this up.

He sighed. It did no good to complain, and he reached for the first piece of trash, knowing this time he wouldn't wait before burning his garbage. It would be gone before the bears could come back to dig through his barrels again.

Then, that woman from California would be gone from his life for good.

Chapter 15

"MAMIE?" Carolina touched her friend's arm. The noise in the dining room was subdued, but there was a lot going on, and Carolina was enjoying that. She was surprised how much of a release it had been to share about Kody the previous evening. It made it much easier to deal with, having someone else who knew, someone she could talk to. Even this dinner was something that she was finding pleasant.

Mamie turned to look at Carolina, and she smiled. "Dear girl, it's so good to have you back at my table. I've missed you so. I want to talk to you about that young man and his surfing, you know."

Carolina smiled. Her shipboard companion didn't miss a trick. "Mamie, you mentioned brocade draperies yesterday." It was the same as the unusual quip Kody had made to her, one specifically tied to General Lee, and more specifically, to a particular movie she and Kody had a shared interest in. It seemed unusual someone else would mention it, also.

Mamie put her hands in her lap and dropped her head. "I was amiss, dear. It's something in my family that we say, just among close relations, you must know, although certainly I don't mind sharing it with you." She laughed. "It was said in the way of encouragement, and I shouldn't have used it without an explanation." She smiled and reached to pat Carolina's arm, and her expression changed, becoming very bright. "Did I tell you I came here to find my grandson? Well, I've found you instead. You're almost as good a discovery, my girl."

Laughing, Carolina thanked her for her gracious remarks. "Yes, you did tell me about your grandson. The brocade draperies, though. What did you mean by that?"

"Oh, my dear, it's most complicated. However, it seems we have all the time in the world, don't we? You see, before my daughter died, she had this movie she loved. You're from the West Coast, you told me, but you may have heard about it anyway. It's a very old one." Mamie nodded as if this were a minor film that had only gotten a small, cult following. "It's also very Southern, telling a story we in the South know well. In the movie, one of the characters has lost all her finery due to a war, and she makes an elegant dress—from velvet draperies, I think. Anyway, she fools no one. At the end, the man she professes to love has had his fill of her shenanigans."

By this time, Carolina's eyes glowed. She knew this movie, and it was the very one she and Kody had shared. How could she not know this storyline? She enjoyed watching the old woman share it with her, though, and she let her continue.

"Well, dear, at the end, this man stands at the bottom of the stairs and finally gives her a piece of his mind, and he does it in no uncertain terms." Mamie looked up with a smile as she finished. "When he does, my grandson and my daughter would always quote the line with him."

Carolina whispered, "It's Rhett, isn't it?"

Mamie's eyes twinkled. "You know this movie. You should have stopped me, dear."

"No, I couldn't have. I enjoyed your retelling. Tell me, Mamie. I don't understand about the brocade part. The draperies were velvet, I believe. Why brocade?"

"We've changed it a bit. The only thing Scarlett has left after the war, the one thing she can use that's important to her, is her draperies. Everything else is gone and we always say to save the brocade draperies." Mamie laughed. "Oh, there's our waiter." She raised a gloved hand to signal him their way.

"That's what Kody said to me," Carolina murmured, looking at her empty plate as it glimmered in the overhead lights. "Kody said General Lee would save the brocade draperies."

However, Mamie's hand had worked, and their order was arriving. She motioned for Carolina to hold her story for a moment.

"Finally we have food, dear." Mamie shook her napkin into her lap. "Now, what was that you said? Your young man said to save the brocade draperies? That's what my Kodiak always likes to say."

At the sound of her grandson's name, Carolina raised her head and gave the old woman a sharp look.

"Remember," Mamie continued, "never let go of what you love. It may never come your way again. That's what I always tell my grandson. Now, where did my napkin go?" She looked around, finally seeing it in her lap. "Oh, there it is. Doesn't this look good, my dear?"

The food distracted Carolina from Mamie's words, and she was definitely hungry. In addition, this time she didn't have to eat it off a stick.

KODIAK rested his hands on the rim of his burn barrel, looking inside at what he'd collected from all the way up the driveway. The wind must have really picked up the previous night, because there was more back in the trees. The bears had never done that before. He'd already cleared all he could find down to the water. Now he wished he'd put his gloves on.

His hands were filthy.

He looked up at the sun high overhead. The day had finally warmed, or maybe it was his too-heavy shirt and traipsing up and down this slope chasing after remnants of garbage. His shirt was also stained from the things he'd carried back to the barrels, and he sighed. He'd once again missed his washday at Claudine's, and tomorrow he needed to be back at work at the shop, clean clothes or not.

Hot, and no longer caring if his hands made the shirt worse, he pulled it over his head and threw it to the ground.

Kneeling down to pick up the burnt end of a stick, his back catching the sun, his thoughts were pulled back to his and Carolina's night on the waterfront. He'd taken her fishing earlier that day, and she'd pleaded with him to let his catch go. He smiled, and he remembered the earnestness of her plea. He'd not seen the sense in it. It was just a fish, and one he'd worked for some time to recapture. However, her face had swayed him, and the fish remained for him to again one day tease onto his line.

Then, they'd had flown into town. He'd known no one would be there, and he'd wanted to have her all to himself. She'd been so pleased with his impromptu meal. They'd sat there, and he'd felt the warmth of the fire at his back. Just for that glorious meal, for that beautiful moment, she'd been his forever, content to spend her life with him in his remote, Alaska retreat.

He reached up to brush an insect from his neck, rubbing away the perspiration. It was the height of summer, and the days could be warm, even this far north, but Kodiak knew his sweat wasn't moisture from the sun's heat. This was frustration from a man who had missed out on an opportunity that had been thrown across his path, and this was a man who had started to love and then let that love escape.

This perspiration was his need for Carolina.

He straightened his back, drew in a deep breath, and squeezed his eyes shut. Then, he opened them and looked out across the water. Wishing wouldn't bring her back to him, and what ifs didn't matter. He couldn't undo what was done, and his property still was not cleared.

Stepping into the trees, he reached to pick up a scrap of plastic, wadding it in his hand, and then off to the side, he saw the packaging from some sort of food. Kodiak grabbed it, too, and gripped it with the plastic. Out of the corner of his eye, he caught a flash of white several trees over. He walked toward it, unsure just what it might be. It seemed too rigid to be food packaging, and he didn't remember having thrown away anything like this.

He knew his trash.

He knelt to pick it up, and before he could touch it, he saw the letters there. They spelled out words that he knew. Altessa Cruise Line. It was the name of one of the ships that stopped in town, the same name he had seen on Carolina's hated phone. Other letters were across the bottom, but they were hidden in the grass.

His heart pounded. It had to be Carolina's, and it brought her back all over again. A bear had chewed the card, destroying one end, and his heart stopped. He touched it, hoping beyond hope that her name hadn't been chewed away.

Kodiak pulled the card from the ground, and he turned it to the back to find a black strip. He knew what was in that black strip. It was Carolina, or at least all the cruise line knew about her. It was in the magnetic particles that were turned this way or that, and it was all that she was. He also knew he had no way of getting at that information. Not only did that require a machine to read the magnetic particles, but the bears had chewed the end of the strip.

He looked at the name on the card, amused to see that it didn't name her as Carolina from California. This was the first time he'd known her last name, and he ran his fingers over the words. Carolina DeAngeles. Carolina of Los Angeles. Caroline of the Angels. He laughed to himself. He'd believe that. She'd certainly been an angel to him, one of beauty and charm. California had finally outdone itself and produced an angelic vision of Southern loveliness and grace.

For some reason, the image brought back his memories of that girl from so long ago on the Savannah tarmac. She'd turned into a dream of his, one that had chased him through a marriage and a divorce. Over the past two days, she'd become one with Carolina. He didn't know but that the dream was part of the reason for the divorce.

Maybe that was why Carolina had run from him.

Kodiak stood, slipping the card in his pocket. He'd keep her with him, even if it was just in this card. He'd burn the rest, because the bears would come again if he didn't. However, this card he would hold on to, even if he never met her again.

Chapter 16

"SEE?" CAROLINA held the ID card up. "You can't tell the difference."

Mamie reached inside her shirt and pulled her card out. "Around your neck, my dear. On a cruise ship, never let it get far from you." She'd already shamed Carolina for throwing her first one away. She had done it with a smile and a wink, but she had shamed her nonetheless.

Carolina laughed. She was feeling better, almost as if her sojourn to the Alaska coast had never happened. At least that's what she told others, and when she was awake, it was even as if it were true. At night her pillow told a different story. However, it wasn't night, and the day had many hours left in it.

"Mamie, I was no longer on the cruise ship, and I thought I'd have to find my own way home. That's why I threw it away. I was so disappointed in what had happened, with being stranded, that I simply threw it in the garbage. You see, though,

I didn't have to worry." She turned the new card in the light, letting it flash across her friend's breakfast plate. "The steward was very conciliatory, and he just whipped up a new one." Carolina knew she was being too effusive, and she knew that Mamie knew. However, she couldn't stop her continual talking and her overly bright manner.

"Carolina, dear." Mamie spoke straight to her with no waffling in her tone. "You may grieve for your young man. It's to be expected. It's the same grief we expect to endure when we face a death. He's died to you, my dear."

Carolina closed her eyes and sat very still, then she spoke very slowly and with exaggerated control. "I have faced a death, Mamie. In fact, I've faced three, and I never should have come on this trip." She looked at the older woman, feeling the need to reveal the reason she was on the ship in the first place. "This is my parent's cruise, Mamie. They were killed only weeks ago, and this cruise would have been forfeited. Kody, that man who helped me, was my lifeboat for a moment, and you're right. He's died, too. At least it seems that way."

"My dear." Mamie reached a gloved hand to rest it on Carolina's arm. "How horrible!"

Carolina forced a smile on her face. "You've been a godsend for me, Mamie. For the rest of our journey, go and look for your grandson, and then sit and talk to me, and tell me what you've found. Let me be overly vibrant, and we'll get through this trip. I don't know how I'll grieve, but I will, in private, if possible."

Mamie cleared her throat. "Dear, I am here for you. That grandson will find me when he finds me. It's you who are important now. Why, when that boy was twelve . . ."

Carolina smiled. Mamie would be just what she needed, that she could see. She laughed at the antics of the grandson, and for some reason they reminded her of her Kody. She knew she must be finding similarities where she wished them to be, but in the stories the two were one and the same. The Alaskan pilot and the small boy with his paper airplanes. That dimpled smile that had split Kody's face in two and the small grandson's infectious grin. A man's Low Country surfboard and a boy playing on a warm, sandy beach.

The first two Carolina could be forgiven for missing, but later she would wonder why she'd missed the third. Mamie couldn't have been any clearer, and neither one of them knew.

THE SHIP'S horn blared its farewells, and the cruise line's dock felt strange after the weeks spent aboard the ship. Mamie held Carolina's bare hands in her gloved ones, and she leaned in to kiss her on the cheek. "My dear, you be careful. If your man from Alaska really loves you, he'll come and find you."

"You're so kind, Mamie," Carolina responded, not really believing her friend's assurances but appreciating them anyway. "I'll look for him. More importantly, if your grandson comes home from Alaska, you send him to me. You have my address. From your stories, I've come to love him as much as my Kody." Impulsively, she grabbed the old woman in a quick hug.

At the sound of a car, Mamie pushed her away with an admonishment. "Your taxi, dear. You'll miss your plane. We must go when the skies demand. Toot!" Then she called as Carolina closed the door, "You'll be in my prayers!"

With a brush of fabric on leather seats and bags stowed carefully in capacious trunks, Carolina was off, and the plane was ready to load. Before boarding, she did look out the terminal windows to see if her boy was there looking for her, but it wasn't that smooth-faced youth from Savannah she hoped to find. It was Kody's face she looked to see, and once again, Carolina began to wonder if they hadn't become one and the same. She needed Mamie's prayers. She felt in her heart that she truly did.

CAROLINA couldn't help but compare the dichotomies in Kodiak's airplane and the giant behemoth in which she now sat. She brushed her hand along the tops of the leather seats, and she felt the air pouring from the air vents over her head. She reached up and twisted the nozzle, turning the airflow on and off, and swiveling the head to aim in various directions. Then she thought of sitting in that small airplane against that Alaska dock, and she remembered the fish Kody had thrown back for her. He'd climbed in the plane as it had sat on that unnamed lake and smiled. His dimples had creased his face, and he'd reached to her.

At first she thought he was going to wrap his arms around her. She'd glanced around the cabin to see if there was actually room for them to be intimate in the confines of the craft, and she'd wondered why he hadn't already approached her on the shore. They were in the wilds of Alaska, and there was no one to watch. She'd been amused at the time, and she'd even thought, except the bears.

Then, with his face pressed nearly to hers, he'd reached, or so she thought, to brace himself against the door on her side of the small craft. All the while, her brain had continued to calculate the possible success of this endeavor. With a quick motion, he'd pushed a lever, and fresh air had rushed over her. She'd flushed with his closeness, and the air had felt good. Kody had smiled, thinking she was pleased with his contribution to her comfort, and she'd touched his hand as he pulled it away.

She touched her hand where it had brushed Kody's, and she wished he was back with her. She wished it desperately.

"There you are! I knew it was you. I was late, and I was checking in when I saw you go through security; but I knew it was you. I hurried so I could get a seat next to you. Look! I'm flying First Class, and I wasn't bumped up, either."

Carolina looked up to see a very pretty girl standing by her seat. She smiled, trying to place her.

The girl laughed. "Blackface, remember? My grandmother and John Barrymore?" The girl glanced at the flight attendant as she whispered to Carolina, "My seat is two rows up, but I told the man you were my mother. Do you mind if I sit here?"

Carolina felt her smile turn a bit sour as she nodded. At least the girl could have said she was her big sister. Oh, well. It was just a flight on a commercial jet, and she had no one for company, anyway.

"Here, let me move my things."

"It was really my great-grandmother in blackface, you remember, but I usually just say my grandmother." The girl smiled and touched Carolina's hand. "That was great, what you said, you know. That about blackface? You see, the people in L.A. called me up. Me!" The girl was beside herself, and Carolina involuntarily felt drawn to her exposé.

"I'm so pleased for you. That must have been very exciting." Carolina put her elbow on the armrest and rested her chin in her palm. Perhaps this trip wouldn't be so tedious after all. She could let herself be distracted by this girl, if it kept her mind off Alaska.

"By the way, my mother was very unhappy with me. I told her about you, you know, and she said I should have given you my name. She said you might be someone important." The girl froze. "I don't think I was supposed to tell you that. Do you mind?"

Carolina smiled, and sincerely this time. "Mind about what? I didn't hear anything."

"Really? I was sure I said it out loud. Anyway, my name is Angela. Angela Caroline Ritchey. My friends and family call me Angel. You can call me that. Would you?" Angel smiled as if she really wanted this total stranger to call her by this familial nickname.

"Sure, Angel. I'm Carolina. How are you doing?"

"I'm fine. Do you have a last name?"

Carolina sat back and laughed. She realized she'd asked similar questions of Kody, and how patient he'd been with her. She would have to be very longsuffering with this girl.

"Yes, I do. It's DeAngeles."

"Cool," the girl said. "You're Caroline of the Angels, and I'm Angel Caroline. I learned that in my classes at school, what Angeles means. That really does make us like mother and daughter, doesn't it?"

Carolina leaned her head back and smiled. "I guess it does, Angel. I guess it does."

The flight attendants interrupted with their safety procedures, and the conversation ceased for a while. However, once the airplane was underway, Angel resumed her interrupted rendition of the events that had overtaken her life since she'd seen Carolina last.

"You know, I was telling you about that blackface thing you said. Well, that's why I'm going back to L.A."

Carolina turned to her, momentarily off track. "Blackface?"

"You remember? With John Barrymore, the old, fat actor. Well, when the studio called," and she grinned at Carolina, "they asked me what I meant by coming from a family of actors. It wasn't really a studio, but nobody else knows. It was just that face commercial."

"A hundred germs, or maybe a thousand on every face." Carolina knew she was way off.

"That one! The girl who called wanted to know about my forms. You see, I had checked that I came from an acting family. I told them acting was in my blood." She leaned her head back and smiled. "I wrote it that way on the form, too. Acting is in my blood. I said it just that way, and they liked it. When they asked me what I meant by that, I remembered what you said." She turned to grin at Carolina. "I said my grandmother was in blackface with John Barrymore." She giggled, causing Carolina to smile at her. "Imagine. Blackface with John Barrymore.

Anyway, she said I had credibility, like it was a disease, but I think it's a good thing. And they want to shoot a commercial with me in it."

Carolina touched Angel on the hand in genuine pleasure. "For the face medication. That's nice."

"No." Angel seemed surprised that Carolina would think she would do a commercial for the face medicine. "For nail polish. They said I had such good hands in my screen test. I'm going to be a hand model." Angel held her hands up to show off her manicure. "They paid for this, even told me where to go to get it done, and they said to be careful not to mess it up. I have gloves they told me to wear, but my nails look too pretty to wear gloves, don't you think?"

Carolina looked away to hide her expression and rolled her eyes. This girl was just too much. Then she looked back and smiled.

"Yes, Angel. They are very pretty, indeed."

KODIAK wiped his hands on the red shop towel he kept in his pocket, and he looked at his truck's transmission. It was lying in disassembly, and his airplane wasn't anywhere near. This was the reason he'd endured that excruciating shift to third gear over the past year. He had to drive his truck to the shop to work on it, and when he had his truck in, his aircraft was at the cabin. He didn't like the idea of asking someone to ride out with him to drive the truck back. Doing so would provide him transportation while his truck was torn down, but then he'd have to repeat the operation when the repairs were done.

No work had come in today—or was expected—so this had been his chance. He'd torn into it with a vengeance, too. He hadn't been kind to his tools or to the nuts and bolts he'd wrestled them against. Then, there had been the rust. His truck was old, and the rust had been everywhere. Spray this to break the rust. Spray that. Then he was forced to endure the rust as it

221

dripped over him in liquid form.

He'd caught glimpses of his face in several of his tools as he'd grimaced in his efforts to move uncooperative nuts from their grip on equally stubborn bolts. He wouldn't want to know himself. He was angry and filthy, and he wasn't being pleasant.

He also didn't expect to find any pleasure in the end result of this repair. He'd know why he'd torn his truck apart, and he'd be reminded of it each time it shifted smoothly into third.

It was Carolina, the woman whose card he carried in his pocket. That was the reason for this transmission repair, and she was the reason he was yanking the parts around as if abusing them could make his heart feel better. He had to work her out of his system.

"Boy."

The voice interrupted Kodiak just as he pulled his flywheel free, and he dropped it to the concrete floor in frustration. "Sheesh!" he called out, the sound echoing in the interior of his shop.

"Don't know that that'll bring her back."

Kodiak burst out in anger, "Flaming bear turds! Bring who back?" He turned to see Old Man Tuck standing just inside the door, a hand resting on Old Red's bumper. He watched a grin grow across the old man's face.

"Got that out? Cause fixing this transmission's not the cure for what's gotcha throwing your tools around." The old man limped toward Kodiak. "You didn't even tell her who you are, did you?"

Kodiak turned to glare at him. He hadn't even heard his old Cherokee drive up.

"What do you mean?" Kodiak reached to pick up the flywheel, and he turned it to inspect its condition.

"You know this girl from way back. I can see that, boy. I watched you and her. There was a spark there, and it wasn't a twenty-four hour spark, either." Tuck walked right up to Kodiak and reached a worn hand to the flywheel to run a finger around the edge, feeling the metal as if understanding the condition of this one part of the boy's failing transmission might tell him something about the person who drove it.

"I had me a woman," Tuck started. "Bet you didn't know that. Lost her, too." The old man paused.

Kodiak watched him, giving him his say, the anger from his own frustration not enough to force him to slice it across this old man. He could see tears in those old eyes.

Tuck continued, "No, I misspoke. I didn't lose her, son. I let her get away. Sometimes I feel I drove her away. We loved each other, too." Then Tuck laughed and turned to the open shop door. "Passionately. You wouldn't know it in this old body, though. There were no children, and I wouldn't chase her when she was gone. I really think she wanted me to. I wouldn't. I always knew I was right, and she should've stayed."

He turned to look at the younger man he was loading up with advice. "Now I'm old, and I'm alone. My pride be damned, because it's all I've got. I wish I had her back, boy." He sniffled. "No, I keep saying what I don't mean. I wish I'd gone after her. That's what I should'a done. Curse this beautiful land they call Alaska. I should'a gone after her."

Kodiak stood with his flywheel in hand. He knew the old man's pain, and he loved this land, too. He also loved his Carolina Low Country, and this girl who'd hooked his heart was from neither. He didn't love California, and Los Angeles least of all.

The old man definitely had one thing wrong, however.

"Tuck, what do you mean about knowing this girl from way back? I just met her the day her ship left her." Kodiak's frustration had been sapped by Tuck's story, and he knew the old man was right in one thing. He should be chasing after Carolina as hard as he could, and he would if it weren't for Julianna. At the same time, he was mystified. How could he have known Carolina before? She was from California, after all, and it was her first trip to Alaska.

The old man paused, and then he spoke, using the boy's name, marking this as something special. "Kodiak, you've got a head on your shoulders." He chuckled. "Except where surfboards are concerned. You're young, too. Think of her face. She's pretty. You'll remember. Just let it run around in your brain. She'll be there, and you'll know. When you get it figured out, go get her, boy. Bring her back, or stay with her wherever she is. Just don't become me. You won't like yourself if you do." He stepped outside, calling back, "My Jeep's down the road a bit. Died and won't start. Give you a ride home if your transmission's not fixed by dark."

Then Kodiak was left alone. The only girl who came to his mind, and he'd already thought about this part, too, was that girl from Savannah. She'd been headed to Hilton Head, and she'd been there in his dreams ever since. The only thing was, he could no longer recall her face. When he thought of her now, it was always Carolina he saw. Tuck had to be wrong about this. They couldn't be the same, not a continent apart.

Kodiak shook his head. He reached and grabbed the tools he thought might help him get Tuck's old Cherokee back on the road. He looked at his transmission strewn across his shop. He just might need that ride home, and the old man couldn't give it if his Jeep wasn't running, could he?

Chapter 17

"MR. WARNER, you've been a dear." Carolina patted his hand. Sometimes she noticed she did that, and she wondered where she'd fallen into the habit. It wasn't something most Los Angelinos did, except Sha'Cretia. Then, Sha'Cretia wasn't like most Angelinos.

Carolina thought of her mother and smiled. She remembered her reaching her hand out to touch Carolina when she'd wanted to let her know she cared. To others, too. Carolina's brother. Her father.

She looked up from where she was standing over her boss's desk to see a glittering set of fingernails ripple and flash through the doorway and disappear. Sha'Cretia! Carolina returned her focus to Mr. Warner. "I'm so pleased to be back at work, sir."

"Just you go easy." He glanced at the door and smiled. "Now, I think Sha'Cretia needs your attention. Go."

Stepping outside into the relative privacy of the hallway,

Carolina was immediately grabbed by two manicured hands. Before she could even greet her, she was wrapped in loving arms and then released. Sha'Cretia ran one long finger next to Carolina's eye.

"Girl, I expected to see happy here. This looks like a sleepless night." Then she stepped back, holding Carolina at arm's length, while shaking her skirt fabric back and forth with one free hand. "What do you think?"

Carolina narrowed her eyes and thought for a moment, unsure what she was supposed to think. She pursed her lips as if in serious thought.

Sha'Cretia prompted, "Well?"

"Sha'Cretia! Is that my mum's Versace?" Carolina laughed. "Oh, I am so pleased. You've brought me my first good thought since returning. I've missed you, Sha."

Sha'Cretia grabbed Carolina's hands and pulled her forward. "To my office, girl. I have to know all the news. Where's that man I sent you after? Did you bring him home packed in your suitcase?" Once in the office, Sha'Cretia pushed Carolina into her chair, and she sat on the desk, crossing her legs and swinging one foot back and forth.

Carolina reached and grabbed the foot. She chuckled. "Are these new shoes?"

Sha'Cretia reached one hand behind her head and moaned seductively, "Klein. Just call me Calvin." Then her face broke into a grin. "At the discount mall, but don't tell. They match the suit perfectly. Now, this man you didn't bring home. I know when a look says there's a man, and you've got it. Now give."

Even thinking of Kody couldn't destroy Carolina's brightened mood at seeing her good friend. She'd tell her enough to satisfy her curiosity, but what she really wanted was to forget every bit of it. It had been no more than a botched Jeep adventure, that was all. Kody had been there to rescue her, and he helped her get back to her cruise ship. Nothing else.

Carolina told more about the old woman with the Southern roots who was looking for her grandson. She shared the stories of the grandson as a boy, and she laughed as Sha'Cretia laughed with her. Later that evening she realized she hadn't been picturing a small boy when she'd shared Mamie's stories with Sha'Cretia. She'd been picturing a face she knew better, and somehow it seemed that the grandson and Kody were one and the same. She had colored the grandson in with her memories of her two days spent with the man of her dreams.

Carolina tossed that night, and she didn't know who she dreamed of. Part of it was the boy she'd seen so many years ago, and part was her Kody from Alaska. However, the next morning, she distinctly remembered Mamie's grandson twisted up in her dreams. As she readied herself to go to work, she knew one thing with crystal clarity. All three men had eventually become one and the same, and that was very unnerving to her.

But she wasn't in love. Nothing like that. She'd been rescued, and she was grateful for it, that was all. As she'd discovered, being rescued on a remote Alaska road was a very big deal.

However, that didn't make it love.

KODIAK trudged along the street. His shop wasn't exactly in town, and he'd been forced to walk to the diner. He wasn't all that clean, but he'd done his best. His hands and face were at least wiped as well as he could get them. He was hungry, though, and Claudine would let him pay later. She knew she would get it back in work around her house if Kodiak was short of funds.

As he approached, he looked up at the sign. Marv's. The sign was old, and the severe winter weather had aged it even more than would seem possible. The neon blinked, and Kodiak could hear it buzz.

Alaska. Marv's. Alaska had even changed the name of the

diner. The last two letters of Marv's name hadn't worked since before Kodiak's father had come up. In a storm, they'd come loose and later were taken down. Now Marv was the name everyone knew the ex-owner of the diner as, even though the menus still said Marvin's across the top.

Kodiak had avoided Marv's since Carolina left. There were too many memories involved. Now, however, he was hungry, and Old Man Tuck's car wasn't completed.

He hoped Claudine would let him pay later.

He stepped to the door and pulled it wide. The aroma of food assaulted him, and he was overwhelmed. The offerings here at the diner hadn't smelled this appealing since Claudine and Marv had split.

Kodiak smiled when he saw Claudine.

Claudine didn't smile back. She lowered her head and looked at him over the top of her glasses. "Kodiak, where have you been?" She reached to an empty chair at her side and pulled it out. "No one's at this table, and now it's yours." She jerked her eyes to the chair and back to him. "Sit."

Kodiak's smile fell from his face. He wasn't sure she was glad to see him, and he knew that couldn't be good.

"Yes, ma'am." He slid into the seat.

She barked at him, tapping the table, still looking over her glasses. "If it wasn't you, Kodiak, I'd slap your mouth off for calling me ma'am. You and your Southern ways. See these glasses on my face? Well, I see you, boy. The trouble is, you've not seen me. Missed you on laundry day last and the week before. Let me smell that shirt." She pulled his sleeve to her nose. "Phew! Tomorrow morning, I want you at my place, you hear me? Pile all your clothes in the back of that rust bucket you call a truck. Show up early, too. I've got my own laundry to do."

Kodiak meekly pointed out the flaw in her plan. "My truck's torn apart in the shop, Claudine."

"Well, you see that it's fixed today. If not, see that Tad

Simmons. I know you put gas in his Jeep that time for that girl, and you never asked Tad for a dime. He owes you for that. Better than seeing him, you just take his Jeep. Don't you dare go ask, either. It's sitting right out there. Two weeks no one's wanted it, and I'm not surprised. Keys are in the ignition like always. You drive it away, and I'll tell him where it's gone." She pulled a pencil from behind her ear. "Now, what can I get you?"

Kodiak grinned with relief. She wasn't angry with him at all. "Um, Claudine. It smells really good in here today. Is something special on the menu?"

Claudine looked at him for a moment with her lips pursed. Then she winked at Kodiak. "Marv's in the kitchen."

Kodiak's eyes widened. "Marv? I thought he was persona non gratis."

Claudine snorted. "Non gratis? You and your big Southern words. Is that like au gratin?" She whipped out a chair, surprisingly agile for her size and age. Sitting on the edge, she leaned in toward Kodiak. "You and that girl got me thinking. You two looked at each other like me and Marv used to before we busted up over that little bimbo waitress. You know me and Marv were sweet on each other when we were kids? Then I went off to beauty school in Anchorage, and Marv fished for a few years. One day we were both back in town, and when we saw each other, it was like fireworks." She looked back at the kitchen door where Kodiak could occasionally see the bulk of a man moving back and forth, obviously intent on preparing a meal. "Took us a week rubber-banding off each other to remember we knew one another, too. I saw that in you two kids. The moment you two walked in, I saw it. Have you figured it out, yet?"

Kodiak was hungry and lost, although mostly hungry, and this was the second time he'd heard this today. The first time had been from Tuck, and now he was getting it from Claudine. It wasn't something he wanted to discuss. He hunkered down in his chair. "Figured out what, Claudine?"

She looked wide-eyed at him as if he were the densest man she'd ever met. "Why, who she is, of course. She's not just that pretty girl you kept out at your place for two nights. She figures in your past somewhere. She was special to you, too. You've just got to figure it out."

Claudine stood and pushed the chair in. "Eggs and sausage, you say?"

"I didn't."

Claudine nodded, the look obvious and exaggerated. "I know you, though, boy, and you need that girl. Get it figured out before she finds someone else."

Kodiak watched as she walked away, and when she stepped into the kitchen to attach his order to the line, she reached over and gave the bulk of a man a peck on the cheek. Kodiak was lost with all the stories he'd been getting from everyone, but he was pleased to see that. With Marv back, he knew the quality of the food would improve. He wouldn't have to wait for Julie to come on duty to get a good burger anymore.

CAROLINA sat at her desk, the whole of Los Angeles spread out before her, distracting her from her thoughts. She knew she could stand and close the blinds, but she couldn't bring herself to face the interior of her office alone. At least with the blinds open, she could imagine she was sharing her world with the millions of Angelinos out there.

She picked up a pencil, wood specifically ordered with real erasers. She never sharpened them. The erasers made it easier to flip through the stacks of reports she had to organize. Opening one folder, she pulled a number of papers out. Picking up her pencil, she idly flipped up several of the loose sheets. Normally, the information in these reports would catch her attention, and she'd be occupied for hours. Today, though, her focus was broken constantly by thoughts of her home.

Her parents' home.

The paperwork had been forwarded to her office while she was gone. It was on her desk hidden by all these files, but that didn't mean it was gone from her thoughts. The new deed was there. Scrawled across the middle was her name alongside her brother's. Carolina. Edward. The names that had been erased from the records were the ones that broke her heart.

And they would never be there again.

In her emails to Edward after their parents' deaths, he'd been distraught, wanting to know about the funeral, the house, and their father's business. Liquidate it all, he'd suggested. Not yet, she'd pleaded, although selling the business might be the wisest thing, she'd finally conceded. Done, he'd replied. He'd sign the house over to her, and share the proceeds from the dealership.

California was her life. She'd become the right hand to one of the most important men in the California electronics industry. She'd helped Mr. Warner through the most difficult time of his life, and he thought of her as a daughter. Her best friend worked at her side, and still, Carolina could no longer find herself here. All she wanted was her home. She stood and walked to the window, brushing tears from her eyes. She didn't even have her Rotten Ricotta Cheese any longer, and right at that moment, he was the one she missed most of all.

All she wanted was to be back in Hilton Head, and she wanted to sit in her window seat. She wanted to see a father throw a small girl a Frisbee, and she wanted laughter to fill the air. She wanted to be those people on the beach, laughing with her father. Then she wanted to run to a campfire, and she wanted her mother and brother to tell stories. The stars would be overhead, and their thoughts would be one. Life would be as it should be.

When Sha'Cretia had come in on her break, Carolina showed her the new deed to the beachfront house. They hugged, and they even cried a bit. Sha'Cretia had her own memories there, and she'd been very fond of Carolina's parents. She'd miss them, she told Carolina, although she knew Carolina would miss them even more.

As Carolina looked out over the city, she owned up to why she was really having trouble focusing at work, and why her identity in her job had become slippery. Yes, it was her parents, and it was the home that they would never visit again, and it was a pet that she loved in spite of all its flaws. Yes, it was those things that were bothering her.

There was more, though.

There was a man who had stopped on the side of the road and spoken magical words to her. *Ma'am. Can I offer you a ride?* It was the graceful lilt of a Southern voice calling her to a home on a distant shore that was no longer hers. It was a dream of a boy who had turned into a man, and he'd brought his golden hair, his dimpled cheeks, and his strong body with him.

Later that night, Carolina tossed in her bed, and her body threw vibrant sensations at her. She felt the heat in her skin, and she remembered the places he had touched her. She also remembered the places she had wanted him to touch her.

In the darkness, she awoke, and her sheets were soaked with sweat. She listened, and outside she could hear that rare summer stranger pounding on her roof. Lightning flashed, and her windows were lit with the fire of the heavens. Her bed vibrated with the thunder that rolled across her beloved city, and Carolina knew what she was. She was alone, and she hated all helicopters. They came, and they carried away. Then they never returned what they'd stolen. She'd been stolen from her Kody, and she would never see him again.

She lay wrapped in her sheets, and she closed her eyes, listening to the thunder crash around her.

She was alone, and still, the storm raged on.

KODIAK pulled the throttle out and idled his airplane to a stop, letting it glide the final few feet to the float. He climbed out and snugged it up to the cleats. The sun was bright once again. It was better than the rain that had pelted the coast for two days. It was cold, though, and he snapped the top fastener on his jacket. It would be warmer away from the water, and he ran up the ramp to the dock. Climbing the ladder to the street and ducking into Koko's, he turned to see a television flickering in the corner. He didn't get much news being so cut off out at his place, so he watched it occasionally when he could.

A weather report came up on the screen, and a red band scrolled across the bottom.

"That's great," Kodiak mumbled. "Probably an early fall storm blowing in. If we're getting snow this early, I'm not even close to ready." He still hadn't cleared the tree from his walk. He hadn't felt like getting anything done. The rain had been his excuse. Missing Carolina was the reason. He glanced out the door and muttered, "And I'm half an hour from home."

He stepped forward to watch the report.

"The storm is tracking to the northwest at forty miles per hour, and it looks to hit somewhere along the Carolina coast. Earlier models suggested North Carolina and the Outer Banks. However, the latest Storm Track Predictions are indicating a hook left with a direct impact on Hilton Head."

The report continued, but Kodiak's mind was frozen. He watched the symbols and the numbers indicating a Category 5 hurricane. He knew not much survived anything above a Category 3. As the image ran the predictions over and over, Kodiak was startled to feel a hand clamp down on his shoulder. He turned to see Koko standing there.

"All of them down there say life's hard up here." She shook her head at the images. "I wouldn't live there for the world. Anyone there's as good as dead. Be glad you're in good old Alaska, U.S.A. At least here, your house is safe from that." She nodded at him and walked away. "Your order is on the counter, Kodiak. It's only the electrical harness. I'll send the alternator down tomorrow." She paused and turned to him before going into the back of the store. "Oh, that new chain for your saw came in. I put it with the harness. I'm eating lunch in the back. Just leave a check." Then she was gone.

"Thank you, Koko," Kodiak replied, turning his head back to the television, unsure if she heard. He was chilled inside, and it wasn't from the air outside. He was chilled, because he realized something. He was in Alaska, but he was here because he'd had nowhere else to run. This was his safe haven, and it had become a good life. However, his home was the place he'd left behind, and the place he'd left behind was going to be destroyed by that storm.

His thoughts were of Mamie. He had to check on her.

He was glad Koko was in back with her lunch, because he felt a sense of desperation in what he'd seen on that television. He'd recently lost one love, letting her slip through his fingers, and it had sapped the life from him. He couldn't bear the thought of losing someone else close to his heart.

Chapter 18

"THE BEACH. You would not play Frisbee today." The voice on the phone was clear, then it would cut out, and Carolina would suddenly hear it again. "Your Rotten is just fine. He has not chewed up any new furniture today. However, your mother would turn over if she could see the one he chewed yesterday. I would like to make an appointment to have his teeth filed off. May I do that?"

Carolina smiled. Margarete was no-nonsense tough, and she'd take care of Ricotta until Carolina could return. She'd love him, too. "No, I don't think so, Margarete. Perhaps we should just get new furniture when the old is so chewed it no longer stands." Over the phone Carolina could hear something hit one of the windows, and then the barking of a dog's voice filled the background. "Margarete, are you sure everything's all right there?"

A pause preceded her answer. "For now. For now." She

could be heard calling to the dog to quiet down. In spite of Margarete's reassurances, Carolina was concerned. She'd been watching the weather predictions. The storm had started in the Atlantic off the coast of Africa, and she'd watched daily as it crawled slowly west, taking out several small islands in the Bahamas. It had grazed Cuba, and everyone had feared for Key West.

Then the storm had turned.

Carolina had also watched the damage reports. There had been those that had cried into the cameras, and the water had been seen flooding the streets. One report that had especially touched her was the picture of a little girl standing in the mud at the bottom of a hill. The remains of her house were in the background, and she was in what was left of her yard. Her arm was wrapped around the neck of a dog that looked very much like Ricotta, and Carolina's heart had cried out.

Now the reports showed the storm was not going to expire helplessly in the middle of the Atlantic. It had changed course and was headed angrily toward the Carolina coast. That was the reason she'd called Margarete. Then she'd heard the storm over the phone. Now she was afraid for her.

"Margarete, you must not stay in the house. Take the car and go inland."

Margarete was resolute. "Your father built a good house. I have secured the windows, and no water is coming in."

Carolina began again, "The storm. It'll get worse, Margarete. You must be safe. Do you wish Ricotta to suffer?"

"He is warm and safe. Be assured of that."

"Ricotta, Margarete. Please think of him."

"Miss Carolina, where will we go? The house is not leaking, and it has never had bad things happen to it before."

"Savannah. No, that's not far enough. Macon. Augusta. No, Margarete, you'll never make it. Savannah. Go to Savannah. That's just an hour away. A high rise hotel. Tall, Margarete. The

236

Marriott Riverfront. It's on General McIntosh. Do you know where that's at?"

Margarete laughed. "Miss Carolina, I know your father's Cadillac. I know OnStar. I will find it. I will go for you."

Carolina let out a sigh of relief. "Thank you, Margarete. I'll call and have you a suite ready. I'll also get Ricotta approved. You don't know how much better this makes me feel."

Her housekeeper snickered. "You do not know how much better this makes *me* feel. Someone else can clean up after me for a change, and the dog will not be able to chew any more of your mother's furniture."

"Go quickly, Margarete. Just go."

"I am getting the keys now. I will pack a small bag and be on the way. Do not forget to call the hotel. Ricotta must be welcome, also."

Carolina laughed. She would call the hotel, and she would pay whatever it cost. She had the money now that her parents were gone. She couldn't handle any more losses, and she'd seen the reports.

This storm was going to be bad.

SHA'CRETIA bundled her things and dropped into the taxi. It was the weekend, and she could no longer stand it. Everyone she knew was following the storm. It was on the opposite coast, so normally it would be academic at best. However, she'd been hearing the latest reports, and she must talk to Carolina. She'd give her a ring, but she'd been out shopping all morning, taking call after call, and now her phone was dead.

It was time to give that girl a visit.

Reaching her destination and pulling her things out of the taxi, she went to close the door and realized she'd forgotten one small package. She called to the driver, "Sweetie, my hands are full. Would you put that on my finger?"

The driver rolled his eyes and reached into the back seat. He hooked the package on her proffered finger and held out his hand. "Twenty-two fifty."

Sha'Cretia paused and looked at all her packages. She smiled. "If you don't mind reaching into my pocket . . ."

The driver laughed. "I'll wait."

Sha'Cretia ran to Carolina's front door, dropped all her packages, and pushed the doorbell. Her hands free, she reached into a pocket and slipped a five and a twenty out. Holding it high, she ran back to the taxi with a grin on her face. "I brought just enough. Keep the change."

The driver fingered it, then he wadded it into his fist. "Thanks!" He rolled up his window and was off, leaving Sha'Cretia alone on the curb.

She ran to the house to find Carolina already at the door with a tissue in her hand. When she saw Carolina's red eyes, she threw her arms around her.

"Baby, you already know."

Carolina pushed her away. "Know what? Just stay well, Sha. I'm fighting the flu."

"Oh," she said, backing away. "I don't want that." She turned to gather her packages. "You do have the news on, don't you?" She dumped all her things onto a settee just inside the front door.

As Carolina closed the door, she sighed. "I'm sick, Sha. Come in and make me some tea."

"With some tasty bourbon?" She purred the words, sounding seductively wicked.

Carolina fluttered her tissue and laughed. "You just make it. I'll drink it. However, if you want bourbon, you'd better call that taxi back. I have none in the house." Reaching a chair, she fell into it and closed her eyes.

"It was just a thought." Sha'Cretia kicked her stilettos off and ran to the television. "Honey, I'm turning this on. You find the news channel." She grabbed the remote and placed it into

Carolina's hand. Then she disappeared into the kitchen.

"Sha," Carolina called. "Do you need any help?" She started to get up when Sha'Cretia's face poked through the door.

"No, you don't, girl. I spent some extra time here when you left for your cruise. I know my way around your kitchen. You just lie there and let Sha-baby take care of you."

Carolina smiled and picked up the remote as Sha'Cretia disappeared again. She called, "Is it the storm you want me to see on the news? Margarete and Ricotta are already in Savannah. They're on the sixth floor. They'll be okay."

"You don't know, then." Sha'Cretia brought a cup of steaming tea in and set it by Carolina's side, then placed one for herself by a separate chair.

Carolina laughed, reaching her hand to run it through the steam rising from the cup. "This is the fastest cup of tea in the West."

Sha'Cretia gave her a mock look of hurt for a moment, then she broke into laugh. "Learn to use your microwave, sweetie. Life is too short to do everything the long way. Now, turn that remote to the news. You'll be absolutely devastated."

Carolina first found CNN, and she watched for a moment, sighing, as nothing looked interesting. "There is no news, Sha."

"The Weather Channel will have it. Now, Carolina."

She looked at the remote and pressed the correct buttons. Then the real story began to write itself across the screen. Even as bad as she felt, Carolina sat up as the news began to tell of storm tracks and warnings to those who were still on the island.

Even Savannah was under onslaught.

"Where did you say Margarete's staying, sweetie?" Sha'Cretia sipped her tea.

"I didn't. The Marriott."

Sha'Cretia gasped. "The Marriott's walled in glass. Oh, sweetie, please say you didn't send them there. No place in Savannah is safe as long as this storm terrorizes your childhood home."

Even the newscaster felt the same. Her very next words said that those who had stayed were already dead. No one within a mile of the ocean would survive.

Carolina looked at Sha'Cretia. Her face was pale, and as her fragile façade finally shattered, Sha'Cretia reached for her, and she was the best friend a broken heart could have. She did what needed to be done, hugging Carolina until her tears were gone.

KODIAK held the card. He sat on his porch and watched the sun as it crawled toward the horizon, and still he held the card.

It was as beautiful a week as he'd ever experienced on the Alaska coast. It had been bitterly cold at night, and the days had been crisp. Soon he'd have to cover his windows and hunker down for winter, but he knew he had weeks, yet. When those weeks began to wind down, then would be the time the shop would keep him busy for days on end as people decided repairs could no longer be put off. Radiators couldn't be topped off as they leaked, and hoods could no longer be raised to jiggle flaps in old-fashioned carburetors. Not when the cold really set in. Then Kodiak would be so busy as to forget this card he held in his hand.

Not today. He'd gotten his surfboard down, and he'd checked it for damage from the heat of the stove. There was none. It had been well made, and he was glad. He'd paid handsomely for it when it was built, and then he'd paid handsomely again when it was shipped to him. As he was pulling it down, he'd thought of Carolina and her West Coast knowledge. Longboards. Shortboards. Surfboards. He'd laughed, and then he'd wanted to stand with her on this board, teach her his Carolina surfing, and take her to his favorite Carolina haunts.

He sighed. She wasn't here. He could dream, though. Now, having seen the weather reports for the East Coast, he could only hope his Low Country home survived, for in his heart, it really was his home, and if it were gone, so were his dreams. His Carolina dreams. His dreams of Carolina. Carolina from California. His dreams of taking Carolina to his Carolina.

Kodiak closed his eyes. He was stupid with the thought of losing her, and all he could think of was how he'd let her go. He raised the card to his lips and held it there, as if that would bring her closer to him.

He turned at a sound from the trees, one that surprised him enough to jerk him out of his melancholy. It was that of a car. He had a visitor, and he had so few, he honestly didn't remember the last one.

He stood and slipped the card into his pocket, correcting himself. He remembered the last one, but none before that. Even his propane tank was something he hauled to town in his truck and hauled home again. His homemade winch for lifting it was something he was proud of.

This visitor in the gathering gloom idled slowly down the driveway in Tad Simmons' Jeep. Over the years Kodiak had repaired it and put gas in it, and when he saw it, his heart jerked in his chest. In that moment, he felt hope. Carolina had driven it once before, and she knew the way to his cabin. Perhaps she'd come back to him.

Then the door opened, and he knew otherwise. It was Claudine. He waved, and he smiled, but he felt deflated and defeated. Carolina wouldn't come back to him, no matter how long he waited.

His visitor walked up the treads to his porch one heavy step at a time. She called out breathlessly, "I've never seen a face so unhappy to see me as you, Kodiak." She gave him a look. "You still haven't figured it out?"

He put his hands in his pockets and rocked on his heels. "Yeah, Claudine. I think I've figured it out. I just don't know what to do."

She snorted. "Then it's not figured out, *Kody*."

He looked at her sharply. "Why'd you call me that?"

She laughed. "You never did tell her who you are, did you?" She motioned, "Can we go in?"

"Not much warmer inside. No fire, Claudine."

"Got fuel for the generator?" He nodded. "Got light, then." Claudine pulled out a stack of newspapers. "Want you to see these."

Inside, Kodiak snorted sourly, "Why's it so important to tell her who I am?"

She sat and pulled Kodiak down across from her. "Kodiak, a lot of us come up here to get away from something. Then we just never go back. Sometimes there's nothing to go back to, and other times what's back there scares the devil out of us. I know you, boy, and I like you. Might even say in private I love you, but I wouldn't want anyone else to hear that." She shot him a sharp look, and he grinned at the unexpected display of affection. "One thing I know, you've run from something, and you've run far. Koko told me about you and the news on her television. She saw you try to hide it, but she's sharp. Your accent, too. I put two and two together. I just came from Juneau. Got the latest news, some just in from Anchorage. Tad let me drive his Jeep out here, and yes, I asked him. Marv's got my Rover." She looked at the papers in her hands. "See this."

Claudine opened her papers and spread them out. Kodiak's eyes were riveted. There were front-page pictures of the devastation. Homes underwater. Downtown Savannah inundated. Roofs peeled from buildings. Piers in the process of collapsing.

Kodiak reached forward in shock. These were the places of his boyhood. His mother had walked those streets. His father. He'd attended that school, and his best friend had wrecked his car right there. That house burning to the waterline, it had belonged to a friend of Julianna's, and before the bad times,

242

they'd spent fun weekends there. Then one picture showed a glimpse of a church through the trees with water everywhere. Holy Family. He would know it anywhere. His grandmother had taken him there as a boy.

Then came the pictures of the airport. Kodiak paused, and his fingers touched the images. He looked for a long time at the destruction. He saw something from his past, something that haunted him still. He saw a girl, and the girl he saw wasn't a girl at all, but a woman, one who liked airplanes and building fires in wood stoves and cookouts on a gravel beach. He saw Carolina, and he shook his head. He looked up at Claudine with tears in his eyes.

Claudine bobbed her head in a brisk nod. "That's your past. I see it in your eyes. You've run from that, and it still haunts you. Who have you left there?"

"My grandmother lives near Savannah." He pointed to the glimpse of the church, and he took a deep breath and looked away.

"Ah. A grandmother." She looked at him, then reached to fold the papers.

Kodiak released all but one, holding onto the paper showing the airport. He reached into his pocket and pulled out the ragged cruise ship ID tag with Carolina's name on it. Carefully, he laid it on the picture.

Claudine reached to him and put her hand on his. Kodiak looked up into her eyes. "What keeps you from going to her, Kodiak? Is it something in that picture?"

Tears began to flood his eyes. "I was married once before, Claudine." He turned to look at their shared reflection in the darkened windows, seeing the colors in the fading sky beyond, and he stared pensively.

She chuckled and spoke to break the silence. "Most of us have been. That can't be it. Not all of it, anyway."

He continued to watch the window. "This was my father's

place, you know." In the reflection, he saw her nod her head. He'd mentioned that to most people at one time or another. "My airplane, too. Julianna wanted more than I could give her. In the end she wanted it all. She didn't know about this place, so I ran here." He turned to Claudine and spoke with desperation. "Even my airplane. She wanted me to sell it to give her as alimony. She wanted to party with her friends."

Claudine squeezed his hand. "Would that have cleared the slate?" Kodiak nodded his head, his eyes still filled with tears. She continued, "So, which is more important? Your airplane or Carolina?"

Kodiak continued to sit, his mind mired in turmoil, and Claudine remained with him, as their reflections grew sharper in the darkening windows. After some time, Kodiak sniffed, and he reached to rub the end of his nose.

"Thank you, Claudine, for helping me figure it out."

She patted his hand and stood. Looking down on him, her glasses hanging from her neck, she nodded briskly. "Good. Go take care of this Julianna woman. Then you find your grand-mother. If she was in this storm, she'll need you. Then you go to this girl." Without another word, she turned and stepped to the door, opening it and closing it loudly behind her.

Kodiak could hear her steps heavy on the treads of his stair-way, and then the Jeep started up. After a few moments, the Jeep was gone and the air was silent. Even the sounds of the insects were quiet in the cold of the night. Kodiak had made his decision. He would go to Julianna, and he would offer her what she wanted. Then, he would chase the woman he had grown to love.

He picked up the ID card, and he traced her name with his fingers. Carolina DeAngeles. Caroline of the Angels. He would find her, and this would be his key.

Chapter 19

"THE DEVASTATION is horrific. I'm standing on the bridge to the island. You can see where the road signs used to be. These beams are designed to hold thousands of pounds high overhead. They're bent like toys. No one is being allowed in or out."

The scene on the television cut to another, one of downtown Savannah in which murky water still stood high on building walls. The narrator spoke of people surviving in hotels without water or electricity while waiting to be rescued in boats. One scene showed a downtown building on fire, and the narrator said that without firefighting capabilities, it would be allowed to burn itself out.

Carolina reached to her remote. At least she was no longer sick. Her flu had been something else, an allergy perhaps, or maybe she'd just cried the residue of the affliction from her body. She felt cleansed, but she did not feel good.

Her finger clicked the reports off. There was no news from

the beachfront. There was a family that had tried to weather the storm, deciding to escape just before it reached its height. They'd been found floating on the deck of their home as it had washed up far inland. Their words as they stood in front of the reporter's camera hounded her.

"No one could have survived," the woman had cried into the lens.

Her husband had wept. "Anyone who stayed is dead. All the houses are destroyed."

Even their teenage children had wailed, "Hilton Head is gone."

Carolina stood and walked to the window. She pulled the curtain aside. It was bright outside and hot even for late in the summer. She reached a hand and pressed it against the glass. Perhaps it was hot because it was late in the summer. Summer here was not like summer in Hilton Head. Here it seemed to go on and on. She paused, her hand beginning to burn with the heat. Summer should be like it used to be in Hilton Head.

Except Hilton Head was no longer.

She dropped the curtain and turned her back to the wall. She'd been able to get no news from Savannah. The reports said all lines were down, and the devastation was spread far to the north and the south. There had been flooding as far inland as Macon and as far north as Columbia. Even Jacksonville had borne much of the storm. Utility crews from as far west as Texas and Ohio were headed in to repair the damage. Margarete and Ricotta were lost to her for now, and it was breaking her heart.

Her heart was indeed breaking. She'd been torn apart in too many ways to bear. Her parents had been stolen from her, and she'd been forced to face the pain without even her brother for support. Her trusted housekeeper and her faithful pet were in the morass left by a devastating storm, and they were dead for all she knew. Most painful of all was the man she could have loved, whom she had loved. She cried out in her heart, the man she did

246

love, and she'd been torn from him.

She couldn't stand this house any longer. She walked to the door and pulled it open. Summer's heat assaulted her, and she walked into it. There was nothing for her in this godforsaken city, and she wanted to go home. Reaching the sidewalk, she turned and began to walk. If her Carolina home were walled off to her by the devastation of this storm, she'd walk to it and fight and claw until she was allowed to be where she belonged. She'd make her feet carry her to her Carolina coast if that was the only way to find the news that no one seemed to know.

A few blocks into her march across the continent, she realized her anger was no match for the blistering California summer, and the heat compounded by acres of concrete made things even worse. She stepped into a convenience store to call for a taxi only to find she'd brought no money at all with her.

"I'm a fool," she said to the man at the counter. "I leave home to walk four thousand miles to the coast, and I do it without money or a phone."

He shrugged, pulling a phone from under the counter, and turning away to let her complete her call.

KODIAK crawled from under his cabin, and he brushed off his coat. Many more trips underneath his floorboards, and he knew he'd need to put it in Claudine's washing machine. Claudine's and Marv's, now. He could smile at that. But not much else. He was feeling too beat down for smiles.

He reached and pulled the metal box from underneath the building, and he hoisted it to the porch, sliding it over the railing. Turning to the lattice he'd pulled off, he lifted it up and set it into place, securing it at the top and bottom. No matter how bad things seemed in his world, he didn't want creatures finding his floorboards to be the warm ceiling for their winter dens. He wasn't that depressed.

He'd known where this box was. When he built the cabin

247

on this slope, he'd understood it would be small on the inside, and he'd known there would be space underneath. For those things he needed to store instead of use, he'd put shelves between the pilings underneath. This box was dusty, but he'd found it just where he'd placed it years before.

He had figured it out. Claudine had been correct. And Tuck. However, Kodiak had already known what they'd tried to get him to see, and he'd just been wrestling with what he'd known was right. Would he have done what he knew to do without them? He didn't know. He'd seen Tuck's desperation in the retrospection of his life, and he'd seen the sparkle in Claudine's eyes. He grinned as he remembered the smells of Marv's cooking that had once again begun to fill the diner. Claudine wasn't the only one appreciating Marv's return. Everyone who visited the diner was.

Kodiak climbed up and sat on the top step. He pulled the box to him and set it in his lap. He looked out at the water in the distance as the sun sparkled on the surface. Although his airplane still floated at his dock, he knew true winter wasn't far off. The tide was running high, and he'd secured the craft with extra lines. Before long, he'd have to pull the float in, and the airplane would go into storage until spring.

He placed his hands on the box and looked up through the trees to the clear blue sky. As long as this box was closed, his airplane was still his. He could return this box under the cabin, and no one would know he hadn't been able to give it up. His eyes blinked as the breeze shifted one branch of a tree, and the light from the sun brushed his face for a moment. He'd enjoyed flying those skies. He didn't know if he ever would again.

"I'm sorry, Dad. This is more important. I hope you'll understand."

Kodiak slipped his hands over the ends of the box and released the catches. Opening it, he pulled out papers and began to set them on the porch beside him. One at a time, the documents piled up. One in particular caught his attention. His divorce papers. He held them in his hand and looked at them.

"Julianna, you've tried to take everything from me," he whispered hoarsely. "My Carolina beaches. My family. My grandmother." Kodiak closed his eyes as his throat choked up. Images of his beloved Mamie flashed through his mind, her hats and her formal suits. The gloves she always wore. The words he had never known how to live. *Never let go of what you love, Kodiak. It may never come your way again. Never, never let go of what you love.*

Kodiak opened his eyes and looked around, the images of his life here on the coast of Alaska blurred with the moisture of his tears. It was a place he'd loved when his father had been here, and it was a place he'd made his own. He did love it, but it wasn't enough anymore. He had to have Carolina, and all the rest was emptiness.

Kodiak ran his hand over his face. He was still a part owner in Julianna's condo on the island. Until he surrendered the funds to clear her alimony demands, he couldn't be cleared from the deed. He was responsible for its expenses and upkeep. He would find a certified copy of the deed in the divorce papers in his hand, too. He laid it aside. The divorce papers were important, but they weren't what he was searching for.

At the bottom he located it. Cessna. Title of Ownership. His eyes glanced at his airplane floating in the water. He'd give up even that for Carolina. Even that.

He put the title aside with the divorce papers, and he placed the rest of the items back in the metal box. Lifting the box in one hand and the papers in the other, he stood and bumped the door to step inside his cabin. He set the box on a table and turned back outside.

He breathed deeply of his Alaska. The crisp air burned its way into his chest. For some reason, his decision made, the very act of holding the paperwork making it real, Kodiak's mood began to lift. He smiled as he pictured Claudine's face. It was Carolina's he wanted to see, but he knew he must take one step at a time, and Claudine would be his first.

CAROLINA stood in Sha'Cretia's office. Her fingers drummed the wood. Finally, she could restrain herself no longer, whispering fiercely, "Sha'Cretia! You have to be forceful. The storm's gone. I've watched the reports. Flights are being allowed into Savannah."

Sha'Cretia reached a polished nail to the corner of her eye and pulled the skin tight. Then she released it and spoke softly into the phone. Hanging up, she looked at Carolina and smiled. "Honey, sometimes you have to be nice to the man. I like to say it this way. Be nice to the man, honey, and the man'll be nice to you." She reached and ran the tips of her fingernails across her bottom lip, wincing at one, and glancing down to look at it carefully. "I just filed this on my break. Hmm."

Carolina rapped Sha'Cretia's desk in frustration. "Sha! The airline! Can I get to Savannah?" She stood and turned to the window, her hand at her mouth. Her voice was broken. "My two most loyal friends are there. I sent them there, and I haven't heard a word. Sha, what if their deaths are on my hands?"

Then two arms surrounded her, and a head rested itself on her shoulder. A voice spoke softly into her ear.

"This friend doesn't count as loyal?"

Carolina turned in the embrace. She hugged her friend with all her strength, the need for physical contact overwhelming her. "Sha," she whispered. "No one has kept me afloat more than you. Without you, I would have given up."

Sha'Cretia released her hold on Carolina and straightened the front of her Donna Karan. She smiled as she lifted an arm and patted one side of her hair back into place. "Baby, that's what I needed to hear. I've got you on a plane, three days from now." At Carolina's pained look, she shrugged. "All the kissing

250

up only gets you so far, sweets. Those flights going in now are for emergency crews. Savannah's opening for residents only then." She chuckled, holding one hand in front of her and pointing with a long and immaculately manicured finger. "I saw that deed, you remember. That's your ticket, girl."

Carolina turned back to the window. "It'll be hard alone." After a moment she called to Sha'Cretia, "I wish you were going with me."

Sha'Cretia leaned against her desk and reached to tap her phone several times, her eyes still on Carolina. "The sweet man said you could certainly take your baby sister. Your deed is my ticket, too."

Carolina laughed. "Baby sister? You scamp! Why not older sister?"

Sha'Cretia vamped back to her chair. Before she sat down, she put her hand to her side and cocked her head. "In this Donna Karan of your mother's? I think baby sister fits the bill just fine."

Carolina rushed forward to hug her again, and then she headed to the door. She called back as she stepped out, "I'll see Mr. Warner immediately."

Sha'Cretia called to her to get her attention before she was out of hearing, but Carolina was already gone. She sat at her desk and moved some files around as she started back to work. She said to no one at all, "I already talked to him, sweetie. But I guess you'll find that out on your own."

KODIAK hit the brakes, and the dust flew. He looked through the windshield at the diner just in front as he shifted the truck into reverse before killing the engine. Now that his gears shifted smoothly between second and third, he'd begun driving faster down the rutted roads. In town, he'd gone faster, still.

At the diner, he was alone. There were no cars, not even Claudine's old Range Rover. The glare on the building's windows kept him from seeing inside, but still, he was pretty sure someone would be around. After all, the sign was on, its gentle flicker reassuringly familiar.

Stepping to the door, Kodiak stomped his feet to clean the dirt. Putting his shoulder to the door, he reached for the knob. When he grabbed it, it was cold against his bare skin, but stepping through, the warmth of the interior wrapped around him like a glove. The diner was as empty as it had seemed from the outside, and he went to a seat where he could watch his truck.

The old vehicle wasn't going anywhere, even though he'd left the keys inside. Things like that weren't a concern here in town. He was simply watching and seeing it today for the first time as it really was. Old Red. More rust than anything else, that and rust preventative paint from a spray can.

It had seemed easy back at the cabin. Take the title to the airplane and just hand it over. That wasn't what would happen. No, Julianna didn't want his airplane. She'd fought hard during the divorce, and she'd been awarded alimony. She'd claimed no job history, not telling the courts of undocumented funds she regularly received from her grandparents. The funds awarded were far above Kodiak's ability to pay. She wanted the cash the plane would bring.

Now, Kodiak's head was tight with the strain, and no one was here. He cleared his throat and called out, "Claudine?"

He grinned to see movement in the kitchen, only to find Marv stepping into the dining room. Kodiak's eyes watched as the bulk of a man walked his direction.

Marv put his balled fists on the table, leaning hard, the knuckles pressing into the Formica. He stood, his breath audible as it moved in and out of his massive chest. Finally he spoke, and Kodiak looked into his eyes to see them shining with moisture.

"Kodiak, boy." Marv tapped the table gently a few times. "Thank you, boy." He shifted on his feet, and it was obvious he was uncomfortable speaking of this. "I wasn't right to Claudine. She came back to me anyway. You did that boy. Claudine done told me what she said to you. I got my advice to add to all the rest. Here's mine."

Kodiak saw Marv's eyes glance to the window, and when Kodiak looked, he saw Claudine getting out of her old Range Rover. It looked even worse than Old Red.

Marv spoke faster, as if he had to be finished by the time Claudine got to the door and walked inside. "A good woman's all there is. Take that to the bank, Kodiak. Give it all up for her when you find her. Hang onto nothing else. I almost lost that." He reached a hand to wipe an eye. "You gave it back to me. Go find her, boy. You'll not be sorry." The big man turned and lumbered toward the kitchen.

Kodiak jerked as the front door burst open, and Claudine barreled through. "Get yourself over here, Kodiak. All this stuff needs to come inside, least if you want Marv to fix you anything. Been to the store." She glared at him as he stood and helped her move the items inside and then to the kitchen. Reaching out to him, she slipped a check in his pocket. "Thank you for the new alternator. I enjoyed getting up this morning knowing the truck had juice."

Finally, she followed him to his table and reached out to the papers he had laying there. She put her glasses on her nose, and she opened them. Then she smiled. "You really figured it out, I see." She glanced up at him over the glasses.

"It's hard, Claudine. I know I have to, but it's hard." He twirled a sugar packet on the table. "I need your help."

"Done done it."

Kodiak's eyes caught a motion in the kitchen, and he glanced over to see Marv in the doorway grinning. "What have you done, Claudine?" He looked back at her.

"John's been in. That stream you fish? That John. Asked me about your plane. Again."

Marv cleared his throat. "Get to it, Claudine," he called.

She cut her eyes to him, her frown showing she'd been enjoying playing this along. She looked back at Kodiak.

"I know you, boy, and you had this figured out the day I came to your place. I knew it, and I had to wait until you knew it. I told him you'd let him have that plane, but give you a few days. He thought thirty-five sounded pretty good."

Kodiak's eyes opened wide. "Thirty-five thousand?"

Marv called, "A bargain at that. I've seen them for thirty with a shot engine. You keep that plane like new. Told Claudine she should'a said forty. She wouldn't, though."

Claudine cleared her throat. "Thirty-five's fair, Kodiak. More than fair, and Marv knows it. You sign that title, and I'll let John know. He's at his cabin now. He'll have your money for you." She called to Marv, "Eggs and sausage."

Kodiak grinned and told her thanks.

She sat and picked up the divorce papers. "Now, about that Julianna. Clear the slate, right? Then you can get your girl." Claudine flipped through the packet of papers. "Called Juneau. They have restrictions getting back to the East Coast. Have to own property to get into Charleston, Savannah, all the way to Jacksonville. Savannah's the worst. Hilton Head most of all. I'm sorry, Kodiak." She looked up at him over the papers, reaching a hand to place it on his. "This paperwork is all showing Hilton Head. Are you still on the deed for this condominium?"

"Until I clear the alimony."

"Good." She looked very pleased. She leaned back and called, "Marv! Call and confirm that flight." She turned back to Kodiak. "It flies out in two days with a layover in St. Louis. Don't know what's in Savannah. Might not be able to get to Hilton Head. Don't know. We'll get you as far as Savannah, though."

Kodiak grinned in relief at having someone else help make his decisions. "Couldn't you at least send me non-stop?"

Claudine stood and looked at him. "You're lucky to get sausage. That's why I went to the store, and all for you." With a hrump from her throat, she turned and walked toward the kitchen, calling back, "And I'm charging you double for the eggs to cover my commission."

Kodiak laughed. She really did love him. Today just proved it.

CAROLINA'S heart pounded. She kept her eyes closed, and she refused to look, even when her attention was demanded. She was on this airplane, and she had to deal with this. However, as long as she didn't look, it was still okay. Her Low Country was sweet and green, and her boy wearing Kody's face would be waiting for her on the tarmac. Her parents would wave and greet her with the love that only parents know how to express.

She knew none of that was true anymore, but to put it off just for the moment was the best she could do. Sha'Cretia, however, was determined not to let that happen.

"My heavenly stars, Carolina. You must look at that. The roof of the airport is gone. Honey, it's just peeled away like a can opener. Hey!" Sha'Cretia wouldn't let this one ride, and she prodded her friend. "There's the men's restroom. I haven't seen the inside of one of those since I was seventeen. There are so many urinals. My stars, sweetie. How do they do that standing up all the time?"

Carolina kept her eyes closed and reached to pat the hand on her arm. "They say the same about you, I'm sure. Just let it go, Sha."

"Carolina, I cannot let this go. You have to see this."

"I've seen urinals. I don't want to see these."

Sha'Cretia's voice got quieter. "No, Carolina. There are boats on the runway. Not boats, girl. Ships. Lots of ships, just pushed aside to make room for us."

Carolina couldn't resist this. She opened her eyes and

255

turned to the window, lifting the shade the rest of the way up. She cut her eyes toward the coast, toward her beloved island. There was green as the land stretched to the sea in the distance, and she breathed easier. Then, she saw the tan within the green, the tan of her beaches as the storm had washed them onto the land. When she saw the debris, the ships and remains of houses and buildings strewn through the green, she could look no longer.

"Sha, it's too much. I shouldn't have come."

Sha'Cretia prodded her to see more. "Look the other way. Savannah. Look across the plane."

Carolina turned her head. Across the cabin, others were filling the windows, studying the scene. Many windows were unblocked, though. The plane was more empty than full. Most people were being kept out of this heavily damaged area.

Savannah looked whole in comparison to the area toward the coast. The biggest structures had survived with little evident damage. An occasional broken window sparkled in the afternoon sun, and water still glistened on the roofs of the buildings. Stretching their necks downward as the aircraft banked to land, additional damage could be seen. Awnings were flapping. The sides of buildings were missing, and cars were sitting on things that no car could possibly drive on.

Suddenly, Carolina cried out in despair, "Sha! There's the Marriott. The building's gone. All that glass. Margarete. Ricotta." Then the Savannah River came into view, and Carolina gasped, "No! Daddy's Cadillac. It's in the river."

As the aircraft leveled out and the view disappeared, Sha'Cretia reached to grab her hand. "It can't be, sweetie. Your parent's house is miles away. I remember that."

"No," and Carolina began to cry. "I sent Margarete to that hotel, and she drove Daddy's car. What was I thinking? It was in the direct path of the storm. I just wanted a building that was tall. I didn't think."

Sha'Cretia stretched to see what she could. "Did you really see your daddy's Caddy? How could you tell?"

"It was a show car for his dealership, stretched, with a special decal in the rear window."

"I don't remember that, sweetie."

"You rode in my mum's car, Sha. That's the one they were in when the accident happened. Margarete drove my father's car in. Oh, Sha! I know she's not all right."

"Sweetie, we'll know when we know." She sat back, reaching to pat Carolina's arm. "We'll know when we know."

KODIAK woke with a start. He looked around. He was on an airplane, and the air was cool. He shifted his position to try to get comfortable. It was very crowded, and there was no room for his feet. He looked up at the ceiling to the small, round air vent there. Had Carolina also had one above her head when she flew from Seattle to her home in California? He reached his hand to it and twisted it to decrease the volume, and then he realized it was too warm in the craft. He twisted it the other way and grew chilled again. He tried once more, swiveling it to the side.

He turned his head to look out the window. Southern Canada. Lakes. He'd seen lakes before, and he'd landed on them in his own airplane. His father's airplane. Now he could only fly on these commercial jets, and it wasn't the same.

Kodiak reached a hand and patted his jacket pocket. Thirty-five thousand dollars instead of the airplane he had treasured for fifteen years, one he had owned for half that. His airplane didn't feel like so much when it was all paper.

His fingers traced the outline of the card that was in his pocket with the money. Carolina. He smiled. It would be a fair trade, just like the one Claudine had brokered for him. Claudine had promised to get Tad out to close up his cabin. Kodiak reminded her to have him pull in the float and the ramp. He'd left his metal box of papers in the cabin, but it would be fine there. The propane would freeze if it got cold enough, and that'd also be fine. Everything would be all right. His cabin would still be there when he found her. Carolina from California. Caroline of the Angels. He wasn't going back until he had her in his arms, no matter how long it took.

CAROLINA and Sha'Cretia exited the airplane. The terminal was roped off with emergency tape, and they were forced to disembark down a rolling set of steps that was backed up to the fuselage on a truck. It was hot, and it was humid. Sha'Cretia stopped and glanced at the sun with dismay.

Carolina looked to her companion and apologized. "It's summer still, Sha." She studied the terminal, and it was indeed in very sorry shape. Windows were boarded up, and trash fluttered in out-of-the-way corners.

The black tarmac directly around the building was clean, though, and Carolina couldn't help herself. She glanced toward the front of the airplane, and her heart knew hope. She looked and wanted to see him step toward her, his face splitting into that grin she'd come to love, and his golden hair shining in the sun. She needed this small bit of reassurance from her old life when her Low Country had still been whole. When she didn't find him, she took a deep breath and looked away, tears already in her eyes. She saw her friend turn to her.

"Honey, it's bad. Don't cry. Keep up your spirits for the people here. They need to see that the whole world isn't gone. They need to see hope. For now, let's hope we can hail a taxi."

Carolina thought of her boy, the one who'd turned into her Kody, and she knew she'd never find him. She whispered, "Sha, there is no hope. Not for me. If he were going to come for me, it would be here."

"Who, baby, the taxi man?" Sha'Cretia looked around, then she laughed. "Honey, no one has a taxi coming. See? There's

probably no taxis in the city. I guess we didn't think about that."
She took Carolina's arm. "I guess we could walk to the river and
see if we could get your daddy's car started. Look, honey.
There's another plane coming in. Think about that. It's almost
like someone's coming to meet us, right here in Savannah. I
thought we'd be the only one."

Carolina hugged Sha'Cretia. "No one's going to be coming
to meet us here. It's just you and me, and all we've got is each
other. I just hope we find we've also got Margarete and Rotten
Ricotta Cheese."

Sha'Cretia reached up and fluffed her hair. "Be strong, girl.
I see a tram coming. Surely it will take us somewhere. Let's go
find us a margarita and some cheese." She marched ahead
boldly, her pumps snapping on the tarmac.

Carolina called after her, "We're looking for Margarete and
Rotten Ricotta Cheese!"

Sha'Cretia wiggled her fingers in the air and yelled back,
"That's what I said, honey. That's what I said."

KODIAK stretched his legs. St. Louis had been hard. The
waiting, not the airport. The airport was big with comfortable
chairs and lots of space. The waiting had been torturous. He
wanted this over with.

At St. Louis, he'd been upgraded to First Class when the
plane had boarded. Not many people wanted to fly into the
hurricane zone. Wanted? No, that wasn't right. Not many were
being allowed to fly in.

He got First Class.

It was nice, too. Leather. Service. He still didn't have his
business finished, though, and that was when he could go look
for Carolina. He'd have to fly back to California, and this was
just an inconvenience that was in the way. He needed to find
Julianna and resolve their divorce so he could move on.

He reached and ran a finger over the ID card from the ship.

He hoped he could take it to the cruise line's headquarters in California, and they'd help him with information. If not, there were always telephone books. Internet, if he learned how to use it. He'd been out in that cabin a long time.

Kodiak felt the wheels as they touched the runway. He raised his shade. After deciding to sell his Cessna, his focus had been on something simple, like getting to the Carolina coast. He hadn't focused on what he might find when he got here. He saw the airport flicker by, and he realized the condition it was in. His pulse sounded in his ears, and his interest was aroused. He leaned closer for a better view.

He used to work here. He knew this airport, and he knew the condition it should be in. When he saw the safety tape and the roof peeled back, he understood the damage he might find. This airport had been built to withstand this, and the Category 5 storm that had hit the coast had destroyed it. With dread, he realized this might not be as easy as he'd hoped, not taking care of Julianna, and not getting to California.

Not getting to Los Angeles. The City of Angels. The city of his angel. Caroline of the Angels.

Kodiak's hands fidgeted over his seatbelt release as the aircraft slowed to a stop. The flight attendants walked up and down the aisle collecting small items from the few passengers, and then the seatbelt lights flickered off. As he heard the whine of the engines fade, Kodiak felt a difference in the air coming through the small opening overhead. He reached to find it had warmed perceptibly. He released his seatbelt and stood, pulling his small case from the overhead.

Waiting, he peered outside. A portable set of steps was being backed up to the aircraft. Then the door was released, and the heat and humidity of a Southern coastal summer surged into the plane's interior. Kodiak staggered. He was used to heat, and his Alaska coast could be excessively humid, but to mix the two was horrendous. He knew he'd lived with this most of his life, but he guessed he'd have to get used to it over again.

Then he was standing and looking over the airport. The sun was bright, and he was surprised to see another airplane sitting not far away. It was larger, and there were more passengers milling around than had ridden with him on his own aircraft. Now that he'd seen the damage, he was surprised anyone else would even try to get into this devastated area.

He did notice two women standing off to the side, one giving the other a quick hug, and then walking off as she waved her hand over her shoulder. The one left standing alone gave Kodiak's heart a familiar jolt. He watched her and had a sudden impulse to go to her, to tell her Alaska had returned, that he'd looked for her over and over the past ten years, and had finally found her.

Then she walked quickly after the first woman, calling out to her. In the next few moments, they approached a waiting tram and were gone. It wouldn't have been her, though; it couldn't have been. Not after ten years. He'd seen what he wanted to see. It wasn't Carolina, either. She'd left him in Alaska, and she'd gone home to California. He was joking with himself if he thought she'd be waiting on him to find her on the Savannah tarmac. That was fantasy, not real life.

He stepped aside as the few fellow passengers who'd ridden on the airplane with him walked out and down the ramp, as dazed at their first sight as he'd been. He knew he needed to follow them, but he couldn't get the woman he'd seen out of his mind. He forced his thoughts back to what needed done, and he looked around him one last time before he started down the steps. This was his life, and with the damage he was seeing this far inland, it couldn't get any more real than this. How he would find his grandmother—or Julianna—he didn't know.

CAROLINA and Sha'Cretia stood at the door to a portable building. It was really no more than a rectangular trailer set on blocks, with wheels dangling underneath. They hadn't even put underpinning around it. However, there was an air conditioner humming away on top, and clearly visible, a portable generator was running merrily off to the side.

"See, Carolina? Just keep our pretty faces on, and civilization comes to us. Air conditioning!" Sha'Cretia had been waving a flattened paper cup at her face. She whispered to Carolina, "I've never learned not to sweat. You Southern ladies have it so lucky."

In spite of the lack of underpinning and the merry generator, a large sign was boldly attached to the side of the building directly over the door, and it proudly proclaimed the name of a prominent rental car company. Off to the side was their fleet of four cars. When they'd asked the tram driver about transportation, he'd assured them the rental companies were fully functional. When he'd pulled up to the portable building, Carolina had laughed. She'd been pleased to see that she could still find humor in this increasingly desperate situation.

Soon packed into the smallest car either of them thought God had ever commissioned, Carolina started the engine. Sha'Cretia laughed.

"Four cars, Carolina, and we got the first. They said another set should be here before dark, but some of those people on that other flight are going to be mighty unhappy." She reached and patted Carolina's hand. "Sweetie, I told you I'd get you on the first flight here." She reached to her waist to fasten her seatbelt.

Carolina had done hers as soon as she sat down. While she knew Savannah, she also knew the airport had been cleaned up. Everywhere else would be worse. She dreaded driving out to the island. She'd already been told that without ID showing a Hilton Head address, she'd have to carry her property deed in hand. Otherwise she'd be turned away. It was on the dash, securely bundled in a waterproof bag.

As she shifted into gear, Sha'Cretia turned the air on high.

Carolina looked forward and murmured, "Thank you, Sha." Seeing the tram they'd ridden out on returning with the passengers from the second airplane, she stopped to let it pass. She glanced at the riders, looking at the expressions on their faces, noting one man with thick, sandy hair looking the other way. It was only a glance, but her heart stopped. Then she laughed as the tram pulled past, causing Sha'Cretia to look her way.

"What, sweetie? What besides this amazing car rental place could you possibly find amusing among these poor, poor people who've had to survive such devastation?"

Carolina shook her head. "I just thought I saw someone familiar. I know better, though. The man I know is four thousand miles away."

Sha'Cretia smiled, pulling down the sun visor. She looked at it, and her face fell. "Baby, maybe we should take this car back. They left the mirror off the visor."

Her driver laughed again. "Sha, some cars just come that way."

"To think, I came all this way for this." She slumped down in her seat before reaching up and flipping the disappointing visor back and forth.

Carolina patted her on her knee. "Sha, you came all this way for me."

She brightened and sat up. "I did, didn't I? Well, that makes it better. Where are we going, Carolina?"

"To find Margarete, Sha. Margarete and Ricotta."

"Good. I'm thirsty and hungry. A margarita and cheese sounds just fine to me."

Carolina laughed a third time, and she wasn't sorry a bit to have brought her friend with her.

KODIAK sat on the tram, the heat blinding in its intensity. He watched as a small car stopped to let the tram pass by. He idly glanced at the interior, seeing the two women from outside the airplane. Just as they were coming into focus, the sun glared on the windshield, and he looked away. A large pleasure boat that had washed up from the river caught his eyes for a moment. When the tram stopped, he turned to look for the car, but it had already gone.

Inside the rental building, Kodiak idly waited until the attendant had rented two more of the cars. He stepped up to the counter and asked what was available. The attendant laughed. "We have more cars coming later, but this is the last one for a while. You are one lucky man." He picked up a set of keys, looked at the tag, and back at Kodiak. "Lucky if you want a minivan."

Kodiak shrugged. "I want wheels. When I rent your mini-van, are they extra?" He turned at the ding of the signal bell hanging on the door to see a distraught-looking older man step inside. Kodiak nodded at him. The older man moved up to the counter, interrupting the rental already in process.

"Good day. Your white van. I'd like it." He made an attempt to smile, but he looked very beat down.

"Sir," the attendant began, "I have a customer here already, and he's taking the van. Aren't you, sir?" He glanced at Kodiak, and without waiting for an answer, he turned back to the older man. "We have more cars arriving just anytime." He turned back to Kodiak and smiled.

Kodiak looked at the older man. He thought a moment, and then he quizzed him. "You need the van, huh?"

The man looked at Kodiak, desperation clouding his eyes. "I've searched the city. Cars I can find. My wife must move her wheelchair. Please, sir."

Kodiak stepped back and looked at the attendant. "He gets the van. I can wait."

"It might be some hours, sir. Are you sure?"

Kodiak looked for a chair to sit on and saw there wasn't one.

He snorted. "Sure, I can wait." He turned to the man. "I hope your wife is going to be okay."

He nodded once at the man and stepped outside the door. He noticed one of the stacks of blocks under the building protruded slightly, and he perched on the edge, slipping his jacket off. It was hot, and he'd only kept it on because of the money in the pocket.

Now, he checked the zipper. He unzipped and zipped it idly, and then he reached inside and pulled out Carolina's shipboard ID pass. He rezipped the pocket and looked at the card, rubbing the chewed places with his fingers, and letting the sharp edges catch on his skin. He remembered passing Tad's Jeep, and then he'd seen her. His eyes misted with longing for that moment. He'd known her for two days, and he was upsetting his entire world just to find her again. He smiled to think he hadn't run to her. He'd run away from her, completely across the continent. Running to her would come later.

He turned to see the building's door open. The older man turned with gratitude in his eyes and reached a hand to shake. "Chalmers. Jameson Chalmers." Kodiak held out his hand to grasp the one offered to him. "What you did in there, thank you." He looked away as his eyes filled with tears. "Can I take you someplace in the van?" When Kodiak didn't answer, he turned back to him. "Please, let me give you a ride. I can drop you off or bring you back. The man inside called, and he said it will be three hours before the next cars arrive. I can return you at that time."

Kodiak smiled. It was obvious that this man really wanted company, his to be specific, and Kodiak liked that. He stood. "I'll be pleased to ride with you." He nodded toward the van. "Do you think it has air?"

Jameson finally smiled, wiping his face with his sleeve. "This is Georgia. It had better." He held the keys to Kodiak. "You drive, please. My heart. It bothers me. I'd like to ride."

265

Kodiak glanced at the door to the building, knowing that when someone rents a car, he's the only one given permission to get behind the wheel. However, in this situation, he was sure that bending the rules was the right thing to do.

"Sure," and he put out his hand.

Kodiak held the passenger's door for Jameson, and closed it firmly before making his way to his door in five loping strides. He folded Carolina's shipboard ID into his jacket and reached to put it in first, only to have it taken from him. Kodiak tossed his bag over the seat into the back.

"Thanks," he said as he ducked inside. "This seems a bit tight after my truck."

Jameson hefted the thick jacket. "Not from Georgia?"

Kodiak laughed. "It's a long story. I just came in from St. Louis, and Alaska before that. It's been a tiring trip."

He reached to start the vehicle, looking for the clutch, then he smiled sheepishly at his assumption. "Automatic." He pressed the brake and turned the key. Both men sat there for a moment as the air began to cool, and Kodiak spoke first. "Where to?"

The man's face sank, and his arms went limp, his hands dropping onto Kodiak's jacket on his lap. "My wife. I was away on a business trip. She was with her nurse. The storm hit, and I couldn't get home. The nurse went out and never came back. Now my wife is alone." He looked at Kodiak, tears streaming down his face. "For two days. I have phone service with her. At least I have that. But the building's damaged. When her battery goes dead, she'll have no one. Even now, the phone service is barely there. Towers are perhaps down. She can't walk."

Kodiak reassured him. "Rescue workers will certainly come." Still, it gave him a moment of anxiety as he pictured his own Mamie. She was strong and sometimes too much there, but he'd begun to hope she'd run from this storm. With no phone service anywhere in the path of the devastation, he'd had no luck calling, and all was guesswork.

"They have. She hears them, and she calls. They can't hear her." Jameson shifted in his seat, and the chewed pass slipped to the floor. He leaned forward to pick it up. He looked at it and held it to Kodiak. "You were with the earlier woman?"

The question caught him off guard. "Earlier woman?" He took the ID and slipped it into his shirt pocket. "Thanks. I wouldn't want to lose that."

Jameson paused as if confused. "Oh," he said. "The woman who signed at the rental agency just before me, maybe two customers earlier, had the same name." He pointed to Kodiak's pocket. "I was certain when I saw the card. Like the dealership."

Kodiak put a hand on Jameson's shoulder. "I've lived in Alaska a long time, and I don't know what you mean."

Jameson reached and wiped his face. "I'm sorry." He looked at Kodiak and smiled. "I don't even know your name."

Kodiak grinned. That he could understand. He reached out his hand to shake. "Kodiak. My best friends call me Kody, though. At least my one best friend did."

Jameson took Kodiak's proffered hand. "Did?"

"Lost her." He slipped the card out of his pocket and held it up before dropping it back inside. "I'm going looking for her." The older man smiled, his color seeming to improve, whether with the cooling air or the distraction from his own problems, Kodiak didn't know. He was glad to see it, though. "You said something about a dealership. What was that about?"

"Where I buy my cars, DeAngeles Cadillac. The woman came in on a tram, you see, like you did, but I don't walk quickly, and she was gone before I got inside. The name, though, I remember."

Kodiak smiled as he shifted the van into reverse. He remembered DeAngeles Cadillac now. A high-end dealership, and not one that Kodiak ever could have afforded to visit.

However, Carolina was from California, and the woman the

267

old man had seen was from here. There couldn't be only one DeAngeles in the whole country, could there? He was here to find Julianna, not Carolina. She was next on his list, but that wasn't today.

As he pulled out onto the road, he began to think on that. Julianna was probably in the condo having cocktails as the world fell apart around her. That's what she'd done before, letting Kodiak's world crumble around his ears, and he wouldn't be surprised to find she was doing it again.

CAROLINA pulled up to the Marriott Riverfront parking lot entrance driving very slowly. The roads seemed to be fairly clear, but in many places it was only one lane. Debris was piled up everywhere. She and Sha'Cretia drove silently, watching the structures that were damaged, often beyond repair. From the airplane, many of the buildings had seemed fine. From below, ground floor windows were shattered, walls were missing, and all that had been inside littered every space except their small cleared path. Occasionally people could be seen walking, and the look on their faces was one of withdrawn hopelessness.

Sha'Cretia reached to Carolina and placed her hand on her companion's arm. "Sweet friend, who could have thought. I knew, but I didn't know."

Carolina whispered, "It must be worse on the island. Be there with me, Sha."

She just squeezed her arm and looked up at the shattered remains of the Marriott. Carolina looked with her. The glass atrium was gone. The ground floor had pieces of the walls missing.

Carolina turned to Sha'Cretia with tears. "Margarete and Ricotta. Sha, I can't bear it."

Sha'Cretia made an obvious effort to put on a bright face and said cheerfully, "Girl, you ain't fat, and I ain't fat. Ain't nobody in this car that's fat. Ain't no fat lady singing that I can hear. Let's not call them dead, yet."

Carolina laughed, wiping tears from both cheeks with the backs of her hands. "Sha, you're so right. Look, the lot has been cleared, and inside I can see some lights on. Let's go see if the valet parking is up and running."

"That's the spirit, girl. I like that. Valet. You think they do margaritas, too? Maybe with cheese?"

Carolina laughed again as the last of the tension in the car broke. She reached and rubbed Sha'Cretia's arm, the fabric of her blouse sliding under her hand. "I'm sure they do, Sha. I bet they'll do that just for you. Now, let's get inside."

She pulled into the lot, and just for fun, they waited a bit, but no valet ever came. They hadn't really expected one to. After all, it was just for fun, and besides, there were no other cars in the lot.

None at all.

"OH, MY WINNETTA. She's had to survive in this," Jameson wailed as Kodiak drove slowly and carefully up the street he'd been directed to. It was hard to recognize specific buildings with all the damage they'd taken. Jameson had earlier pointed to one, thinking it was his home, only to realize they were on the wrong road.

Kodiak's heart pounded in his chest. From the airport, he'd expected to find damage in the city, but this was beyond belief. Some buildings he could see were washed out all across the ground floor, and many of them had the second floor sagging dangerously. Surely Julianna had taken the sense to run from this. He was now convinced he should have waited before coming here. He had so wanted to find Carolina, and now he was in a different kind of hell.

"Look, there. See? Back behind that building. The glass hotel. The Riverfront, it's called. We could see that from our balcony." Jameson paused, his next words barely whispered.

"The glass walls. They're gone. My poor Winnetta. She loved to watch the lights shine there." He watched as Kodiak drove past another building. "There, stop."

Kodiak looked at the building. There was no ground floor left, and one end had no support under it at all. It was sagging and looked as if it would collapse within hours. He turned to Jameson. "Are you sure?" It was surrounded with tape to keep people out.

Jameson looked to the building and nodded, his eyes watery. "The end where it sags. There are windows only on the back. One small window on the end, too, our bedroom. She's there, Kody. You must help me." The old man withdrew a cell phone from his pocket. "I know each call may be my last. Please, I'll let Winnetta know I'm here."

With a shaky hand, he punched in his numbers and held the phone to his ear. Kodiak could hear it ringing, and then an equally shaky voice answered. He knew Jamison must have the volume very loud.

"I'm here, my dear." Tears began to run down the old man's face. "I've brought help." He turned his eyes to Kodiak as he waited for an answer. After a moment, Kodiak reached and took the phone. He looked at it to see the display was blank.

Kodiak chose his words carefully. "Jameson, the battery's gone on your phone. However, I heard your wife answer. Are you sure this is the place?" He reached to the door, readying himself to get out.

Jameson looked at the building and pointed to three large numbers at the top. "See? Four. Three. Five. This is where we'll find my wife."

Kodiak gave him a resolute look. "Then someone must go in and get her. You stay here, and I'll go see what needs to be done."

With a swift motion, he released the door, and he walked to the tape that surrounded the collapsing building. Ducking underneath, he carefully walked the perimeter to assess a way inside. Then, with a look of satisfaction on his face, he ran back to the van and slapped it on the hood.

Opening the door, he said, "I'm there, Jameson. You stay here, and I'll get her out." He looked back to the building, evaluating, and he turned back to the van when Jameson called to him.

"I'll say a prayer for you as you go."

"Jameson, I assume you go to church?"

The old man nodded. "On the island. Holy Family."

Kodiak grinned. "My grandmother's church. I used to go with her. I trust your prayers. Pray me a good one, Jameson." He slapped the door, shut it, and was off at a run.

Chapter 20

CAROLINA pointed to a hand-lettered sign on a battered staircase wall. Up. There wasn't much else on the ground floor, and she and Sha'Cretia could see through the building to the other side. Off one direction a huge industrial generator was chattering away. The noise obliterated any conversation as they started up the steps. As they came to what must have originally been an interior corridor, the chattering lessened in volume, and the two friends could finally hear each other talk. The corridor was warm and muggy, and a portable sign showed directions. Following the arrows, they finally opened up a door into a meeting room where portable tables for operating the hotel were set up. They were relieved to find the air conditioning in this part of the building was running. A trim and youthful hotel employee turned to them.

"Marriott Riverfront. Please pardon our distress. How may I help you?" He smiled.

Sha'Cretia laughed, turning to Carolina. "How cute! I didn't know I'd like this so much." She winked.

Carolina just waggled a finger at her and shook her head. She spoke to the young man. "We're just in from California, and we're needing some information."

The young man laughed, rolling his eyes. "Ma'am, you picked a really good time for a vacation. However, we do have plenty of rooms. If you noticed, the atrium is a bit under the weather, but if you don't mind that." He shrugged. "The hotel generators got flooded, but we've brought in temporaries. You couldn't miss that."

Carolina saw Sha'Cretia's hand motioning for her attention. She laughed as Sha'Cretia mouthed, "He's adorable." She turned back to the hotel employee. "No, we don't need a room, or at least I don't think we do, not yet, anyway." Carolina waved her hand at Sha'Cretia to quiet her when she saw her nodding her head rapidly. "A friend was staying here when the storm started."

The employee paused, thinking. "A number of people weathered the storm with us. Do you have a name? Our computers are inoperable, and all our hard copies went down the river." He grinned. "Literally. However, we've gone from room to room making a list." He pointed to a clipboard on one of the tables, and he reached to pick it up.

Sha'Cretia jumped in. "Sweetie, perhaps this would help. We're looking for a very big dog. About eighty pounds worth."

The employee tossed the clipboard back down. "Say no more. Follow me." Going down a short hall, he reached to open a door. Inside the room on a king-size bed, a large brown head turned, and Ricotta barked twice and leaped for Carolina in one bound, his deep-throated calls of excitement filling the air. Laughing, she threw her arms around his neck and began to cry.

Eventually she looked up and asked, "The woman with him?"

273

The employee rolled his eyes for a second time, and he grinned. "She's taken over the kitchen. Rather, I should say, she's created a kitchen for the guests, pulling a salvaged stove from below and moving in several guest refrigerators from unused rooms. Margarete, I believe."

Carolina laughed. "That's her. Heaven help you if you keep her around too long. She'll be running the hotel."

The young man sighed as he rolled his eyes once again. "I think she already does."

KODIAK jumped over the tape, and running around the building, he grabbed a long timber lying behind the structure. He raised one end to an exposed balcony along the back of the building, and he left the other resting on the ground. Stepping back from where it pressed into the matted, yellowed grass, he started to run, and building momentum, he loped up the suspended board.

The building sagged with Kodiak's additional weight, and it rocked with each step. The windows had been shattered in the storm. Inside, the carpet was wet, and the draperies fluttered in the breeze. Glass crunched under his feet. He walked gingerly. He knew that if the building went down, he went with it.

He called, "Winnetta?" Hearing no answer, he ventured farther in, adrenalin pumping in his veins. He hoped the old man had the correct house. It would be a shame to die in a collapsing building when the person he wanted to find was still one street over.

"Winnetta?"

Finally, forcing a door into the room that must be the bedroom, he heard a voice from a bed in a darkened corner.

"Winnetta?" he called once again.

"Jameson?" The word was barely there. Kodiak saw an arm move on the bed. "I'm so thirsty, Jameson." In the air an opened cell phone glowed gently in the near darkness.

He went to her, and he held her hand for a time. It was obvious she had lain here unattended for days, but saving her was what was needed. He looked around for a way to get her down from this dangerous building. There were no stairs, and he didn't think he could carry her on his makeshift ramp.

Then he remembered the draperies. He'd built a winch to raise and lower his propane tank. It had been very heavy. He thought he could do the same for this wisp of a woman. Before walking away, he comforted her with his words, and then he set out to get her down.

When Kodiak carried the old woman to the van, Jameson was outside waiting. Kodiak watched him drop a rosary into his pocket. With a trembling hand and reddened eyes, Jameson reached to touch his wife's face. Kodiak held her as she rested a wavering hand on her husband's arm. Then Kodiak stepped forward to lay her gently into the van. As he pulled the van to the corner and stopped, he smiled at the words he overheard Jameson whisper to his wife.

"I prayed, and the Father sent his angel to you, my Winnetta. He sent his angel, and you're safe." Kodiak glanced in the mirror to see him give her a kiss on the forehead.

Kodiak smiled, his face still flushed with the rescue he'd performed, and he wished that something as simple as a prayer could send his California angel to him. He murmured as he sat there, not sure where to go, "God, Mamie believes. Jameson does, too. If you're there, please bring my Carolina back to me. I don't know how I was lucky enough to meet her in the first place, but I lost her, and I sure do need her back." He took a deep breath, hoping his prayer worked.

"Jameson," he called, loudly enough to get his attention. "Where's the hospital?"

He looked up from his wife where she lay in the back of the van. "Just follow the angel," he said, and then he turned his eyes back to her.

At that moment there was a loud noise, and Kodiak turned. Where Jameson's house once stood, the entire building had just come crashing to the ground.

"Jameson! That was your house."

The old man didn't look up this time. His voice was clear, though. "I told her you're her angel. You kept her safe, Kody."

"Well, this angel can't find the hospital without directions." Then he noticed something. In this city where nothing worked, someone had found a way to let the remaining populace know where to go for medical help. There, floating in the sky, was an unusual balloon in the shape of an angel. Kodiak chuckled. It was probably attached to a hospital, too. He glanced up at the couple in his rearview mirror, and he thought of Jameson's directions.

Just follow the angel.

Well, Jameson, you were right, and I didn't even see it. What I wanted was right there in front of my eyes all the time. Kodiak took his foot off the brake and eased the van forward, keeping his eyes on the angel leading him to his destination.

CAROLINA sat in the suite that had protected Margarete and Ricotta throughout the hurricane. It faced inland, rather than over the water, and she marveled that it looked pristine, as if no storm had been through, and it was simply another day in Savannah.

"I told them." Margarete dipped her head to show she'd been forceful in her demands. "I did not want another room. The view in the other, it was beautiful, but the wind. The rain was leaking at the windows already. Not like at your parents' house." Margarete pursed her lips. "Your father built a good house. I told that man at the desk I wanted on the opposite side. You should see that other room now. No windows. I made them fix me up here, and this is still a good room." She reached and brushed her hand along the edge of a finely finished table. "No damage."

Carolina ran her hand across Ricotta's head and idly rubbed his ears between her fingers as he shifted position next to her. "Was it bad, Margarete?"

The old woman nodded her head, the severity of the ordeal wrapped up in that one motion. "Very bad. The whole building shook for hours. When the glass ceiling fell, I thought we were gone. The whole city was dark, but we had light. Then, the water made the generators quit. I was very afraid, and I remembered your father. He would say his soft prayers when bad things happened, and I wanted to do the same." She paused, her eyes moist.

Carolina leaned to her and placed a hand on her knee. "It's okay, Margarete."

She waved a hand at her and reached to wipe the corner of her eye. "My rosary. The one from the old country. I left it behind." She smiled a guilty smile. "I prayed anyway, and now we are all safe."

Carolina felt a pressing loneliness at the mention of her parents. She stood and walked to the window. She was glad this room didn't face the river. Her father's car was visible there, a monument protruding for all to see. She looked down to see Sha'Cretia helping the young man from earlier place a sign near the street. She could make out the word *Open* on it.

She called back to Margarete, "I see we're open for business." She watched the two for a while, then she spoke quietly, "Have you been to the house? I've heard no news at all. No one has. I came first to find you." She looked down as the large brown dog dropped at her feet, causing her to smile. "Ricotta, too, of course."

Carolina looked up, trying to blink away the tears she felt coming, and her eyes soaked up the blue skies overhead, ones that were the same color as the skies she had flown in Alaska. She smiled through her tears, thinking, Kody from Alaska. She needed to be with him, and he was thousands of miles away.

She whispered, "God, can you do that for me, bring Kody back? Please?" Then something caught her eye. "I didn't see that when the plane came in. Margarete, what's that object floating over the city?"

Margarete stood and walked to her, pulling the drapes aside. She had a satisfied expression on her face. "Good. It is finally there. I have been with your parents since you were very small. Your parents were very strong, resourceful people. Much like my family in the old country. When the storm finished, many people needed help, and no one knew where to go. I told the hospital, put up a sign that all will know. They asked me what, and I told them. It must be a sign of who you are. Angels. You are angels to the people you help. Put up an angel." Margarete tapped the glass holding the Savannah heat outside. "People can see that, and they know where to go. Everyone is telling everyone to follow the angel, and people are safe." Then Margarete shrugged. "We do what we can do."

Carolina gave her a hug, causing Ricotta to shift his position on the floor. Not yet comfortable, he stood and lumbered to the sofa, jumping up and laying his head down to look at the goings-on at the window.

Carolina spoke softly as she squeezed Margarete's shoulders, "You take care of me, and when I'm not around, you take care of Savannah. Margarete, this city needs more people like you."

Margarete pushed her gently away, a smile on her face. She straightened her simple clothes and quipped, "More people like me? One is more than enough, and they already have me." She glanced at her watch. "It is dinner time, and I am the one preparing it. It is time to go downstairs. Rotten Cheese, come with me. Your downstairs room needs you for company." She looked at Carolina. "The furniture was damaged anyway. What are a few more chew marks?"

Carolina laughed. Margarete had things under control, and that's the comfort Carolina found in her. Her prayers? Perhaps she had some power there, too. Maybe her parents' home was safe and sound, as well-built as Margarete claimed.

The thought of that brought tears to her eyes, but she brushed them away. She was convinced no prayers had that much power, and if not, at least she had Margarete.

PULLING up to the hospital, Kodiak looked to where the angel was tethered to the emergency room portico. Someone had made this, and hastily. From shower curtains, possibly, or sheets, and they'd found a way to float it. Party balloons filling the inside, possibly. He didn't know how many it would take to float an angel, or if the hospital even had the means to make their own. It was a good idea, though.

"Jameson, we're here." He reached and turned off the engine. Opening the door, he stepped out into the heat of the Savannah evening. He looked at the sky, and he knew he'd missed his opportunity to return to the car rental building to rent his own vehicle. His hand moving to release Jameson and his wife from the van, he had no regrets. He paused and smiled. Maybe he'd been a bit of a rescuing angel after all. He liked that idea.

He slid the door back, and he waited for a moment to let the old man finish his ministrations to the woman he adored. Then, Jameson moved aside with a final whisper.

"Winnetta, your angel is going to carry you. He'll protect you, and nothing bad can happen to you when his arms are around you. Rest easy, my love."

"Trust me, Jameson. I'll take care of her, at least as far as the doctors will let me." Kodiak reached in and wrapped his arms underneath the woman he'd rescued from her collapsing home. She placed her hand on his arm, and she smiled and closed her eyes. Kodiak looked up at Jameson. The old man pressed his wife farther into Kodiak's arms.

"She's safe with you. Go. I'll follow when I can gather my strength." He was pale, and he massaged his left arm.

Kodiak carried Winnetta swiftly and smoothly to the door. Glad to see lights inside, he pressed the large lever that triggered the door to open. When a nurse ran to him to offer her help, he motioned with his head.

"Outside in the van, my friend's heart."

With efficiency, more people were soon on the way with a gurney to help Jameson, also. As they rolled him in, the old man reached his arm out, and Kodiak moved to grasp his hand. He could see the old man smile, and then the nurses wheeled him away. The final one through the door stopped and spoke to him.

"You'll want to move your van. Others may need to come in the same way." She paused, her eyes glancing around as if considering. "To your left. A lot has been cleared there."

She moved as if to follow the others, then she turned back to Kodiak and placed her hand on his arm. She looked him in the eyes and spoke with conviction. "You've saved these people. Thank you." She turned and paused one more time, looking back at Kodiak and calling out, "You are truly an angel." Then she was gone.

Kodiak chuckled to himself. "I'm a funny angel standing here in my filthy clothes getting ready to drive away in someone else's car." However, he knew he was leaving Jameson and his wife in good hands for the time it would take to move the van. He'd park the vehicle, and he'd return to the hospital.

When he could no longer help, then he'd look for Julianna. She didn't need him, anyway. She was good at surviving just fine on her own.

CAROLINA held the drapes aside with her hand and looked out at the darkened city. There were islands of lights here and there, but it was eerily black. She glanced up to see the angel and

280

smiled at the beacon floating in the darkness. Margarete had finally shared her part in making it. The hospital had helium, and they had balloons. Margarete had used sheets to make a rough angel, and she'd helped the hospital employees fill the balloons that went inside. Tethers were attached, and someone had come up with an idea to light it with a spotlight.

"Follow the angel," Carolina whispered into the darkness. "I wish I could find my angel. God, my prayer still stands. You show me what I need to do, and I'll . . ." She stood still for a few minutes, then let the drapes fall, her prayer unfinished, as the room deepened into blackness. Her heart was empty. Her angel was in Alaska, and she didn't know what prayer to pray to remedy that. On the island, her parents had attended services, often with Margarita, too. However, prayers had always been a convenience for Carolina, and they'd never seemed to work. Her need for Kody was overwhelming, but she knew she didn't believe in that prayer, either. She felt hollow, and she had nothing else to grasp to, not even her long-ago memories of her young man at the airport.

She pushed her hair from her face, trying to find her way through all this. She moved across the room until she felt the bed against her leg, and she sat. After a few moments she lay down in the coolness of the air conditioned room and drew the blankets up over her body. Her thoughts wandered to a man's dimpled face laughing as he held a fish, and her pleading for second chances.

She squeezed her eyes shut. *I need a second chance, God. Just show me. That's all I ask.* Then she let the darkness lull her to sleep.

KODIAK stood at the hospital desk and waited. He idly rubbed the chewed card he'd earlier slipped into his pocket. Up and down the halls were beds with the less severely injured propped up or attached to various types of hardware.

The nurse turned to him. "I'm sorry, sir. I don't see a Jameson Chalmers or a Winnetta Chalmers." She smiled at him as she brushed her hair back to reveal an exhausted face. "However, our computers haven't come back up, so they could be anywhere. See the big white boards?" She pointed, and he turned to look. "We've been listing what information we can there. You'll see those everywhere on the main floor. You'll find where your friends are listed by their names, if you come across them at all. A red slash means they didn't make it. I hope you don't find the slash. Too many people have since all this happened."

Kodiak thanked her, and as he turned away, she called to him again, "Sir, there are a lot of good people in this city, but I can tell you're from out of town. You're not beat down like the rest of us. Thank you for coming to help. God must have sent you, you know, and I'll say a prayer that you'll find the one you love."

Kodiak smiled. "Ones. I'm looking for two people."

She returned his smile. "Two. That's right. Godspeed." Kodiak turned, but he caught her next words as he walked away. "Find the people you love. That's what counts."

He smiled at that. He wished he could. It seemed everything was getting in his way, but he was trying. He looked up, thinking, *God? A little help might be in order here.* Then he chuckled sourly and stepped to the board to begin searching the names.

"BABY PUMPKIN, this is Savannah sunshine."

The curtains flew open, and light assaulted Carolina's eyes. She felt Sha'Cretia sit on the bed.

"Honey, you have to see me today. I'm going to be rough and outdoorsy, just for you."

"Just for me?" Carolina sat up, and she blinked her eyes against the light, before squeezing them tightly closed. She moaned. "Sha, I don't think that's possible."

A hand pushed against Carolina's shoulder to make her point. "Open those eyes, sweetie. You're just not looking. I have pants on." She stood and sashayed across the room. "Carolina! You're not watching."

Carolina dropped back to the bed, pulling her covers over her face. Her voice was muffled. "I was, too. It takes more than pants, Sha. You have to act differently."

She came and sat at her side. "Well, there's only so much I can change at one time, and today my pants will have to do. My little friend from below, he's going to take us to your beach today. His name is Trent, just so you know."

Carolina sat up. She narrowed her eyes at her friend. "You haven't been messing around with him, have you? Sha . . ." Carolina was relieved to see a horrified look on her friend's face. Sha'Cretia reached to Carolina and put her hand on her arm.

"Honey, you devastate me. I'm as clean as a new-mown flower. You know that. At least I hope you do. He said they wouldn't let you out there, so I had to tell him about your deed. He's so sorry about your parents. I hope that was all right, sweetie."

Carolina grabbed Sha'Cretia's hand. "Sha! Your nails. Where's your manicure?"

"Sweetie, my womanicure is history. It was a really good one, too. I chopped them all off last night. I'm outdoorsy, now. Remember?" She held her hand up to look at her nails. "I really liked the color, too. Oh, well." She brightened. "Nothing really goes with denim, does it?"

"Denim? Sha?"

"Are you looking now?" She stood and walked to the door, placing each foot carefully and deliberately. "Better? My walk, I mean. Yes?"

"The denim? Where did you get denim?" Carolina could see

she had on faded blue pants in a well-worn fabric.

She waved and called as she walked away, "Better not to ask, girl," and she was gone.

Carolina looked out the window. From her view, the sky was clear, and the tops of trees graced the horizon. She lay back down and put the day off for a few moments. The beach. She wasn't sure she could stand what she might find there. However, she must, in spite of her misgivings. She guessed her resolute attitude was the Southern iron in her blood. Either that or Margarete.

She laughed and threw back the covers. She couldn't spend another moment lying around. She could see the hospital's angel hovering in the sky, and she was finally inspired. Maybe she would find her own angel today, and the rest of her life would be perfect. She did pray last night, and maybe today would be when God would choose to step in and be there for her. She could only hope, that and depend on her friends . . . as well as try to trust in God, just a little bit.

KODIAK stood by Jameson's bed. It was in a hallway, but at least it was a bed. Others had been given air mattresses on the floor. Jameson was lucky.

The old man reached to Kodiak, and in a whispered, cracked voice he asked, "Winnetta?" The hand shook with worry and age.

Kodiak held the hand until it stilled, and he spoke quietly, "She's gone, Jameson. During the night. The doctor said nothing could be done. I was with her at the end. I stayed for you." He felt his eyes burn. This was bringing back his mother, and the memories were overwhelming. "She was at peace when she went."

Jameson pulled at Kodiak's hand. "She was held by her angel—" His old man's voice choked off. Then, his words surprisingly strong, he released Kodiak's hand and began fumbling at his side. "Take this."

Kodiak glanced his way and frowned, puzzled. Everything the man owned had been lost in the storm. What could he possibly find to give away?

Then Jameson held his hand out to Kodiak. "I overheard the nurses. They've made an angel to take to the island. Holy Family. The angel must float there. Go with them. If you're there, they'll find success. Go."

Kodiak reached to take what was in Jameson's hand, and it was the small rosary from the previous day. "I can't take this." His eyes were moist, and he looked away, tracing the tracks of the ceiling tiles with his eyes.

Jameson placed his hand over Kodiak's and wrapped the beads in the younger man's fingers. "An angel's prayers are stronger than mine could ever be." He released Kodiak's hand, and with a deep breath, he let his head sink back on his pillow. His eyes watched the ceiling as if he could see something there no one else could.

A nurse down the hall caught Kodiak's attention, motioning to indicate the man at his side. She raised her eyebrows as if asking a question. Kodiak nodded his head to tell her to come.

As he waited, he pressed his lips together, and he whispered to the man in the bed at his side, "I'm no angel, Jameson." He looked at the small rosary, aware of the approaching nurse.

His eyes still on the ceiling, now unfocused, Jameson reached to place his opened palm over the rosary. The strength he had shown for a moment was gone, and his voice was that of an old man once again.

"The Father doesn't always ask us what we want to be. The job is just there, and we have to do it. You are an angel, even if you don't know it yet." Jameson gasped, and his hand pulled back to flutter at his chest. The color drained from his face. His next words were strained, as if a great weight was pressing upon him. "Go. This city needs angels. Go." He relaxed his hand and closed his eyes, his lids fluttering erratically.

Kodiak looked frantically for the nurse and motioned urgently. Then he moved aside as she stepped up. He was certain it must be the end.

After a moment, the nurse spoke to him. "Sir, I'll have to ask you to step to the end of the corridor." She spoke into a small device at her side, and he watched as others came and wheeled Jameson away. Then he was alone with his emotions.

Unable to focus, and unable to sit still, he walked the halls of the hospital, finally standing in front of one of the white boards as he watched a nurse put a red slash next to Jameson's name. Jameson's words flooded through his head.

"You are an angel, even if you don't know it yet."

Kodiak's grief at the old man's passing ripped his rebuttal from the depths of his being. "Angel? I'm no angel. God? I've lost my own angel. How can I be an angel for anyone else? Are you there?"

He stood for several moments unsure what to do next, his eyes glancing across the board, caught by the number of red slashes in front of him. Then one name jumped out at him. Leberge. He looked again, and was stunned to see what he hadn't noticed before. Leberge, Julianna. 222A. Kodiak shook his head. It must be his ex-wife, but she wasn't Julianna Leberge anymore. Her maiden name was Frankston. The name change was in his divorce papers.

His thoughts flashed to the paperwork out in Jameson's van. His divorce papers. His airplane. The alimony. She'd started using Frankston, but legally he supposed she must still be Leberge until he followed through on the payments she'd fought so hard to win. He flicked his eyes up and down the corridor, wondering if he should search out 222A. He'd come looking for Julianna. Maybe his search was over. He hated that it had to be here.

At the end of their marriage, she'd fought him, and she'd

beaten him. Then he had run. However, not everything about their life together had been bad. It was the money that had driven them apart. He didn't wish her dead, lying in this hospital with her name written on a whiteboard. He'd come back to forgive her, to pay his obligations, and to move on. He no longer hated Julianna. He loved Carolina. That was all the difference in the world.

He had to find her. He didn't know where to go, and he wandered the corridor looking for someone who could give him directions.

Seeing a nurse working inside a room, he leaned through the door. "Room 222A?" He hesitated, unsure of himself as she looked at him in surprise. "I'm sorry. My friend just died, right in the corridor. I'll find someone who's not busy to help." He looked away, his grip tight on the doorframe, giving himself time to get a handle on his emotions.

"Sir, the front desk is where you need to go."

He tried to explain. "My wife. My ex-wife. I just learned she's here, also. Her name is on the board."

The nurse laid down her clipboard and told the man in the bed she'd be right back. Pulling Kodiak outside, she closed the door.

"I'm sorry, sir." She looked up and down the hall as if deciding how much to tell this man. Then, looking at his face, she whispered, "We've had so many injuries, we've had to section off a wing for the severest. Room 222 is one of those assigned to our critical unit for the most traumatized. You do know about the boards and what the red slash means?"

Kodiak nodded. "She didn't have one. I was just there."

The nurse put her hand on his arm. "Wait here for a moment, sir." She turned and motioned to a man down the hall wearing an orderly's smock. When he got to her, she told him, "Please take over for me in this room. I need to take this man to the critical wing."

The man looked at Kodiak, then he cut his eyes away. With one swift, efficient motion, he was inside the hospital door and safe from what Kodiak would be forced to endure.

The nurse took Kodiak's arm in one hand. "Quickly, follow me. I'll be frank with you. We mustn't wait if you want to see her alive." She began to lead him expertly through the maze of people strewn throughout the corridor, and coming to a door marked employees only, she released him and strode through, not watching to see if Kodiak was following. Heading up a set of stairs, she carefully opened the door to a new corridor, and seeing no one blocking the way, she moved confidently down the hall.

There were no patients lining this passageway.

She turned to Kodiak, and as they walked, she talked. "With so much damage and so many injuries, the injured come in, and no one comes to find them. Everyone is injured. You've come for someone you love. Or loved." She smiled at him and took his arm. This time she squeezed it and held it for a minute, pausing and shutting her eyes. "You've seen our angel outside. It's become our symbol, our way of telling others where help can be found." When she next looked at him, her eyes were wet with tears. "That's become our term for anyone who goes out of their way to provide assistance to the injured. Angels of mercy. You did say ex, correct?" Without waiting for his answer, she turned to the plate by the door and tapped it with her fingernail. "Room 222. Julianna Leberge?" She paused and watched his face. At Kodiak's nod, she opened the door. "We nearly lost this one last night. First bed. Be prepared. She was afraid to die alone, but she knows what's coming." Leaning to him before walking away, she whispered, "At least someone's prayers are working this morning. You're here for her. She'll appreciate your presence." Then her steps carried her away.

Kodiak stepped into the room. Both beds were occupied. If the nurse hadn't told him which one was Julianna, he wouldn't have known. He moved toward the bed, questioning, "Julianna?"

He was relieved to see her turn his way, and he recognized her in the one undamaged eye she focused on him. "Kodiak?" He also recognized the smile that ghosted her storm-torn lips.

"I expected you to be safe." She was broken, and he didn't know what to say. His emotions were at the bursting point. It was as if nothing was right with the world anymore. "Mamie. Do you know where she is?"

"You came." Her eye moistened with welling emotion, and her voice was strained and broken. "I didn't mean for this to happen. The storm was too strong. One minute I was holding my cocktail in my hand, and then the windows were gone. I should have evacuated, but I didn't want to be alone. I'm so sorry, Kodiak. I'm so very sorry." She closed her eye, and a tear ran down her cheek.

"Mamie? Have you heard if she stayed or evacuated?"

"I don't know. We haven't spoken in months." She coughed several times.

"What can I do, Julianna?"

"My hand. Hold it, please." When she felt his touch, a steady stream of tears began to flood from her one good eye. "We were all right once, Kodiak. Long ago. Then we grew apart, didn't we?"

Her words were interrupted by ragged coughing, and Kodiak reached to pull a tissue from a box, using it to wipe blood from her mouth.

"Don't talk," Kodiak cautioned. His heart was torn two directions by a remembered love and the anger that had followed. He couldn't hate this, though.

"I know what's coming, Kodiak. The doctors have been frank with me. I won't live. My injuries can't be fixed. I just didn't want to be alone. All I ask is that you forgive me. I want to be at peace."

Kodiak felt his eyes moisten, and he looked across the room. He remembered his anger and running across the continent to save his airplane. He had the proceeds from its sale in his jacket pocket. It all seemed so unimportant now.

"There's nothing to forgive, Julianna. I've made my peace with what happened between us, and I've let it go."

"Thank you, Kodiak." Her coughing was worse this time. When her body was still again, she whispered hoarsely, "Hold my hand, please. Do that for me. I want someone to touch my hand as long as they can."

Kodiak sat on the edge of her bed, and he kept his hand in hers. He watched her close her eye, and he let the rise and fall of her chest tell him she still lived. Finally, the heart monitor wailed its distress, calling a nurse into the room. Kodiak sat as Julianna had asked until he felt her hand grow cold in his. Then, the nurse pulled Julianna's hand from Kodiak's warm one, asking him to step outside, and if he knew the next of kin.

Kodiak closed his eyes as the tears fell. "I am. I'm her husband. I was her husband, anyway."

"Sir," the nurse inquired softly. "If you'll follow me."

Kodiak did, and his hand moved when the pen was given him, but he had no idea what he signed. Death had crossed his path three times that day, and all he could remember was the chill of Julianna's hand as her life faded away.

"THAT DOG will not fit in your car." Margarete was firm, and her frown brooked no nonsense. "It is the smallest one I have ever seen. You should be driving one of your father's Cadillacs."

"Margarete, they were all washed away. I'm sorry. Sha?" Carolina hugged Ricotta around the neck and looked at the ruggedly dressed woman who had traveled across the continent to be at her side. Her eyes pleaded for her support.

Trent coughed, and in his best hotel voice he tried to

intervene. "Damage on the island is very severe. A good dog is a necessity to prevent accidental injury."

Sha'Cretia burst in, "Dead people, too, Margarete. Ricotta can find them. Trent said so."

Margarete mumbled, "Smells like himself. Rotten. That dog cannot even find himself some days. Then, I am staying here." She turned to Carolina. "You go to Holy Family. Say a prayer for your poor mother and father. Lock the doors when you leave your mother and father's house, and close those windows. You must not let the furniture ruin."

She turned, but not before Carolina saw the tears on her cheeks. She stepped to her, giving her shoulders a squeeze. "I do love you so, Margarete. I'll do everything you ask." She turned to Sha'Cretia and Trent. "Men?" Sha'Cretia beamed at the word, and Trent, red with embarrassment, looked around as if he wasn't sure who Carolina was talking to. Carolina pointed to him. "You, too, hotel employee. Let's go say a prayer for Margarete and check out my house."

Sha'Cretia laughed, attempting to be more masculine than she normally was. "Your deed, Carolina. You won't get very far without that." She had her thumbs hooked in her belt in an outdoorsy swagger.

Trent nodded. "Yes, ma'am. You must have that. You'll be turned back without it."

"Very well, boys and Sha. Let's see what's out there. My leash. I need my leash. Ricotta, did you eat your leash when you were downstairs? You ate everything else in that room."

With a bark of excitement, Rotten Ricotta Cheese bounded up at the mention of his name to show her he already had it around his neck, and it was in very good shape, indeed. Carolina knelt to his side and whispered to him, "Boy, you're going to keep us safe. You know that?" She whispered her next words to him. "Be good, and bring me home a man, Ricotta. I lost the one I found, and I need you to locate me another. I can't be the last lonely single girl."

Sha'Cretia turned, and as she was walking out the door, she called back, "I heard that, Carolina."

"You shouldn't be listening, Sha. That was for Ricotta's ears only." Carolina stood and looked at the empty door.

Sha'Cretia poked her head back inside. "Baby, I'm always listening." Then she was gone, her laughter ringing down the hallway.

Carolina looked down at Ricotta. She snorted. "Sha's right. I need to get me a real man before my best friend beats me to it."

"I heard that, girl."

Carolina rolled her eyes.

KODIAK sat on the front steps of the hospital, Carolina's card in his hand. He was lost. He'd come to his treasured Low Country to find Julianna in order to set things right. He'd found her, that was true, but things hadn't gone as expected. Now he didn't know how to proceed. He'd always believed the best thing was to do what was right in front of him, to act on the next thing that needed done, and now, there was nothing in front of him. Even the van he was driving was rented to someone else. The infrastructure here was in such a shambles that he wasn't even sure if he would be able to get back out to the real world again. Then, how could he chase Carolina without matters here being resolved? He felt he should have stayed in Alaska and kept his airplane.

Now he didn't even have that.

He looked up to see several hospital employees struggling with two large air tanks. At last there was something that needed done. He stood and walked over, stepping in to help them set the heavy tanks up straight.

"Oxygen?" Kodiak knew there were certain to be people who were homebound who couldn't make it to the hospital for care.

"Helium." One of the men reached to take a large bag from a woman who had walked up. "For the angel." The employee glanced up, and Kodiak looked to see the angel floating over the hospital.

"Another one's going up?" Kodiak smiled. He fingered the rosary in his pocket as he remembered Jameson's words.

The employee grunted. "They're opening up the bridge. We're taking this to Hilton Head. We'll be managing a triage station there, and this'll tell people where to come." He turned to see a small car drive up. The driver climbed out and popped the trunk.

Kodiak looked at the tanks and the bag. "Are you people going, too?" He knew what Jameson had wanted him to do. If so, this might be his opportunity. He could provide help and get to the island at the same time.

"Yeah," the employee said. "All of us."

"Not in that, you're not." Kodiak ran his eyes over the small vehicle, one side of his mouth pulling back into a grin. This car was small. His van was not.

"It's all we've got. We have to fit." The man hefted one of the tanks and tried to fit it in the trunk. No matter what, it simply wasn't going in.

Kodiak asked, "If I have a van, can I ride along?"

The employee continued to work on the tank as he responded. "Property owners, only, are being allowed to cross the bridge. You own property on the island?"

"Got my deed in the van." He stepped back, waiting on the man's decision, and reaching for his keys. When Kodiak pulled out the rosary he'd been given, he thought about what Jameson had said. *If you're there, they'll be successful.* He grinned when the employee looked up at him in surprise.

The man glanced at the others who were going with him, and he smiled. It quickly grew into a laugh. He said, "Man, where's that van? You're taking us to Hilton Head."

CAROLINA held her deed out through the window of her car. The officer flipped through the stack of papers attached to his clipboard. "Ma'am, you're not on my list. Was the deed put in your name recently?" He looked up as Carolina answered.

"My parents died in June. June fifteenth, to be exact. I inherited the property, but I live in California."

"Do you have a valid California driver's license?" Carolina reached in her purse and pulled it out. "All right." The officer found a particular sheet and checked something off. "I have you marked as entering the island. You have to check back out today. You cannot stay after dark. Has everyone signed the form?" He reached into the car and took the second clipboard. "Be careful in there. It's dangerous."

"Thank you, officer. We will." Carolina handed Sha'Cretia the deed and her license. She rolled up the window and began to drive slowly forward.

Sha'Cretia leaned back, huffing. "At least Ricotta didn't have to sign. He's the lucky one."

Carolina looked in the back seat where Trent was comfortably leaning against the big dog. She smiled before looking back to the roadway in front of her. She pulled slowly around a sailboat whose keel blocked one lane. Then she accelerated and began to climb up the bridge. She'd seen the damaged houses back off Fording Island Road. Those areas had been protected by the island itself. She knew the beachfront would sustain the majority of the damage, and that was right where they were headed. She took a deep breath and looked at Sha'Cretia. With a dance of her eyes to the mirror, she caught a glimpse of Trent, now staring pensively out the window. Carolina turned to her friend.

"Ready, Sha? It's here," she whispered.

Sha'Cretia patted her arm. "We'll be all right. Just you

drive. Be brave, girl." She turned to look at Ricotta in the rear seat. The animal grew excited with the attention, and his ears cocked up at the sound of Sha'Cretia's voice. "At least one of us is fine."

As the car began to move along streets lined with damaged buildings and debris, Carolina called to Trent, "Are you doing okay back there? You're very quiet."

He caught her eye in the mirror, and his face was pale. "I have friends here. I think they all got out, but no one knows. I just saw my mother's antique shop back there. There's only the roof left."

Carolina responded in a sympathetic whisper, "I'm sorry. I should have thought. This is your first time since the storm?" He nodded, unable to answer, and he looked back out the window.

Louder, Carolina announced, "All right, now. Holy Family, first. Boys and Sha, that should be easy to find." She gritted her teeth. "Cross Island to Pope. Just follow the road around. It'll be past the circle, and then we'll be able to orient ourselves."

She talked to reassure herself, because she didn't know if she really could find her way. So much was gone. Plantings, street signs, and parts of buildings. The gas station canopy she was used to seeing was gone, blown to the other side of the street, and just the poles were left. Stores had whole sides missing. Cars were buried in the median, with only the windows showing.

After rounding a circle, Carolina whispered to Sha'Cretia, "That must have been Sea Pines Circle I just went around. Look for Woodhaven. It's on the right. That's where we'll find it."

Trent murmured, "I can't see any of the streets at all. It's all sand."

Sha'Cretia cried out, "There, Carolina. The sign is still there. It's Holy Family." She paused, and quieter, she continued, "It was Holy Family. Oh, you poor baby." She looked at

Carolina with sympathy.

Carolina turned and pulled into the parking lot. The trees were gone. The parking area was full of sand. The beautiful cross had fallen, and the entire church sagged on one side. The storm had washed the ground from under the foundation, and the street side was a good two feet below the west side. Carolina closed her eyes as she thought of her parents' funeral services held there just months ago. At least the bulk of the church was standing. She was thankful for that.

She was surprised at the number of cars in the lot. She pulled onto a sandy patch that seemed as if it should be a parking space, and the four of them crawled from the car. Sha'Cretia rushed up to put one arm around her shoulder and hugged Carolina.

"Remember, girl. You've got me." She looked behind her. "And Ricotta. Trent, too, you know. Be brave." She glanced around. "It's packed, honey. What do you think is happening?"

"A special Mass, a thanksgiving Mass, Sha. These people survived. I wonder how many didn't. Let's go inside."

The windows on the collapsed side of the church were shattered, and the worst had plastic sheeting taped in place. Inside, someone had been very industrious. The pews were lined up neatly along one side, and the carpet had been pulled away. Folding chairs had been gathered and set out for a small assembly. Carolina turned to see Trent standing at the door with Ricotta. She called the dog to her and knelt. She wrapped her arms around his neck, and her throat was tight as she whispered to him.

"Poor Ricotta. You were forced to wait outside the last time we were here. Not this time. I want you with me." She stood and thanked Trent for taking care of her treasured pet. She was puzzled when she heard someone call her name.

"Carolina, my dear. What in heaven's name are you doing here in this place? I thought I sent you home to sunny California.

You do have a knack for getting lost in all the wrong places, you do know that?"

Carolina turned, and there coming toward her were two well-known arms wearing very familiar gloves, a head covered with a broad hat, and a smile larger than life.

KODIAK'S van was filled. In addition to the angel materials, cartons of medical supplies packed the back of the vehicle. They had even squeezed in a small generator and a still smaller refrigerator. It was cool with the air conditioning running in the van, but he knew it would be hot when they arrived. However, the generator would go for more necessary needs rather than air conditioning, such as refrigeration and lights, probably.

The first item on the agenda was the scouting of a good location for setting up the triage station. When Kodiak suggested Holy Family, one of the employees was surprised.

"You know the island, then."

Kodiak laughed. "I grew up here. Holy Family is my grand-mother's church. It's about as central as you can get." He also remembered Jameson's words, and he could feel the rosary in his pocket. Holy Family was the place to go.

Kodiak was surprised not to have to show his deed to the condo, but when the medical team flashed hospital credentials, all they were required to do was sign a list. Then they were waved on through.

It wasn't always easy going, and although Kodiak had grown up here, he'd been away for a while. There were several starts and stops, and one wrong turn. Finally, however, Holy Family came into view.

"MAMIE. I've missed you so." Carolina rushed up to the woman, and she refused to let a simple kiss suffice. She wrapped her arms around her, and then she stood back and laughed. "How do you manage to have spotless gloves on in circumstances like this? That suit. It looks just pressed."

Mamie pursed her lips and glanced around. Then she smiled. "Enjoy it, dear. This is my last clean set. I pulled this out for the Mass."

"Thanksgiving Mass?"

Mamie stopped and looked at Carolina, as if surprised she didn't know. "For the angel. We're calling it our Follow the Angel Mass, and we're sending another angel aloft. We're not sure just where it'll be, but it's on the way. All the churches are gathering. If you didn't know, then tell me, dear. What brings you here?"

Carolina's eyes teared up, and she knelt to put her arm around Ricotta, finding some familiar comfort there. She dug her fingers into his fur as she answered Mamie's question. "My parents loved this church. Their services were here just last June."

"The DeAngeles' services. Oh, my dear." Mamie turned to look around the building, as if seeing what had been there just months ago. "I was on that cruise with you, and I never knew. I never paid attention to your ID card. I never asked, and there was no occasion for me to read it. I'm so sorry. I wish I had made the connection." Mamie fluttered her hands, flustered at her social gaffe. "I was at the services, dear. Your mother was always so charming, and I regularly bought cars from Delcroy. Three, in fact. Oh, the world is so small. How did you ever get to California?"

Carolina laughed, her tears drying as the conversation turned. Her fingers against her cheeks helped. "Running away from a boy, I think. I've prayed to get him back, but he just runs from me now."

Mamie nodded her head abruptly and with determination. "Come with me, dear. I saw you walking up with your two friends. They may join us, also. We'll get you a prayer that'll work. The Father listens, you know. You've just got to know how to do it." She marched back to a small apse surrounded by mosaic windows of Holy Land fields and grape arbors. She reached up and stroked the statue of the Holy Family centered there. It had been shifted slightly out of alignment by the storm, but it was otherwise undamaged.

Mamie continued, "I brought a small candle. I'm a part of the Ladies Guild, and I helped bring this statue here. I don't think the Holy Family will mind if we burn one small prayer candle in their presence. It won't matter if the flame stains the ceiling now, I'm sure."

Mamie pulled the small candle from her purse, and she took out a book of paper matches. She turned to Carolina's two friends, and she motioned them forward. Handing the matches to Carolina and wrapping them in her hand, Mamie drew in a deep breath. "You need to be the one to light it. You don't need to pray out loud, but it helps, I think."

Carolina laughed. "Mamie, I've knelt and prayed here before. Not for a man, but I have prayed. How can this candle make a difference?" She glanced at Sha'Cretia for support.

Sha'Cretia patted her arm. "Honey, just do it. I want you to. We need some kind of help here, and it looks like a higher power might be the way to go."

"Please," Trent added. "For all of us."

Carolina sighed and relented. She looked at Mamie. "For you, Mamie. I'll do this for you."

Mamie held out the candle, and as Carolina lit it, she whispered, "For my grandson, Kodiak."

Carolina glanced at the old woman with a frown, but Mamie laughed and called to her, "Quickly. You must take it and let the wax drip. Then set it in place. Everyone, bow your heads. Carolina must pray."

Carolina did pray out loud. It was a simple prayer she'd practiced the night before, one with only eight words. "Just show me, God. That's all I ask."

Then they stood in silence. Sha'Cretia reached forward and worked her fingers into Carolina's. After a few moments, Mamie stood tall, and she took a deep breath. The candle burned gently, spreading a soft glow on the faces of the Holy Family.

"Good, Carolina. Very well done. You're an angel to this old woman. Prayers do get answered, you know. When I saw you last, I prayed that you would be safe, and that I would see you again. Here you are. Trust the Father, my dear."

Mamie turned to face the ruined interior of the church. She stood with the young woman she had befriended on the cruise ship. As Carolina's two companions walked away to survey the damage and hopefully enjoy what beauty remained, Mamie tugged Carolina down to whisper in her ear.

"Dear, why does that dark-skinned woman have men's pants on?"

Carolina truly laughed, causing others in the church to glance up in surprise. "Mamie, I adore that question, and you don't even know why. However, for Sha's sake, I won't answer it."

One of the windows the direction of the beach still had its glass designs in it, and sunlight reflected through it from a passing car, catching Carolina's eye. She turned to look. It had been her mother's favorite window. Taking a deep breath, she put her hand on Mamie's arm. "I think I'll walk to the beach and see what's left of my parent's home. I suspect it's gone." Her emotions once again seemed to be on her sleeve, and she felt her face reflecting them.

Mamie murmured, "I suspect so, dear Carolina. Will you ask your friends to go with you?"

"I'd like to go alone. Please let them know where I am if they ask. I'll have my Ricotta with me." Mamie looked puzzled, but Carolina simply reached and rubbed his ears, unable to find the energy to explain. All she said was, "My Rotten Ricotta Cheese." Feeling her face give way, she quickly turned and strode from the church without looking back.

"NO!" THE SIGHT of the church hammered Kodiak. "I thought this at least might survive," he exclaimed. "My grandmother's church."

He studied it as he turned into the parking lot. The building seemed on the verge of collapse, one end, anyway. He was sharply reminded of rescuing Jameson's wife, then hearing that building as it had given way minutes after he returned to the van.

He pulled forward into the lot. Then he stopped as a young woman with a brown dog walked briskly out of the church and passed by in front of the van. The dog was huge, and it seemed to occupy much of her attention. She appeared to be crying. Kodiak didn't seem surprised at that. However, he did feel a surge of adrenalin as she passed. If not for the location, he'd swear it was Carolina. His eyes followed her for a time as she headed in the direction of the ocean.

"Do you know her?" His companion in the seat next to him glanced at her before turning his attention to his seatbelt, unclipping it as he spoke.

Kodiak let out a laugh. "She looks familiar, but the woman I know is in California. She's got a long way to walk if she's headed to the beach. We're blocks away."

"Maybe she needs time to herself. God knows a lot of people have a lot of loss to deal with after this storm."

Kodiak nodded. "I'm one of them." He pointed toward the church. "The building's very damaged. What do you think?" In spite of Jameson's request, the church building did have to be functional to be suitable. "Does it look stable enough for your triage needs?"

Several of the team fell into a discussion, and after a few minutes, a decision was reached. The preliminary visual verdict was that the largest portion of it seemed mostly stable, and if it wasn't actually collapsing, it would probably be satisfactory. Who knew if they would find anything better? They only required a short-term solution. As soon as the injured could be stabilized, they'd be transported directly to Savannah. It was decided to unload the van and then to look at the building more closely.

Kodiak backed the van up as near the building as possible, and he helped the men unload. Helping them identify the old cross mounting on the front steps as a sturdy anchor for the angel, he left them to their business and pulled the van forward. He parked it near the smallest car he guessed Detroit's auto engineers had ever considered possible. He chuckled as he looked at it. There wasn't even room for a dog inside, much less one like that horse that woman had been walking. He looked around, wondering what she'd been driving. His eyes bounced over the license tags, surveying each one, but none were from California.

He walked toward the church. He remembered when this building was built. He'd only been a boy, but he'd been so excited at the glass walls and the tall ceiling. He'd enjoyed the stained glass well enough, but the wide outside steps in front to run up and down had been even more thrilling to him as a child.

He stepped to the front doors, and he moved inside. His first thought was whether his grandmother's carved Holy Family statue was still standing in the apse. When he looked that way, he didn't see the statue. Instead, his eyes caught a broad brimmed hat, a tailored suit, and a pair of long gloves. Mamie was facing the opposite direction with her back to him, but he'd know her style anywhere. With a smile breaking across his face, he bounded into the building and wrapped his arms around her from behind. With a great laugh, he called her name.

"Mamie! I should have known you wouldn't run from something so trivial as a storm. You're as irreverent and stubborn as the day I first loved you. There's been a hurricane, and the island's destroyed. Yet here you stand in your gloves and a crisply pressed suit."

She broke free, turned around, and slapped him on the arm, her voice not welcoming at all. "Kodiak, you bad boy. I went to Alaska to find you. You didn't show up. Now you come home and find me. I wasted all that time."

He bent down and looked in Mamie's face. "When did you make it to Alaska, you impossible thing?" He knew his grandmother was liable to do anything, and he wouldn't put this past her. However, he never thought she'd try to find him on the other side of the continent.

"Weeks ago." She looked at him hard. "I lost a girl up there, too. I hoped you'd find her."

Kodiak laughed, wrapping his arm around her again. "I was in Alaska, and yes, weeks ago I did find a girl, Mamie. I lost her, though."

"You expect to find her here? Do you think the hurricane brought her to the Carolina shore?" Mamie pursed her lips, as if daring him to answer her question.

"I don't know, Mamie. I think she's a whole continent away, but I intend to chase her until I find her." He kept his arm around his old grandmother. He had lost too much this day, and he needed this connection with someone warm, breathing, and alive.

Mamie pushed him away, though. "Are you here to see Julianna?" She looked hard at him, only growing sterner when she saw his body sag. "What, Kodiak? Don't try to hide this from me. You ran away from her, I know that. You also ran from me when you ran from her. Don't keep this from your grandmother." She narrowed her eyes at him. "I would have given you the money for Julianna if you'd asked."

Kodiak's eyes jumped to the old woman's face. "Mamie, I didn't know."

"You're too much like your father. Independent. He told no

303

one where that faraway place of his was, and no one knew if you'd gone there. I did, though."

Kodiak looked at her carefully, studying her for clues. "How did you know, Mamie?"

Her features softened and she smiled. "Alaska? Cool."

Kodiak laughed. "You remembered that old phrase? I haven't said that in years." He reached to hug her again, but she put her hands up to stop him.

"No, you don't, Kodiak Leberge. Not until I'm finished with you. Did you know Julianna dropped her petition for all the money you owed? Every cent. I'd like to say she did it voluntarily, but that wouldn't be Julianna, would it? After you left, her grandparents' support came to light, and a judge rescinded all the alimony. Have you seen her?" When he paused and didn't answer her question, she insisted. "Well, have you seen her?"

"Yes, Mamie. I saw her today."

"Did you get it worked out?" She glared at him, daring him to give her any answer other than the one she wanted.

He sighed. "Yes, Mamie. We worked things out. In a way, I guess you can say we shook on it."

She smiled broadly and gave him a hug of her own. As she held him, she murmured, "I told her you'd come find me if only she stayed by my side."

When she released him, he quizzed her, "If who stayed by your side, Mamie?"

"I told you, dear. That girl. The one that got lost. Did you freeze your brain up there in Alaska? Listen when I talk to you, Kodiak." His grandmother turned from him as if irritated. Then she pivoted back, surprisingly agile for an old woman who had survived a hurricane and its devastating aftermath. "She made me promise to do something, but I'm not sure I should. I'm not a matchmaker, Kodiak. You know that. You're too stubborn to let me do that. However, I did promise, even if you don't like it."

He smiled. "What did you promise? I'll try to like it very much."

Mamie bobbed her head to show she'd made a decision to do as she'd been asked. "She made me promise that when my grandson came home, I'd send him to her."

Kodiak laughed again. "You are so good for me, Mamie. I've had a very hard day. A hard summer, for that matter. Tell me, where is this girl? I won't mind meeting her for you, even if I do have another to find in California."

"And if you already have?" Mamie looked him in the eye, her gaze steady, and she began to smile.

Kodiak chuckled. "What does that mean, you conniver? Met her or found her? I never could keep up with you."

Mamie didn't bother explaining. With her perfectly tailored arm, she just waved in the direction of the beach. "She's that way with a big brown dog. Rotten cheese something."

Kodiak shook his head with a frown. "Rotten cheese?"

"You heard me. You must have seen her. She just left. She's been the angel to me that I needed. After all, she brought you to me. You walk right out of here, Kodiak, and you follow the direction my angel went. She needs you, and you need her. Go on, now. You follow the angel with that big brown dog. You can't miss her."

Kodiak looked toward the beach. The day was beautiful, and he knew the girl his grandmother referred to. If she was looking for a familiar place on this island, she'd have a very hard time, and she didn't need to do it alone.

That decided him.

"I'll go, Mamie. I can at least keep her company. Don't leave without me, though. I want you by my side when I get back."

AS HE STEPPED away, Mamie whispered, "I'm not the one

305

you need by your side. That dear girl Carolina is. Don't let her get away, Kodiak."

She turned as a voice spoke her name. "Mamie, who was that good looking man?"

She found Sha'Cretia at her side, and Trent was with her. Mamie said, "My grandson, Kodiak." She reached and pointed a strong, Southern finger in Sha'Cretia's direction, telling her in no uncertain terms, "Girl, you need to get out of those men's clothes. You'd be beautiful in a dress." She bobbed her head as if that settled it. When someone started singing a tune, she pointed a gloved hand in the direction of the assembled chairs.

"Mass is starting. Join me, children. We can all say a prayer for the lost and the homeless." She walked away, leading her tiny flock into the church.

Chapter 21

CAROLINA stood on the beach. As the wind ruffled her hair, she squinted into the sun. She hadn't needed to walk to her parents' house. There was no cause. The closer she'd gotten to the water, the worse the damage had been. The roads were the only safe places to be, and now, even the beach was cleared only where the tide had scoured the sand. She'd walked around pieces of people's lives that had been twisted and flung about by the storm, and she knew those lives had been devastated. She'd only thought it was bad in Savannah. Here, things had been destroyed so completely that if she didn't look back at the debris behind her, the island was as if civilization had never touched the land.

Her life had become like that. She reached down and unclipped Ricotta's leash. She wanted him to run free. Her life had become like this island. Her past was littered with lost dreams she should have held close, and she'd learned the hard way. Hold on to what you love, because it may never come your way again. It seemed she'd heard something like that somewhere.

She turned to look for Ricotta, and she saw him chasing a stick with an unfamiliar man down the beach. She laughed. Even Ricotta could find a man. She'd asked the animal to bring a man home for her, but playing fetch wasn't exactly what she'd meant.

Carolina walked out to the water. She reached to pick up a shell, rubbing her hand over its surface, and admiring the shine. Then she tossed it far out into the water. She knew she shouldn't kick her shoes off because of buried storm debris and possible glass shards, but she wanted to. The sand had to be sifted for broken glass and other particulates to make it safe. She wanted to roll her pants up, walk barefoot in the sand, and let the water wash over her toes. She sighed, and she looked up at the sky. She searched for Someone she wasn't even sure was there. In the solitude of the nearly deserted beach, she breathed her despair to Him.

"I prayed for you to return the man I loved and ran away from. Where is he?" Her eyes flooded with impending tears. The end of her emotional rope was growing dangerously frazzled. She had lost everything; she needed Kody; and she didn't know how to find him.

Without warning, Ricotta nuzzled her hand, and Carolina looked down. She knelt and wrapped her arms around his neck.

"Did you have a good time with that strange man, you old rotten thing?"

As she grabbed his collar to hook his leash back on, she found a tag attached to it. One end of it was chewed up. Mystified, she turned it over to see Altessa Cruise Lines across the top and her own name across the bottom. Her vision narrowed, and her heart raced. He couldn't be here. It was impossible. Then she remembered her prayer. *Just show me, God. That's all I ask.*

308

With her hands holding Ricotta's collar, she turned and looked behind her. She felt her face flush in anticipation, yet there was no Kody to be seen. Standing, she reached to shade her eyes from the midday sun. Without warning, Ricotta bounded away from her.

"Ricotta!" Carolina started after him, dismayed to see him disappear over a rise in the sand. Just where he'd disappeared, up in the sky, she could see they'd finally gotten the angel floating above the church. Well, if that dog needed religion, he'd certainly run the right way. She could hear him barking, and then there was a sharp whistle. His barks immediately quieted.

"Ricotta!" Carolina called to him, the leash dragging in the sand at her side. She stepped forward, filled with a mixture of anticipation and frustration. What could that dog have gotten into?

Carolina's heart jumped when she heard a familiar man's voice call out to her, and she looked to find a recognizable head of golden hair coming over the sand. Dimples split his face, and by his side walked a big brown dog.

"He's right here. Never let go of what you love, Carolina. It may never come back to you."

Carolina's heart was whole again with the sound of that voice. Her feet began to run in the sand straight toward her rescuing angel, and soon her arms were wrapped around him.

Her voice was ragged with emotion as she whispered, "How did you find me?"

With his head next to hers, and his eyes closed, Kodiak answered her question. "A wise old woman that I've known forever gave me the best advice I've ever been told."

"What was that?" Carolina didn't really care about his answer. It was simply his voice she needed to hear. She'd dreamed of him, and she'd prayed for him to come find her. She held her Kody, and he was all she needed.

"She told me to follow the angel. I did, and I found you."

Epilogue

CAROLINA reached and brushed the sand from the dimpled face at her side. She smiled at the golden streaks in that tousled head of hair. She knew the girls would never be able to resist the siren call of this boy's beautiful face.

The sound of laughter caught her attention. She tore her gaze from the dimpled face she loved so much, the face that had become as familiar to her as her own, and she looked down the beach. She smiled a second time. She remembered her wish from so long ago. She'd sat in her parents' house in her window seat, and she'd wished to hear her father call to her as he threw her a Frisbee over the sand. There it was, being lived once again.

A man's skin sparkled in the sun, his swimsuit still damp against his body. He laughed at a small girl's antics, obviously his daughter, throwing her the Frisbee he'd just retrieved from the waves, and he reminded Carolina of a boy she'd met once.

That boy from all those years ago had been on a Savannah

airport runway, and he'd drawn his head out of an engine cowling to smile at her. They'd only spoken a few words, but Carolina knew his name, now.

He knew hers, too.

She turned her attention back to the face lying asleep beside her. How could she have missed it? That Carolina surfboard, and that Low Country softness in his voice. She'd seen his face and known that wild Alaska man for her own Savannah boy, and yet she'd dismissed the connection with a wave of her hand.

Carolina smiled, looking back at the man and his daughter. He'd done the same. After all, she was Carolina from California, and not even Rhett and Scarlett had been able to bring them together.

As Mamie had said, though, sometimes the draperies were the important things to save. Together they'd managed to rescue those brocade draperies. Maybe it was General Lee who'd pulled it off. Maybe he'd finally won the most important battle after all.

Carolina was startled as a wet tongue drew itself across her face. She reached a hand to brush it away and turned. "Ricotta!" She put an arm around his neck. "You rotten cheese, you. You'll get sand all over me." She gave him a quick rub around his ears, then she pushed him away.

Carolina glanced out across the beach and was dismayed to see the father and his daughter were gone. She'd so enjoyed watching them play. Seeing them there reminded her of her own father and herself from so long ago, and it was a memory she had learned to find pleasurable. It was also something she'd been glad to see others enjoyed sharing, also.

Then Carolina gasped as water began dripping down her back. She turned to see the small girl from the beach standing behind her with a cup of seawater in her hands.

"Angela Caroline Leberge! Stop that. Your brother's asleep. If you wake him, you get to carry him back to the house."

Carolina reached to grab the grinning girl with one arm, and she pulled her face down to hers and whispered, "He's too much like his father. He gets cranky if he's awakened unexpectedly." Carolina glanced around and frowned at her daughter. "Your father? Did he go to the house already?"

"Mummy," Angela whispered. "He followed me to you. Look the other way."

Carolina turned her head, and a dimpled face, the mirror of the one asleep at her side, looked into her eyes.

He kissed her and whispered, "He's my son. I wouldn't want him to wake cranky like his father. I'll carry him to the house." He knelt to slip his arms under the little boy.

As the boy shifted in his sleep, finally nestling into his father's arms, Kodiak whispered softly to his son, "Come on, little Kody. There's already two bears on the beach, and that means your mother might get frightened if she's left alone with them. We can't leave her alone with the big, bad bears, now, can we?" He cut his eyes to Carolina and grinned. "Someday we'll fly Daddy's new plane to our Alaska retreat, and we'll find plenty of real bears there."

Angela tugged at her mother's shirt as she stood. "Mummy, what does Daddy mean by bears on the beach? There's no bears here."

Kodiak and Kody were moving away from them as Carolina folded the blanket, and she felt free to laugh out loud. She looked at her daughter's face and saw herself there, just as she'd seen her husband in little Kodiak as he'd lain sleeping beside her. She reached and hugged her daughter.

"Yes, dear Angela. There were two bears here. It's just that one was a papa bear, and the other was a baby bear. Kodiak bears."

Angela laughed and pulled away from her mother. She'd heard the joke before. She began skipping across the beach after her father and brother. Her high-pitched chant rang out in the early evening air as sand flew from underneath her feet.

"My daddy is from Alaska, and bears can live there, too. If they come out and growl at night, just kick them with your shoe."

Carolina shook her head. That one would be a songwriter someday, that or perhaps an activist. She looked up at the house that stood where her parents' had been. The blinds were open, and the glass doors were thrown wide. There was no ivory inlay in this house to be damaged by the sea breezes.

As the sun dropped and the sky continued to darken, she could see Margarete through the open windows, and she watched Kodiak hand their son to the housekeeper. Then he stepped outside to the deck to wave at her.

Words from long ago flashed through her mind. "Follow the angel." Kodiak had come and found her, but Carolina sometimes thought there was more to it than that. Margarete had no doubt what had happened. She'd told Carolina, "I prayed a strong prayer for you, girl. God brought your man back to you, all the way from that Alaska, even if he had to stir up a hurricane to do it. Do you believe, yet?" Carolina's prayer had been simpler. "Just show me, God." Then, Kodiak had stood there on her beach, right under the angel.

Carolina waved back and moved toward the house. The church, hers and Kodiak's now, had a new apse. It had a new foundation, too, thanks to the money from Mamie's estate, but her final wish had been to build a new apse. She'd wanted it surrounded with images depicting a stained-glass hurricane. Kodiak had been delighted to spend part of his sizable legacy from his grandmother constructing it in her memory. Inside was a Carrera marble statue of an angel. Mamie's final wishes had been explicit in what was carved underneath.

Follow the Angel.

Carolina smiled as she stepped onto the deck and wrapped her arms around the man she loved. She had followed the angel, and now he was hers.

Did you enjoy this book?

Find more by this author at:

 THREE SKILLET

www.ThreeSkilletPublishing.com

www.ingramcontent.com/pod-product-compliance
Lightning Source LLC
Chambersburg PA
CBHW071104250626
47159CB00002B/601